The Next Time I Go To Heaven I Will Not Be Back!

D1607613

My Journey to Heaven

By

Willie Agnes Chennault

DEDICATION

For my husband, Lazarus Sr., my children—Lazarus Jr., Otis, Pastor Henra, Dr. June, and my daughters-in-laws—Skirkea, Kianna, Esq., First Lady Taurika, my grandchildren—Semira, Olivia, Otis Jr., Callie Blue, Caia, Hannah, and a host of family members, friends, clergy, Doctors Hospital, Select Specialty Hospital, and Wilkes Memorial Rehabilitation Center's doctors, nurses, other medical staff members, housekeeping and food service staff who helped me along this journey, but most importantly—my Lord and Savior, Jesus Christ.

CONTENTS

ACKNOWLEDGMENTS

A special thanks to the Emergency Medical Technicians (EMTs)—Rebekah Echols, Dennis Weaver, and Lindsay Hughes of Washington, Georgia in Wilkes County for their care while transporting me to Doctors Hospital in Augusta, Georgia. I special thanks to the Willis Memorial Rehabilitation Center. Also, a special thanks to the Doctors Hospital team— Dr. Guillermo V. Amurao, Dr. Jon C. Gibbs, Dr. H. Hubert III, Dr. Kishan M. Khera , Dr. Amy M. Sprague, Dr. Robert H. Webbs Jr., Dr. Brezina C. Barton, Dr. Allison Buchanan, Dr. Kailash B. Sharma, Dr. Kerrthi Ponugoti, Dr. SMA Zheed Hassan, PAC (Physician Assistant-Certified) Paul Coffman, the emergency room Registered Nurses at the Doctors Hospital— RN Beth Hartman, RN Megan Laflam, RN Kayla Broom, and RN Tara H. Boysen, RN Amy, RN Rosa, RN Christina, RN Allison, RN Andre and to Rev. Matthew Harden and other Respiratory Staff members. A special thanks to Beverly Jarrell, she is the primary Physical Therapist (PT) at Doctors Hospital; Beverly is an overall wonderful person that I will never forget. We cried together and we laughed together. Beverly Jarrell saw first-hand all of the hard work that I put forth daily to recover from my illness. I want to send a special thanks to PT Tamar Ellen, SW Yvonne M. Puckett, and Kimberly G. Snyders from Doctors Hospital. I want to thank the amazing Dialysis team at Doctors Hospital and Select Specialty Hospital. I would like to give a special thanks to the entire staff at Select Specialty Hospital. I want to thank the Director of Pharmacy, House Supervisor, House Keeping Staff Members, Rehabilitation Therapy Manager, Wound Care team, Respiratory Therapy Manager, Nurses' Manager, Case Managers, Director of Case Management, Chaplain, Dieticians, PT Alica Metts, Vicki Cognet, Susan S. Bell, and Holliman. I thank everyone for being so kind to me. May God specially bless each one of you. I want to send a special thanks to all of my follow-up doctors—Dr. Mac Bowman of University Cardiology Associates, Dr. Brezina Barton of Nephrology Associates, Dr. H. Fechter of Eye Guys, and my Primary Care Physician, Dr. Robert Clark. A special thanks to all of the clergy—Rev.

George Edwards of Thankful Baptist Church, Rev. Timothy Bell from Rocky Mount Baptist Church, Rev. Lance Pitts from Gibson Grove Baptist, Rev. Kenneth Norman, Rev. Joseph William, Rev. Charles Lacy of Nebo Baptist Church, Park Avenue Baptist Church Clergy, and many other clergy and church families all around the United States that had a role in my recovery. I will be forever grateful for the many prayers and thoughts that were spent during my recovery with me on your mind. Lastly, but not least, I would like to thank my husband, children, grandchildren, sisters, brothers, aunties, nieces, nephews, cousins, sisters-in-law, brothers-in-law and my neighbor, Troy Bell for his undying support of taking care of my home while my family and I were at the hospital. I thank you, God, for picking out my team for this test and journey that I had to take.

Chapter 1

MY PRAYING GROUND

Two months before I got sick, I told my husband I had to go back to where I use to live and he said, "Okay." I called this place, "My Praying Ground," which I will explain later. My journey back to this house was around March in the year of 2017. It was cool, and the wind was blowing. I had been thinking about going back to see the house where I grew up; this house was on my mind. I had to go back! This house is down the road from me where I live in Washington, Georgia. I felt as though I had to go back to this place before I leave this earth. I have always told the Lord when I get grown and married, please let me live on this road known as Metasville road and he did!

One day in March, I went back over to where the house was found on my road. It was a white house where my mother used to work and there was still a lady named Ms. Mary Ann Garrard in the house. She lived there; this is the niece of the lady that my mother worked for about 38 years. My mother was a housemaid for Miss. Fannie Lue Garrard. This is the house where I grew up; it was behind the pecan trees—a half of a mile behind the Garrard's house. We lived down in the bottom; the Garrard's own this house. My father paid twenty dollars a month for us to live there, which included myself, my mom, my dad, my four sisters, and my five brothers.

My husband and I drove up to the house. As I drove up, all kinds of memories came running in my mind. I walked these roads as a small girl bare-footed and hungry. I could see my mother sweeping the patio off and she would have on her white apron. She always had to wear a white apron to work. She would wash her apron and starch them. She would wash her apron with potash soap that she made and every evening she would put her apron in a black iron pot outside of the house around a man-made fire pit. She would let her aprons boiled in white starch that came in a red and white box. This starch was very popular, and this is the same white powder starch that people would eat. I never knew why people ate this starch. My mom would iron her aprons until they go stiff looking. This apron was white as snow. My mother was a beautiful woman. I guess I look more like her than the rest of my sisters. I think I do anyway. She and I were very close. I saw her in Heaven. I will never forget that she made it to Heaven.

I asked Miss. Garrard could my husband and I walk down to the house where I used to live. She said, "Surely." Miss. Garrard taught my children in high school; she taught English. If it had not been for the Garrard's fruit trees and pecan trees and with my mother working up there, I do not know how we would have survived; it was hard on my father to feed 10 children not even including himself and my mother. He was a

2

hard-working man. He was strong and he had a good heart. He loved the Lord, and my mother did too. He was a man of strength and power.

My husband left our Blue F 150 Ford pick-up truck parked in the front yard of Miss. Garrard's house. I had all these memories running through my mind, but my mind was in a daze. I had to go back to this house. When I met the Lord Jesus Christ, I walked down the road below the house, and I went back to that praying ground where the Lord touched me on my shoulder. I had to go back even with tears in my eyes! I had to go back! I have not been over there in 55 years and the house is still standing. I went to the place where the Lord touched me. I had to go back there because I had not been feeling right in a while, but I was not sick. I just had to go back, and I laid on the ground, which was the same spot where I stood as a child praying in the woods about a third of a mile from my old house. I told my husband to wait there on the porch. I told him that I would be back in a while. He did not know what was going on and I did not tell him.

Sometimes you cannot explain things; this was one of those things. I laid on the ground in the same spot and I cried looking up to Heaven and the Holy Spirit came over me so strong. I was so light it seems like my body raised off the ground. I cried and I prayed; I said, "Oh, Lord have mercy on me. Lord, I have served you! Oh, Lord! I gave my life to you as a little girl. Now I am a grown woman, but I come to you as a little child knowing something is about to happen to me, but I do not know what it is. Immediately, the Lord told me, "I got you!" I laid there for a while; I do not believe in long prayers, because the Lord knows our need before we ask, but I ask anyway.

I came back to where my husband was on "My Praying Ground." He was in the back of the old house. It is still standing after all of these years. I went to the back of the house to the old meat house where my dad used to put the hogs. I stood there as a small child watching my dad as he went to the hog pen. He had a very sharp knife, a long knife. He would cut the hogs neck and let all the blood run from the hog's neck. I stood there looking with my brother, Joseph. My father threw boiling hot water on the hog. First, he put a copper sack on the dead hog, and he would scrap the hog clean. After my dad cleaned the hog, he put him on a pole with the head hung downward. He cleaned the hog. The first thing my dad got out of the hog was the liver. I would be standing there with a pan to put the liver in the iron pot inside the house and I gave it to my mother. She would cook it right away. She fried the liver and made thick onions and gravy. You are talking about good. That liver was the best thing I had ever tasted in my life. Oh, how my siblings and I did eat; we cleaned our plates. My mom was always a good cook. She cooked and cleaned for the white folks up the road.

Laying here thinking back to my comfort, my childhood. During my childhood, I knew nothing else. I did not know anything about nothing. My siblings and I just lived to survive in a situation. My father killed two hogs every winter. He let some parts of the hog cure out; some hog parts that did not have to be cured out very quickly. My dad put a box of salt on the meat in the meat houseback in the back of the house. I noticed that parts of the house had fallen in some places. After he cleaned the hogs, he stored the hog meat in the old meat house outback. He would hang the hogs up until they become stiff and then about a few hours later; he would cut the hog up into pieces. He finally laid the hog meat on an old wooden table inside the old meat house and then he would put lots of salt on the hog meat. The salt purified the meat. I would always be standing around looking along with my brother, Joseph, helping my dad. I loved to help my dad. We would work outside; I guess I was a Tomboy—I loved the outdoors. There was nothing I could not do; I climbed trees. I noticed the cider tree that I use to sit on in the front yard as a little girl. I used to pray while I sat on the ground by this tree and the Holy Spirit would come right to me as I prayed for a better life. I would also look at the fancy houses in the magazines that read by this tree. The magazines came from my white neighbors—they would always give my mom old magazines and newspapers.

As a little girl—I would play in the dirt and look up the road for my mother to come home from work because I wanted to be the first one to run and met her—hoping that she would have some food for me. She always had a piece of something in her pocket—a cheese biscuit, piece of fish or cornbread that she had cooked for Miss. Garrard. It was so good; my mother was an excellent cook. Every time after work each day, she would lay her apron on the bed, wash her hands, and go cook supper for my siblings and me.

When I looked inside the old meat house, it seemed like I could hear my mother's voice just as I walked around the old house. I walked around the house; I could see all 12 of us in there—myself, my five brothers, four sisters, my mom, and dad. The house consisted of four rooms, no bathroom, no running water, just a wood stove inside the house. I walked all around; I looked at all the pecan trees; they looked old. Wild hogs had rooted up the land where the pecan trees were; they did not produce any pecans anymore and all of the fruit trees were gone. It looked like a ghost town it was so lively when all of us were living there. I had to go back and just touch that place where the Lord touched me. I took all kinds of pictures and I walked through the house. I saw that part of the backroom had fallen off, but the front room was still there.

All the writings that my siblings and I wrote on the back door by the kitchen were still there. Our names were scratched on the wall—Charlie, Jessie, Mamie, Daniel, Racheal, Willie, Joseph, Alberta, James, and Barbara. At the back door, there was a tree, it was usually tall; right at the back step that took my attention. The old shutters were on the window barely hanging on the hinges, but some of them were still standing strong. I walked around all over there for a while. Life was simple and comfortable back then. Even though we had mediocre living conditions, life was still comfortable.

I went back to the well. It is still standing. I took a picture of it. We used to pull all kinds of things out of the well in the water bucket—old shoes, clothes, sometimes even rats and other rodents. We still had to drink the water. Sometimes we could not get any water, because everything would fall into the well. We had to keep drawing the water until it was clear. If it was too dirty—we had to go to our neighbor's house about a mile and a half away to get the water. During this time as a little girl, I had never heard of a phone. My family never had a phone at that time. I only knew of and seen a phone at the white neighbor's house up the road where my mother worked. It was a black rotary phone. I used to call my classmates from Miss. Garrad's phone when she went to town. This is the house where my mother worked all day. I wanted to look as though we had a phone, but we did not. I never gave my classmates Miss. Garrad's phone number. I only called them.

Also, during this time, I never heard the words "cancer, stress or being bored." We never ate hamburgers or hotdogs at this time. I never heard of McDonald's or had fast food. I thought of how I had to clean possums for my mom. She always loved fried possums and fried turtles! Someone in the community would always bring my mom these creatures. We ate them and they were delicious. I remember one time it snowed for a long time, and we had no food. My mom cooked possums on the wood stove and that is all we had to eat for meat. We ate it with pear preserves. We had lots of sad lonely days, but God took care of us.

I never had toilet paper or paper towels at this time in my life. The only paper my family and I used to clean ourselves after using the bathroom were old newspapers from the white peoples' home. It was a struggle—we had to struggle. We were all struggling to survive for food, which was our main issue. I am glad we struggled because it made me the person I am today, but I hope my latter part of my life will be better than my beginning. This scripture from Job 8:7 in the Bible sustained me to keep going, "Though thy beginning was small, yet thy latter end should greatly increase" (King James Version).

I took pictures all over the house with tears running down my cheeks. My father and mother slept in the front room. This room is seen from the moment you enter the house. My parents' room had a wood heater in there. The room was so small. The white neighbors had given my mother a baby bed. I had never seen a baby bed before. It was white and the paint was chipped all around the baby bed. The babies slept in the bed by the wooden heater in the far right of the front room. Two babies slept in the bed at one time. One baby at the foot and one baby at the head of the bed. My parents never allowed children to sleep in their beds, because my dad was six feet six inches tall—the bed was too small for children and my mother. The rest of the children always slept on a cot bed. A cot bed was a bed with one mattress on iron springs. The springs would protrude through the hard, thick cotton. The mattress had blue stripes and it was a gray. The mattress was about 10 inches thick. The second room of the house is where I slept with my two older sisters, Rachel, and Mamie. I never got any sleep, because I slept in the middle and I got crushed by my two older sisters every night. I always slept in the middle of the bed—I remember this room being our living room because it had one sofa in it. In the back room was the refrigerator, this room had two beds in there, a small colt by the wall, and a trunk for housing all the children's clothes. The trunk was a small size trunk. It was two feet in width, four feet in height and about five feet in length.

We did not have a lot of clothes. I only had two pairs of shoes, but most of the time I did not have any shoes. My siblings and I went barefooted most of the time. My mom and dad hung their clothes on the back door that entered the kitchen on the inside of the house. There was an old chifforobe in the corner behind this back door. My mother kept her personal items in this chifforobe, items such as her pocketbooks, high heel shoes, special plates that we never ate off, and little, white gloves that she wore to church on Sunday. My two older brothers, Charlie, and Jessie slept in the backroom on the cot bed by the back wall. In the other cot bed, my brothers, Daniel, and Joseph—slept next to the older brothers. My youngest brother, James, slept in the same in a corner by Himself on a small cot bed. My youngest sister, Barbara and my middle sister, Alberta slept in the front room on a cot bed. Some of the cot beds were stuffed with three bales of hay out of the white folks' barn. My brother Joseph and I had to pull the bales of hay out of the barn on our backs. We found old worn-out mattresses at the trash dump, but it was not worth the trouble, because the next morning from sleeping on hay mattress; our bodies were very sore! My oldest brother, Charlie, would snore so hard; no one got any sleep.

His feet had a horrible stench; his feet smelled like a rotten potato.

I am laughing as I think about these memories. The house was so small; it was a mess at times. However, things worked out somehow! My father and mother were incredibly beautiful people. They were very smart when it came to common sense. Whatever my parents told me—I did! They told me to be honest, be kind and treat people how I wanted to be treated. My parents told me to keep my circle small with good, honest people. I remember them telling me to never tell lies and always pray! When it rained, we could not get outside. There was so much mud. The roads were a big mess. We could not get in and or out.

My Aunt Essie known as "Aunt Nee" would always come by our house and she would help my mother bath us and comb our hair. She did not have a home; she just walked from house to house, which was her brother's and sister's house. She would walk from my mother's house—her sister, to my uncle Jimmie's house—one of her brothers, to Aunt Lue's house— one of her sisters and Aunt Clifford's house—her sister, to Uncle Willie's house—one of her brothers. Her brothers and sisters did not live far apart, but it was a daily 10-mile walk on foot. She walked all the time; she never learned how to drive. She walked everywhere and she was always happy She carried a bundle of clothes on her back. She did not care about how hot or cold it was—she would walk at any point and time throughout the years. She never wore socks or shoes. She was always barefooted; she caught shoes under her arms, but never wore them—her feet had a double layer of skin on them due to her not wearing shoes. Her feet looked like alligator skin. She stayed where she could, and she would always help my mother with us. She would comb our hair and help us to get wood in and haul water from the spring. She would carry the water on her head. She went to all my aunties' and uncles' homes to help with the children. She was a tremendous help with my siblings and me, ten children; she did not have any children of her own, but she helped to raise all of her nieces and nephews. I saw her in Heaven. She made it in the kingdom.

Aunt Nee got married early around the age of 19 years old. She had a child, a daughter with this husband, but sadly the child passed after being only a day old from natural causes. My aunt's last name changed from Brittain, which was my mom's maiden name to Wooten. She went to Detroit, Michigan with this man, and she fell into hard times after she split from this man. My grandfather, Jessie Willie Brittain when I got her, and she lived in Wilkes County ever since the 1930s. I saw her husband when I was 19 years old when he came to visit my dad. He grew up with my dad. My mom told me that was Aunt Nee's husband. I had never seen Him before while I was a child. My mom also told me that he wandered off somewhere in Detroit, Michigan to start a new family.

Aunt Nee would help us clean our house. She helped with all the chores. She would sit by the woodstove, and she would get one biscuit and soaked up the all the grease that from what my mom fried for breakfast, lunch, or dinner. I remember when my siblings and I were sitting on the front porch, and we looked up the dirt road and we would see Aunt Nee. She would have an ear of raw corn in her hand; she ate half of the raw corn—the juice of the corn would be running down the side of her mouth. My siblings and I would fall out laughing. My Aunt Nee would start laughing too. She would pick up corn from the white neighbor's property on the way to our house. The cornfields were close to the road. When she arrived at our house—she would finish eating the corn after she sat and rested from her long walk. She walked all the time—all of her life.

When she spent the night with us, she slept in the kitchen by the wooden stove. She slept on the bare floor, and she never asked for a blanket or pillow. She never complained; she had a good nature about her. She was very smart and funny. She did not finish school—she made it to 6th grade just like my mother. Aunt Nee just loved a cigarette! I never have seen anyone enjoy cigarette smoke like her! She made smoke come all out her nose. When she came to our house she always sat on the edge on the porch and had one cigarette. She carried one pack of cigarettes for a long time. She only smokes one day. She did not have money to keep buying cigarettes. She always carried her clothes tied up in a bundle on her back. She wore plaid all the time. I saw her that way in Heaven. She has a good heart. It was a blessing just to see her and talk to her! I love her and I respect her! The Spirits of all of these Brittain women is indescribable. Aunt Nee lived to be 87 years old; she lived with Aunt Clifford, my mom's other sister until she passed away. Aunt Nee died from old age—not from the disease Emphysema she endured all her life. She is in Heaven now with Jesus. I saw her; she was so happy, and she was full of smiles when she saw me. All she went through in this world; she was saved in the Glory of the Lord. Hallelujah! Praise the Lord! He is mighty! He knows our hearts and intentions. Romans 8:18 says— "For I reckon that the sufferings of this present time are not worthy to be compared with the glory, which shall be revealed in us."

I wondered did everyone live the same way we did; I came to find that most black people lived in poverty the way we did back in the late 50s and 60s when I was a child—I was born in 1956. So, I prayed, and I prayed, and I always walk down to this place—"My Praying Ground," where I had to go back to after 55 years. I had to go back now. I am now 62, but I had to go back. Something was just pulling me to go back and walk

14

those ground--it was just like I knew death was coming or this ended for me soon. I told all my siblings where I had been—I sent all of the pictures of the old house. They were amazed and shocked! My youngest brother, James was so amazed. He had to go over there to the old house and then he came to my present house, which is about two and a half miles from our house we grew up in. He said he still saw our names on the wall. I wrote all the names on the wall, my name, and my siblings' name.

I walked around for a while. I stood in the house. I sat on the porch. I cried and I prayed here. So many memories flashed through my mind. I remember when my father taught me how to drive when I was 11 years old. I used to drive out of this driveway. I almost ran over the fence many times, but I still learned how to drive early. My dad would be sitting on the passenger's side, and he had so much confidence in me. He never said much. He just told me to press the brakes and change gears. In a week, I learned how to drive. I would drive in the deep woods where we lived, and I drove my mother and siblings around in the car to the store early in the morning or evening time when my mother got off work. My dad would be gone in the pulpwood truck; he cut trees all day. My parents never mentioned any about a driver's licenses to me. I just drove. I was only 11 years old. The car was a long, white station wagon. I learned to change the gears in this wagon from my dad.

When I was not driving—I was walking. I walked the dirt road. My siblings and I had to walk a half of a mile or more to catch the bus every day. As my husband and I stood on "My Praying Ground," I noticed that there was no plum trees or peach trees on the side of the road like it used to be. When my siblings and I would get so hungry, we just found plums and peaches to eat from these trees or we climbed the pear trees for pears to eat. My brother, Joseph and I always climb to the top of the pear tree and got the ripest, sweet pears at the top. My brother, Joseph is my closest sibling—we are best friends. We ate, but sometimes we could not find anything to eat in the house. My siblings and I were always hungry—we never got enough. Joseph and I would go fishing; we were incredibly young. I was seven years old, and he was six years old at this time. Nothing bad ever happened to us; we never got snake bit.

One time I fell in the pond, but my brother did get me out. I was trying to unhook my fishing pole—the fish I caught got stuck on a tree limb out in the water and I tried to get it. The water was too deep for me. I did not know how to swim. My brother saved me! We were fishing in the cow pond by B. Booker's house—our other neighbor. The Booker family, a black family, lived about a mile from us. They were exceptionally good neighbors to us. If my mom needed little flour, salt, sugar, meal, or fatback meat—the Booker family would share with us. We also did the same with them.

I prayed and prayed when I walked to the edge of the woods, where I use to pray down the hillside. I cried and said, "The Lord is my shepherd. I shall not want." This is the first verse of Psalm 23. I always said Psalm 23 and repeated the Lord's prayer. I just walked around on this land of my old childhood house, "My Praying Ground." I was stood there; I looked up in the sky. I looked at the wooden structure on the outside of the house. It was still good; it was amazing. This old house still had so much life in it!

When we came home from school, my mother would sometimes divide the food and have our plates prepared for my nine siblings and me. When she did not fix our plates—the food got eaten up by some siblings more than others. She would cook as soon as she got in from work when we were children. I remembered she was so tired from work; she worked as a maid all day. She left for work at 8 a.m. and she got off at 2 p.m. sometimes at 4 p.m. I asked her one time, how much money she made, she told me 20 dollars a week, but I did not know the value of money. I am sure that she got paid more than that as the years went on. She worked as a maid for 38 years.

Laying here still in the hospital bed, thinking about my childhood and "My Praying Ground." I stood there in my old childhood yard looking down through the pecan orchard. The trees were close to our house and a bob wire was in the front of our house, but cows were in the pasture where the pecan orchard use to be. For many days, I was so hungry. I walked down through the pecan orchard and found me some pecans after the season was over in February. I found enough pecans to fill my hungry soul. As I look and think about all the good times, we had fun; the ten of us, my siblings and me. We used a wash pan to bath in as children. We never had a foul body odor, because whatever we ate was all natural with no artificial ingredients. All ten of us—my siblings and I got along very well; we had no major problems, but we are all different.

The word "love" was never mentioned in our house, but we knew our parents loved us. I never heard that word, but I tell my children, I love them! I always have and I always will, every time my children and I speak on the phone—I tell them, "I love you." Their father, my husband, do as well. Children need to hear, "I love you" from their parents. This just came in my Spirit to say this. When my first child was born, I made this a habit.

I am laying there thinking about all my siblings. My oldest brother, Charlie, who is deceased would have been 74 years old and the next brother, Jessie, who is deceased as well, would have been 72 years old. My oldest sister, Mamie is 67 years old and the next brother, Daniel, is 65 years old and the next sister,

Rachael is 63 years old and I am 61 years old and the next brother, Joseph, is 60 years old and the next girl, Alberta is 58 years old and the next brother, James, is 56 years old and the next sister and youngest is 54 years old.

My husband walked on back to the house where Miss. Garrard lived—this is where my mother worked for 38 years, cooking and cleaning for Miss. Garrard. My mother would sit on the back steps of Miss. Garrard's house to feed her babies—my siblings. I walked up there plenty of days pulling my younger baby sister and brothers to nurse in a wagon that my siblings and I had made out of wood we found and old wheels at the trash dump. This was awesome. I am just thinking about this as I walk around the house looking at the trash can that me and my brother, Joseph, ate out of as children. We ate out of Miss. Garrard's trash can plenty of days. We found half-eaten fruit such as apples and bananas and half-eaten bologna sandwiches. We never found anything to drink in the trash can. My brother, Joseph and I took apples from the tree where the man, Chester Hall, lived—but he only came down on the weekend. He was married to Miss. Fannie Lue Garrard's other niece. Mr. Hall owned cows in the pasture next to the pecan orchard. He often gave his cows beautiful, red apples and sometimes my brother and I would be so hungry we would get us an apple apiece and eat the apples. I thank God that Mr. Chester did not put any poison in the apples; some people would have done that—my mother did not know anything about this. We never told anyone!

As I walked around the house, I noticed the pink faucet where my siblings and I use to get water. Sometimes we walked a mile in the dark; we could barely see our feet. My dad would come home, and we did not have any water in the house. My brother, Joseph and I would have to go over to our neighbor's house at 2 a.m. and get water—no one went but Joseph and me. I was so mad! When it was thundering, and lighting— Joseph and I still had to get water. My mother told my father do not send them out there. She would say, "Do you see it is thundering and lighting"? He did not respond to her. What my dad said to my siblings and me was the final word. I prayed that the lighting and the dark, bad clouds would go away.

The storm was so bad; we never got struck by the lighting. We walked about two miles over to the neighbor's house to get a milk can of water in an old wagon that we had made from old tires and other materials we found at the trash dump. We pulled the wagon back home, but half-way home the water wasted out of the milk can because we hit a rock; it was pitch, black dark and we had to turn around in the late night and go back and get some more water. I was praying the whole time asking the Lord to take care of us. I asked the Lord to have mercy on my father for sending us out to get water after nightfall. I do not know why we did not get water before dark came. We were afraid to get water at the white folk's house that time of night; we might have gotten shot. So, we went to our black neighbor's house, B. Booker's house. Our neighbor came to the door and turned the light on, and they felt sorry for my brother and me. I was a little girl, but this made me strong. I am glad to be strong and not weak. I praise the Lord all the time because in a way He is all I have and still He is all I have in away. He has shown me a favor all my life.

I remember standing in the yard looking down through the bushes. Oh, how we had to find fire starter sticks to start the fire in the morning. My brother, Joseph, and I had to find these fire starter sticks or lighter sticks. They were found from broken tree stumps. We put them in a Croker sack, and we dragged it home. Oh, Lord, have mercy! I thank the Lord for all of my hard times. It made me the woman I am today! My hard life and my husband's hard life shaped us. We educated all of the children to the fullest. We taught them how to trust God beyond all else. We all have problems, and we always will, but with God—we will grow in our problems to serve Him. That is all that matters! So, my husband talked to Mrs. Garrard, she told us to come back again. I told her I would. This happens two months before I got sick in March of 2017. □

Chapter 2

GOD'S DIVINE ORDER

The whole week before I got sick on May 19, 2017, I was truly busy. Just, as usual, I was busy helping a sick friend of mine; she had Parkinson's disease. I took her to physical therapy on that Wednesday and we had a good trip there and back. During that week before I got sick, I had to pray. I would go outside and look upon the sky. I would say Psalm 23 and I would tell the Lord, "If I have any hate in my heart to remove it!" For days and days, I would go outside and pray. I looked up in the sky. My husband would see me.

He said, "Are you going crazy?"

I did not say a word. I just kept on praying and saying Psalm 23 and asking God to give me a clean heart and give me the right spirit. I always pray early in the morning. It is the first thing that is on my mind as soon as I awake from sleep. I say bits and pieces of scripture and I pray all through the day that is every day. I would not dare shut my eyes without praying, asking the Lord to help me, and praying for other people that I hear are having trouble. They do not have to know you are, that you are praying for them. This is when your prayers will be heard; you have to pray for someone other than yourself. I told my husband that I was free. If you are holding on to hate or harboring hate, you are only hurting yourself!

I told my husband two weeks before I got sick that I was free. I knew that something was not right; I could not put my finger on it. I walked around the house like I always do, but this week I prayed more than usual. I would walk around the house looking in the sky praying that God's Spirit just shines on me. I got too full of His Spirit. I always had church outside alone thanking Father God for his many blessings. I always took Father God back His word, because He cannot lie. I walked down to the garden spot where my husband and I have had a garden for the last 38 years, but this time the Holy Spirit said to me plain as day, "You will not work in the garden this year." So, I told my husband.

He said, "I am going to plant me a garden you do not have to help."

I just stood there looking at the garden spot. I just was not excited about my garden as usual. My husband planted Him a row of peas anyway. During the first part of May, I had to keep my granddaughter, Callie Blue, because her mother had to go into the hospital to have her sister. My husband and I took care of Callie Blue for one week then she went back to Atlanta. I was busy as usual. I went for walks around the park and recreational track. I went to church on Sunday and did usual grocery shopping.

We go to Atlanta to visit the children and grandchildren often. I did regular chores around the house. My husband and

I went fishing on our neighbor's pond. He let us fish there whenever we wanted too. So, coming up to the third week of May that Thursday I was feeling okay that morning. I went to town; I went by the bank, and I had a few words with my sister who works there and drove off. I went home. I cooked and cleaned up my house. My son called me that morning to tell me he was going to bring the Callie Blue back to spend a few more days with my husband and me. She was four years old currently. I told him to just call me, and I would meet him in Greene County. It is about 40 miles from my house to Greene County. He called me and told me he would be there around 8:00 p.m.

On my way to Greene County, I was feeling okay. I was riding along listing to my gospel music, and I was driving a blue Ford F150 truck, my husband's truck. I got happy. The Spirit of the Lord came to me just like usual. I began to pray, thanking God for all His many blessings. I was thinking about my children and how He had brought them through college, and He did let no hurt, harm or danger come upon them. I was praying for healing for my sick husband and asking God to give strength to his body. He has been sick before. I was riding alone. My husband was supposed to go with me, but he was pulling in the yard as I was leaving out, so I went alone. I sat there at the gas station, and I waited for Pastor Henra. He called me and said he was running late so I patiently sat there, and I waited there until he came to meet me. I was feeling okay. I did not feel sick or nothing. He showed up and he hugged me like usual. My children always hug my husband and me every time we see each other. That is how I raised them. When my children come home or whether I go to their home in the city; we always hug each other.

Pastor Henra got his daughter out of his car, and he put the car seat in the truck, and he put the baby in the truck. I drove to the backside of the gas pump, and he pumped some gas for me. My grandchild and I started to my home a few moments later. It is 40 miles to get home. The time was 8:30 p.m. While on my way home, I stopped at a few miles up the road on the right; I pulled into Ingle's grocery store and Callie Blue got out and we went into the store. I was feeling okay, nothing out to the ordinary. We went inside and picked up a few packages. We came out of the store, and I put Callie Blue in her car seat, and I started up the truck. I remember sitting at the road turning towards home and that was it. I do not remember anything else. How did I get home? I do not know! I have no remembrance of driving. I do not know how I got home. I remember nothing.

I was lying there in the hospital about three weeks later listening to my voicemail and my husband's voice was in the voice mail. He called three times to see where we were, my granddaughter and me. I did not know he had called me that night; I did not hear my phone rang that night. I do not remember driving home Thursday night. I have no remembrance of even getting home. I did not know I had gone to pick up my grandbaby. I do not remember getting home. I asked my husband, "When did I get home?"

He said, "I cooked Callie Blue some cheese and eggs and then I told him I was going to bed."

An angel drove me home. I got home safe; my granddaughter was safe. I remembered nothing! I do not remember sleeping that night. I went blank, but I woke up the following morning and I talked to my daughter like I do every morning. She called me. I was feeling okay. Then my granddaughter came walking down the hall. I asked my husband where she came from, he told me that I had gone to pick her up. I said, "When?"

He said, "Last night."

I did not remember that, so I told Callie Blue to go into the den and watch her cartoon shows. My mind was trying to think, trying to remember picking up Callie Blue. I did not think about it much and I stood in the bathroom so my husband could cut my hair. I was standing up and I made a stutter back toward Him; I almost fell. He said, "Have you gotten so old you cannot stand up?" I did not say a word, feeling a little tired, but nothing out of the ordinary. My husband got me a stool to sit on and he begins to cut my hair. I did not look at my hair after he had completed my hair cut. I was feeling tired. I told him to go and fix Callie Blue some cereal. I told my husband that I was going to take a shower. I vaguely remembered taking a shower. I do not remember putting on my clothes, but I had some on. Over 30 days went by before I would take another shower.

I came and sat on the sofa in the living room. I coughed one time and I went back into the bathroom. I spit in the bathroom sank and I wondered why in the world would I be throwing up blood. I got nervous and I told my husband to drive me to the hospital in Augusta, Georgia knowing I was probably too sick to ride in an automobile. My husband went into the bathroom after me and he asked me, "Why is all of that blood in the toilet bowl?" I did not say anything. I did not know blood was in the toilet bowl. All I knew was blood was in the sink. I was surprised when he told me that blood was in the toilet bowl. I got so sick every second. I got so sick so fast. I told him to call 9-1-1 and to hurry. I was losing my breath so fast. My husband had his oxygen tank sitting in the living room in the corner. He has been on oxygen for about 14 years. He has pulmonary fibroids; he was exposed to asbestos. Usually, he would put all of his tanks of oxygen in the backroom; that week he had one of them sitting in the corner, it been sitting there all week and I did not move it. This was May 19, 2017, on a Friday morning. My life changed all in one day, one morning. I did not know what was happing to me. I was feeling fine all week and busy as usual doing household chores.

So, my husband called 9-1-1; while the 9-1-1 operators were on the phone, my husband put his oxygen on my nose. I could hardly breathe with the oxygen on my nose. I could not breathe with the oxygen on my nose. I remember pulling the oxygen mask off, but my husband put it back on again. I was too sick to pray; all I could say was "Lord have mercy on me." I thought about my prayer life. I am glad I pray many times a day. I did not worry too much about praying. I was not able to pray. I had to go to my faith believing in God and His will for me. I know He was going to take care of me whether I lived, or I died. So, the EMTs came in the door. I was almost gone; every second, I got worse and worse. I saw these two EMTs coming through the door to get me. The EMTs were angles. One EMT was the driver, a female, and a male EMT worked on me in the back of the ambulance. When I arrived at the hospital—I was told there was an EMT from Washington, GA already there waiting on me. She helped to put me on the stretcher. God had sent them to pick me up; I have not met them yet, but I am going to meet them because they are special. One of the EMTs said, "Hello, Mrs. Chennault." They asked me what I had taken, and I said I had some green tea with cinnamon. I heard my husband tell the EMTs that I always am the one to be picked up, never my wife. He told the EMTs that he had been picked up a hundred times since he due to his illness.

I have no remembrance of getting on the stretcher, but the last thing that I remembered was that the door shut. I left this world, and I went to Heaven so quickly. I went to Heaven before I got to the hospital. The EMTs did ask me what hospital I wanted to go to. I told them University Hospital, but my husband told to me that the EMTs could not make it to University Hospital because my heart stopped once I entered the ambulance. So, the EMTs had to stop at the Doctors Hospital; I did not know what I had or what I was diagnosed with. I was gone to Heaven. Let me go back a bit before I tell you more about Heaven.

I did not have any idea what was wrong with me. I know I was not supposed to be throwing up blood. Whatever was going on with me, I knew my God had it covered because He has never let me down, why would he do it now? The scripture says,

There hath no temptation taken you, but such as is common to man: but God is faithful, who will not suffer you to be tempted above that ye are able; but will with the temptation also make a way to escape, that ye may be able to bear it (1 Corinthians 10:13).

The EMT male said, "Mrs. Chennault have you taken anything?"

I said, "No, I have not eaten anything or took any medication."

That morning, I felt light-headed and tired, very tired. I tried to catch my breath. I could hardly wait until the EMTs got there. I heard the fire truck coming. I knew whatever sickness I had was very serious, because all of the blood was coming from me coughing. My husband was moving very slow and was in grave shock when I told him to call 9-1-1. He did call 9-1-1 and they got there very fast, to our home. I do not remember the ride to Augusta, Georgia; This is where the Doctors Hospital is found. I do not remember anything, because I left my body, and I went to Heaven. All of my life, I always helped other people—whether I cleaned houses or took some of my old friends to the doctor. I always had checkups and I went to my primary care doctor. I went to my primary care doctor every two months. I had regular checkups with my heart and blood pressure doctor. I went to the gynecologist and the eye doctor often. My sickness slipped up on me so quickly and in a matter of a few hours, I left this world. My children and husband told me that I stayed in a coma for ten days. I did not know that, and I was in shock when they told me that.

When all of this happened to me, I felt like my back was up against a brick wall. I could not go backward, forward nor sideways. I was stuck in a moment in my life not knowing that I had been walking around with double pneumonia for three weeks. My husband has been sick for 13 years. He has been to the doctor's time after time, in and out of the hospital month after month. I was very busy waiting on Him; he has lung disease Pulmonary fibrosis and Restrictive lung disease secondary to asbestos and silicosis. It has been hard waiting for Him. He has these flares up with his Pulmonary fibrosis, but most of the time he pops right back up and a few months later he is sick again. No matter what you are going through—God knows all about it. I just had to be strong for myself and Him.

Thinking back on May 12, 2017—I was in Atlanta, Georgia at my daughter-in-law, Kianna's graduation from law school. The doctor reported I had double pneumonia for at least three weeks. I could hardly believe that, but that is what the doctor said, and it has to be true. The doctors thought at one time that I might have Leukemia because my blood was being eaten up. Kianna said the doctors did not want my small grandchildren around me. The doctors were not sure about what disease I had when I first entered the hospital.

I went to the graduation ceremony, and I had to walk about a half of a mile to the Georgia State University Law School where the ceremony took place. I was feeling a little touch of fatigue and that is the way I always feel in Atlanta—visiting the children and grandchildren, all they want is mama and dad in town. We always have a wonderful time with the children and grandchildren. We all eat together at mealtime. In the city, it feels so good just to sit there and listen to the conversations between my children and their children.

It was so hot that evening of graduation, but I was excited just to have a lawyer in my family. Our daughter, Dr. June, is a Doctor of Education. Our oldest son, Lazarus Jr., is a Physical Education teacher and basketball coach. Our second son, Otis, is a Network Engineer. My youngest son, Pastor Henra, is a great preacher and a Premier Banker One. We call Him, Pastor Henra. Pastor Henra's wife, Taurika, is a teacher, and my other daughter-in-law, Skirkea, is a cosmetologist. She is married to my oldest son, Lazarus Jr. Kianna, the lawyer, is married to my son, Otis. That evening after graduation, we took a lot of pictures. We went to the restaurant to eat in downtown Atlanta. There were lots of people, all of her family from Maryland, our family, and some friends. We were all there about 50 people; that was the same day of the graduation.

I was feeling somewhat tired, but nothing out of the usual. The next day my daughter-in-law and my son had a pool party for her graduation. I felt tired and restless, ready to go home and lie down—thinking about my bed in a peaceful country. That Sunday we all went to my son's church in Grant Park of Atlanta at Park Avenue Baptist Church. He performed a Christening ceremony over our first grandson, Otis Jr. and a lot of pictures were taken of this occasion. I was smiling and Monday morning my husband and I headed back home.

On May 6, 2017, my husband and I met my son Otis and our granddaughter, Semira in Augusta, Georgia. She ran track all summer at various track meets around the area including Atlanta. She is a very good runner. A grandmother would say that, but no joke; she is fast. So, we met my son at the track meet; we stayed there all day and then that evening we went to dinner. I also had my 4-year-old granddaughter with me I had been keeping her, Callie Blue is her name. She had been with me all of the weeks because her mother was in the hospital having her sister. I was feeling soggy. We spend the night in Augusta because the next day my granddaughter had another day of track meets. It was hot. I brought Callie Blue a big sausage dog. She loved it. I do not think she has had one quite like that before. I felt very fatigued while I sat there at that track meet; it was so hot, but I enjoyed every moment of the track meet. I always enjoy my grandchildren. I thought about Semira as I looked upon her running around that track praying for her as she grows up in the world, asking God to put a hedge around her. I am thinking about the letter Semira wrote to me even before I awoke from my coma. She told me in the letter about how she loves me, and she told me there is no way that she could go on without me. She told her mother, Valerie and her father, Otis that she could not go on without me, grandma. Her parents told her that I was in God's hands and whatever He decides to do was right for me. Semira told me how she cried and prayed and how she said Psalm 23 over and over. She told me that her life was going to be very empty without her grandma. She told me that I was the one who always taught her how to pray and I would always tell her about boys. She told me that my grandma always told me how to always make good grades in school and that she loves her grandmother so much. She told me that I had to see her graduate from high school and college. She told me that I had to be at her wedding one day. She said, "Grandma I can't lose you! Please grandma come back to us! I need you my sweet grandma!" She told me she kept repeating Psalm 23.

I had to have been sick at this time around May 14, 2017, but I did not notice anything out of the ordinary. That week I started to eat things that I knew were healthy for me. I was not feeling right, but I could not put my foot on what was wrong. I helped one of my friends to clean their house that week and I also went to church as usual. My mind stays on the Lord more than usual, because I always pray many times throughout the day. I sing hymns and listen to preaching on the television, playing gospel music in the truck as I drive throughout the day. It always keeps my mind on the Lord, and I pray, and I would say Psalm 23; I know eight times every day and the Lord's prayer because everything I need is in those two prayers.

On May 19, 2017—a Friday at 10:46 a.m. my life changed forever, or should I say I had a chance to go to Heaven—my miraculous journey to Heaven began. I cannot feel sad or angry, because this happened to me. I know that—

The Lord is my shepherd; I shall not want. He maketh me to lie down in the green pastures: he leadeth me beside the still waters. He restoreth my soul: he leadeth me in the paths of righteousness for his name's sake. Yes, though I walk through the valley of the shadow of death, I will fear no evil: for thou art with me; thy rod and thy staff they comfort me. Thou preparest a table before me in the presence of mine enemies: thou anointest my head with oil my cup runneth over. Surely goodness and mercy shall follow me all the days of my life: and I will dwell in the house of the Lord forever" (Psalm 23).

When I got out of bed that morning, I thought about nothing earthly. I was in a whirlwind—all I said, or thought was "Lord You know my heart and I know You love me because you told me so when I was a little girl standing in the woods one day and I know You got this." This is what I thought about. I could not think at all, but I knew whatever was wrong—it was not good. I was not afraid! I was just depending on my God, who I met many years ago. I knew He had this; whatever was wrong. I did not have the strength to react to the fear of this, so I am depending on God. I know I am not talking about what someone has told me about God; I met Him for myself. One of my favorite scriptures is Proverbs 3:5-6— "Trust in the Lord with all thine heart and lean not unto thine own understanding. In all thy ways acknowledge Him, and he shall direct thy paths."

I had no idea what was wrong with me because I always went to my doctors' appointments. I never missed a checkup in all my life. The EMTs asked me what I had taken—I said, "Nothing." Thinking back on May 19, 2017—I did not eat breakfast; I could hardly see the EMTs who entered my home—I only saw their legs as they walked in. I do not know how many people came; nor did I see their faces. I was too sick to look up. I did not see anyone in the ambulance. I barely saw the door close and what they did to me in there; I do not know. I felt nothing at all. I was fading away. I do not remember them pushing me through the front door or off the porch to get to the ambulance door. I do not remember getting on the stretcher in the house. I only remember my husband and Callie Blue standing at the end of the ambulance. They waved goodbye to me. I do not remember the ride to Augusta. I looked at the report; my husband called at 10:46 a.m. The unit was on the scene at 10:53 a.m. The ambulance left the scene at 11:10 a.m. with an arrival destination to Doctors Hospital at 11:55 a.m. I was not aware of anything that was going in the ambulance that day, even though the EMTs stated I said a few words to them. I do not remember talking to them.

I have no remembrance of being inside of the ambulance.

Thinking back on this Friday morning some more. My husband always uses oxygen. I was sitting in the living room all of that week. In a corner, we never keep the barrel of oxygen in the living room, but that morning it was sitting there in the corner. It had all of the parts already hooked up to it because my husband uses the oxygen box. He only uses this particular oxygen box when we are traveling away from home, but that morning it was sitting there, and my husband put it on my nose and I still could not breathe, so I pulled it off. He put it back in my nose, but I was almost gone at that moment. My memory was going and coming. I was coughing up blood in the paper that I had in my hand. My children came to my mind, but I was too sick to even stand up. When I first told my husband to call 9-1-1, he hesitated and looked at me as if I was crazy because he had never had to call 9-1-1 for me; I always call for Him.

On May 19, 2017, according to the EMS; they were on their way to the hospital in Augusta. The hospital in Washington, Georgia is a good hospital, but my case was too large for them. My husband had been in the Washington hospital close to a hundred times, and they treated Him good, but my situation was very tough. At 11:50 a.m., I was five minutes away at this time from Doctors Hospital. I did not open my eyes anymore according to the report from the EMTs. All the while I am riding and being transported to the hospital, the EMTs are working very hard to save my life. They had to run very fast! My son, Pastor Henra, told me that the ambulance had to drive on the shoulder of the highway to get me to the hospital. The God that I served already had planned for this and God knows all things even before it happens.

I am reminded by Psalm 139—

O Lord, thou hast searched me, and know me. Thou knowest my downsitting and mine uprising, thou understand my thought afar off. Thou compasset my path and lying down, and art acquainted with all my ways. For there is not a word in my tongue, but, lo, O Lord, thou knowest it altogether. Thou hast beset me behind and before and laid thine hand upon me. Such knowledge is too wonderful for me; it is high, I cannot attain unto it. Whither shall I go from thy Spirit? or whither shall I flee from thy present? If I ascend up into Heaven, thou art there: if I make my bed in hell, behold, thou are there. If I take the wings of the morning, and dwell in the uttermost parts of the sea; Even there shall thy hand lead me, and thy right hand shall hold me.

On May 19, 2017, this is what the EMTs reported—

The EMS called to the residence for patient who says she woke up fine this morning, and about 50 minutes prior to calling EMS she began coughing and having difficulty breathing. States she started to cough up blood. Finally decided to use one of her husband's Albuterol and Nebs with his Nebulizer machine. Spouse states were not getting any better so notified EMS. Patient was slightly Diaphoretic in residence. Patient denies any chest pains. Asked if she had something showing what the blood looked like, she coughed into a rag and noted blood-tinged sputum. States she took her Atenolol this a.m., but not any of her other meds. Patient up and into the EMS unit and prepped for transport. Lung sounds wet. Patient hooked up to monitor and into place at this time. Patient finished up her treatment and placed Albuterol and Atrovent in the nebulizer and continued in line. Patient prepped for transport. States she wanted to go to university, if possible. Patient vitals stable and respiratory effort controlled. EMS unit en route to university. Code 3 at this time. A-0, B38 labored. Lung wet rhonchi noted in all fields inspiratory and expiratory. Skin moist and warm, CRT<sec. B/P 182/128, Pulse 94, OX 94% with Neb and CPAP. Denies any pain, pupils ERRL. Patient was given Albuterol treatment and placed on oxygen. Albuterol/Atrovent given to patient when her Neb ran out. 40 mg IV Lasix given. Patient was given Xopenex

Via Nebulizer in line with CAPA. 70 ET tube placed at the 21 CM mark at the teeth after BVM used and suction. Patient's Lungs sounds still the same with wet rhonchi sounds propitiated all the way to the bases bilaterally. Patient was given Xopenex via inline nebulizer 10 minutes after the Albuterol/Atrovent complete. Patient tolerated CAPA well and patient loc assessed while EN route. Patient still with Tachycardia and HTN noted with her vitals. Patient not as Diaphoretic at this time after getting on I-20. While passing weight station on interstate patient still responding to EMS alertly and sat around 86%. Increased CAPA pressure to 7.5 CM/H20 support. SAT bumped to 90%. Advised University of Patient at this time. After report given. Re-Evaluated patient coming up to Belair Road and she is only responding with painful stimuli.

I do not remember ever being in the ambulance. The last thing I remember—I saw my husband waving at me as the ambulance doors closed. What went on in the ambulance? I have no idea. The EMTs say I was talking to them; I do not remember that. I do not remember any of these occurrences. It is hard for me to read this report, so I just paused for a moment. I pray and thank Father God, who I serve daily. I pray to Him throughout the day, every day always. I did not start praying after I got sick; I have been praying all of my life.

I said this prayer after I awoke from my coma—

> Oh, Father God, the God of this whole universe, the God of Abraham, Isaac, Jacob. I come to You low and humble as I lay at thy feet. Thanking You for saving my life and all of those stripes that You carried up cavalry for all of us, for the entire world. Lord, You spoke the word over every situation I needed help in, with my family members, friends, my enemies, and my neighbors. Lord, if I had ten thousand tongues; I would tell you to thank you for those many times at one time. I am no stranger to you; You know me. I talk to You all through the day and that is every day. Lord, I never missed a day or an hour from talking to You. Lord, thank You for sending those angles to pick me up. You already had them in mind when I had the biggest test to take. Thank You, Father God.

Back to the EMS report, I got so happy sitting here typing and thinking about the goodness of God's Mercy and His Grace.

Diverted to Doctors ER due to rapidly decreasing patient conditions. CAPA removed from patient, and she had frothy pink sputum coming out of her airway. Suctioned patient and placed BVM on patient and began bagging. Patient at this time on monitor showing bradycardia with

PVC'S at 56. Patient's Increased to 68 with BVM. Patient prepped for intubation at this time. Patient HYPER oxygenated and suctioned copious amount of frothy pink sputum placed in 7.0 ET visualized passing cords and immediately had pink sputum pouring out of ET tube. Cuff inflated and began bagging patient with good equal rise and fall of the chest. Once arrived at the ER Dockable to secure tube in place via tube tamer at the 21cm mark to the teeth. Lungs sound auscultated in the top and bottom of the lung fields and absent over the epigastrium. Patient HR at this time had increased back to 100 with her ventilations being assisted at 16 Last B/P 138/110. Patient into ER and to room 16. Arrived in and moved over to ED stretcher while holding tube manually. Respiratory in room and ED Physician also. Report given to the nurses' staff and Physician while patient Loc was Improving. Patient began to try to pull at the ET tube and was looking around. Patient assured to allow EMS and Resp to ventilate for her and to relax. Physician ordered versed for patient and resp place patient on ventilator at this time. Patient is unable to sign Medicare forms due to resp. EMS unit in service at the time. The doctor on call at the Doctors Hospital reported a 61-year-old female with resp. failure. She was given Lasix, nebulizer treatments CAPA per EMS en route. She stops breathing, becomes unresponsive, heart rate decreased from

126 to down to 70's. In the emergency department, hypotensive 89/70, pulse rate 132 reportedly sinus tachycardia, respirations 23, pulse oximetry 99% in place, cardiomegaly obesity, bilateral infiltrates suggestive of pulmonary edema but hard to exclude pneumonia only 139. She was on mechanical ventilation, given additional Lasix Levaquin after cultures, was also noted to have copious secretions, pink frothy/slightly bloody. She had a fever/diaphoresis, and she was felt more to be septic rather than in congestive heart failure. She was then given fluids per sepsis protocol, and also needed Levophed at this time. Temperature was 37 degrees cel, pulse was 132, respiration at 23. This was at 12:09 p.m. in the afternoon, condition critical, stable, primary impression. Respiratory failure Admitting notes: (Doctor notes) I have explained the patient's condition, diagnoses and treatment plan based on the information available to me at this time. I have answered the patient's and or caregiver's questions and any concerns. The patient and/or caregivers have a good understanding of the patient's diagnosis.

I remember none of this. I never saw anyone in the emergency room. I did not know I was even there. Here is more from my doctor's report— "Condition and treatment plans can be expected at this point. The patient has been stabilized within the capability of the emergency department."

What is going on here according to the definition of my illness? What did I have? I went into a Septic Shock diagnosed with Severe Pneumonia, and Pulmonary Edema with Sepsis Protocol. What is Sepsis? From what my doctors explained— Sepsis is poisoning of the blood. It is inflammation throughout the body due to a blood infection. The causes of Sepsis can be bacterial, viral, or fungal. People with Severe Sepsis require continuous monitoring and treatment in a hospital intensive care unit and proper medication.

Back to the doctor's report on May 19, 2017—

Patient critically ill, very guarded prognosis, a high risk for deterioration/complication/death neuro; sedation, analgesia per protocol, paralytic prn (severe resp. failure) Critical care time spent 45 minutes so far today, records/meds/labs/tests/vent, discussion with patient family/ICU team/consultants/ED staff. Plan discussed with spouse/partner/sons/daughter/family, admitting physician, nurse, interdisc care team. A 61-year-old female presents respiratory failure with septic shock secondary to sepsis, hypovolemia, or cardiogenic cause. Patient is currently; however, on the ventilator sedated. She also presents wht pneumonia. The plan was to continue to treatment of Pneumonia with antibiotic therapy. Continue treatment of the Septic shock with antibiotic therapy. Patient would benefit from an ID consult. At any rate, if she had an underlying coronary disease that has now manifest itself as a non-STEMI infarct certainly this along with poor LV function could be accountable for renal decline and liver decline. The patient also has thrombocytopenia with platelets of 71000. Patient additionally has renal insufficiency either acute or subacute with a creatinine of 2.31 down from 4.3. Certainly, the patient would be at risk for the further renal decline and possible dialysis if we were to give her a contrast dye at this point. Additionally, if she were to have catheterization and need a coronary stent with her platelets being 71,000 at the start, she with certainly with any stent platform need additional long term anti-platelet therapy which would be necessary would likely worsen be additive to the intraoperative anti-platelet therapy medications that would be necessary to be administered during the angioplasty and stenting procedure: i.e., angiomax, integrelin, etc. Given her overall increased risk for invasive procedure at this time would like to continue with antibiotic therapy for sepsis to see if any improvement in her renal function continually as well as her LFTs. Would also like to see if there is some improvement in her platelet count. At the present time, the patient appears to be DIC. Cathing her under the circumstances would be less than optimal. All of the above was explained to the patient's family. They are aware of the circumstances and the multi-organ failure and high level of acute illness of this patient. Will continue with therapy as outlined by the ICU team at the present time. If patient cannot tolerate with bleeding or worsening of her platelets, we may need to discontinue it.

I was in a coma at this time. I do not remember any of this. I was in another place. I will tell you about that place a little later on in my story. Sitting here typing—I have never read these notes before I am reading them for the first time. I had to stop, cry, and listen to a few of my favorite songs like "Peace in the Midst of a Storm" by Shirley Caesar and "God's Grace" by Rev. Luther Barnes. I had to read a few scriptures—Isaiah 41:10 reads:

Fear thou not; for I am with thee: Be not dismayed; for I am thy God: I will strengthen thee; yea, I will help thee; yea, I will uphold thee with the right hand of my righteousness.

This verse played over and over in my mind—Isaiah 26:30 says, "Thou wilt keep Him in perfect peace, whose mind is stayed on thee." I also read Mark 4:41—"And they feared exceedingly, and said one to another, what manner of man is this, that even the wind and the sea obey Him?"

Back to the Doctors report on May 21, 2017—

The patient does have pneumonia, which is currently being treated with antibiotics and also has septic shock secondary to her sepsis. The patient is critically ill in the ICU on Ventilatory support but does open her eyes to tactile stimuli. Patient's family is around her bed and is very supportive. Patient vital signs: She is afebrile at 98.4, pulse rate is 89, blood pressure is 154/69 and she is 100% on a ventilator. General: She is in bed. She is intubated, with no bleeding. She opens her eyes to voice. Cardiovascular: Regular rhythm and rate.

What is going on in my body at this time according to the doctor? I do not remember any of this. I will tell you where I am a little bit later on. Sitting here typing this book—I am feeling so warm. Oh, I got to stop and pray; thinking God call Him Father God, who holds the whole world in His hands.

I pray to thee for laying Your hands on my sick body, healing me Lord. I fall to Your feet no other name that I can call on to say thank you, but You Father God. You know me, there is nothing that I can hide from You. Oh, Lord as You spoke to that great storm to roll away. Lord, I am here today to say use me. Oh, Lord anyway that You will! Lord, I am yours! Lord, I am not my own, but your Lord. Oh, Lord! I am thinking about you.

I woke up! Glory hallelujah! I am awake! I will tell you where I have been in a few.

Back to the doctor's report on May 28, 2017—

This is an awake, alert 61-year-old African American female who is morbidly obese and in no acute distress. The patient is weak but is able to move all extremities actively. She is awake alert, answering questions. Focused examination of the patient's sacral region reveals a stage II pressure ulcer, which is noted to have a red moist wound bed. There is some scattered yellow slough, but no active sign or symptom of infection. Stage II pressure to ulcer to the sacrum. After today, the patient will be started on Bactroban and Xeroform to the wound daily. The patient should be washed with soap and water prior to application of this dressing. The patient will be monitored closely while she is admitted to the hospital by our services on Tuesdays and Fridays. She will be placed on a sidewise alternating pressure mattress as well as a turning and repositioning program every 2 hours. She will wear Prevalon boots at all times to further pressure reduce. She was examined today with direct supervision. Family is at her bed side.

Pausing here for a moment, thinking about my waking up. The first thing I did—I looked around the room wondering, "Why were all of these people in my room?" Family members I had not seen in years were standing there looking at me. I was so sick. I did not know a human being could get as sick as I was and still be living. It did not make any sense. I did not know what was wrong with me; no one had told me a thing. Some of my family folks were just walking in and out of my room. Some of them came up to my bed and spoke to me. I looked around still in shock to see all of those people. Some called to see how I was doing.

I know the Lord. He loves me and I love Him. I am thinking about Jeremiah 33:6—"Lord bring health and a cure to every area of my life and give me the abundance of peace." After the doctors told me what happened to me; I did not say a word, because my God, the God that I serve took time out of his busy schedule to come and see about a poor peasant woman like me. I was just thinking about all of the billions of people that have died and who are with Christ Jesus. And all the billions of people that live here on this earth. Jesus Christ took time out of his schedule to come by The Doctors Hospital to room 16 in ICU to see about me, even though I was not there in that body until several days later. I left that body before I got to the Doctors Hospital. I left that body five minutes before the EMS got to my house. What happened on the way to the Doctors Hospital? I do not know! I vaguely remember telling the EMS where I wanted to go. I am glad that God already had made plans for me to go to the Doctors Hospital. I had three of my children there, so they knew my blood type and they had my records.

I will explain where I went in a few. Oh, it was something! I did not feel any pains until I came back to that sick, sick body of mines. I am glad I came back. My husband and my children were not ready to let me go. "The Lord restored health unto me and healed me of my wounds." This is Jeremiah 30:17. My mind was on where I had been, and it is still on my mind. I think about it all the time, but I will tell you about it a little later on in this book. This is the biggest battle I had ever endured in my life. I gave it to the Lord. He got a purpose for this battle that I have to fight, and I have to pass this test. It is a million pages long, but I must pass this test and I will. So how will I pass this test? We need not fear what comes against us but stand firm in our faith in God. He knows the whole situation. Though we feel overwhelmed when we look at our circumstances, the Lord sees the whole picture and sees the way out for us. We need to let God have control and fight the battles we are fighting. He has promised that He is with us and that He will bring us through. I read Christian Devotional on the Lord Fighting our Battle by M.S. Lowndes. When I awoke, I was amazed about where I was in a mess, but I know I had the ball in my court. I kicked it in the direction I wanted to go; it was up to me. I know that He showed me many things. God is real! Why me Lord? Why not me? He used me to bring a great miracle through.

I was in really bad shape when my Spirit came back to my body. I was not in any pain. Where was I? I was in Heaven. I will tell you about this a little later in my book. My children looked so tired, but they stuck with me, and their father did too. My family was standing there just looking at me. When I awoke—I think two of my sisters laughed at me the way I was trying to talk, my voice sounded like a very old lady that had been out in the cold all day. It was okay. I remember the nurse pulling all of those tubes out of my throat. Funny thing, my throat was not even sore, but everything else on my body was a mess. The nurse gave me a half cup of ice to eat, which was the best ice I had ever tasted. The nurse said that also. She also gave one spoon of ice cream, and she threw the leftovers in the crash can. Oh, how I wanted the rest of that ice cream! I had been sleeping for a while for about 10 days. That is a long time to lay still. I stepped out of my body, and I went to Heaven. I will tell you all about it later on.

I have never been a person to give up or complain! I just had to do what had to be done and hold on to Jesus Christ where all my help comes from, because I will never give up on my Lord; He will always see me. God has been with me through all of my storms and sometimes the storms got so bad I had to pray and sing hymns of praise and wait. If you want help you just got to wait on God, no matter how long it takes sometimes. He comes quickly and sometimes he will come in the morning, but you do not know how long that morning will be. Just wait on Him and praise Him while you are looking for what you are asking for. When you ask God for something, you just got to wait and keep your heart open for the answer. He will come in a way you will never expect Him to answer, but the way He will answer will be in His will for you because He knows what we need before we ask. When I awoke, I was too weak to sit up. I know my four sisters and my brothers were so hurt to see me in this condition! I just looked at their eyes and sick as I was, I had to say, "Lord have mercy on them!" I prayed these scriptures:

Keep me as the apple of the eye, hide me under the shadow of thy wings. I will take heed to my ways, that I sin not with my tongue. I will keep my mouth with a bridle, while the wicked is before me (Psalm 17:8; 39:1).

I was too sick to even sit up! I was so sick I would have fallen out of the bed if it was not for the rails. My husband says that he called me several times on my way back from picking up Callie Blue, but I never heard the phone ringing. About three weeks later, I listened to my message, and it was true he had called me three times. He said, "Are you coming home tonight?"

Chapter 3

BLESSSED BE THE TIDES THAT BIND

I was holding onto that big wheel turning in the middle of the sky. When it turned, it was like thunder roaring in the elements. It sounded so loud! "Lord, have mercy on me! Where am I?" I have never heard a noise like that. I was holding on. Every time the big wheel turned; the chains were breaking in the sky. I held on so tight! I could not let go. I saw my son, Otis, he was flashing in front of my eyes.

He said, "Hold on mama! Hold on, mama!"

I said, "I can hardly hold on!" I had to. Otis told me Otis Jr. was sick!

He said, "You got to hold on so he can get well!" I did not say another word. The wheel turned two more times and Otis said, "You are almost there, mama." I was in another dimension. The sound got so loud! The sounds were just clapping together.

"Oh! My God! Where am I?" I saw Otis face flash in front of me again. I was in another dimension at this time.

After that, I found myself at my gravesite. My son, Pastor Henra, was standing there. I was standing in the front of my casket up on the hill at Thankful Baptist Church. I only saw my youngest son, Pastor Henra, at my funeral. I felt myself going down into the ground. It was fun going down in the ground! I saw dirt on each side of me. It is just like riding a roller coaster! I road through the earth. Pastor Henra said to me, "Come back!" This was a five-second ride in the ground! I came to the other side. I come came out through a tunnel. The light was so bright in the tunnel, and I was by myself. Oh, my God! I was so happy! This happens while I was still in an ambulance on my way to the Doctors Hospital. I stepped out of my body, and I went to Heaven. I stayed over there several days. I was not in my body when I got to the emergency room in Augusta, Georgia.

A lot of things happen to us, but in the human mind, there is not an explanation for the situation. I had no pain in this body. I was smiling and very happy. When I got to the river in Heaven, I saw my mother. She was standing on the other side of the river. She was looking the other way. She told me to go back. She said, "It was not my time to come yet." I laid in the water on my back, and I was looking up at the beautiful skies in Heaven; I did not sink in the water. My whole body was healed from this water. The water felt so warm and smooth. I stretched both of my hands out in the river. I cannot explain this feeling. I was so happy! I can see myself in the water now! The water was like Jell-O. The water was a darker blue and shiny. It is different from the water here on earth. I was looking back on top of the hillside and Pastor Henra was saying "Mama come on back you are not dead." I looked at Pastor Henra and I smiled at Pastor

Henra. I know I wanted to stay. He said, "Come on back, mama!" He was using his hands to reach out; he was up high on the of the hill looking at me starting to cross the river.

I looked to my right where my mother was, and I saw my two aunties, Essie, and Lue. Essie is "Aunt Nee," which is the name we called her all of her life. She said, "Is that you, Willie Agnes?" She always called me that. My mother thought she was having a boy, so she named me, "Willie." My parents named me after my uncle, Willie Callaway. Once they found out I was a girl at birth, they added "Agnes" to my middle name after my Aunt Agnes Butler. I looked at the hill where all those children were playing. I saw all those children; there were all races of children, but they were all dressed alike. They had on jumpers (overalls) they were blue, and the jumpers had light blue flowers on them. All of the children had on white, short sleeve shirts. My aunties were sitting there watching the children play. I looked at the trees where the children were playing, and I noticed how beautiful they were.

My body is well in Heaven; I am not sick here. When I stepped out of the ground, I stepped into the light. There is nothing dark here. The color of the tree bark is like deep chocolate, brown. The bark was extra thick, and it was so shiny like gloss was on the trees. Some trees were tall and so huge. A lot of children were playing under these types of trees. I looked at the trees and they were extra wide than any other tree I have seen on earth. The green leaves were a spring green—very bright. I looked down through the path where the river ran off and there was shining gold on side of the streams where the water was running it was so peaceful. You do not have to breathe there in Heaven. The sky was bright and seem like you can touch the sky. There is no sun or moon in Heaven. I did see any stars. I looked up at the sky, it is lower than here on earth. The sky did not seem as though it was so far away from the ground like it is here on earth. The grass looked like plastic; it is so beautiful. The dirt on the ground just glowed—it was light brown. I saw a whining road of thick, shiny gold and when the road straightened out it led to me large buildings—many mansions. It was yellowish and shinning. I look at these mansions—stones were going all around the door and windows. The stones resembled amethyst, jasper, rubies, sapphires, diamonds, and crystals. I am reminded by 2 Corinthians 5:1-5—

For we know that if our earthly house of this tabernacle were dissolved, we have a building of God, a house not made with hands, eternal in the Heavens. For in this we groan, earnestly desiring to be clothed upon with our house which is from Heaven: If so, be that being clothed we shall not be found naked. For we that are in this tabernacle do groan, being burdened: not for that we would be unclothed, but clothed upon, that mortality might be swallowed up of life. Now he that hath wrought us for the selfsame thing is God, who also hath given unto us the earnest of the Spirit.

I laid my whole body in that water over there. It healed my body. I remember I had to change into my Spiritual body before I got to Heaven. When I left my physical body; my Spiritual body took over. My mother and my aunties were young. My Aunt Lue just looked at me and I smiled, then I went to another place in Heaven—it had to be another dimension. I got to stop here before I tell you about the other part of Heaven that I had a chance to visit; I had to stop and thank God for me being here. Sitting here listening to Dr. C. J. Johnson singing "I know it was the blood that saved me!"

I was just walking along, feeling good, and enjoying myself in Heaven. I do not know this world while I was in Heaven. I did not know that I lived in this world at this time. I am only thinking about Heaven and enjoying what I see here. I did not even know that I was sick. I had no idea. In Heaven, there is only peace. While walking in Heaven, I came upon a large wheat field. I saw people gathering the wheat. There are garden tools in Heaven. I saw pitchforks and rakes. The two oxen that I saw were off-white with light brown stripes running down the side of their backs. They were full of God's glory. The wooden wagon was light brown wood with the same color stripes. There were hooks across the oxen's head so they could pull the wagon. The wagon wheel was made of wood. It had about 12 spinners inside the wheels. I stood there and I look at all those people gathering barley and wheat and places the bundles into the wagon.

I saw men with satchels around their waists and with knives hanging at their sides. The garden tools look at the tools of old in the Bible days. They were trying it up in little bundles in the field. I am standing there looking at the people. The people look just like the ones in the Bible days. The men had on fieldwork clothes and wore sandals with belts tied around their waist. The men had on hair scarfs or rags around their heads. They had stuck in their hands to guide the animals. The women had very long hair and wore scarfs on their heads. The women had on saddles and shawls. Some women had on field working clothes others were dressed elegantly. One woman had a white long dress that went down to her feet. She had pretty brown hair, very wavy and long. She stood there looking at me, fixing her headscarf. Was this lady Jesus' mother? She was extra beautiful.

I believe I saw Simon of Cyrene that carried Jesus' cross up Calvary. Well, I know I saw him! He is African. He carried Jesus' cross when Jesus could no longer carry His cross up Calvary. I saw this man. He had sachet around his waist, and he was standing with the other people out in the field. He was tall and skinny. His skin was milk chocolate in color. He had on metallic brown color pants and brown boots. He had on a plaid shirt. He had natural hair, an afro, not too much hair on his head. The Bible talks about Simon of Cyrene in the book of Mark chapter fifteen. I also saw this Lady; I believe this was Mary. She had on a long, white gown and a scarf around her head. Her hair was wavy and long. She was extremely beautiful. She was tying her back around her head when she looked at me. I am walking; they are looking at me. I am young about 30 years old, slim, and strong. I am not sick here. I looked up at the bluish sky. I am feeling so light; my body is like a feather. I was in Heaven enjoying myself not knowing that my husband, children, family members, and friends are wondering how my sickness is going to turn out. I did know I was going back to my body. I had nothing to do with that. I did not know that my body was sick.

Back to Heaven—As I was walking, I saw oxen with wagons on them. The oxen were huge. People were putting the wheat or barley on the wagon. They looked at me, but they did not do say a word. Oh, the feeling! The oxen had gloried in their eyes! I cannot explain it! It is an unbelievably exciting feeling! I walked on over to the end of the field. I saw this man—he looked at me most compassionately. This man was sitting on a rock. I walked upon Him. When He saw me, He looked at me for five seconds than He looked away. When that man looked at me, I cannot explain the feeling I felt! My God! Who was that man sitting on that rock, I got to tell the world about Him? He had a rag or scarf of some type tied around His head. The inside of His eyes was like the ocean, bluish water was running up on the side of His eyes and parts of His eyes were very clear. He had a beautiful cheekbone structure in His face. His nose was perfectly made. His skin was gray and pink mixed together. He had on clothes, a robe—fine, satin linen—it was eggshell in color, not exactly white. His robe gleaned and laid against His skin so softly. He had a belt around his waist. Lord, have mercy! I am getting happy with the Holy Spirit telling the world about this man I met sitting there on a rock. The rock was dark brown and glowing. It looks as though it was a glass rock. I looked at His legs and I saw that He had sandals on; they were dark brown with leather straps wrapped around his feet. One thick strap from the saddles went across His feet—the middle of His feet. The other strap went around His ankles and buckled on the left side of his feet. His saddles were old and thick. His head rag was the same color as His sandals—dark brown. I looked at His ankles and long leg bones. His legs were usually straight and did not see a curve in his leg. He had hairy legs. I saw His knee cap. They were glowing and they were medium size.

He looked about 6 feet tall. He was slender in size. He had dark, brown rings going around His toes—possibly dirt from the ground. His toenails were clear—looked like fish scales, not like human toenails. I could see through His toenails. I saw the meat of His nail under His toenails. The same color as his skin. His chin was that of the men in the Bible days. His chin was oval-shaped. His face was beautifully constructed—He had thin lips. His nose was mildly pointed. He had a beard on his face—not thick. I could see His skin through his beard. His hair on His head came to His shoulders. His hair was thick and bushy and had the color of dark chocolate brown. His hair was combed back off of his face. I saw that His hands turned into his gown. I saw His index and middle finger of His right hand. He had long fingers. I saw a half of a scar on His right hand. What were these marks? Were those marks from Him hanging on the cross? His arms were long. His robe covered his arms and came to his wrists. Oh, His eyes had water moving around inside of them. I asked the question, "Who was this man?" I see Him in my mind every day. I see this man sitting there. I walked upon Him; He turned His head and looked at me. It was like He was controlling my eyes to what He wanted me to see concerning Himself.

When I walked upon Him, it was a few seconds before He turned His head and looked at me. I will never forget that man sitting on that rock, was that Jesus? I believed it was Jesus! Who else would it be? Why would Jesus show Himself to me? I am nobody in this world. Why would He look at me that way? I am a peasant woman. I kept to myself. I love Jesus; I always have, and I always will no matter what I have to go through, I will always love Jesus! One day I am going back to that rock and the next time I will not be back! Until then, I am going to keep praying and trusting God. I do not know why this happened to me, but I do not need to know. Everything cannot be explained. I always tell the Lord to use me any way He wants to use me. I am Yours, Lord!

While back in the hospital, I heard the angels singing all around my bed and clapping their hands. I never heard of the songs or heard singing like that, it had healing power in every clap and every word. I was laying there sick, real sick. The angels who were marching around my bed had on white gowns. The angels just sang one song a day and then they vanished from the room. I was in another dimension. I saw myself in the hospital bed with no tubes hooked up to me in this dimension. I was laying in the hospital bed with real white pillows under my head; the pillows were radiant white. My whole hospital room was shining bright. The light from the brightness bounced off of the windows. In this dimension, I also seen two angles come to the hospital to check on me. The angles came twice a day to check on me. They fixed my pillows, and they were talking to each other as always. The angles would say, "She is all right; we will be back." These angles look like the nurses back in the 1950s. They had on uniforms with the white stripes going across the shoulders with white stockings and white shoes. There was a man angel that came as well. He had on a white jacket, black pants, and a white shirt. Their faces had a radiant glow about it. I will never forget any of this, what I saw. It will be with me until the day I die! I am going to tell everyone who wants to listen, that there is a Heaven and God is real! I already know Him! He just had another test for me to take. The closer you get to God, the more tests you will have to take. Lord, I take nothing away from my journey--all the pain, heartache, disappointments, all of my mistakes, and failures. I am going to count it all joy.

Sitting here reading the Bible—

There was a certain rich man, which was clothed in purple and fine linen and fared sumptuously every day: And there was a certain beggar named Lazarus, which was laid at his gate, full of sores, and desiring to be fed with the crumbs which fell from the rich man's table: moreover, the dogs came and licked his sores. And it came to pass, that the beggar died, and was carried by the angels into Abraham's bosom: the rich man also died and was buried: And in hell he lift his eyes, being in torments, and seeth Abraham afar off, and Lazarus in his bosom. And he cried and said, Father Abraham, have mercy on me, and send Lazarus, that he may dip the tip of his finger in water, and cool my tongue; for I am tormented in this flame. But Abraham said, Son, remember that thou in thy lifetime receivedst thy good things, and likewise Lazarus evil things: but now he is comforted, and thou art tormented. And beside all this, between us and you there is a great gulf fixed: so that they which pass from hence to you cannot; neither can they pass to us, that would come from thence. Then he said, I pray thee, therefore, Father, that thou wouldest send Him to my father's house: For I have five brethren, that he may testify unto them, lest they also come into this place of torment. Abraham saith unto Him, They have Moses and the Prophets: let them hear them. And he said, Nay, father Abraham: but if one went unto them from the dead, they will repent. And he said unto Him if they hear not Moses and the prophets, neither will they be persuaded, though one rose from the dead (Luke 16:19-31).

67

I had to put this scripture in my book. There are so many people in this world that are outside of the safety of God. God requires all of us to repent, believe, and be saved before it is too late. Who would want to miss Heaven? It is a beautiful place—no more pain, tears, sorrows, no more disappointments, or sickness? No more doctor appointments, hospitals, tragedies, troubles, no more jealously, or fear, hatred, or worry; nothing evil will be allowed in Heaven! No more lies will be told on you! Every day will be racism-free! "When all of God's children get together, oh what a time it will be!" I listened to this song by Dottie Peoples often.

I love Psalm 16:11, which says "Thou wilt shew me the path of life: in thy presence is fulness of joy; at the right hand there are pleasures forevermore." Also, I love Revelations 22:14—"Blessed are they that do his commandments, that they may have right to the tree of life and may enter through the gates into the city." After I awoke from my coma, I had more rivers to cross. Sick as a human being could get without being dead; I have come back to my body after being in a coma ten days. The devil showed up to my mind and said, "Why don't you just go ahead and die! You are almost dead, anyway! No one cares about you!"

I started to feel bad inside, questioning God. How could I question my Savior when I just came from Heaven? How could I? I told the devil, "I just came from Heaven, and I belong to Jesus Christ! Leave me alone!" Oh, the devil will try you, but he cannot stand the name of Jesus! When you talk to people, all you have to do is bring up Jesus' name and tell them what He has done for you, see how long most of them will stay. Very few!

I am too sick to blink my eyes. I was completely broken. I was in little, tiny pieces and I had to be put back together. My God had done what he had to do. I had to do the rest—me, myself, and I. The only thing I could do was rest in the Lord and keep on praying. I was pitiful, sad, and sick, but I knew God is with me because he told me so. I am like Job from the Bible. Job 16:12 reads: "I was at ease, but he hath broken me asunder: he hath also taken me by my neck, and shaken me to pieces, and set me up for his mark." No matter what shape I am in; I am going to praise my God because I have no strength of my own. I am not my own. My life belongs to God.

Just lying here—my children, my husbands and one of my granddaughters standing here looking at me. I look terrible, but my heart is beating. I am thinking what in the world have I done to be going through all of this suffering? I never suffered like this before—crying every day after my family leaves, that is my immediate family. I did not want them to see me cry so much, because I already know that they have cried themselves to death, they were not ready to let me go yet.

You got to say your prayers all through the day; Do not ever wait until night! I always pray before my feet hit the floor in the morning. I look at the Bible studies on television when I wake up about 5:00 a.m. and I pray. I pray while I am bathing and I pray all through the day, this is every day. I listen to sermons and I play gospel music especially when I am doing my housework. Please do not ever wait until nighttime to pray! You might die before night comes! Always store up prayers, because it might come a time when you cannot pray! I could not pray when I got sick, because I was too sick to pray. I got sick so quickly and in the blink of an eye, I was gone. The Lord ran across my mind, but I could not pray. I was gone. I have always tried to live a clean and good life. I did not have time for messing around in my life. I married at 18 years old and had a child at 19 years old as well as four more over the years. I lost a child at birth; his name is Noah. I will tell you more about Him later in this book.

I had a lot of work to do raising four children. I had to make sure that I put the right stuff in them. You have to start very early with children. I had to make sure that they knew Jesus. I had to make sure they were around the right people; their morals and values had to be intact. I always told them to treat other people like you want to be treated. I had to make sure that those four children of mines had a good life. I did not play. We had fun. They had a good childhood; when my parents were living, and their dad's parents were living, they spend a lot of time with their grandparents before they passed on to glory! They had a chance to see their grandparents on both sides. All of their grandparents had strong beliefs in the Lord. I always told them at an early age that the first commandment was to love the Lord with all of their heart, soul, and mind.

I had to be careful, because we may think we are better than someone else because we do not do what they do. Oh, yes! I thought that because I prayed all of the time; I got special favor and I do but be careful—the same way you judge another God will judge you. Matthew 7:1 says, "Judge not, that ye be not judged. For with what judgment ye judge, ye shall be judged: and with the same measure ye mete, it shall be measured to you." "I do not do that or this," but you are doing something wrong.

You have to discern that Spirit that tells you ahead of time about trouble; when it comes around an antenna should go up, but you have to be close enough to God to feel this. Laying there in my bed, so sick—I question the Lord and told the Lord that I have lived as close as I could to His word, "Why am I so sick"? We should not question God, but I did! I did not mean to, but I was not sick until I came back to my body. I always know people get sick enough to leave the body because I did it before, but I saw different things; I will tell you about it later on. No matter what situation we are in, we must always give God thanks. I thought I was going to die again, when I came to the Doctors Hospital—the doctors never had any hope for me.

One of my doctors came into my room and told me about my family; he met my children and he told me how wonderful they were and how they loved me. He said that he knew how they felt because he loves his mother so much. He says he was supposed to check on me, but he did not come in there, because he did not see a way that I was going to live. He was a very nice doctor, but I do not know his name. I know was so honest. He said, "Mrs. Chennault I had to come by and tell you this." I could not say a word. I was too sick to say much; I just nodded my head. I was on so many machines, but I never have seen the ventilator on me when I awoke. I had a lot of other machines and all kinds of wires hooked up to me.

I was a sick woman. I had bit my lip and swallowed up all of the skin on the inside of my mouth due to the peeling on the inside my mouth. I had splits or cuts on both sides of my mouth. I almost swallowed my tongue. All on the inside of my mouth; I had sores. My gum had sores, but my throat was fine. That was strange to me. My eyes looked like a sick animal that had suffered for a long time. I never looked at my eyes until several weeks later; I was too sick to look at this time. Oh, my family; my immediate family looked so tried. I did not have an idea when I awoke that I had been sick. I remember I left my body. I was not sick in Heaven. I did not even know what was wrong with me. All the time, I was sleep. I felt no pain! None at all until I came back to my physical body. Lord, have mercy on me! I almost felt like Job from the Bible, but God let me see Heaven and the people in the Bible days. I was so weak. I remember what Job said, I know part of what he was feeling.

After this opened Job, his mouth and cursed his day. And Job spake, and said, Let the day perish wherein I was born and the night in which it as said, There is a man child conceived. Though he slay me, yet will I trust in Him, but I will maintain mine own ways before Him (Job 3:1-3; 13:15).

I was not worried, and I knew I still had a long journey. I was on the floor where they kept the hospice people. I did not know that. My husband knew that, and he told me some time after I got home. I did not know that I was so sick; I thought I was going to die at any given minute, but I knew God did not bring me that far to leave me. He does not work like that; If I was going to die, I would have stayed over there with Jesus when I saw Him sitting on that rock in the field. He looked at me in a way I will never, never forget. Oh, if you do not know Him; If there is breath in your body, please get to know Him. His hand is stretched out to you! One thing about the Lord, He will accept you! He is a forgiving God!

Looking back over my reports for the hospital—I saw these words on my records, "Streptococcus Pneumonia Antigen." This was on May 20, 2017. My report read:

Patient's temperature was 37.3 F°. A 61-year-old female with acute respiratory failure, acute renal failure, pneumonia, cholelithiasis elevated transaminases. Patient is not a surgical candidate, if it is felt this is acute process of the gallbladder, then only option would be a cholecystectomy tube.

When I awoke, I was just like that frog that you see on the front of this book. When I came from the hospital, I was looking just like her. The same day that I came from the hospital, I went to the back of my house just looking around still on my walker, because my strength was not back yet in my legs. So, I looked down in this large barrel of water that I use to water my flowers with—just standing there praying and thanking God for letting me get home again! I had to tell God how mighty He is, and I just love Him. I am praying to Him while lifting my hands to Heaven and thanking Him for letting me see a glimpse of Heaven, praising His name-calling Him a "Doctor in a Sick Room," a "Healer," calling

Him "All-powerful," "All-knowing," calling a "Lily in the Valley"!

I looked down in that barrel of rainwater and I saw this creature down in that can of water; the can was half full of water. I stood there just looking down in there at this little frog trying to get up to the rim. I thought, "Oh how is this frog going to get out?" Every time she made it to the top of the barrel; she began to slide, and she would slide back down again into the water. I am just looking in that barrel of water. I stood there; I know for ten minutes. I felt so sad! It reminded me of my struggle to walk again. I looked and all of the times that frog tried to get out of that big barrel. I know she developed in that can of water and lived in the country in the woods.

This little frog touched my heart. I know she made eight tries to get out of that barrel. I had my phone in my pocket, so I took this picture—the front cover of this book. The Holy Spirit was already upon me, and the Holy Spirit told me to put this picture on the front cover of the book. When that frog struggled to finally get to the top of the rim of that barrel; she just sat there. I am just calling the frog she because I am, she; I was her.

As this beautiful frog is sitting there wondering which way to go; she just sat there looking around. She was afraid of this world because she has never known this world. It is a mystery to her. I am just looking at her. You could look at her and see the fear in her big shining eyes. That frog just sat there looking at me. I stood there looking at her until I got tired of standing due to being on a walker at this time. It came to my mind I did not want her to fall back in the water because she made all of that progress of struggling out of this barrel. The frog's struggle was like the same struggle I had to do when I had to learn to walk all over again just like a newborn baby. It was one of the hardest things; I had ever done.

So, I said to myself, "I do not want to rush this frog to jump to an unknown place." She knew nothing about this place. If we do not take a jump in life or go out on the limb, how can you ever know what is out there for you? We all have to take risks in life. Life is a risk, a dream, a vapor. "After you struggled to get to the top of that rim, little frog—where do you go from here?" The frog had entered an unknown world that she knows nothing about; she never did hop by herself, I had to give her a little nudge. I do not know what way she went; I have never seen a frog that looked like that before. She was very beautiful! She was a diamond color and shining white like a rock. God gave me the title of this book. I called all of my children and I told me what the title of this book was going to be and all of them were amazed by the title—the title that the Holy Spirit gave to me.

A lot of times it is just you and God. I prayed this prayer while I was watching the frog in the barrel of water. I was seated on the bench in the back yard. I prayed this prayer.

Lord, I have my mind on Thee. Lord, what can I say to You? Lord, You know my heart and you know all about me. You knew me before I even knew myself. Lord, You know I had to take this test. This test was unhuman for any human being. I thank You, Lord, for taking me out of my body. You showed me, Heaven. You let me see "You" most of all. You let me see my mother. You let me see my two aunties. You let me walk around in your glory. Your glory was everywhere, even in the oxen eyes; I saw Tour glory. I saw all those peoples from the Bible days. I knew the old lady Hannah was among the group. I know Paul was there. I know Peter was there. I know David was there. I know all of the other prophets were there. I know Abraham, Isaac, and Jacob were there. Why me, Lord? Why did you choose me for this test? What made me so special to You? Lord, You gave me a vacation to Heaven, and You brought me back from Heaven. It was so real. It was not a dream. I was with thee. I saw You Lord, as You looked at me so compassionately. I stood right beside You. You took care of my children and my family members while I went through this test. You did not let Lazarus Sr., my husband, get sick or have to go to the hospital. I just want to say thank You! I thank You for giving my children traveling grace back and forth to the hospital and Lord, You kept them strong. I just want to say thank You. Thank You, Lord Jesus! This test I took, Lord Jesus. I will tell everyone who wants to listen. I know You did not want me to go through all of this to keep this to myself. I am Yours, Lord. Use me anyway You, please! Hold my hand as I continue to walk with thee. But the next time I come in Your presence; I will stay. Lord thank you! I am glad; I was afflicted. I am free! Amen.

We cannot depend on our love ones or our pastors, or our parents, or our church family, to be in the favor of God. For God to give us favor—we all must stand before God for ourselves! We must make our own choices. While I was standing in the backyard looking at this frog trying to make up her mind which way to leap, tears of joy began rolling down my face because the Holy Spirit was present. I always had church in my back yard most time.

It is just me and my dog, his name is Fuzzy. He just sits there and watches me hold up my hands to Holy God and I always thank Him for what He has already done for me all of these years from my cradle until now. I tell Him, I do not have any strength only what He gives me. "Oh, mighty God! I ask you to hold my husband, my children, their children, my daughters-in-law, my ex-daughter-in-law, and her family in Your hands."

I tell God about whatever is going on in my heart. I tell Him if I have anything in my heart that is not pleasing to Him, to please remove it. I tell Him, Lord, if there is any unforgiveness in my heart to remove it and give me a clean heart. I always pray before my feet hit the floor in the morning thanking Him for waking me up. I ask God to give my children and the rest of my family traveling grace to work then I tell Him to bless my friends, my enemies, and my neighbors. I pray for my brothers, sisters, brothers-in-law, and sisters-in-law. I pray for my nephews and my nieces. I always pray for my cousins, aunties, and my uncles. I pray for my doctors that touch me! I tell God to lay His mighty hands on the doctors that touch my family members. I pray for the people that I meet daily in the grocery store and the drug store. People come up to me and tell me their problems and I pray for them on the way home. I think about all of the people who are sick, and I pray for them. I pray for the families that have lost loved ones. I pray all through the day that is every day, about seven times a day. I repeat Psalm 23 and the Lord Prayer's because everything is in those prayers that you will need. I always pray for myself last and again, when I pray; I always tell God to let His will be done in my life. Lord, I tell Him—"I am yours Lord use me anyway You want to!" I do not wait until night to pray. I pray all day, every day. My husband asked me why I pray so much. I do not know; I just hunger, and I thirst for God's presence. There is nothing that I have found in life that can fill that space. There is a place in my heart that no one in this world can get to, no problems or pains can enter that place in me that place is in my Spirit with God.

I am reminded by 1 Corinthians 4- 4: "For I know nothing by myself; yet am I not here justified: but He Judgeth me is the Lord." I read Luke 12:48 often throughout the day, which says—

But he that knew not, and did commit things worthy of stripes, shall be beaten with few stripes, for unto whomsoever much is given, of Him shall be much required: and to whom men have committed much, of Him they will ask the more.

The closer you get to God; it will cost you some things. The closer a person gets to God the more they will have to endure.

When I awoke from my coma, I saw this beautiful girl. She was just helping the nurse to turn me over and she put some cream on my lips. I asked her, "Who are you?" She was just working on me; she had the sweetish Spirit; her Spirit was very humble. Her hair was very wavy, hanging down her back. She looked like a nurse. I asked her what is her name?

She said, "April!"

I said, "Is that you, April?"

I had not seen her in a while. I smiled at her, and I thanked her for what she was doing for me. April is my niece—Alberta's daughter, my second youngest sister's daughter.

I had the best team in the world looking after me. God had everything in place for me. What God does for you, no one can redo what God can do. I was okay. I am all right. My immediate family was always by my side. My other family members called me throughout the week, but this battle; I had to fight it alone—Just me and my God! Jesus walked with me! I was not worried! I was sick as sick could be in a human body. That was me! Some of my family members came by my bed and spoke to me. I am sure some of my family members and friends had decided that I was not supposed to wake up all, all odds were against me! However, life is not over until God says so! No matter how dim it looks to the human eyes.

There were so many doctors and so many nurses in and out of my room all day and all night. It was time for my children to go back to work; they had been out of work for a long time. I looked across the room at my husband and my granddaughter, Hannah; they both looked so worn completely out so I told them to go home and get some rest, but my husband said he would go in a few more days. My daughter stayed with me along as she could. My husband was sick Himself. He has been sick for 14 years with a terrible lung disease. He would be in and out of the hospital about five times a year. I had no appetite. My son told me if you do not eat, you will never get out of here. That was easier said than done! I was always laying there thinking about the things that I had seen in Heaven. If people only knew how it feels to be in Heaven. There are no words to describe Heaven; it is more than amazing.

The doctor came in to see me and he looked away some of the times when he was talking to me, but I would be looking straight at Him in his eyes. He told me that your kidneys are not working, and your blood is not clean. I did not make any gestures. I heard Him! I was not worried about it at all, because I know the God that I serve has not brought me this far to leave me. I prayed, and I prayed! I anointed myself with the oil my daughter and I had prayed over. I told my daughter to bring me my Bible the one that is in my bedroom at home on the table by my bedside. She retrieved my Bible for me, and she gave it to me, and I turned it to Psalm 23, and that Bible stayed with me openly on the table in the book of Psalm—the 23rd chapter.

Soon after, another lady doctor came into my room and said in a few minutes; we will be taking you up to dialysis. I had been on dialysis all the time while I was in a coma. I am awake, and my kidneys are still not working. So, this lady doctor came to my room to tell me what time my dialysis will be taking place. She told me a story about her husband and how he had to have dialysis. She told me that her husband had to have the three cycles of dialysis. She said after that his kidneys went back to working just fine.

I had no fear! I was thinking about Heaven and how Father God speared my life. I thought about my family; they needed me, especially my husband—with Him being so sick. He always depended on me. My daughter told me that he had been crying ever since you got sick mama. At this time, the doctors have left my room. I am laying there thinking about a verse in the book of Matthew 8: 5-8—

And when Jesus was entered into Capernaum, there came unto Him a centurion, beseeching Him, And saying, Lord, my servant lieth at home sick of the palsy, grievously tormented. And Jesus saith unto Him, I will come and heal Him. The centurion answered and said, Lord, I am not worthy that thou shouldest come under my roof: but speak the word only, and my servant shall be healed.

I closed my eyes thinking about these words. I was just like someone with palsy. I could not turn over. I had to be turned every two hours. I put myself in the same position as this sick servant. I told Father God if He would just speak the word. I always take Father God back to His word if I want something from Him. He cannot lie. Just try Him and see want He will do it.

So, an hour later the dialysis people came to get me. They asked me, "Are you ready to go?" I nodded my head. The Spirit of the Lord was upon me. They rolled me out of my room, and then we got into the elevator. They pushed the whole bed out of my room because I could not turn over at that this time. I would slide down to the foot of my bed and I could not slide myself back up to the head of the bed. We went to some floor. I do not know what floor I was on in the dialysis unit. When I arrived in the unit, I looked all around. I never seem a dialysis place before. When I got in there, the lady who was pushing my bed, she called out, "Mrs. Chennault is here!" The dialysis nurse looked at my chart. She told everyone in the room that I was the "Lady from the Dead!" Everyone just looked at me and I made no gestures.

I just laid there in my bed looking at the nurses put all of those tubes in me. The other nurse lady told me, "You were already over there, why did you come back here?" I did not answer, but I was praying to thank God for His grace and mercy. I laid in my bed during dialysis thinking about what I had seen. I was thinking about being at the graveside listening to Pastor Henra telling me to come back. I then went through the ground; it was fun riding through the dirt. I was laughing at that time. I laid there and I thought about that man sitting on the rock with those brown saddles on his feet looking at me. I know it was Jesus, but why would He have shown Himself to me? I got to tell the world about that man! He is real! Oh, how he looked at me! The dialysis took a long time. A lot of other patients were there.

I laid there thinking about my family and whether I was going to live or not. God had opened my eyes, so I did not doubt that anymore. I had to fight until the end. Remembering the scripture James 5:13-15—

Is any among you afflicted? let Him pray? Is any merry? let Him sing Psalm. Is any sick among you? let Him call for the elders of the church: and let them pray over Him, anointing Him with oil in the name of the Lord: And the prayer of faith shall save the sick, and the Lord shall raise Him; and if he has committed sins, they shall be forgiven Him.

I told my daughter about the oil, and I touched myself with my oil using my finger beside my thumb. This is the only finger you should use to anoint your body. So, I am laying there thinking all of this while the dialysis machine is just running my blood to the machine back to me. Oh, Lord why me? This feeling did not last long. Why not me? Our God has no respect of person. He calls babies home early; he knows what is best for us every second of the day. Hours went by and I am sick as sick could be. When I got back to my room, my granddaughter, Hannah was there with Lazarus Sr., my husband, was sitting by the window looking worn out. They spend several more nights with me. My husband going to the waiting room every four hours to take his breathing treatments. He has been taking breathing treatments for 14 years now. It was sad to see both of us taking breathing treatments. He would bring his machine to the hospital. You never know what is coming your way in life, so it is best to keep hold of God's garment.

Never let go! Hold on, because it will come a time in your life where it will be just you and God. I had to have breathing treatments every four hours. There was a family friend from my area that I knew—Pastor Matthew Harden. He was one of my Respiratory Therapists and we had church every time he brought me my breathing treatments. It was good to see Him! He waited on my mother when she was in the Doctors Hospital before she passed away. My oldest son came that same night along with his wife, helping to turn me over along with the nurses. My other two sons had to leave because both of them had young babies, and the other children and my daughter came back. She was moving at this time, getting ready to go to five different states to run STEM summer camps at various colleges. She stayed with me around the clock. The children were so much help. Every pain that I felt in labor showed itself in my children while I was sick. I had all of them without medication. I had all-natural childbirths; 19 to 20 hours of hard labor.

While I am going through all of this, I know God has a plan for me. Everything I am going through God is getting me ready for something that only I can do for Him. So, He can get the glory. Give God all of His glory! We cannot even blink our eyes if He did not say so. Thanking God for just being alive; protecting my family. Glory Hallelujah, the storm is passing over; but this storm will pass over slowly. It will pass! This brings me to Psalm 46:1-3—

God is our refuge and strength, a very present help in trouble. Therefore, will not we fear, though the earth be removed, and though the mountains, be carried into the midst of the sea; Though the waters thereof roar and be troubled, though the mountains shake with the swelling thereof Selah.

The condition is still critical, but stable at the moment. I am coughing every minute. I am sick as sick could be without being dead. I do not have enough strength to get my food off of the tray. My daughter feeds me. I am still coughing at this time. My arms and hands are very weak. I try to reach out to the food, but I am too weak at this time. I am at one day after being in a coma. I am spitting up black mucus all day. There are lots of suction tubes hanging down in front of my face. All kinds of doctors are attending to me. Many nurses come into my room throughout the day. We get to talk about Jesus and how good and mighty He is. Most of the nurses are Christian people that work there in the Doctors Hospital because a lot of them tell me about the Bible stories.

There might come a time in your lives when you cannot pray so it will be a great blessing to give your praises every day to the Lord. There is nothing so important to you in this world that we cannot put God first in our lives. It is time to pray! Pray when you do not feel like it; take all of your worries to God. He is only a hand lift away. Send up your prayers every day! I was too sick to pray! I was not worried, because I pray, listen to sermons, read my Bible, meditate on God's words daily, and I try to treat my fellow man right. My youngest son is a Pastor. He always tells me how important it is in a person's life to treat someone as you want to be treated in life. I tried to instill in my children to always treat people as you would want to be treated. And I can see that it took root in each one of my children.

My husband told me about my granddaughter, Callie Blue. He told me that she was picking at him crying on the way to the hospital; she was there at my house when I got so sick. I thought it was Hannah, but it was Callie Blue. My husband drives down to Augusta, Georgia behind the EMS, but not too close behind, because he had to get his breathing machines, put Callie Blue in her baby seat, and lock up all the doors to the house. He told me that Callie Blue picked at him calling him, "Cry Baby Papa." He kept on crying, and she kept right on laughing. She did not understand why Papa was crying. She had never seen her Papa cry before, and they ended up at the University Hospital. They told where I wanted the ambulance to take me. I do not remember saying another word to the EMTs. University hospital is a few miles from the Doctors Hospital. So, when I got there to Doctors Hospital no family members were present except my husband and Callie Blue. My children live in Atlanta, Georgia and one lives in Gainesville, Georgia. So, no one was there. I think, my son, Otis was the first on to get there. He will tell that story later in this book.

Back to myself, laying there thinking about Father God—What have I done in my life to be suffering like this? He said, "Nothing!" My mind went to the book of Job.

For the thing which I greatly feared is come upon me, and that which I was afraid of is come unto me. Man, that is born of a woman is of a few days and full of trouble. He cometh forth like a flower and is cut down: he fleeth also as a shadow, and continueth not. Seeing his days are determined, the number of his months are with thee, thou has appointed his bounds that he cannot pass (Job 3:25; 14:1-2; 14:5).

All odds were against me, but God! I will keep on trusting Him. No matter how many rocks fall in your pathway, kick them out of the way and keep your eyes on the dream. My eyes were to stay on my goal and my goal was walking out of this hospital even though I am lying here. I cannot even turn myself over. I cannot even stand up. I am too sick to sit up in the bed, but I got my mind on my family. The place that I had seen—I saw my mother, my aunties and all of those children running playing on that beautiful side, Heaven.

Most importantly of all, I saw this man sitting on a rock. I will never forget this as long as I live. I want to tell the world that there is a Heaven, and it is a wonderful place. There is no fear there, but peace. There are no worries at all, and you do not even have to breathe over there. You are just there enjoying your love ones and they will know you by your name. My mama called me, "Willie."

One of my aunties called me "Willie Agnes," which is what she always called me while she was living.

My other auntie just looked at me, Aunt Lue. My Aunt Lue was named Lucinda Cullars. She was a quiet woman. She had a lot of wisdom. She loved my mother, and they talked a lot about how she loved Jesus. She was married twice, in the first to this guy, named Jake. She had three children by Jake and many years later the first husband, Jake, died then she married Marshall Cullars. She had two boys by Marshall. I never knew her to smile much; she just had a look of calmness on her face at all times, she never really looked sad or happy. She looked the same in Heaven. I looked at her with a smile, but Aunt Lue turned her head and looked at me, but she did not say anything. Both of my aunties heard my mother talking to me; she told me, "To go back they need you over there!" My mother was standing on the other side of the river, a small gulf of water. My mother emphasized her words. I know that was Jesus Christ telling her to tell me I had to go back. When I saw Jesus I to stop in my tracks, I was standing besides, "The Breath of Life." My aunties and my mother all had new bodies. They were not sick over there. They are having fun with each other. They are together with no men beside them, but this is what the Lord wanted me to see. Their husbands could have been there! I recognized and saw men and women of the Bible days. I believe I saw the inner circle of Jesus—Peter, James, and John.

My Aunt Lue had on a blue shinning two-piece suit and her hat. Her skin was smooth like my mom and Essie's skin. They are at peace now and happy! I was so amazed when I saw them. I smiled a lot in Heaven! All of the time I smiled! If there is any doubt about Jesus, please seek Him! He will make Himself known to you personally! He comes to each individual personally! There were three chairs at the table where my mom and aunties were sitting. My mom was already waiting on me at the river by the time I stepped out into Heaven. They all were younger. They did not have the wrinkles they had on the skin when they left earth nor the gray hair. They were radiating in glory, the Glory of God! And I was younger also! I did not know anything about this world at that time. I had no memory of this world, while I was over there until I came back to my sick, sick body. I have seen the streams that flow with the most bluish water with gold on the sides of the streams. I stood there with a smile on my face looking down through the meadows. Oh, who would not want to go there! I am so glad that God has the last say, no preacher, no one but God! Do not spend all of your time enjoying all this world at any cost, make sure your soul is fixed in Jesus Christ. Everyone does not have to like you or love you, just treat everyone right as far as you can according to the scripture. Do not agree with people who you know are wrong just to be their friends or make them feel good. No one is worth missing this place that I saw, and that place is Heaven. I was over there for a while. I do not know how long I was there, but one day is like a thousand years and a thousand years is like one day (2 Peter 3:8-9). I had a lot going on in my body; all of my organs shut down completely and my blood was poisoned due to my illness.

Sitting here writing my book; my heart is always heavy, but I trust God. I have to keep my trust in Him! The Lord showed me, Heaven. I am thinking about Psalm 139:13-14—

For thou hast possessed my reins: thou hast covered me in my mother's womb. I will praise thee; for I am fearfully and wonderfully made marvelous are thy works; and that my soul knoweth right well.

I only felt pain for a little while and that was right before the EMS came. I could not breathe at all. My chest was filled up with blood and fluid. I am now back in my room after the dialysis treatment. This is the first one I remembered, and I am sure they had me on dialysis while I was on the ventilator. I am looking at my husband and my granddaughter, Hannah. They are sitting by the window, and they are looking at me with the saddest faces I have ever seen. I turn my head to the other side of the room thinking about a song that I love, and I sing the words to myself. I just love this song, "Let Your Power Fall", by James Fortune and FIYA. I told the Lord—

So, this is what I need you to do; fight this battle for me, fight this battle for me…So I can tell all of my friends that You have won, you, you did it again. I said you have won, again. You won again. You brought me out so many times. Over, over, and over again…I said Hallelujah! Somebody give Him glory now (Hallelujah). Somebody ought to give Him glory (Live Through It, 2014).

I just was thinking about this song with tears running down my face. I love these words! I always listen to this song by James Fortune and FIYA. I was glad; praising God for not letting me have brain damage. I have the right mind. I did not wake up a vegetable or unable to know myself or my family members and friends or even that I had been to Heaven. I do not care how much you pray, go to church! Trouble is coming into this world! Every one of us is in a battle or coming out of a battle. This makes me think about Jesus and the hymnal, "Must Jesus Bear the Cross Alone" by Thomas Shepherd (1693). The first few words of the song are: "Must Jesus bear the cross alone, and all the world go free? No, there's a cross for everyone. And there's a cross for me." No cross! No crown! No matter what comes my way; I am going to keep pressing in my faith.

I am laying there in my bed and my mind flashes back to my childhood. My mother told me to go over to the neighbor's house next door and ask her to send her a little piece of fatback meat. We were very poor! Everyone else we knew was poor also! We did not have anything, almost nothing. So, my brother; the one under me—Joseph and myself ran about a mile and a half to get a small piece of meat for my mother. It put my mind back in my childhood! My mother was standing in the kitchen in this old shack; no running water, no bathroom, no nothing. I have not started to go to school yet. My brother and I did not have any shoes! We just had some raggedy looking for clothes. We had fun running to our neighbor's house to get that piece of fatback meat for my mother to cook with pinto beans. It was fun! We stopped at the white folk's apple tree and ate us a few apples. We both rubbed our stomachs.

Laying there in the hospital; my mind goes back to my childhood. I found peace for healing there. All kinds of hospital staff were coming in to see me all day, every day, every minute. I had to have something done. I was not worried. I woke up! God has a plan for me! How can a human endure all of that suffering? I was not worried! I counted it all joy. God has access to us, every one of His children. I laid there and cried day after day and hours after hours praising God. I felt sorry for myself laying there. I could not even stand up by myself about two days after I awoke from being in a coma. The physical therapist came to my bed and asked me to sit up. I was too weak to sit up! He was a tall, strong man. He put my legs on side of the bed. I just fell over to the other side of the bed. He put a belt around Himself, and he put the belt around me. I am facing Him right in his face, breath to breath. He was trying to make me stand up. My legs were just dangling. There was no life in my legs at this time. I tried and tried! I was sick as any human being could be without being dead. I asked the Lord, "What I have done in my life to be suffering like this?"

He answered me quickly! He said, "Nothing."

My mind then went back to the stable where Jesus was born. I got inside of that stable with Joseph and Mary and the Savoir, laying there looking at baby Jesus. He was lying in a trough that the pigs ate out and the rags that they clean the horses with were those was the one that he laid his head on and for his blanket as well. He was laying on those rags for this poor sick woman! No matter how low you get; He is there for you. All of that straw! The smells of the animals using the bathroom all around Him. I put myself there and then I went back to that field where I saw Jesus sitting on the rock. I stood there looking at those people gathering up wheat or barley. I looked at the string tied around the little bundles.

The physical therapist unhooked the belt from around him and he unhooked the belt from around me. I just fell back in the bed. I could not even lift my legs back in the bed. "I am going to make it!" I told myself. I have never given up on anything that I went after, and I was not going to now! God woke me up and I am going to finish this race that is set before me. I know in my heart that I am covered by the Blood of Jesus. I always prayed all through the day no matter where I am! I always pray! I pray for others! I always pray for myself last.

While there in the hospital—The nurse and my family members help bathe me. My children were always there. I do not know what I would have done if I did not have those children and my husband always by my side. It was hard to let the nurse pan bathe me because I had sores all over my backside—going down my buttocks. My buttocks were full of big sores at the very top of my buttocks and big sores all over my hips. The nurses put on all kinds of cream throughout the day. Blood was all over the bed, coming from those wounds. My body had begun to break down from laying in the bed so long. I was fading fast, but God! Seem like there was a sharp knife stuck under my ribs. I was not worried, because the God that I serve had already brought me this far. He will never leave me. I am going to walk out of here! I kept on telling myself that.

At this point, I have a long road to go. I thought about standing. I am very weak at this time. I cannot even get my food from the tray. I tried to tell my arms to pick my hands up to get my food. The first few times that I ate, my food came back up out of my mouth; the food went halfway down. I felt so helpless looking at my plate! I did not have enough strength to even open any of the seasons that were on the tray, so my daughter feeds me. She stood there looking into my eyes with the most patience as if I was her baby. She waited until I tried to chew my food. She did not hurry me at all.

Back to a child again, that is me! Here I am! I cannot worry about anything, because there is nothing to be worried about! I still do not think that those doctors were expecting me to live. I always found a way in Jesus; He is always there! Sometimes He may seem far, but He hears every mumble that you say, every prayer you lift to Him, and tears that you shed. He knows your heart. No one can fool, Father God. My children are standing around my bed, touching and agreeing on some of the healing scriptures. Pastor Henra standing there along with his two brothers Otis and Lazarus Jr., Dr. June and their dad, Lazarus Sr. praying, reading, and praising on some of the healing scriptures. Pastor Henra found the scripture that he wanted to read, Mark 11:22-24—

And Jesus answering saith unto them, Have faith in God. For verily I say unto you. That whosoever shall say unto this mountain, be thou removed, and be thou cast into the sea: and shall not doubt in his heart but shall believe that those things which he saith shall come to pass; he shall have whatsoever he saith. Therefore, I say unto you, what things so ever ye desire, when ye pray, believe that ye receive them, and ye shall have them.

He read more scriptures: Psalm 103:3—"Who forgive all thine iniquities, who healeth all thy diseases."

We all touched and agreed!

He read more scriptures, James 5:16, which says—"Confess your faults one to another, and pray one for another, that ye may be healed. The effectual fervent prayer of a righteous man availeth much."

And he read Isaiah 53:5—"But he was wounded for our transgressions, he was bruised for our iniquities; the chastisement of our peace was upon Him; and with his stripes, we are healed."

He read my other favorite verse, Psalm 6:2—"Have mercy upon me, O Lord; for I am weak: O Lord, heal me; for my bones are vexed."

Lastly, he read from the scripture of John 15:7—"If you abide in me, and my words abide in you, ye will ask what ye will, and it will be done for you."

The Spirit of the Lord showed up and out this evening!

I was not worried about a thing! I was too weak to pull myself back up in the bed or turn over! I could turn my head! I had to use the bedpan! The nurse pushed me over a thousand times from side to side to put the pan under my body when I had to use the bathroom, that was a very hard job! My children would help me when they were there. I thank God for those children. My husband worked right along with them—waiting on me, but he was sick Himself. Lord, when it rains it pours! I do not care how bad it storms; it has to pass over. I always sing to myself, "The storm is passing over, hallelujah!" I keep my mind on Heaven. I am thinking about what I had seen in Heaven. I am still thinking about Heaven. I think about it all through the day! We will know each other in Heaven! That is a fact!

Death does not change our identity. We will be able to recognize our friends, loves ones, and others in Heaven. When we get to Heaven, we will know each other. Jesus talks about Abraham, Isaac, and Jacob lived and existed as persons by their name (Matthew 22:31-32). Also, in Chapter 17 of Matthew—Peter, James, and John knew Moses and Elijah when they appeared on the mountain during "The Transfiguration" of Jesus. Thus, we will know and recognized each other in Heaven. We will have names and faces.

The scripture says that Jesus in His resurrected body went up to Heaven and will return in the same recognition (Act 1:9-11; Titus 2:13). We also will receive new bodies that will be truly transformed from what they were before in this life on earth (Corinthians 15:12-57). When a Christian dies, he or she finds themselves in the presence of Jesus Christ who is in Heaven (Luke 23:43; 2 Corinthians 5:8) Although our bodies remain in the grave, our souls find themselves in God's presence and we who are still living and awaiting resurrected bodies will be renewed during the rapture when Jesus comes back (Thessalonians 4:15-17; 1 John 3:2).

When I awoke, I saw this man with a whitish shirt on. I asked him, "Are you one of my doctors?"

He said, "No, I am Pastor Lance Pitts!"

I said, "You are Pastor Pitts!"

He said, "Yes!"

He mentioned to me that he had been there several times before to see me at the hospital, but I was sleeping. He was a tall man. Pastor Pitts is my pastor from my home church, Gibson Grove Baptist Church, where I grew up. He has come to pray for me again. He said, "Wait, pray for yourself first!"

I said, "Ok!" I said my favorite prayer, Psalm 23, and the Lord's Prayers. He was holding my hand while I prayed and then he said a prayer for me. I was glad to see him. My children told me several other ministers came by to pray for me, but I did not see them, or I did not hear them. My children told me who came by to pray for me while I was in the hospital. Pastor George Edwards, my pastor where I am a member of the Thankful Baptist Church, came to pray for me. Pastor Timothy Bell told me that he came, and his wife came to pray for; he told me some weeks later that he laid his hands around my bed, and he prayed for me. He is from the Rocky Mount Baptist Church. My husband and I go there often. Pastor Joseph Williams came by to pray for me, but I was sleeping. I did not hear a word. Pastor Charles E. Lacy came by as well from Nebo Baptist Church. My nephew came by and prayed for me, Pastor Kenneth Norman. My son, Pastor Henra Chennault was there as well. I know he cried over me every day all through the day. Zoah Methodist Church's Pastor Howard Harmon came as well. All of these pastors prayed for me and came to see me. They were all are praying for me. Many prayers went up for me from all the churches near my hometown, Washington, Georgia. Churches all over prayed for me—the Lyonsville Baptist Church, Trinity Baptist Church, Pleasant Grove Baptist Church, and Pole Branch Baptist Church. All of these churches! Oh, how they prayed for me! Forgive me, please if I missed any church family or any other pastor!

At this time, I was too weak to sit up in the bed. I saw my family standing around my bed. As I mentioned before, I did not know what was going on or why I was there in the hospital; no one has told me a thing. All I know was that I was sick as I sick could be. I was laying there thinking about Heaven. The Lord has brought me back to earth, back to this world. I was so glad to see my children, my husband, and my other family members. All of my family just looking at me with this strange look on their faces. I wonder why they are looking at me like that. My sister-in-law Brenda told me that I made it. A friend of mines said I made it back as well, her name is Gloria. She said, "I am glad you are back!" We used to work at the primary school in Washington back in the day. They were all just looking at me!

My brother, Joseph said, "Boss Lady is back!"

I smile! I was too sick to speak! My hands shook like leaves on a tree. I had nervousness in my voice! I sounded like a one-hundred-year-old woman. My sisters were laughing at me with tears in their eyes, but I count it all joy.

God got me! I know that; I have always known that! When I awoke from the coma, about two or three days after—the nurse asked me, "When was I born and what city was in?"

I told her, "I was in Smyrna, Georgia."

She said, "Try again?"

I had to think, and I never got it right!

So, she told me, "Surprise! I was in Augusta, Georgia."

Most of my children lived in Smyrna, Georgia. I had no idea where I was; I did not know what my sickness was; I had no idea what was wrong with me. Because in Heaven I was young and, strong and I looked about 30 years old. I was sick. I was happy, very happy. I did not have pain in my body. I was just walking around Heaven. Oh, it is so beautiful; who would not want to go? I got to tell the world that Heaven is real. The beautiful color of green that I saw in Heaven; it is not the same color green as here. All of those beautiful colors. It looked magical and of those children playing on the hillside; they have all dressed alike. I walked among those people in the wheat fields. They were just working in the wheat fields.

I was just looking at them, but soon after I saw this man sitting on the rock. It was Jesus Christ, the son of the living God. His eyes, His color, His robe, His feet, His facial structure, His brown saddles, and the length of His feet, about 10 ½ inches long. Those straps that went across His feet looked like old leather. Jesus looked at me with a look I have never seen on this earth. That look of compassion. He did not say a word to me. He just looked at me. I was smiling! I was young and skinny, full of strength. His eyes were like the bluish ocean, clear and shiny. This will be on my mind until the day I die. I can hardly believe that I saw all of this, but I have already told many people about this, so it will not be a surprise to them when they read this book.

I laid there thinking about all I am going through. I do not know why? All I know is that Jesus has won again. Oh, I was so sick. The medical staff pushed me onto another floor. I did not know where I was going. I was too sick to think. I was wishing I could feel better. My husband told me later on that I was on the hospice floor. I did not react to the statement. I was too sick! I have never been this sick in my life. I saw my nephew pass by my door. I was too sick to speak. I thought I was going to die any minute, but I said to myself I have already died because I have seen my Lord and Savior Jesus Christ. I asked Otis how the baby was doing because in one dimension that I was in I saw Otis Jr. very sick, so I had to suffer until he got well. If only anyone could have seen what I saw when I stepped into Heaven. You would not waste any time accepting Lord Jesus Christ as your Savior. It is easy if we look at Ephesians 2:8-10—

For by grace are ye saved, through faith; And that not of yourselves, it is the gift of God: Not of works, lest any man should boast, For we are his workmanship, created in Christ Jesus unto good works, which God hath before ordained that we should walk in them.

Who deserves grace? Grace is a pouring of favor on those who do not deserve it! I was given favor and grace. Laying there in the hospital—coughing up black mucus and barely able to speak. I told my children I did not want to see anyone outside of my immediate family. I was sicker than sick. Wires everywhere, but I am alive! Wow, look at my family praising God; thanking Him for letting his mercy fall upon me! I wondered, "Why I am suffering in this way?" I cannot question Father God, because He has the power to do whatever He wants to do. I am using the bathroom in the bed. A strong woman like me laying here. I cannot even reach back and wipe my buttocks after using the bathroom in the bed. Oh, Lord! I am not worried about a thing! I am blessed. I laid there in the bed, in this situation, thanking Father God for all of His blessings. Pray for other people. I always pray for others more than I do for myself and then I say Psalm 23 and the Lord's prayer. Why me Lord? I cannot question the Lord; I am alive! I have always been a very strong person. I started to think back over my life; I go to church. I have church at home every day. I pray throughout the day and that is every day. I am a straight-forward person. I do not like to cut corners. I love the Lord with all of my soul, my heart, and my mind. What else is there to hold on to, but Father God? I am going to hold onto His unchanging hand. The wind may blow, and the storms may not let up for a while, but I am going to hold to that hand that touched me when I was eleven years old.

I woke up in my right mind! Oh, what a blessing! At this time, it may be the first of June; I am on lots of medications. IVs running of all kinds—high blood medication, vitamin shots, all kinds of pills, about 15 pills at a time. I was amazed at how much medication ran through my body. I cannot put this into words. It was hard to eat, but I forced it down. I did not want food, but I told myself, I got to get out of here. I was too weak to sit up in the bed. Every time my sons and my daughter would come, they would try to move and exercise my arms and legs. I tried to think in my mind if I only could turn over. My hands were shaking badly. People say they know you! They do not know the parts of you that matter to God. God only knows the heart. That is what is important! A tree is known by the fruit it bears. My God knows me! No one else knows me, not even my husband. God got my mind, my soul, my life is in His hands.

We are just like a bubble on the water. We might pop anytime; that is why you must send up prayers every day. I laid there in the bed. I went back to my childhood days where there was no stress. Our biggest concern back then was finding food. Thinking back to the 1960s. Thinking back to how I use to walk barefooted down the dirt roads. Most of the children went barefooted at that time. I never heard the word, "bored," or "stress." We had a good time! Our parents did not have to keep their eyes on us. We knew we had to be home by dark whether we were fishing or visiting cousins. We ran through the woods home alone. I walked through the woods by myself at the age of eight or nine years old. I was lying there in that hospital; I and my mind went back to a certain place. My childhood was one of those places. My mother, father, five girls, and five boys. I was the sixth child. My mother had lost some children. I would have been the ninth child. We had to suffer to get up. We had to draw water from the well. The well had everything in it. Sometimes we would go up to the white people's house to get water, but not all the time. My father would haul water in the back of his truck. There was a lot of fruit trees. I stopped on my way home. Laying there in my bed sicker than sick.

My brother Joseph and I use to sit up in the apple trees eating apples until our stomach push out and then we would fill our pockets up with apples and go home. My mind went back to the cornfields and how we use to pick corn and peas. My mother was a smart woman. She always cooked bread if there was nothing else. We had some biscuits to eat. She could go in that kitchen and make some food. We ate a lot of syrupy biscuits. We had to work hard—all of us, ten children.

My mind and my body went back to the back yard where I use to swing as a kid. In the backyard, a bullfrog was holding on the side of the back porch. My brother, Jessie, would catch the other siblings and me some bullfrogs and he would skin them. He ate the two back legs. I remember he gave me a piece. I was about seven years old. My mind went back to those days and my body began to heal slowly. I felt my life in a whirlwind with a feeling I cannot describe! I could not go forward sideways or backward. Every morning my husband would get up spitting up mucus. This has happened every day for the past 13 years. I have to make him this special kind of tea to keep the mucus off his lungs so much. I always see about him, my husband. I forgot to see about myself. I listen to my children and their problems and my friends' problems. I do not have many friends; they are all older folks. I had to help them out when I am available to help them.

I was standing by the stove one day fixing my husband some tea. I told the Lord how tired I was becoming and feeling funny. I got off of my diet. I had to gain weight. I started eating anything and everything. I felt terrible inside my mind, but I kept on going back and forth to Atlanta; that is where my children and grandchildren are, and one is in Gainesville.

I was not paying attention to my health, but I always went to the doctor every month. I just had a check-up at the doctor on May 5, 2017. My primary care doctor did not do any blood work. She just checked my heartbeat and that was it. I always tried to eat right. I would go for long walks, and I went to the gym. I always planted a garden like I always do, but this year in 2017 I went down to the garden spot and just looked. I knew I was not going to plant a garden at that time because the Spirit told me standing there looking at the garden; So, I did not plant a garden. I never slept much in the hospital. I was too sick to sleep. My mind went back to Heaven throughout the day. The air there is so smooth; you do not have to breathe. You are just there enjoying nature. I was so happy; remember I am out of my body. I have been out of my body before. I lost a son in childbirth. I will tell that story a little later on.

Do not try to understand everything that happens to us in life; there are things that we will never understand so do not worry about it, go on with your life. God always knows what is best for us. I had on my grave clothes and Pastor Henra, my son, preached my funeral. I went down in the ground, and I stepped out in Heaven. Sitting here typing, I remember a second after coughing up blood in a towel and in the sink in the bathroom my husband asked me, "Why is all of that blood in the towel?" I do not remember spitting up blood in the towel, but I do remember the blood in the sink. I just had got out of the shower, but I do not remember that; I do not ever remember putting on my clothes. I do remember sitting on the couch. I could not breathe at all even with my husband's oxygen mask on hooked up the oxygen tank. I still could not breathe. I was sitting there feeling my body fading away fast very fast. I could not pray! I had little time to think about prayer. I talked to the Lord. I said in a few seconds, "Lord, I have served you! I am in your hands!" That is all I could think, and I was about gone. It all happened that quickly!

Sitting here with tears running down my face as I write this book. Thinking back over my life; I told the Lord; I have served Him. You know everyone will not love you when you give your life to Christ. Do not focus on this just do what is right in God's eyes and He will put the right people around you. I never really cared about what the world thought of me. I try to love everyone and treat everyone like I wanted to be treated. I always told my children that was the golden rule around the Chennault's house. God knows my heart. I know He had me! There was nothing I could do for myself at this point. It was all in God's hands; He had already laid the plan out for me. He did not let me feel any pain at this time in the ambulance. Oh, when I came to Room 16 in ICU, I was sicker than sicker. I thought about the scriptures in the Bible,

"But seek ye first the Kingdom of God, and His righteousness; and these things shall be added to you" (Matthew 6:33). "But without faith [it is] impossible to please [Him]; for he that cometh to God must believe that he is, and [that] he is a rewarder of them that diligently seek Him" (Hebrews 11:6).

Wrap your mind, body, and soul in Jesus Christ while there is time; while you are still breathing because after the breath leaves your body it is too late. My nurse would come by and tell me scriptures like these most of them at the Doctors Hospital would talk to me about Jesus Christ. A lot of times people feel offended to mention Jesus' name, but not those people at the Doctors Hospital. The Holy Spirit would stay around my bed every time I said the Psalm 23and the Lord's prayer. The Spirit of the Lord would come to me and run His hands over my sick body; all I had to do was just think about scriptures from the Bible and little by little each day I would get a little bit of healing to my body. Breathing treatments after breathing treatments, shots, and pills after pills. The nurses would turn me from side to side to let me use the bedpan; there is no way I could get up because I was at risk of falling; I had that band on my arm, a green band I believe.

On a Friday, June 2, 2017; I was transferred to another hospital that night about 9:30 pm in the ambulance to another hospital since it was a long ride from the Doctors Hospital to the Select Specialty Hospital in Augusta, Georgia. This was about a 20-minute ride. I felt really sad, and I was so sick. The nurse monitored me very close while riding in the ambulance; I was hooked up to the oxygen machine. The nurse was checking my vital signs. It seemed like a long ride. We finally arrive at the Select Specialty Hospital. It looked so strange in there; all I saw were very old people; they look so weird none of them was moving. All of the patients I saw were laying very still as I was being pushed down the halls. I was just looking and wondering what in the world am I doing here? I did not know how long I would be here, but it was all up to me at this point; the ball was in my court. I had to play with the ball. When I got to the room, the number on the door was 201.

The EMTs from Doctors Hospital rolled me from one bed to another. It was so quiet in this hospital. A man nurse came in to help me. He said, "I will be your nurse for tonight." He looked very strange, but he was nice to me. He checked my blood pressure. it was 204/85. I had a fever of 105 degrees Fahrenheit. I knew it was high because the nurses wrote it on the board. I was feeling hot, so I told the nurse to give me a washcloth and some ice. So, he gave me what I asked for and I put the ice in a washcloth, and I put it around my neck. and I broke my fever for the moment. He told me that they were saving me a plate of food. I did not eat, but two bites; I was too sick to eat. This is about five days after I awake from the coma. I was a sick woman. I felt low. None of my family members were there at the hospital at this time. I felt so low; all I did was cry.

I could not question God, because I know this was His plan for my life. Why? I do not know. I cried awhile and I prayed a while. I cried happy tears for a while and sad tears. I was glad! I was alive, but barely. I thought about my grandchildren. I had two very young grandchildren; one of them was just born a few weeks ago. I had my Bible with me. So sick at this time, I could hardly see, but I put my glasses on and I found myself some scriptures with tears running down my face. I was not worried, because I was going to walk out of this hospital one way or another. I had been to Heaven. I saw our Savoir Lord Jesus Christ. I wondered why he would show Himself to me. I am nobody to see Jesus! Why me? Why did He look at me in such a calm, compassionate way? Why did He let me go to Heaven and see all of what I saw in Heaven? He brought me back to earth. I think about Him all of the time. I found some scripture. I always say the 23rd Psalm. I say it over and over and then I told the Lord what He has done in the scriptures.

Sitting here typing this book, it is another day that my God has kept me waking up every morning. I have already had church this morning like every morning. My husband and I have church together—I pray, and he sings, some mornings I sing, and he says the morning prayer. Some mornings we have our own church. I can walk this morning. I can fix my breakfast; I can bath myself. There was a time I could not even stand up by myself. Oh, praising God, He is mighty! He is a powerful all-knowing, all-loving. This morning I am sitting here telling a true story; it is unbelievable, but every word of this story is indeed true. I am sitting here remembering and thinking back about one of my nurses. She asked me, "Why did I come back? You were already over there!" I told her simply as I could I had nothing to do with it; whether I stayed in Heaven or I came back it was out of my hands.

What God has for you; it is for you! She just looked at me with the strangest look. I am sitting there barely able to see. My eyes are very cloudy because I have an eye disease. I have had this for about 30 years. I have Glaucoma. I have implants in both of my eyes, but I always give my God the glory thanking Him for my sight all of these years. The nurse told me patients do not go as far as you did and come back in your case. She said it is very ray. I just laid there sick, sicker than anyone could be. I thank God for bringing me this far. I am so glad to be here with my family. Glory

Hallelujah! I am at the other hospital, Select Specialty
Hospital at this time. The June 3rd doctor's progress notes:

Assistance with management of AKI requiring dialysis.
Mrs. Chennault is a 61-year-old African- American female.
She had coughing spells when she called the EMS, she was
emergently intubated bEMS and upon arrival to the
Emergency Department was diagnosed with a NSTEMI as
well as Septic shock related to pneumonia. She was noted to
have elevated transaminase levels related to shock liver and
rhabdomyolysis. Her admission was complicated by the
development of AKL secondary to ATN thought to be
related to shock and rhabdomyolysis. She was initially
receiving CRRT but was converted to IHD on 5/25/2017.
She was also noted to have anemia which was felt to be due
in part to DIC as well as thrombocytopenia related to Zyvox
and Heparin. She has been delayed MWF and was
transferred to Select Hospital. She has been given multiple
transfusions as recently as yesterday on dialysis. She has a
fever overnight.

I laid there feeling sad, sick, and lonely. None of my
family was here at this time. It is about 11:00 p.m. and I am
feeling terrible, but I know it was just me and the Lord. It
comes a time in every person's life where it is just you and
the Lord. I did not want my family around so much, because
my children had to go back to work. I do not know how

long they had been out of work. I was too sick to ask. I was glad to just see them when I could. Oh, my God! I had to carry Him back to his word. I always do when I want to get a prayer answered quickly. I have always taken the God that I serve on a minute-by-minute basis. I pray all through the night. When I wake up in the middle of the night, I start praying and I have been doing this all of my life ever since I came to know Father God. Even when I was a young girl, eleven years old when I accepted my God as my savior. I cry for a while and I told myself I have no business here in this shape, but I am alive. I took my God back to his word. Here is what I told Him. I told the Lord how he had raised Jairus' daughter from the dead and I told the Lord how He has healed the woman who had a blood disease. How I told Him how He had open blinded eyes! I told Father God that He healed the Leper and how he heals the brokenhearted, and how he has healed the paralyzed man. I told the Lord that He does not have to come in this hospital, "All You have to do is just speak the word! And I will be healed like the centurion who was healed when you speak Your word, Lord!"

I was just too weak; I did not know a human being could get that sick. I also told Father God about Lazarus, the one who He raised from the dead. I was dead for several days longer than Lazarus my body started to deteriorate.

Sores had formed on my body. My mouth, my buttocks, and inside of my body had begun to waste away, but I was in Heaven already and like Lazarus; Jesus called me, and I came back to my sick body. I had to take the pain of my physical body, but while I was in Heaven, I was young and strong. I cannot explain it! No one can hardly believe it! It is hard to believe.

I got dentures in 2014, but in Heaven, I had all my teeth. My mother wore glasses before she died due to her eye condition, but in Heaven, she did not need glasses. She did not have them on in Heaven. I have told all of my family and my friends. Who else wants to listen? I laid in the water in Heaven. It is not like this water here on earth; it is more like the water that Peter stepped in when Jesus said to Peter to come to Him. I walked around in my young body. I did not weight much in Heaven. I looked like I did when I was about thirty years old. I was smiling all the time. I did not know I ever live anywhere else besides Heaven, but I saw my family on my mother's side. I did not see anyone on my father's side. I saw my grandson who died a few years ago. I saw a lot of those children over there. Nothing, but children playing on the beautiful hillside. They looked at me for a moment. Oh, this boy looked at me real hard and he went on with the other children to play. I have a son over there his name was Noah Chennault. I will tell you about Him later on in my book.

Please know that time or death waits for no one. Time and death do not adhere to our deadlines or timelines. However, when death enters our world whether, from friends or family members, we have to adjust our daily routines for death, we have too! When a funeral procession happens, we must move our cars to the side of the road; this is a sign of respect. I am reminded by Luke 7:11-17—Jesus found Himself at the entrance of a town called Nain. A large funeral procession was happening for the son of a widow with only this one son. Jesus went to the mother and asked her not to cry. He went to the casket of the young son and told Him to get up. The funeral procession ended just like that! "Whoever believes in me, though he dies, yet shall he live" (John 11:25). Death will not wait for anyone. Jesus is a forgiving God, a giver of life, and salvation. He tells death to step aside and presents to us the gift of eternal life.

That night when I got to the other hospital, I had to use the bathroom. I had a man nurse. I did not pay much attention. He was my nurse. I was wondering," How did I get here?" We do not know what we have to go through in this world. It is best to stay humble and stay prayed up. We brought nothing into this world, and we surely will not take anything away. I carried nothing with me to Heaven, but my soul. I look like I am thirty over there. You do not have to prove to the world that you know Jesus. Those that know Jesus, can see Jesus in you! A tree is known by the fruit it bears (Luke 6: 43-45). I did not want that male nurse to wipe my buttocks, but I had no choice but to let Him do it! I could not do it. My hands were so weak. I could not reach behind my buttocks to clean myself after a number one or two. I was so pitiful. I was so sick, sicker than sick. I was weak. I have never known sickness such as this for myself. The Bible says once a man and twice a child. Here I am a child again. I tried to clean myself, but my hands shook so I could not hold the towel paper in my hand. How was I doing at this time according to the doctor's notes? Here are the notes:

Vital Cardiac: Regular rate and rhythm, no gallop or murmur, Lungs: a few scattered rhonchi, otherwise clear. Abdomen: Positive bowel sounds, soft, nontender, no organomegaly or mass: Extremities: no clubbing or cyanosis, does have edema Distal Pulses Impression. Status post hypoxic respiratory failure to Pneumonia and Sepsis. Bacterial pneumonia with Leukocytosis. Acute kidney injury requiring hemodialysis. History of Cardiogenic shock resolved. Transaminitis-improved. Hypothyroidism. Gastroesophageal reflux disease. Accelerated Hypertension: Hyperlipidemia the Plan is we will continue IV and consult

ID to continue to monitor the patient. We will continue with an aggressive Pulmonary toilet. We will adjust blood pressure medicines to help her achieve better control. We will monitor blood sugar, etc. We will consult nephrology to continue with the patient's hemodialysis. We will follow patient's blood counts if any pain issues that may occur. We will monitor her cardiac status and continue current medications. Also, we will continue with dialysis while monitoring for evidence of renal recovery. We will need to follow urine output and daily weights. Anemia-due to DIC in the setting of AKI. We will check an iron panel in the morning. Fever: she has multiple lines so we will check a set blood culture. Report from the doctors. AKI requiring dialysis in the hospital.

The doctors from the wound clinic came to look at my wounds twice a day and they took pictures of my wounds. They gave me a cream to put on the wounds twice a day. I have had so much done to my body at this time since I have been awake. I do not know what happen while I was in the coma. I did not hear anything on earth that was going on. I was in Heaven having a good time looking around. I was walking around. Who would not want to go? I feel sad if anyone would miss that journey. What I saw just looking at the trees and the flowers and all those beautiful, shining buildings were amazing. It cannot be explained! You cannot get into Heaven in the flesh. You got to die first. Heaven had nothing to do with the fleshly body. It is all about the Spiritual body. The fleshly body will be finished once the soul leaves the body. It about what is inside of you! God cannot use the fleshly body! It is all about the Spirit that God can use once we step out of it. These fleshy bodies will be no more. They are useless to us.

I died and came back to my body; this is when all of the pain and weakening started. I had no memory of this world. My mind and my body were in Heaven all the while the doctors were here working on my physical body. I was not in it, my physical body. I was gone! I had to take all of the kinds of vitamins and liquids like Ensure every day with every meal. I had to drink Javen three times a day, which is a liquid vitamin drink that I drunk three times a day along with my meals. I took Nephro-vitamins once daily and a lot more vitamins every day. I had lots of IV running through my neck and arms. I had tubes in my right hip for dialysis. I had all of the wires hooked up to me. So many wires! I always get wrapped up in the wires and I could not unwrap them. The nurse always helps me keep them straighten out.

At this time, I am too weak to sit up in a chair. I cannot turn myself over. If I slid down to the bottom of the bed, I could not get back up to the top of my bed. The nurse would always pull me back up to the head of my bed. They pull me up a thousand times. When my family was there in the hospital, they did it. My children, my husband, my granddaughters, and my daughters-in-law helped me a lot when they came; it was a blessing to have a good family and they were a great blessing to me all while I was sick. I thank God for them every day.

On June 2, 2017, the Physician's Orders were: "For my eyes Lumigan, Timolol Maleate Ophthalmic Solution, Clonidine HCL Patch topical Q7 days, Hydrazine 50mg, Levothyroxine sodium 50 mcg. Metoprolol 25 mg, Preservation Areas, Oxycodone 5mg, Piperacillin 3.375 gm IV, Simvastatin 40 mg". These were some of my medications, but I had a lot of IVs and I had to have more blood and my blood pressure is so low. My head felt light, so they gave me two more pints of blood. It took a long time for the blood to run in my body through the veins in my neck. I did not need to complain! I am still alive and thank God all through the day, looking at my children, their spouses, and my grandchildren, and my husband. It was so good just to look at all of them! They looked so tired, but I looked the worse at this time. My lips were peeling, and they were filled with pus. My lips were swollen; they were very sore, but I am alive.

Chapter 4

HOLDING ONTO MY FAITH

"I am going to get out of here as soon as I can!" I keep on telling myself this. My daughter and my husband came the next morning; they stayed a few days for about four days. My husband was tired! He had given out. He was not looking right at all. He helped me wipe my buttocks just like he did our children when they were infants. He told me that he was tired of wiping my buttocks. He said he never thought he would be wiping my buttocks so soon. Remember at this time, I could not walk or turn over in my bed. My bed moved all of the time like a waterbed. I was so sick! I did know a human being could be this sick! I was not feeling good all. I was so sick; I could not even sit up in a chair at this time. I could not talk or text on the phone because I could not hold it in my hands. I felt about 100 years old. My hands would shake like the wind blowing a leaf on a tree, but I am still alive! Pills and more pills! A cup full of pills! I had to take so many pills. I also had to wash my mouth out three times a day every day with a solution ever since I awoke from the coma. My mouth had sores in it. I had to swish, swish and swallow. The solution tasted awful, but I had to do it so my mouth could heal on the inside. My mouth was full of black mucus; it was the smell of pus and death. I cried out to the Lord to let this cup pass from me. I remembered when Jesus Christ cried out in Matthew 26:42. It states that Jesus "went away again the second time and prayed, saying O my Father, if this cup may not pass away from me, except I drink it, thy will be done."

At this time, I needed someone with me every minute. I was so glad my family was there for a while. I told my husband to go home and do not come back, he looks awful. He has turned a shiny, dark color. He is sick himself; he has to have breathing treatments every four hours. He had to bring his medication to the hospital with him so he could help me. He would go out to the waiting room with his breathing machine to take his treatments then he would come back to the room to help turn me over. My sons came in and out of my room. My daughter was there. My daughter-in-law helped me. My other two daughters-in-law had young babies so they could not do much. They came to visit off as often as they could.

My husband was looking so worn out. I told him to go home, do not come back until I could call him. I know him. I meet him in the 9th grade. I have been with him all of my life. I have been married to him for 43 years, so I know how he supposed to look. He was at the point where he was exhausted, and I did not want him to have to go into the hospital while I was in the hospital. He always goes to the hospital at about twice a month for his lung disease, but one thing for sure he did not have to go to the hospital all while I was sick. At this time, I cannot even stand up on my feet. I got enough strength to pull by the rale on my bed. I try to pull myself up, but it is so hard to do. I never imagined being in this shape. I have always been on the move because I had my children to keep me busy all of my life. My first child was born when I was 19 years old, so I never really got any rest since then. Then I had three more children with my husband. We had to work hard with those children to make sure that they will be worth something to society. I had to make sure that they get the best education. I was always busy I did not have time for foulness. I had to keep my eye on them. We had to pray, go to church, and keep our eyes our goals.

My mother told me one day, "Willie, you cannot put all of those children through college! You do not any money to send them to school." I told her—I know my God was going to send all four of them to college because I ask Him every day to make a way for all of my children to be college graduates. I prayed and I prayed! We worked toward that goal, and it became a reality. Laying there in the hospital bed, thinking about how good the hospital staff members are treating me with every valve in their heart. They are doing all they can do; I look at each one of them. They all have a very simple personality. How hard it was for me and my husband to raise our children! We were so busy! We always work together as a family. If their dad told them something, they knew it had to stick; they could not play one against the other one, me and their father. Whatever you put in them that what you will get back! Their personalities will be just like you. What your children think about things or other people it will be just like yours. You have to instill hard work in your children. Again, it is what you put in them!

Laying here, I cannot even turn over. If I could only get up and walk to the door and just lookout in the hall. I never imagine that I would be in this shape. I am not worried! You know why? I have seen Jesus and I saw my mother, aunties, and some of the other people of the Bible days—men, women, and children of all races. I saw my grandson who died a few years ago and some other children that belonged to the family, who died in birth. The children told me who they belong to, but I will not say their names in this book. Laying there in the hospital bed with a thousand wires hooked up to my body, I feel happy to be alive! I am looking at my husband knowing if I did not make it, he was going to give up his fight. He said, "He cannot make it without me." I said, "Yes, you can; you just think that!" If only I could stand up and go over there to the sink and wash my face, tears are running down my face, but I am glad I am alive. If only I could go to the bathroom. Laying here calling the nurse a thousand times saying I got to use the bathroom that means the bedpan. It is hard to use the bathroom in a pan in the bed, but what choice do I have. I did it for a long time. I am not able to comb my hair at all. I cannot remember the last time I even look at my head or combed my hair. I could not comb my hair, because I could not hold a comb in my hands.

If only I could sit up in the chair. I could not sit up. I felt like I was such a bother. So much work has to be done with me at this time the week of June 2, 2017. I anointed my body all through the day with my oil. I call it my healing oil. I was already healing. I just had to get this physical body back working. I laid in the river in Heaven. I laid on top of the water as Peter did; I was healing at that moment. I went back to my physical body, and I found it in a mess, but I am not worried. I have already been healing. Every day I just feel my strength returning to me fast. The nurse always asks me what was in that bottle. I told them that I had to touch my body with that oil every day. They just smiled. Most of them just smiled at me. The good thing about it was that I had the same most of the same doctors that I had at the Doctors Hospital as well as some of the same nurses. I had to come here to Select Specialty Hospital. I felt in my heart that my doctors did not expect me to heal that fast, because they told my family that I had a very low chance of surviving this double pneumonia with sepsis.

When God has His hands on you, no devil in hell cannot do a thing to hurt you. So, I tell the world to be careful in judging people, because you cannot do God's job. No one expected me to live, no one! People prayed for me all over! My children called all of their friends. Churches everywhere were praying for my healing. God had the final say as to whether I would live or die. I was all in His hand! He had the best team picked out for me starting with the EMS team. God picked those special people to pick me up. They were all in God's plan. God was driving the EMS. He told them what to do for me on the way to Augusta, Georgia. He had the hospital staff picked out. I told the EMTs University Hospital that is where I wanted to go before, I left my body, but God said the Doctors Hospital. I had my children there years ago; thirty-three years ago, I had my last kid at the Doctors Hospital. God picked out all of the doctors, nurses, the other staff members, and even the junior who cleaned my room day after day. The food service people who brought my food were also picked out by God. The physical therapy team and all of the other staff members who I cannot call by name was picked out for me. This was the biggest battle that I had ever fought, but I had a similar battle I had to fight; I will tell you about it later on.

I am telling the whole world, "To get your house in order!" My vision was blurry, but now I can see it very clear. You can fool people most of the time, but God; you cannot do a thing with Him so be real! Do not be a fake! Live your life based on a personal relationship with Jesus Christ. When you die, you want to step out in the light, not darkness. You want to meet Jesus Christ, Lord, and Savior. I had to wait until the nurse came to bathe me. If my children were there, they would help me. My husband stayed a few more days with me. I told him to please, go home and see about himself. This was the first week of June. I was so sick to even sit up in a chair. The nurses were checking me; I was too sick to go to sleep and too sick to relax, but I had no worries because I was going to get out of here as soon as I could. Just because you have been in church all of your life, you will not be exempt from trouble or sickness. I know I have tried all of my life to keep the ten commandments and I tried to live holy, but we all come up short. I have tried to raise my children in the way they should go in the Lord's way, and I trained them while they were young. you cannot bend a full-grown tree, bend it while it is bendable.

My husband teased me all while I was in the hospital. He told me that he was tired of wiping my buttocks. He knows I have been waiting on him for 13 years. I never complained because he has been a good man to me. He is a good husband, but a good friend first. He is the best dad in the whole world to his children and grandchildren. He should get the "Grandfather of the Year" award. I could not do any better at this time. I was praying to the Lord. No doubt about it, I have been to Heaven and back to earth. Oh! What a great joy! No cross, no crown! If He brought me all of these years, He was going to bring me again! I am going to get out of here! He has brought me all of these years. I laid there going back to my childhood where I use to walk to the end of the road where I lived as a child and get me a peach off the tree. Sometimes I would just walk alone on those long roads. I remember one day my sister and I went up to the white folk's house and we took my baby sister to the back door, the place where my mother worked every day. My mother would sit there. I was young. I would stand there looking at her come out to the back to feed my sister. My sister breastfed for about 30 minutes. My oldest sister, Mamie and I carried her back home. I was very young about seven years old. My mind always went back to different times in my life while I laid in the hospital bed. We were very poor, but I did not know it at this time. The neighbor lived so we just lived too; we did not know any different.

The doctors would come in and tell me your kidneys are not working and your blood is not clean. I did not make a gesture about what he had said. I just listened to the doctor, and I thought in my heart I am not worried because I know the Chief of Staff. I know a man who is over all of the doctors. I said these things to myself and then I went to the scripture where the four friends carried the friend to Jesus. Each one of my children had a corner in the hospital room and my husband walked in front of my bed. They carried me to Jesus, and I crawl through a crack, and I laid behind Him listening to Him teach. In the scripture, they tore the root out, but every day I went there to that scripture. I laid behind Jesus. A crack was life to me, just enough for me to crawl through.

Mark 2:3-4 reads—

And they come unto Him, bringing one sick of the palsy, which was borne of four. And when they could not come nigh unto Him for the press, they uncovered the roof where he was: and when they had broken it up, they let down the bed wherein the sick of the palsy lay.

I went there every day. My mind always stays in Heaven. I did not have a choice whether I stayed or not it was not up to me. I had no say in the matter. I just love Heaven. I got something to look forward to. I will return there one day. I can see the field where the wheat was tied. I can see the soil on the ground; it was dark chocolate brown and shining. I can see the string that had the wheat tied up in small bundles. I walk among those people who look like the people in Bible days— dressed in Bible clothes, but I had on regular clothes. My mother and my aunties had on regular clothes. My Aunt Lue had a hat on her head, but my mother had pretty black hair just like she wore it here on earth, it looked the same. Aunt Nee's hair looked just like as she wore it here. My mother and aunties were just younger.

I saw the place where I would return one day because I was told that I would return to that same place. My mother looked at me sideways; she told me to go back, you got something else to do! She said, "You cannot come with us yet!" She did say what it was, but I will know this year. I was sent to Select Specialty Hospital. I had to continue my IVs. I had lots and lots of IVs. I was given antibiotics after antibiotics to try to clean my blood from that infectious disease that took over my body. I had physical and occupational therapy. I cannot walk at all at this time. I finally learned how to stand, and I was tried to sit in a recliner. I was still too sick to sit up, but I am tired of that waterbed moving. The hospital bed had to move so my body could move. I was on twelve different medications including lots of IV. I have lost a lot of weight. How much? I do not know. I had been in a coma for 10 days. I only know what my children and my husband told me. I did not remember any of this. I did not even know that I had lived on earth.

I only know about Heaven, because I walked upon Jesus Christ, our Savior of the world. I cannot explain it, but He looked at me with those eyes. I looked at Him good; he looked away and I noticed everything about Him. I look at His cheekbones, His robe, His belt around His waist, His face structure, His sandals, and His head. He had a scarf tried around His head. His feet look like he wore about a ten and a half size in sandals. He looked away, but I was still looking at Him. Before I got to Him, I was looking up in the sky. It looked like it is much closer to the ground and much bluish than the sky here on earth. You do not have to breathe there; you are just there.

I saw all of those beautiful children playing on the hillside. All of the children noticed me when I stepped out of the ground. When you die in a blink of an eye, you are in the presence of the Lord. If you make it in, I want to tell everyone to make sure that your house is in order. You do not have to prove anything to anyone. This is a very serious matter! It is all about that personal relationship with Jesus Christ. No one knows your heart, but Jesus Christ. So, make sure your soul is anchored in Jesus because we will spend more time with Him than here on earth. Do what is right no one has to agree with you! Do not follow the crowd! Sometimes they are not right! Follow Jesus! The Bible is the road map. It will tell you how to live from earth to Heaven. I am not perfect, but I tried the Lord. I know I have to try harder. Sometimes the harder you try to live for Jesus, the more you will be knocked down by believers. So, ground yourself in Jesus; He is the only one who can help you. He will send human beings to help you. He had my whole medical team picked out to help me from the ambulance to the hospital. I do not know why this happens to me, but I do know it is all working out for my good. I will tell you about this a little later on.

It is now June 5, 2017. I got to have dialysis for the first time at the Select Specialty Hospital. I had it at Doctors Hospital as well. I know the children told me that I had to have dialysis when I was in a coma, but I do not remember anything about it or any of those machines coming in my room. It was so scary, but I know it had to be done. It took a long time, just one dialysis took four hours. I had nothing to do. Where was I going at this time? Just lying there looking and thinking about my family, my children, and my grandchildren—they were just born on the last day of April and a few weeks ago.

I remembered that I was in Atlanta on May 12, 2017, at my daughter-in-law's graduation. She graduated from law school from Georgia State University. I walked a long way across the street and after that, we went out with the family to eat. I was feeling a little tired, but nothing out of the usual. That Sunday I went to church with the family for the christening of my grandson, Otis Jr. at my son's church, Park Avenue Baptist Church. I took pictures. Oh, we went to a pool party at my son, Otis, and daughter-in-law, Kianna's, condo after graduation, but I did not swim. I do not think anyone took a swim. It was just a party at the pool for my daughter-in-law's graduation from law school. I was feeling tired, but nothing out of the usual.

Laying there during my dialysis, thinking back during the week I got sick—I helped a friend of mines do a light cleaning of a few rooms in her house. My husband, myself and my granddaughter Callie Blue came back home to Washington, Georgia on that Monday. I was busy all of that week. I was babysitting Callie Blue because her mother just had her baby sister. I am just thinking while laying here undergoing dialysis. I thank God for His goodness. He woke me up, so I am going to be fine. I just have to get out of here! I have no business being here in this shape! "Why me?" I ask myself. I am not worried! I have been to Heaven! I feel good in one way and bad in another way. I have IVs running from my neck and the inside of my hip. I am fighting to get out of here. I know my family is tired. My daughter, Dr. June is by my side and two of my sons, Pastor Henra and Otis, had to go because their wives, Taurika and Kianna, just had newborn babies, but my oldest son, Lazarus Jr. is here and his wife, Skirkea. I had to send my husband home and my granddaughter, Hannah, went with Him. I think God school is out for my Granddaughter, Hannah because she kept my husband company at home while he tried to get some rest. I did not want Him to have to go into the hospital while I was in the hospital because he is always in the hospital every month. He will be sick with his lung disease.

I had dialysis three times and my kidneys went back to working. Oh, Lord! The nurses and I had Church that day. The nurse came in and took all of those tubes out of my hip so my IVs could just run through my neck because I already had some other tubes on the side of my neck. I praise the Lord for letting my kidneys go back to work! This is a miracle in itself! I just love the Lord! He has been good to me all of my life.

I laid there in the hospital bed, and my mind went back to the late sixties during my childhood. I laid there and remembered when my parents did not have electricity in this old house that we lived in; it was too small for ten children and our parents. One night we were all sitting there in the dark and this man came looking for my dad. My dad was a sport; everybody loved Him. This man was the sheriff of Wilkes County. His name was Caesar Moore. He did not tell my mother what he wanted with my dad. We were all sitting there in the dark like sardines in a can. The only light we had was a kerosene lamp. The sheriff told my mother the electricity people would be here in the morning to put electricity in the house. It was so dark, but there were peace and joy in the house.

The next morning, we had electricity. I remember standing there standing in the door looking up the road with my mother with my very nappy hair as usual and with raggedy clothes on with my mother. I remember all of those white trucks coming to give us electricity. I will always remember that the sheriff of Wilkes County kept his word when he told my mother he would get electricity for us. He wondered why we were all just sitting here in the dark; he felt so sorry for us. We were in bad shape, but that was all that we knew. We did not know anything about electricity. Most black people were in the same shape as us. My siblings and I only put good clothes on to go to the church. I was in school at that time. My mind went back to these moments while I laid here in the hospital bed. Oh, my God! When my dad came from work, he was glad. He was very happy we had electricity. A big white light bulb was hanging down with a string tried to the bed to turn it on with.

Laying here in my hospital bed, listening to the lady next door to my room just crying. She has been crying ever since I got here at Select Specialty Hospital. The lady is saying— "Oh, Lord! Please come on! Please, Lord! Please come and take me with you!" I always stop and pray for this lady laying there in the room next to mines. I listened to this lady. I never heard a person beg God to come and take her soul away from her body. It was so powerful for me to hear this lady day after day, all day. She cried all of the time, begging God to come to take her away. She cried all day long! I never have seen her face, because I could not get up and walk. I do not know what she looks like. She begged and begged! I had to block her out and just pray for her. I said, "Lord whatever is bothering her please help her. Oh, Lord! If it is Your will, please calm her Spirit and heal her body. Lord, I plead the blood of Jesus over this lady. Lord, please help her!" She cried and she cried. She did not bother me, because she reminded me of a person who needed Jesus right away.

My children and my husband had to stop and pray for her also. I could not do anything for her because at this time I could not even walk to the next room to see her, nor could I move close to the door. She would stop crying at night. I guess the nurses would give her some medication so she could rest and sleep at night. I could feel her pain through her cries. I was in so much pain myself; I had to pray for both of us. She sounded like she was a middle-aged woman.

Laying in my hospital bed singing to myself; everyone is gone. My family will be back tomorrow. I am remembering this old song that I love so much singing, "Hallelujah! The Storm Is Passing Over! Hallelujah!" I would hum the words, sing to myself, and then cry tears of joy. The Spirit of the Lord is upon me. Remembering when I heard the angels singing all around my bed—the sound of sweetness. Oh, it sounded so sweet! All around my bed, I heard the angels singing, singing to me! I am thanking Father God for His many blessings!

Laying in my hospital bed, I am still praying for this lady next door to me for many days. Finally, I saw her bed pass by my door, and I did not hear her anymore. The medical staff carried her somewhere. I do not know where, but I did not hear the crying anymore. I still think about her. I hope she got better wherever she is; she is in God's hands like all of us. We have no strength of our own, only what God's grace, mercy, and favor has in store for each one of us. I always wanted plenty of mercy, grace, and favor. That is why I spend a lot of time in prayer each day of my life. I do not wait until trouble comes; I pray ahead of time. I am glad no one can interrupt my prayer to God.

It is up to every person to have a personal relationship with Christ. Most people think that just going to church will do it. It will not! Study the Bible for yourself, pray for yourself, you can have your church and sing songs of praise by yourself, and treat people right. Love people even if they do not love you back. Love them and keep praying to Father God. He will guide you into all truth; He will talk to you in a still voice. Many voices will try to talk to you, but the one that speaks the loudest—that is the one to follow! Father God will speak, and He will speak. He will keep on speaking if you do obey His voice. You should follow His voice.

I know so great joy is coming out of this storm because this storm was tough. I am sicker than sick at this time, too sick to sit in a chair at this time. All of that glory that I have seen, I wondered why that rich young ruler from the Bible days could not give all he had to the poor to follow Jesus. He had a chance to talk to Him one on one. The Heaven that I have seen is amazing! It cannot be explained, but I am going to do my best in this book. Who would not want to go to Heaven? Just in the blink of an eye, you are in eternality. Your friend will not go through the ground with you! You go down and then you step out into eternality. The brightness of Heaven is unusual, very bright colors. You would not believe it! I will never forget as long as I live! I am not trying to prove anything to no one. I just had to tell the world my true story.

At this time, I asked my daughter to explain to me what I had; I did not know! No one ever told me what was wrong with me up until this point. So, I asked her as she was lying next to me on the cot on the floor, "Now what do I have?" I asked her this question.

She told me I had "Double Pneumonia with Sepsis." I never heard of the word "Sepsis." My daughter, being a Doctor of Education explained it to me. I was too sick to listen to. She always does a great job explaining things. I was too sick to listen to all of what she was saying. She told me from what the nurses and doctors reported to her:

Sepsis, once diagnosed, is a medical emergency. Your immune system has been compromised due to an infection, it could be fungal or bacterial. It can take place in the Lungs resulting in Pneumonia, in the Kidneys, the bloodstream (bacteremia) or the abdomen can lead to

Sepsis and be potentially life-threatening. There are three stages of Sepsis. The first stage presents a consistent temperature of 101 Fahrenheit or 38.3 degrees Celsius. The second stage results in the risk of organ failure. It is important to catch Sepsis early due to organ failure. The third stage presents very low blood pressure along with the patient being unable to respond to the replacement of fluids in the body. Low platelet count and abnormal cognitive behavior are also present in stage three. Other symptoms include a hard time breathing, low urination, and irregular or abnormal heartbeat. Sepsis shock happens in the third and final stage. The patient is not able to respond to fluid replacement. Half of all patients die from Septic Shock. Sepsis affects mostly those adults 65 years and older. Sepsis can go to semi-serious to very serious very fast. Issues due from Sepsis can promote the formation of blood clots. The restriction of blood flood happens during the last stage and the patient can lose their fingers and toes due to gangrene.

I had to take a deep breath after hearing about Sepsis. I experienced all the stages. My organs failed due to Sepsis. I am going to trust God as I have always trusted Him. He knows what is best for me. He can use me any way He pleases. "I am yours, Lord! Try me and see! I do not belong to myself; I am Yours, Lord. Try me and see!" What happened to me is not only for me. It is for every eye that looks upon me; for everyone to see Father God working a miracle through me. I am going to stay humble. I have a long way to go at this point. I am still at the Select Specialty Hospital. I left the Doctors Hospital, but later on, I will return to the Doctors Hospital for rehabilitation.

Now at Select Specialty hospital laying here on June 5, 2017—The progress notes stated:

> The patient has uneventful weekend except for soreness of her throat and mouth which has been since her intubation. She has no chest pains, shortness of breath, nausea, or diarrhea. Her blood pressure has been stable. Temperature is 98.4 rr-20 HR. 72 Bp 135/73.

Laying in the hospital bed, my family is sleeping at my bedside. All of my children were at my bedside at this time and some this reminded me of when they were very small. When a storm came up and all of them would come into my bedroom and ease in the bed beside me and their father. We always be still when God was working and at this time all of them were there sleep in my room along with their dad. I was very ill at that time. I was still unable to walk or take care of my personal needs.

My renal progress notes:

> Neuro: asleep/arousable, conversant Skin: dry, intact
> Lungs: clear to auscultation with good air entry Abd: soft,

no guarding, bowel sound present Ext: no edema, right femoral trialysis. we will continue with AKI: means requiring dialysis in the hospital. AKI-related to ATN from septic shock and rhabdomyolysis. we will continue with dialysis MWF-while monitoring for evidence of renal recovery. We will need to follow urine output and daily weights. Anemia- due to DIC in the setting of AKI. Her iron level is low however her ferritin is elevated. Her hgb is improving. I will start Procrit 5,000 units SQ every Wednesday Metabolic acidosis-due to AKI. This will be corrected with dialysis today. Hypokalemia- this will be corrected with dialysis today. Hyperphosphatemia- I will start sevelamer 800 mg TID with meals. NSTEMI-conservative management including metoprolol and Lipitor. will defer to the doctor. Hypertension-controlled. Fever. Blood cultures were drawn on Friday and are pending.

On June 7, 2017, my assessment notes stated, "Patient (PT) is sitting up on the side of the bed talking to her daughter. Talking a little plainer." My wounds have not healed at this time. I continued to use wound cream twice a day. The nurses always help me. It was to use on my arms at this time. When my daughter was there in the hospital room with me, she would help put the cream on me and also my husband and my granddaughters. I had to drink Ensure three times a day along with Javen, a nutritional drink. Those sounds that came from the IV when it was finished, even when they had stopped, I could still hear them, that sound got trapped in my head. Too many to count! My buttocks are very sore. My hair feels like a fish cord, my hip on my right side has no feeling in it, my chest feels like a bomb is getting ready to explode, but I am not worried; I have been to a place where I am going back to one day. I got my mind on living. I am awake so I am going to live. I never knew a human being could be this sick and still be alive. I saw all of those mansions. John 14:2 states "In my father's house are many mansions: if it were not so, I would have told you. I go to prepare a place for you." There is such a place, believe me! There is a place! Who would not want to go? The Bible tells each one of us how to get there. The Bible is the road map from earth to Heaven. John 14:3 states "And if I go and prepare a place for you. I will come again and receive you unto myself; that where I am, there ye may be also."

Here I am reading my Bible. I am laying here. I cannot walk at this time; I am still very weak. I know there is a Heaven. I have to tell the world that Heaven is real. Do not put all of your time in foolishness. Praise God while there is time and talk to Him on a personal basis. Tell Him all your troubles. Talk to Him when you have no trouble. Talk to Him when He is blessing you. Every day is a blessing. If you wake up, that is the biggest blessing for them that day. I woke up, but I cannot get up. A grown woman laying here, I never thought I would be in this type of shape. I have lived a life pleasing to God and He knows that in my heart. He loves me. He always tells me that He has no respectable person. What He does for one, He will do for the other! No matter what you are going through, He is always standing there with a hand stretched out. He said come to me and I will help you, but you have to come to Jesus just like you are—do not try to fix yourself up. Let Jesus do it because we cannot fix ourselves up. We are all filthy rags in the sight of a Holy God. We have all sin and fell short. The fruit of the Spirit must be planted in our soul by Jesus Christ. "But the fruit of the Spirit is love, joy, peace, longsuffering, kindness, goodness, faithfulness, gentleness, self-control" (Galatian 5:22).

The word "Spirit" means that the nine fruits are coming directly from the Holy Spirit, not from ourselves. God's peace, joy, and greatness are placed into your minds by God. His divine qualities will start to move into our Spirits. God the Father, Himself wants us to connect to His divine Spirit. He moves into our soul. Jesus has already told us that He is the vine, and we are the branches. The branches draw their life from the vine. We draw our light and love from Jesus. Jesus will release His divine Spirit into us through His Holy Spirit.

Chapter 5

SHINE ON ME LORD WITH YOUR GLORY AGAIN, PLEASE!

It is the seventh of June, and my daughter has worked with me consistently. I am here at Select Specialty Hospital. Every minute, she looks so tired. My other two sons have to go home because they have young babies, but the oldest one and his wife is still here. They come every afternoon from Gainesville, Georgia, which is a very long drive to Augusta, Georgia. Dr. June, my daughter, is here. She goes and gets me some fresh fruit from the farmer's market every day. She would bring me some peaches and some watermelon often. I had to make myself eat. Looking at my daughter's face, she is exhausted, but she is here sleeping right beside me in my room. She is sleeping in the recliner. She is the best daughter anyone could ever ask for in this whole wide world.

Laying here thinking about a lot of things—thinking about the rich young ruler who could not do what Jesus asked Him to do and be saved. Did he understand what he was giving up? He did not like so many people in this world, did not understand. They have put all of their hope in money, but we do have to have money for a decent life. The young man told Jesus that he had been keeping all of the rules since he was a child. He thought he had earned a place in God's kingdom by keeping the commandments. Then the young ruler asked Jesus if there was anything else, he should do. Jesus told Him that he needed to sell everything he owned and give all the money to the poor. Then follow Jesus. Now the rich man heard a commandment that he could not keep. God should have been number one in his life, but God was not first in the man's life all of his stuff was more important to him. All of his stuff was blocking the way to his relationship with God. Having money is not a sin. Loving money is a sin. Matthew 16:26— "What will it profit a man if he gains the whole world and lost his soul." To gain the whole world is to receive all the world has to offer, which is money, fame, pleasure, power, prestige, etc. To lose one's soul is to die without a right relationship with Christ and spend an eternity in the Lake of fire. In Matthew 16:23— Jesus then spoke to the crowd and reminded then that there was nothing worth more than one's eternal soul. Rejecting Christ means temporary earthly gains, but it comes at the worst possible price.

These are the stories that would be running through my mind, and I laid there looking at the rain sliding down the window. As I looked to my right a large window there are no curtains over the window, because the nurse told me I was up on a high floor. It was so high up. I saw the top of the trees. I am sicker than sick, but I am alive. I thank God for bringing me back to earth, but I want everyone to know I had nothing to do with me coming back from Heaven, it was all in God's hands, not mines because I had no remembrance of this world. Laying there my hospital bed, the nurse is checking my blood sugar, blood pressure, and temperature. The nurse was straightening out all of these wires that are hooked up to me. Wires are in my neck, my arms, and my groin. The nurse said my sugar is okay this time. I do not need any insulin this time. Everything in my body was poisoned. I had a fever and kidneys were not working well at this time, but we will see later on how things are working. There are wounds on my buttocks that are healing. I got to use some cream twice a day called Silvadene cream. The wounds are still sore. My body was beginning to break down as I laid in a coma. It does not take long for the body to begin to break down. The doctor orders a collection of urine for 24 hours, this was on June 7, 2017.

The nurse collected the urine and the next day she was just smiling about how much urine she has collected from me. It was so much when she measured it. She poured it into a tall container, and she went out of my room. We were joking about how much she had collected. The next day the same nurse that was working on me at the Doctors Hospital was at this hospital, the Select Specialty Hospital. I had mostly some of the same doctors that I had at the Doctors Hospital. This nurse said to me that they were going to take the tubes out of my groin for the dialysis treatments and she told me I did not need them anymore. My kidneys had begun to work again! Oh, how we praised the Lord! We were both so happy! I cried out to the Lord. Thanking Him for helping me! He allowed kidneys to work again! I just praised Him and the nurse praise Him! I said Psalm 23 over and over again and the Lord's prayer. I was so happy! Dialysis is no joke! The Lord has smiled on me! I was laying there after all of the nurses were gone and I thought about one of my favorite songs. The title of this song is "You know My Name" by Tasha Cobbs. I sang this song to myself, and it goes like this:

You know my name; You know my name. You Know my name. He walks with me. He talks to me. He tells me I am His own. You Know my name. Oh, how you comfort me! Oh, how you counsel me! It still amazes me that I am your friend. So now I pour out my heart to you, yes, here in your presence I am made new. You know my name. Oh, how you walk with me. You know my Name. Oh, how you walk with me. Oh, how you talk to me, you tell me I am your own. Oh, God, you know me, So I trust you with my life. No fire can burn me. No battle can stop me. No mountain can stop me. I walk in your victory. Your power is within me. You know my name. Oh, how I talk to you.

This was one of the songs that my I sang with me children and the Spirit of the Lord shined in that room, the whole room! The whole hospital was filled with the Spirit of the Lord on this day. Singing and praying with my children and my husband! This is a milestone that I cannot express! This is a wonderful blessing! My kidneys are working again! Praising God! I have always praised Him every day of my life ever since He came into my life. I never had time for foolishness. If I know something no could change my mind, I had to do it, because the God that I served always tells me I am His own. I cannot follow the crowd! I never had time too! Everyone should be persuaded by their minds. I always had my mind. I had to follow it, but I had to ask Father God about it first no matter what it was; simple things like Lord, "Where should I park my car?" I asked Him, "Who should I let in my circle of friends?" I used to try to fit in with that crowd, but I could not. I just keep encouraging myself like the Prophet David did.

I love people! I have to because God is love, but you do not have to associate with everyone, just love them! This is a song that I love by Tasha Cobb, "You Know My Name." I did not sing it all the way right word for word, but I told God, "You know my name!" This song is one that I always humble myself to. I am not worried; people are praying for me. I know that my God has the final word over my body. People put your time in serving God. I know when you are serving people, helping them, and praying for them; you are serving God, but do not build your hopes on the things of this world! Build your hopes on eternal things. I do not call on Father God when things happen in my life or trouble come, I call on Him while things are going well. Whether I feel like praying or not I pray anytime, anywhere. I do have to say fancy words because God always knows my needs before I ask Him, but I always tell Him how mighty He is, and I always take Him back to His word.

I always pray to the Lord, "Let your will be done not my will! If Your will be done it will be all right not my will, because Lord you know what is best for me in any given situation!" That I am praying about. I am still not sleeping well at all. I am too sick to go to sleep. My body is still in a whirlwind so many wires! I do not know how many wires I had on my body in ICU, but my daughter-in-law told me that she has never seen so many wires on one person in her life. I told her I did not see those wires because I was not there to see no wires. I was in Heaven with a big smile on my face, enjoying and exploring Heaven! There is so much to see around Heaven. My mother told me, "To go back, it is not your time to come yet!" I see Jesus sitting on that rock. Can anyone imagine seeing Jesus sitting on a rock in the field? I did! I have told everyone that wants to listen. I cannot tell the whole story until they read this book. It was unbelievable! I have told my children and my husband so many times; they just stop in their track.

Heaven is real. Five minutes after you shut your eyes, you will know where you are. I hope everyone steps out into the light as I did! I am going back one day when I finish telling men, women, boys, and girls that there is a Heaven! God is waiting for everyone to believe and trust in Father God! He is real! He looked at me! I was a young woman! I got the picture here in this book that I took when I was 30 years old. I look just like I looked in that picture in Heaven. I walk upon Jesus sitting on that rock! I will never forget this as long as I live! I always ask myself, "Why did I have to go through this? It is because God gives the hardest test to the strongest servants. I know this test was the hardest, but I have another test that I went through I will tell you about it later on in this book. Unbelievably, it happens 41 years ago. I am at peace with God; He has shown up again in my life and shows completely out again! What is so special about me? I keep on fighting these huge battles. There are three more I will tell you about later on in this book.

On June 12, 2017, I am still at the Select Specialty Hospital. The kidney doctor has ordered Sodium Bicarb 650 MG tablets because the acid in my kidneys was high. I take one tablet twice a day, but I do not have to take these anymore. The doctor told me if you come out just taking this for the rest of your life it will not be so bad. Sitting here writing my book from my notes that I got from the two hospitals, I cannot believe a human body could go through so much! Oh, my God! Lord, have mercy on me! Lord, I have served you all of my life! I pray at least 20 times every day and when I awake at night; I pray until I fall back to sleep. I go out in the yard, and I gage up into the sky and I pray. I sing my favorite gospel songs and listen to my sermons while I am driving in the car. I have done this most of my life. I brought 45 gospel records when I first got married 43 years ago. I brought all of the old gospel records. These songs are what I raised my children on. I listened to all of those old sermons and gospel songs.

One of my children told me a couple of years ago. He was teaching Bible study at his church; he told them how he met the Lord Jesus Christ. He told them that he meets Jesus walking through his home. He told me about it, and I said praise God that is when he accepted Christ as his savior, and he is my last son the baby of the four children, and he is a minister. When I could not tell my children about Jesus, I got a lot of tapes and sermons and I pick the song and prayers go up I told them about Jesus. It was a busy job raising four children and getting them all through college. I got them through college on a schoolboy's lunch. That was through Jesus Christ because my husband did not have a penny to educate four children. I always asked God would he please make a way for all four of them to be educated. We worked hard praying and they studied hard; I saw to that. I was a tough mother, but they knew I loved them with all of my heart and their father did too. We worked and we worked, and we prayed. I prayed on my knees when I was tired at times; I would just fall in the bed and fell to sleep in five minutes. I had a vision one night that I seem all four of my children walking to get their college degrees in a black robe and believe me that it came to pass.

My mother told me one day on my way home from work that I was too busy. I had stopped at her house for a little while for a conversation as I always do. I could not say anything; I was too busy, but I never quit. I had work to do; I had to make sure that my children would not end up poor. I was very poor when I was a child. I could not have my children coming up in a world where there are so many opportunities to be successful and live a good comfortable life, so I told my mother I did not want my children to be poor. She just looked at me. She said that there is no way in this world that you cannot send your children to college. I said, "The way has already been made, all of them will finish college, mama!"

So, I went on home I lived a half block from my parents down the same dirt side road off of Metasville Road. I laid there thinking about how good my children have been to me so far. All of their hard work has paid off so far. They would always try to exercise my body when they came to see me in the hospital. They would turn me over. The nurses did not have to do so much for me when my children were there. With them and my husband standing by my side along with God; I was in peace. My children are so good to me, and my daughters-in-law are the best. At this time, I am learning how to sit up in the recliner chair. I am too weak! The first time that

I sat up, I almost fainted! My heart sped up; I could hear it beating outside of my chest. Every time I am sitting here at this computer, I am praising Father God for letting me live.

I was in Heaven. Why did I come back? I know that my time on earth was not out yet. There is something that I got to do! Laying here thinking about Father God and how he showed up and out! My God healed me in a supernatural way when I laid in the river. My mother standing there on the other side of the river telling me to go back, moving her hands tell me to go back! She said, "It is not your time yet to stay here! You got to go back to you! You can't come with us yet."

It looked like the same place where John the Baptist baptized Jesus. I laid there on my back smiling happily as I could be I looked about 30 years old. When I laid in the river, I did not sink. My mind is always in Heaven, but I got to live on until my end come and then I will go back one day. My aunties were sitting on the hillside watching the children play. I will never forget how beautiful it was over in Heaven! All of the pretty houses, flowers, trees, and the water ran differently from the water on earth. Gold is on each side of the river. It shines! I stood there after I got out of the river. I stood upon the water, and I walked out, but I did not sink.

Laying here sicker than sick but making progress every day. Thinking about people who are not saved, there is time to be saved while there is still breath in your body. Laying here thinking about all of those who do not know Christ. If you do not know Christ, you are on the outside of His safety. If you are please come into Christ before it is too late! Who would want to miss Heaven? What is the point of living if you will not go to Heaven? No one can deny that God was not on my side when I was sick, even the doctors were puzzled about my case. I am still alive even though all of the odds were against me, but I am here today telling my story, a true story! I never through a human could be so sick. I did not feel pain while I was in a coma. I left that body, and I came back to that body. After I awoke the doctors still did not have much hope for me to live. I was so weak! I know the God that I serve, the Lord and Savior Jesus Christ was not going to leave me! He has brought me too far to leave me now! Laying here praying and telling the Lord, I am your Lord! I am not of my own! I am your Lord! You have tried me through the fire, and you brought me out shining like pure gold. I was standing beside Jesus. He was sitting on a rock in the field, and I walked upon Him. I cannot describe all of that glory that was in His eyes. He looked at me with more compassion than I have ever seen. I am repeating myself in telling this experience, but this was the high point of my whole life. It was more than amazing it was shocking. I am a living testimony! I am a living testimony!

Why me, Lord? Why me, Lord did you use me to let everyone see a miracle? I am laying here at this time. I can barely stand up. The physical therapist comes in my room trying to help me stand up. I have a band on my arm that shows that I am at risk of falling. So, I am not even supposed to try to get out of the bed or I could fall. The nurse brings me lots of medications through pills, shots, and IVs running through me. I am at peace! I am happy! I am thinking about my children and my grandchildren. I just love to play with them. I have the best husband in the whole world and the best children! I did all I could do for my children to have a good education. My children had to know who Jesus was first; if they did not know who Jesus was then they could not make it in life! It is as simple as that! Knowing Jesus will keep your mind right as well as studying the scriptures, praying, and going to church, but you have to put all of those into action.

I laid there looking at all of these doctors, nurses, housekeeping staff, and the food staff; they are all so nice to me. We talk about things especially the word of the Lord. Most of the nurses tell me about Jesus! Most of them are Christian people. Some of them tell me how hard things are for them and they are asking me to pray for them. I tell I will, and I tell them to do the same for me. So, I always start praying for whoever asks me. I have always loved Father God ever since I was 11-year-old. We are all sinners saved by God's grace and His mercy! "As it is written, There is none righteous, no, not one:" (Romans 3:10). I love the Lord! Just like He says in Mark

12:30, "And thou shalt love the Lord thy God with all thy heart. and with all thy soul, and with all thy mind, and with all thy strength; this is the first commandment."

Laying there some of my people told me I knew you were going to wake up, but I know that they did not know that because my children told me that they doubt it. No one knew, but Father God. I still cannot believe all of this is happen to me, but I always tell Father God to use me anyway that He sees fit. "Lord try me and see!" I always tell the Lord this. "I am not my own, I belong to you. Lord, I pray all through the day and that is every day!" I always pray for other people more than I do myself.

Laying here in this bed, looking at my husband changing me as if I was a child or a newborn baby. I have been waiting on him for 13 years, hand and foot since he was diagnosed with his lung disease. I never knew what it was to get rest. I worked all the while I was a child: carrying wood or water from the well even before I started to go to school. My siblings and I had a lot of chores to do, working in the garden were the main thing we did. We were always looking for food. There was never enough when all ten of us were at home, but as some of us got grown; it got a little better. I am this type of woman. I never got much rest at all. When my last baby was born, I had a baby at home, two in diapers and two more to take care of; I never really got any rest.

I was always busy with four children, working three jobs at one time for some years. I worked part-time jobs, which consisted of cleaning and washing clothes. I cleaned house after house with tears in my eyes hoping that my children would have a better life than I had. I would not trade my past for anything. I want my children and their children to have it better than I had because I have a vision for my children. God gave me the vision. I have to run with the vision. I told my husband of this vision. He ran right along with me, and it came to pass. I give God all of His glory.

Laying here thinking back when I was a child on a Sunday at church, we got full on a Sunday when we had dinner. All of those sisters from the church would put dinner on the table on the outside of the church especially on "Homecoming Day!" This day symbolizes that day that those who have relocated from their church home come back home the same time every year to reunite with other members that have remained a part of the church. Oh, what a time we had praising the Lord! These days the Spirit is not as high as it was then, but one thing for sure we had a full stomach that day. We all carried a big plate home with us. Thinking about my childhood while laying here in the hospital brings peace to me! Those were the best years of my life in a way and things were very simple back then! We did not have electricity, but we got some, later on, no running water, no television, no phone, at this time. We had nothing but a few clothes the white folks gave us. My aunties in Washington D.C. sent us a box twice a year. We could not wait to open it! The mailman brought it and that means we got some clothes to wear to school, but they did not last long my sisters and I wore each other's clothes. No one had their clothes. One day I wore them and the next day my sisters wore them. You can blink your eyes one time. That is how quick you can be in eternity. In just ten minutes after I got sick, my soul left my body; I was gone.

I went to different parts of Heaven. I saw so many different things; it is very hard to put on paper, but I am trying. Reading 2 Peter 3-8—

But, beloved, be not ignorant of this one thing, that one day is with the Lord as a thousand years. and a thousand years as one day. The Lord is not slack concerning his promise, as some men count slackness; but is longsuffering to us-ward, not willing that all should come to repentance. But the day of the Lord will come as a thief in the night; in the which, the heavens shall pass away with a great noise, and the elements shall melt with fervent heat, the earth also and the works that are therein shall be burned up.

At this time, I have learned to stand up. I have learned to put my sock on with a sock slider and I am sitting in a recliner still sicker than sick. The nurses are very patient with me. My children coming in and out. June is getting ready to leave. She has worked with me day in and day out. So, she is very tried, she has been right by my side--bringing me some fresh fruit every day. She goes to the market and brings me fresh fruits and vegetables. She looked so tired. My daughter looks exhausted, and my sons do as well, but they are so happy. They are willing to do what it takes to get me back on my feet. I look at each one of them. All I have been through raising them it was all worth every second. So much is going on with me I cannot put it into words.

At this time, I have learned to stand up using the pot that is beside my bed it is always close to me. I cannot reach it. I always look at the sink on the right side of me, but I cannot get over there to it to brush my teeth. All of my family has gone at this time. My husband looks sick. I sent him home again; he looks very tired. I told him to go and do not come back until I tell you to come. He looks really bad. My granddaughter has given out also. She is looking after her granddad. She is staying with him. My daughter has to go back to work. She has to go to five states to work at the colleges. Before she left, she laid on the floor next to me on a pad and blankets. I would look at her at night—she was so tired and worn out completely. I had to go on, me and Father God. The doctors were excited about my progress and my physical therapist was excited that I could walk to the door. It was the hardest thing that I ever had to do; to try to walk to that door. I had to do arm stretches and legs movement sitting in the recliners chair. It was the hardest thing to do. "Once a man twice a child," this is me at this moment. My daughter brought me two of her blankets from home to put on me, because I was always so cold. One of my doctors looked at my blankets and said that his daughter would love those because they have some pretty bears on them. I just looked and smiled at Him.

I often thought like Job 13:15 "Though he slay me, yet will I trust in Him; but I will maintain my own way before Him." Job 14:14 states, "If a man die, shall he live again? all the days of my appointed time will I wait, till my change come." It is coming I am going to get out of here sooner or later. This was just a test. If you get so close to God. He is going to use you the most. I have been so many times. This is one test that God passes through me. I had nothing to do with it. It could have easy went the other way, because I was already in Heaven. Why did Father God bring me back? I will know when I get this book published. This bed moves all of the time. It has gotten on my nerves. I move so much. I never sleep in this bed. I am too sick to go to sleep. I did not know a human being could get this sick. There is a mirror on the right side of me, but I never look at that mirror. I do not how I feel. I cannot look much better than I feel. My hair has not been washed since I got sick, and it has been 25 days now and I am still not able to walk. I can make it to the door and back with a walker and the nurse by my side. The nurse comes into my room.

The physical therapist is trying to help. They always tell me I am doing great. My muscles are getting strong again. It is the hardest thing I have ever done--learning to walk again. I have to get to number six in strength before I can move on. It is like finding a nickel in a hay staff trying to learn how to walk or to stand up because my heart rate shoots up every time I try to walk. My blood pressure shoots up, but I got to keep trying. I got to get out of here. Father God has brought me this far. He will not leave me now. I got to fight the fight. I got to get home. I will get home one day soon. I am not worried about anything. I am trusting in the God that serve and that is the Lord and savior of this world. Every time the doctors would tell me something like my blood is not clean or my kidney is working; I did not say a word, because I know a man who I have seen sitting on that rock and he has all powers in his hand. He said so when he got up for the resurrection. All powers in Heaven and on earth were in God's hands, stay humble and pray to treat people right. You do not have to agree with people when you know in your heart that they are wrong, because it is coming up again.

Please the Lord, no man, because one day in a blink of an eye you will be in eternity. I never felt any pain until I awoke; I did know this world. The world that I was in, I saw all of the races of children playing on the hillside. They looked at me. I saw brown children, black children, white children, and red children. I saw all of the races that are here on earth and all of them were very happy and playing together. I stood there and watched them play. Father God is God of us all not some of us, but he created us all in his images. All I can do is to hold on the same God that has been with me ever since I was eleven. I used to sit in the woods alone and I would always go sit in the woods as a child. We live in the country in the woods. We did not have people living close to us. No one bothered us or hurt children. I would always sit in the woods and pray.

One day in the summer of 1968, I was praying, and someone touched me on my shoulder, and I know it was the Lord. I will never forget that. That was the same summer that I accepted Jesus Christ as my savior and Lord of my life as long as I live. And when I die, I will be with Him again, I have been to Heaven two times the next time I go I will stay there forever more I will tell you about the first time I went a bit later on. The devil will always tempt you to stay strong in the word he will still tempt you, but he wants to get you unless you yield to his calling when you go to pray, he will interrupt you pray I always say get behind me Satan. I belong to the Lord Jesus Christ I always say that when I am praying, and my mind will wander at times but most time I go into a deep word like Psalm 23; I say it several times a day that is every day. I repeat the

Lord prayers several times a day. I think God for when he has done for me and my family. I always carry Father God back to his word when I am sick. I go to the healing scriptures. If I am feeling lonely or sad, I go to Psalm 23 and I think about what the Lord has already for me. I feel happy. It is just that simple and I say the Lord prayers. One scripture that I always say when I know the battle is not mines it belongs to the Lord. Isaiah 53:5 states that—"He was wounded for our transgressions; he was bruised for our iniquities; the chastisement of our peace was upon Him; and with his stripes, we are healed."

I say, "Lord what have I done I my life to be suffering like this?", but in a still voice, the Lord said, "Nothing! I got to use you!" We all have sinned and fell short of God's glory. I have always been the person who tried to live a perfect life in front of the Lord. I try, but I know it was impossible, but I tried. No cross, no crown! I laid there day after day crying happy tears not sorrowful tears, but tears of joy. Every day I made some progress. Looking at the door trying to get ready to go home, but I have a long way to go yet. I still cannot walk at this time. My husband has not gone home. I told him to not come back until I call him, he looks worn out. I know my family got tired of helping me get on the pot, but after they left; I dragged myself out of bed. I pulled the bed pot close to me. I have made some progress. I have used the bathroom on myself plenty of times, but now I make it to the pot. I cannot stand up long. I drag myself to the pot.

I called the nurse a hundred times and day and all night seem like it to use the pot because they always give me a stool softer and when I have to go, I have to go. I am at risk of falling; I should not try to get out of bed, but I do. I called the nurse to help me and most of the time they are right there, but some of the time I get bold, and I try to drag myself out of bed. I have so many wires hooked up to me; I cannot get far if I wanted to. I get all wrapped up in wires. I try to get them unrumpled, but I cannot; so, I just lay there until the nurse gets there. Most of the time if some of my children are here, they keep them straighten out. They have pulled me back up from the bottom of the bed a thousand times. I slide down to the bottom and I cannot pull myself back up at this time, but I am sitting up now in the recliner. The first time I sit up in the recliner I got so sick; I had to get back into bed. I was too weak to hold my head up. I surprised the doctors. They looked at me sometimes as if I was done, but I got the best team in the world working on me.

The last thing that I told the EMS to take me to University Hospital, but God said to you is to go to the Doctors Hospital because I was too sick to make it to university hospital God wanted me at the Doctors Hospital. I did not know where I was, I did not even know I was sick because I was in Heaven I life my body before I got to Augusta, which is where the Doctors Hospital is, I left my body I have no remember or even riding to the hospital. Whatever my body was feeling I did not feel any pain I look at the Ems report that picks me up from my home and took me to Augusta Ga. where the hospital was on the way it said I went through a lot of things. I did not feel anything, because I was walking around Heaven enjoying myself. I did not have any remembrance of this world. I know I was in a wonderful place because I was exploring Heaven. I was young; I looked about 30 years old. Whatever I went through on the way to the hospital in Augusta, Georgia, and whatever happens in the ICU; I do not know! I was there I went to different parts of Heaven. There are parts of Heaven. I heard nothing that was going on around me; I mean absolutely nothing because I was not there.

When I awoke, I wondered what in the world where all of those people were around me; I thought I was in Smyrna, Georgia. I did not even know what was wrong no one told me what was wrong with me. I was well in Heaven. There is not any sickness there; I did not see anyone who was sick. I saw children playing. I saw my mother and my two aunties. They were not sick. I did not know the word sick in Heaven. Everything is so different. You will recognize your folks, but there is some kind of glow. You do not think like here on earth it is more majestic. You are light and you move in joyful motion. I cannot describe it is amazing. Who would not want to go there? There is much peace in Heaven. I look up at the sky; it is bright and more blueish bright. I look at the ground and the trees; they look very different than these here on earth. The ground and trees more beautiful and simpler; the same color, but shining colors of brown and beautiful greenish colors? I had no remembrance of the things here, but I recognize my family over there. Oh, they recognized me! Also, my auntie called me, "Willie Agnes" like she always did here when she was living here on earth!

God made me a target, so I know he knows me because he heals me in a spiral way. I still had to struggle my way be because my physical body was a mess to ugly to look at. The devil is always standing around, but I have never been worried about the devil because my God tried me hard and I got to hit the floor running I cannot give up. Never, never will I give up no matter what happens will pray on and see what the end will be. God knows what he is doing with me I do not, but I will know when I finish this book, I live for God every day of my life I always have I did not need the approval of people I love everyone I hate no one whether they hate me or not. I do not want that feeling in me, because it is not worth it! Hate makes you look ugly, inside, and out. There is a purpose for all of this I place myself like Job. You are talking about a sick person I am still very sick weak as a newly born animal. Philippians

4:13— "I can do all things through Christ which strengthens me." Philippians 19—"But my God shall supply all your needs according to his riches in glory by Christ Jesus".

Reading my scripture, my Bible stays by my bed. Ever since I woke up; I am reading it and praying to God, because I have seen the glory of God. I will never forget it was amazing in the blink of an eye you are in Heaven. I looked at my mother and my aunties and the children in Heaven. I walk on little father I saw all of these people dressed in the days of old just looking at me, but they did not say anything. I walked on a litter farther and I saw this man sitting on a rock, he did not look my way until I walk upon Him. And he turns his head and looks at me. Oh, my God, who was this man?

And he said unto me, my grace is sufficient for thee. For my strength is made perfect in weakness. Most gladly, therefore, will I rather glory in my infirmities, that the power of Christ may rest upon me. Therefore, I take pleasure in infirmities, in reproaches, in persecutions, in distresses for Christ's sake: for when I am weak, then am I strong (2 Corinthians 12: 9-10).

The last thing I think about at night before I go to sleep is Father God and I pray. The first thing I do in the morning is pray, and I read my Bible and I listen to my gospel music that is every day and every night before I got sick. I pray all the time in my car and the shower. I pray when I am walking and exercising in the gym. I am praying sitting in church. I talk to Father all of the time whether good times or bad times. Laying here wondering why this happened to me? I am a countrywoman. I do not socialize very often with other folks. I am what you call a to "myself person" other than being my husband, my children, my grandchildren, and my daughters-in-law.

Laying here looking up in the ceiling of this hospital wondering why God let this happen to me? Why not me? God has a plan! I am a praying woman. I prayed all of the time. My husband asked me, "How do you live? Every time I see you it is something about Jesus." I pray outside looking up in the sky. I sing hymns in the shower or the bathtub. I pray while driving alone. It is a hunger and a thirst that I got to have and there is nothing in this world that I have found to replace my hunger and thirst for the Lord and Savior Jesus Christ. I got to have Him all day, every day in my life. I cannot wait until Sunday! That is not enough for me! It all day; bit and pieces of the Jesus, reading His words.

On June 14, 2017, my progress notes were—

There were no acute issues noted overnight. She continues to have a good appetite. she has no chest pain, shortness of breath, nausea, or diarrhea. Her blood pressure has been stable. Temperature 98.4, BP- 128/74. Sitting up in

chair eating dinner, the family is at her bedside.
awake/alert/ conversant, skin very dry, Lungs clear to
auscultation with good air entry No edema AKI- related to
ATN from septic shock and rhabdomyolysis, her renal
function has improved. and is now stable. Anemia-due to
DIC in the setting of AKI. Her hgb is slightly lower this
morning, she has been ordered to receive a transfusion
this morning. Metabolic acidosis- due to AKI. Her level is
improving on supplemental bicarbonate so I will follow
for now. Hypomagnesemia. She was started on
MagOx400mg BID. Hypokalemia-continue with
supplementation. Hyperphosphatemia I will discontinue
sevelamer and follow. Hypertension controlled.

These were my progress notes at this time. I have a long
way to go. I still cannot walk. I use my walker and the nurses
help to get to the chair beside my bed. My children and my
husband always help when they are here. God uses anyone He
wants to use. We always think He can only use certain people,
but God knows the hearts of everyone. A poor man can die,
and they will have few flowers at their funeral; if any, it might
be the only flower that is on top of the casket, but when a
person dies who thinks about going to Heaven. Those who are
big in the community; we try to put them in Heaven, but God
is the only one who can judge the heart. He has the last word

over you. He has the last word over me; He saved my soul a long time ago. He always hears my cry! How many tears do we have in Heaven? God knows how many tears each one of us has in Heaven. Some people do not care about going to Heaven. If I could only explain what I saw; I walked around Heaven all day long for days. I never knew I had lived here on earth. I did not have a mind of earthly things. It is so different in Heaven. We will look the same. I recognized my family—my mother, and her two sisters. They had a glow all around them. When your feet touch the ground in Heaven, it does not feel the same as here. When your feet touch the ground in Heaven, you are so light. It feels like you are floating on air.

I have a little strength to wash my face in the pan of water that the nurse sat on the table. It is so hard to reach down to wash. The nurse would always help me. If my daughter or my husband were there with me, they would help me. Everyone is getting so tired. They are exhausted, but they do not pretend to help me or love me. They love me with all of their hearts. My children love me with their actions. They always try to help me even when they were small children. They helped me fold up clothes, wash dishes, and cook. They would clean the house. They loved to mop the floors. They all have been so helpful, all of their sweet lives. My husband sits there sick Himself; he told me that after all of these years that you have been waiting on me, you never said a word or complain or even made an ugly face at me—since I have been sick all of these years. He always goes out to the waiting room and takes his breathing treatments. He brought all of his breathing medicines and machine to the hospital. I was on some of that same medication that my husband was on. I have been helping him fix his medications all of these years and now look at me laying here taking breathing treatments also. Lord, have mercy! We must be careful in this world how we treat sick people especially our spouses because the leaning tree does not always fall first.

I lay there reading a Psalm that I have marked in my Bible. One of my doctors told me that he had five critically ill patients all with Bibles in their rooms and they are the ones that are improving the fastest. I read my scripture, thinking of the other patients and praying silently for them. Psalm 119: 153-154— "Consider mine affliction and deliver me: for I do not forget thy law. Plead my cause and deliver me; quicken me according to thy word."

I cannot ever give up a lot of people who do not want to go through the door to Jesus Christ, but he is the only way to the father. Knock and I shall be open, seek and you will find, ask and I shall be given I believe this with all of my heart. I may not be what you ask for, but it will be best for every believer that loves the Lord. I put myself with the paralyzed man that was on his sick and his four friends carry him to Jesus on a cart they was consistent in getting their friend to Jesus and they did I was this person on the mat and my children carried me to Jesus every day for something and I didn't get in through the roof I saw a very small crack and would crawl thought the crack and I would lay behind Jesus the room was full with sick people, but I touch a thread that was on His garment. I was sicker than sick, so sick. I did not want to think that I was going to die after I woke up. I know it was my time to fight. I had already been to Heaven. I was died according to one nurse who spoke from the dialysis team. She asked me, "Why did I come back here? I told her with pride, "I had nothing to do with it!" It was God's doing not mines!" I am so glad He brought me back! This makes two times He has brought me back! I will tell you about the first time later on.

Why me Lord? Why me Lord? You chose me to work a miracle through me for everyone to see. I went back to the EMS in Washington, Georgia. I was on my way to the gym both days. I told the EMTs my story. I went here to get my report from my ambulance ride so I could put the notes in my book. The lady sitting there getting my report ready for my book; I told her my story. She went across the hall, and she got the other man that worked there. I told him what I had told her, and we all had church. We were all crying, and the Spirit of the Lord showed up in that EMS building. I asked her about the people that came to pick me up and she told me that they were not there. She told me to come back tomorrow. She looked at my report and she shook her head. I heard the man say from across the hall that no one has never come back and thanked them for picking them up. I told them about my story of how I went to Heaven. They all got happy and were filled with joy. The next day, I went back to meet the people who came to pick me. Who were these angels that God had already picked out for me? I did not have much time; my children told me about how fast they had to drive to get me there to Augusta, Georgia. That story will be told later on.

Getting back to the angels that up picked me up in the ambulance; they were predestinated to be working that day May 19, 2017. Their names on the EMS Dispatch reports are Rebekah Echols, Advance Emergency Medical Technician Role; Driver, Dennis Weaver, /EMT- Paramedic Role Primary Patients Caregiver, Lindsay Hughes. So, I went back, and I met all of these people. The lady has already told them that I would be coming by and all of them were just sitting there waiting for me. The first man that I met in the other room before I went to greet the EMTs, said that he was the one who talked to my family about my condition, but he had no idea that I had made it because they move me to another Select Specialty Hospital. He said, "You made it?"

I said, "Yes!" and I went in where all of the EMTs were sitting; they were looking at me as if I was a ghost. They were not blinking their eyes. I shook their hands and I told them to thank you all from the bottom of my heart. I am sitting here typing this story and crying about now. Praising God! I am getting on with the story about these angles that picked me up; they had to be God sent.□

Chapter 6

STRENGTH RETURNING

I told the EMTs about my visit to Heaven and how I was so happy that I had a wonderful team of EMTs! I got so happy and the other EMTs that were sitting there got so happy and emotional. I told them that I would never forget their faces. The Spirit of the Lord showed up again. They could not believe that I made it, but God did; it had nothing to do with that because I have always been in His hands. I know He was not going to leave me. Oh, what a time, we had in this place! One of the ladies handed me a napkin to wipe the tears out of my eyes. All of them were emotional. I died at the time I got into the ambulance. I do not remember riding in the ambulance. The last thing that I saw vaguely was the door shutting and then I stepped out of my body into glory! All of the time the EMTs were working on me in the ambulance and at the ICU in the Doctors Hospital. I felt nothing, but when I awoke several days later. Oh, my God! I will tell you more about that later on in this book. The EMTs knew my address; they had been out here to my address hundreds of times picking up my husband up, but never me until this time.

I live in a town of about 5000 people. Everyone knows everybody! I worked in the school system for years and in the factories. I did housework to see that my children get the best education that my husband and I could give them. It is a great town to live in, if you are at the age of retirement. All three of my boys played sports, got scholarships, and worked. Nothing came easy! We all had to work toward that goal and my daughter; I wanted her to have the best education. Also, my husband and I started early telling them that they were going to college and that was it! I did not care what they study or what they chose to be; all we know was that they had to go to college, and that was my prayer to the Lord and Savior Jesus Christ. It did come to pass! Glory, hallelujah! My husband and I thought if we could get our children through college our grandchildren would have a chance at going to college also. After I left my regular job, I cleaned various peoples' homes to help my children, but I did not want them to have to do what I did. I wanted better for them because they had a tough mother and father to push them. They all were great children. I was almost sorry when they left home going to college, but I know it was time for them to leave the nest and go out into the world. I have tried to prepare them Spiritually, mentally, and physically to meet the world.

Around June 16, 2017, at Select Specialty Hospital, I signed for more blood to be given to me. I can eat independently at this time. I have bruises on my upper arm from turning myself. I am turning myself and if I slide down too far in the bed, I can hold on to the side rails of my bed and pull myself back up. My family and the nurses have pulled me up from the bottom of my bed a thousand times with wires everywhere. The wires got so tangled one day; the nurse asked me what in the world has happened to me. She was laughing and then I started to laugh too.

When she came into the room, I was wrapped from my neck to my feet in wires. I could not get the wires separated so I just laid there praying until the next morning. The nurses come all through the night, but a few hours before day, they do not come anymore until the next morning. The left side of my buttocks still had sores, but they are healing. The nurse put cream on my buttocks twice a day. My buttocks were so sore at one time; blood was all over the bed sticking to my gown. My skin had broken laying there in the hospital bed. I did not know I had bed sores; they were everywhere. All in my mouth and on my gum had sores. I had to rinse my mouth out with this medication three times every day. It tasted so bad, but after a while, it healed the wounds in my mouth.

It is a long, hard journey. I have given it all to God. He knows what He is doing, and He knows what tests I should take because I am not my own, I belong to the Lord and He can use me any way He wants to; I am yours Lord, try me and see, I am your Lord. I am sitting here thinking about Roman 8: 28-32—

And we know all things work together for good to them that loved God, to them who are called according to his purpose. For whom he did foreknow, he also did predestinate to be conformed to the image of his Son, that he might be the firstborn among many brethren. Moreover, whom he did predestinate, them he also called; and whom he justified, them he also glorified. What shall we then say to these things? If God is for us, who can be against us? He that spared not his own Son, but delivered Him up for us all, how shall he not with Him also freely give us all things?

This was very hard for me, but I got a chance to see Heaven; it was all worth it! Yes, I say all of this was all worth it! I will say it a hundred times over; this was all worth the illness! I got a chance to see my mother again. I got a chance to see my aunties. I got a chance to see Heaven; there is no night there. I did not see anything dark. I saw everything very bright and shining with light beautiful colors. I just stood there gazing at all of the beautiful plants, animals, and people. I did not know that I lived anywhere else. I had no remembrance of this world.

I am crying most of the time, it is joy unspeakable joy and peace that I feel now! I get sad when I think of how my family is suffering and dealing with all of this, but they all have seen a miracle. God worked right in front of their eyes. I can barely stand up at this time. It is so hard trying to learn to walk again.

I cannot put my clothes on; my daughter went to the store and brought me a pair of pants and a shirt. She put it on me before she left; she has to go back to work. There is a strength coming back in my body, little by little. I can wash, a little. The nurse gets me a pan of water and sits it on the table by my bed. I am at risk of falling. I should not get out of bed, but I drag myself to the bedpan at night. So many wires are still hooked up to me. I can walk to the door on a walker with the help of physical therapists. I hate to see these physical therapists coming because it is so hard to try to walk, but I know what I got to do it. I got to get out of here and get home as quickly as I can. Everything is fair, at this time. Sitting here praising God for all He has already done for me and my family! Praying! You must always pray for others! When Job prayed for his three friends, that is when God healed his body.

I am feeling very much like Job, still sick as I can be, but I am improving every day. Sitting here thinking about Heaven. I did not stay, because I got something else to do down here on earth. I will know when I finish this book. I always have told people about Jesus even before I got sick. Every time I go out to Bilo or Ingles; I might get in a conversation, and I tell people about Christ. I ask them, "Do you know Him?" They always tell me their problems and I would tell them about my experience with Christ. I tell them to try Jesus! He will help anyone, just give Him your life, confess, believe, and live out your faith in Him!

I did not wait until I got sick to pray. I did not pray any more than I do now. I always pray every day, all through the day and before I go to sleep. I listen to sermons, and I listen to the Bible studies on television. I pray for everyone that I have come in contact with me that day along with my family members and friends. Laying here just thanking God, because He has smiled on me! Why did He show me His glory? I am not the big shot in the churches. I am the one who will hardly get noticed because people in the church pick out who they think is saved and that is sad news. Humbleness is the way to the Lord.

There were no pains in Heaven. I had no pains; there I was light and free. I had no remembrance of this world, but I recognized my folks over there. I always think about this man that I saw sitting on that rock. He has long legs. I stood there looking at His saddles and His legs were longer than usual. He was a beautiful man. He had brown hair hanging from up under the rag that was wrapped around His head. He turned his head and looked at me with the most compassionate look I have ever seen. This will be with me until I go back to Heaven. I tell everyone who wants to know that there is a Heaven! Live your life so you will live again because you do not want to miss Heaven! It is so peaceful. I cannot explain it, but I am trying.

My husband said to me that the nurses and doctors said that I could hear, but they are so wrong. I never heard a word; I was in Heaven. I heard nothing when I awoke in that hospital room. I thought to myself, "What in the world are all of these people doing here? I have not seen some of them for a long time. What are they doing here around me? I thought what in the world is wrong with me? I did not know I was sick. I felt no pain where I was, none at all! I heard nothing and I felt nothing. Oh, the pain started when I returned to my body.

Sitting here typing this book little by little, I type each day then I stop, and I cry, reading my records from the hospital and praising God. Heaven is real! I am reading Revelation 20:12—

And I saw the dead, small, and great, stand before God; and the books were opened: And another book open, which is the book of life: and the dead were judged out of those things which were written in the books, according to their works.

I have to live to do God's will. You have too as well! Laying there in my hospital bed, my mind always went back to my childhood. I remember when we use to shook all of that corn; we always had a garden. My mother would be in the kitchen of a four-room house with ten children cooking fried corn, fatback meat and two large pans of homemade biscuits. At this time, I had never seen a brought biscuit from the store. Old school mothers always cooked biscuits when there was nothing else to cook. They would go in that kitchen and find something to cook. I knew that when there was not anything in there to eat; we all ate fried corn, biscuits, and fatback meat for breakfast.

Fatback meat was very popular back in the 1960s. Some mornings, I remember I got nothing to eat in the morning; all my other brothers and sisters beat me to the kitchen plenty of times. I ate the scrapes around in the plates trying to find some scrapes left; that is how I made my meals. Life was simple then! We just knew little. We had no radio, television, running water or a telephone at this time. Life was simple, but I found joy just thinking back to these days. We never talked loudly. My father would never let us talk loudly; he could not stand the noise with ten children in the house. There was no noise in that house. When he left home, we talked and when we heard Him coming home, we got silent. We had good parents; I mean good Christian parents.

Laying there thinking about how in the world did I get from here to there? I was always a strange child and that is the way my other siblings treated me. I stayed in my world, but I followed my brother, Joseph, the one under me, a lot. If he climbed a tree, I did too. We went fishing together. We were about eight or nine years old. I never caught anything on my fishing hook, besides Minnows, which were too small to cook, but we cooked them anyway. My mind ran back to my childhood. I walked in the rain barefooted all of the time. The mud came up to my knees. We never wore shoes, my siblings and me. We did not have any shoes. We always found some shoes to wear to church. I always remember wearing beautiful can can dresses. The white people up to the road and gave them to us, me, and my sisters. We shine our shoes with cow butter. Cow butter had a smell so loud, very loud like sour cheese. It tasted so strong like sour cheese. I do not think butter is made with that smell anymore.

At this time, my sores are healing, and my mouth is healing. My lips had all of the skin peeling off of them. They are healing. My daughter put something on my lips from the health food store. My lips felt pretty bad. My mouth was cracked open on both sides; it is healing. My buttocks are sore. The burn doctors come twice a day to check my wounds. Sitting here thinking back to my childhood, I found comfort thinking back to when life was simple. I did not worry about anything.

Every Saturday: almost every Saturday, my mother would let one of us go to town with her. We took turns going to town; going to town was a big thing in the 1960s and 1970s. I remember going to the five and ten cents store. It would always be this man in there. My mother would give me one whole dollar. She would be down to the old jail with her friends; she would have a beer. I would walk uptown to that store to get me a big bag of popcorn and a slushy drink. I still had change left. I would buy me some candy at the grocery store before we went home. I do not know where my father went, but he would put us out at the old jail café. They sold beer, hamburgers, hotdogs, and fried chicken. The people would be in there having a good time.

There was another place called, "Laura's place." They did the same thing there. They had lots of fun and dancing. Everyone would be dancing and having fun. I never saw my mother dance. She was strictly business, but she sat there, and she enjoyed beer after beer. She was a hard-working lady; she kept all ten of us cleaned. We used to bathe outside in a tub. We caught the rainwater and bathe in it. That popcorn was the best I have ever eaten until this day; I still think about those popcorn sitting here in this recliner.

Thinking back to these days, I found comfort there. Since I saw Heaven, I cannot describe how I feel, because my mind stayed; there even now it almost a year after I am sitting here writing this book. It is two months from being a year after my sickness. I am back at the Select Specialty Hospital. The Renal report states:

There were no acute issues noted overnight. She had no had dialysis since June 9, 2017. She has no cramping, itching, chest pain, shortness of breath, nausea, or diarrhea. She has noticed increased urine output; Her blood pressure has been stable. sitting up in the chair eating breakfast skin dry, AKI-related to ATN from septic shock and rhabdomyolysis, she appears to have regained function. I will check her BMP this morning and if her renal indices are stable; we will remove her femoral line.

At this time, they are moving the femoral line for dialysis. I had to stop and shout right here! Just me and the Lord, He is so awesome! He already has healed me! I just got to go through the physical process of this. When I laid in that river; I was already healed. That is why every day after I awake, my body starts to heal in the process of quick healing. I know it is hard to understand what I am saying at this moment, but all this I am going through is not only for me; it is for everyone that has come in contact with me while I have been sick. This is for every eye that has looked upon me. Everyone, I mean every one of the doctors, nurses, and all of my family members, all of the visitors who were standing around my bed when I woke up; it was for them. I was alone that evening when they took the line out of my neck.

I had church alone just me and the Lord! You know it is not about just going to church; it good to go to church! I have been in church all of my life, but that is just one-third of what you need. You have to find the other parts; there is a bigger part that I know of and that is to have a personal relationship with the Lord, one on one! You do not have to have any one's approval of how much you pray or how much you read your Bible or how much you listen to the gospel on the television. You do not have to discuss with no one what you tell the Lord; it between you and Him. It is not all about just going to church and following the crowd most of the time. The crowd is completely wrong most of the time. Follow Christ and let Him speak to your heart. He will accept anybody; He does not care about your skin color or your education or how much money you have in the bank. He loves all of us; He has no respect of person, what He does for you; He will do for others, just try Him, and see what He does! He is it for me!

I am not a popular person! I keep to myself! I had to raise my children so they would not be poor. I did not want them to be poor. I told them even when they were babies that you have a bright mind, and you will use it. The struggles I had in my childhood; my children could not go through these struggles. I had to do everything to make them strong and I prayed all of the time to God to help me on my way. I was a very young mother. I was 18 years old, and my husband was 18 years old when we got married; both of us had just finished high school. We had four children; I lost one of my children because he was stillborn. I will tell you about that later on because a miracle happened then in my life. I lived through it!

I was thinking about my childhood when we went to town. My mother always took one child at a time to town with her, because we only had a black truck at this time. I would be in there, my mother and father, and one of the older siblings would be in there. Sometimes we would sit in the truck body; my father would have a bench back there in the truck body. That is what they called it at this time in the early 1960s. Thinking back to those days, I remember going to the grocery store, a man name Deal ran that store. It did not look like the stores today. It was an old store; it had a wooden floor and all kinds of other items like big bags of flour and cans of lard that what we would always buy. He also sold that old greasy sausage; my mother would always buy about seven pounds of that sausage. She would put several large pieces in the skillet and when it got done; there would be a skillet full of grease and a piece of sausage as big as a golf ball. All of that sausage gone, and all of the grease left in the skillet. We ate that all of the time. It was hard to feed ten children. We were strong because we suffered throughout our childhood. It was good for me that I suffered in my childhood so I could help my children. We had a good time! We had peace and joy! We did not know much about the world or what was going on like children today, but we went to church, we prayed, and we had church back then. It is not like it is now; some people are pretending that they know Christ and live a whole other way.

A few minutes after you shut your eyes, you are going to step out. I felt myself going through the ground. I saw the earth on both sides of me. I was so happy. It was just like riding on a roller coaster through the earth and then I stepped out in the light. Oh, what a place to see! Pastor Henra, my youngest son, was standing at the grave. He told me I could go, but I have to come back. Then, I went through the ground. It is no danger if you die in Christ. Please do not step out in darkness! Give God your heart! It would be so bad to just live your life down here and then go to Hell! I am so glad I got a chance to see Heaven again, I will explain later the first time I saw the light. I could not stay in my body; I was too sick to stay there. All of my organs had failed, and all of my blood was poison. I could not stay, so the Lord let me come with Him for a while. Oh, I can feel the joy! I had no remembrance of this world, but I did recognize my folks.

I believe the Bible because it is true! Love God! Follow what is right no matter who is saying do wrong. It will come up again; we will all reap what we sow (Galatians 6:7). So be careful how you live and treat people! God is keeping a record; I know people do not believe this, but Heaven and Hell are real. I was so glad when I stepped out in Heaven, the angel told me that I am coming back to this place when I die. I am not worried about anything. I have been to Heaven. Why did God show me all of this? I will know when I finish writing this book.

Laying here at this time, it is just me and the Lord. I got a long way to go! I told my family to go, my husband and my granddaughter, Hannah looked so tired; they all have been through the wringer. My daughter has to leave; she had to go back to work. She is nervous herself; she had to do so much for me. I am a child again. I am that now! I cannot walk, sit, or stand up, but a few minutes at a time. My hands shake. I am nervous and my body is still very weak, but my vital signs and my organs are beginning to function better. I have been in the hospital for a long time now, but I am improving. I got to stop and pick my Bible back up! I always read the scripture; it always gives me strength that I always needed to continue in life. No one said it was going to be easy; you cannot get through life on "flower beds of eve. Battle after battle, we must be dressed up for the battle. I am reading my favorite scriptures laying here in this bed. The scriptures add strength to my body. Ephesians 6:10-18 states:

Finally, my brethren, be strong in the Lord, and the power of his might. Put on the whole armor of God, that ye may be able to stand against the wiles of the devil. Stand therefore, having your loins girt about with truth, and having on the breastplate of righteousness; And your feet shod with the preparation of the gospel of peace. Above all, taking the shield of faith. Wherewith ye shall be able to quench all of the fiery darts of the wicked. And take the helmet of salvation, and the sword of the Spirit, which is the Word of God, praying always with all prayer and supplication in the Spirit and watching thereunto with all perseverance and supplication for all saints.

I read on to Revelation 1:18: "I am he that liveth, and was dead; and behold, I am alive forevermore." Amen! God has keys of Heaven, hell and of death! Sitting here still reading so many scriptures.

The Lord is not slack concerning his promise, as some men count slackness; but is longsuffering to us-ward, not willing that any should perish, but that all should come to repentance. But the day of the Lord will come as a thief in the night; in the which, the heavens shall pass away with a great noise, and the elements shall melt with fervent heat, the earth also and the works that are therein shall be burned up (2 Peter 3: 9-10).

I got so happy reading Isaiah 40:31—

But they that wait upon the Lord shall renew their strength; they shall mount up with wings as eagles; they shall run, and not be weary; and they shall walk, and not faint.

I am not worried about anything, anymore! I am free, very free! I do not hate anyone! I am free! God has me in His hands. He has worked a great miracle through me! Why me, Lord? I will understand it better as the days go by. I had nothing to do with it; I have no strength of my own. "I am yours, Lord. Use me, Lord, anyway, You please! I am your Lord." I have been low as any human can get. Why did this happen to me? I do not know, but I have an idea! It is dangerous to get so close to the Lord! My mind stayed on the Lord all the time! I have to accept Him and meditate on His word!

My progress notes for June 16, 2017, reads—

There were no acute issues noted overnight. She received blood yesterday without incident. Her headache is improved. She has indigestion this morning after eating bacon and drinking milk. she has no chest pains shortness of breath, nausea, or diarrhea. her blood pressure has been controlled. Her Hbg has improved since yesterday following transfusion, activity tolerance is fair, sitting tolerance is fair, standing tolerance is fair, mobility level is a 5, Rehab potential for stated goals; Good.

I can get to the pot, and I can walk to the door and back with the physical therapist and with a walker. I can only stand up for three minutes. My heart rate and blood pressure go up when I try to move around. This is the hardest thing I have ever had to do is to learn how to take care of myself and learn how to walk. I am feeling very sick! I cannot sleep at all! I am too sick to go to sleep, but I am alive thinking about my family. They have to go, but some of them always come by on the weekend. I need time alone. It comes a time in everyone has life where it is just you and the Lord. We all need that so you can hear from the Lord. He speaks to you in that voice that is very still. Several voices will speak but listen to the one that talks with the beat of your heart; that is the one to listen to. The Lord keeps right on talking to His children all of the time. He loves all of His children just like a parent loves their children. You cannot fool your parents any of the time. They know your heart; they know you!

I should not try to get out of bed, but sometimes I just slid myself to the edge of my bed and I reach out to my bed pot; I pull it next to me and I use the pot. I could not use my hands that well. I look inside my hands, and they were so white; my blood was so low. I know the nurse got tired of me calling them, but they always came to see me. I felt bad calling them all of the time, but they were right on time. I would be glad when some of my children were there, they would help me.

Semira's mother, my ex-daughter-in-law, Valerie, stopped by one day with her sweet, little girl Bella and she helped me do everything that morning. She helped me take a bath. She got me some water in a pan, and she helped me change my gown. She made my bed while I sat in the recliner, and she did so much for me that day. I was so happy to see her. She worked at the hospital in Atlanta, so she knows what to do. She stayed a long time with me; she said, she never through I would make it, but here I am in the flesh.

My husband and my granddaughter, Hannah, came in to visit me and I told my husband who had come to visit me. He said, "That was great!" He sat over by the window; I was resting a bit. I looked at Him and I remembered the first time I saw Him when he came from Tignall school to visit Washington school. My friend, Mildred, and I said we were going to stand out here and see how the Tignall boys look. We were in the eighth grade. So, Mildred and I stood there. Mildred was one of best friends from school back in the day at this time. The boys got off the bus; they came down one by one.

My eye caught this pale looking bumpy face boy. I looked at him. Mildred said, "That they are not so cute!"

I said to Mildred, "You are so right!" In the ninth grade, I have seen this boy again in the library. We had to study hall at this time and this boy was sitting there and the other boys from

Tignall. The Librarian said to them that she was not going to keep telling them to be quiet. She told me that she would put them out of the library if they kept on talking. The librarian's name is Mrs. Clara Sutton. I was sitting at the next table beside them. I looked up at them and a still voice told me to look at the one in the middle and that he will be my husband for life. I still think about this until this day, forty-seven years later; it came to pass. We are still married. I did not have time to date around. In my tenth-grade year, he was in my homeroom class, Mr. Lance was our teacher. He wrote me a letter and he handed it to me, and I threw it back to him. About a month later, he wrote me another letter and I read that one and that was it. I am still with him until this day.

Glory hallelujah! God is still in control of my life. My husband is sitting there looking out of the window. I got out of my bed and used the pot beside the bed, but I could not wipe myself. He looked at me and smiled. He said, "I am tired of wiping your buttocks." I did not say anything but smile. He said that he had been sick 13 years and I never said a word, no matter how tired I got sitting up all night with him. I rubbed his back. I beat life back into him when he stopped breathing one day. I cook his food. I help him take a bath. I drove him to the doctors. I sit at the hospital for years at a time in the waiting room and his room. I never said a word and he looked at me with tears in his eyes and he said, "You did! Yes, you did all of that and so much more!"

I know he was tired. That is why I sent him home. He did not have to go to the hospital all while I was sick and that was a blessing in itself because he always has to go to the hospital due to his lung disease. He has one lung that only works about 46 percent, but God is good. He will not put more on you than you can handle. The doctors wanted to put him in the hospital 12 years ago, but my children and I would not let them. He is doing well. I make him all kinds of teas for his lung disease. The doctor told him that he has lived over his limit for his illness. The God that I serve says, "He will live!"

I cry a lot, but most of the time they are tears of great joy. I am not questioning God; He let me see Heaven. I am going to tell the world about Heaven and what I saw over there. It is beautiful over there, unspeakable peace—just calmness. I had no thoughts of this world—nor anything or anyone of this world. There are lots of sick people in the world. I got sick for a reason. God got me. When I was 11 years old, I would sit in the woods behind our house. I always went there to pray, and we moved when I was in the 7th grade to another old house in the woods with no running water, but we did have electricity. We had no phone until when I was in the 10th grade. "Good Times" was my favorite show. We had black and white television, but we did not have running water. We caught rainwater to bathe in and we had to walk a half of a mile to get to the spring water that came up very clear. Every animal drank from that spring, and we did too!

If you went down the hill to get the water from the spring, it was very hard to come back up. It was a high hill going down but coming back was so hard to get up plenty of times. We would waste our water and we had to go right back to spring again. It was hard getting back up the hill, but what does not kill will help you grow.

My neighbor came to pray for me, Mr. Troy Bell, and he prayed a wonderful prayer. Troy was so good to my husband. He kept our grass cut and he helped to hold my husband up in the hospital. Troy gave him gas money to help out. He said a very beautiful prayer over me while I was in the hospital. Everyone in view stopped and listened to that prayer.

At this time, I am still on a long list of medications such as Magnesium Oxide, Sodium Bicarbonate, Heparin, Atorvastatin Calcium, Levothyroxine Sodium, Hydralazine, and many others. I came off a lot of medications as time went on and I got stronger.

Sitting at this computer on April 4, 2018, just typing and thanking God for all He has done for me. He has been awesome to me. God loves us all. If you get close to him, He will be closer to you! I try to stay close to the Lord, putting on a show to the world does not mean anything to him! I always

want to be real. I always love people whether they love me or
not. That is the way Jesus works! He always loves us in spite of
how we are feeling! His grace, mercy and His favor are always
in place for those who have confessed their sins and believe in
Him. You must pray for other people! If you do not pray for
other people, how can Father God help you? I would never
think of going before Father God just for me and my family.
The people who I meet daily, I always pray for them; even
people who I know hate me. I make sure I pray for them. On
this day, I have all of my records laying on the table and the
floor in my dining room looking at them trying to put all of
these records together. I cannot put all of them in my book,
because it is so many. Just unbelievable!

It is June 13, 2017. My medical records say that "my blood
count is 7.0 and my heart rate is 130 during physical
activity…". I tried to get to the sink in the bathroom. It is the
hardest thing I ever have done. It is just so hard to stand up for
a few seconds. I am putting all of my body weight on the
walker. My leg has no strength in them. I cannot even pick
them up; dragging myself along like an animal with two legs,
but I will not give up! I come too far to turn around now. God
has brought me too far to leave me now! I got to fight! I mean
fight!

Looking at the doctors' faces when they come to see me;
they are surprised to see me come this far. My blood is so low

at this time. My head is hurting something terrible. Trying to perform hygiene with the nurse right by my side, because I am a high risk for falling and I do not want to fall; I have so many wires hooked up to me. I cannot stand up in the bathroom, but for a few seconds. The bathroom sitting stool was right behind me, but I am going to try to stand up to wash my face. I do not do too much. I did not want to look at the mirror in front of me, but it is okay; I will get there. I have never in my whole life given up on any tasks that would benefit me or my family. I always had to work hard, and I told my children to work hard and pray continuously. If you put the Bible in their hearts early; I mean early, your children will make it along with good values and morals. They will make it and I will too. I am so sick, sicker than any human being could ever be, but it is okay; I am going to beat this and be stronger than ever before. It is Father God over my body, and He owns my mind because I gave it all to Him. I was trying to wash my face, holding the rag, and trying to pick up the soap. I had to hold on to the walker; I was giving out of breath, breathing weakly as a newborn chicken. It is okay; I have seen Heaven and I think about it all the time, but it was not for me to stay this time. I look at my eyes and just glance at myself.

I had left home on May 19, 2017, and so that has been 25 days ago. I am still here at Select Specialty Hospital. One of my nurses came to me and said that I had no business here. "You can move well." I thought about it, and I know the doctors had done for me all that they could do. I know I surprised them. I can tell the way that they looked at me. I can sit on the toilet, but I cannot get up; I pull up with the walker. This is the first time trying to use the bathroom. I cannot use the pan to wash. I cannot go to the bathroom alone. I did not go anymore at this time. I was too weak! The nurse helped me bathe out of the pan. I had a sock slider to put my socks on with. You can easily feel like a burden in this shape.

I am always praying; why did I have to go through all of this suffering? I am glad; I did sit here writing this book. I can see things very clearly now. The glass was cloudy, but now I can see lots of things. I will explain this later on in this book. My balance is getting better. I can wash. I can apply deodorant and brush my teeth, my hands are still shaking, but not as bad. I need a lot of rest breaks in between because it is very hard learning to do simple things. It is hard to think of a grown person in this bad shape. Giving up never crossed my mind, but I think about my grandchildren, my children, and my husband. I got to fight on; not giving up here. Each session was very hard. No one is here at this time, but me. I told everyone to go get some rest. I got this and the Lord; He is so close to me. My skin was so dry. I was too sick to rub some skin cream on me or comb my hair. I have not seen my hair in about a month. I do not know what shape it is in; I was too sick to care for my hair at this time. Sitting up this morning, getting blood through my neck; a lot of IVs going through my neck. Blood is going in my body through my neck.

This morning, June 15, 2017; it took a long time for blood to go in my body. I am just sitting here looking at the blood drop by drop entering my body. God already knows I was going to meet this day. He knows everything even before you enter your mother's womb. Yet and still, He gives us all free will to serve Him or you can reject Him. It is up to you, but somethings we have no control over. All we can do is live a life pleasing to God and praise His Holy name because he knows each one of us by our name. He knows your heart and your motives. He knows who loves Him and who does not! How can any human being not praise a Holy God; we cannot hide from Him. I would always pray, and I know in my heart, my God, the one that I serve would help me along the way with raising my children with their good father; with both of us walking with Jesus He would provide and help us if we walked along in his ways.

On June 16, 2017, I was walking 25 feet slowly and steadily then stopping and resting on the way. Not about to give up. A lot of things are going through my mind and one of them is walking through my front door. Sitting here is the chair looking at the blood drip by drip. I thought about all of my classmates that have gone on before me. I do not know why, but thcy will always be in my heart. One day one of my classmates came by the Doctors Hospital; he was a pastor. His name is Reverend Dennis Joe Quinn. He did get a chance to pray with me because I had to go to physical therapy. He told me that he had heard so many things about my condition; he had to come by and see how true the rumors. He asked me had I had a stroke? I told Him, "No!" I had double pneumonia. He asked me how I made it through all of that. I was sitting there in the wheelchair eating at this time. He did not have time to pray, because I had to go to physical therapy. He asked me why my eyes were so red; I told Him I had glaucoma.

Sitting here typing my book, thinking about when I was in the first grade. I walked down the hall with seven plaits of hair on my head. We always had recess at the back door by the chinaberry tree while at school. My classmates and I would climb that tree down by the red hill and eat chinaberries. My mind went back to this moment in my childhood. All the children of the same color played together, even though we were all black children playing at school. The integration of schools had not happened yet at this time. Sometimes the lighter skin children with longer hair did not too much play with me much. If you had decent clothes to wear or if you lived in town, you got treated differently. The country children who looked very poor; the other children did not want to play with them. I was one of them; so, plenty of days I just stood on the wall until the bell rang. All of this ran across my mind! Even the teacher treated you differently if you looked a certain way. The teacher would always call on the lighter-skinned children to take the lunch report to the office. Or if the teacher knew their parents very well, those students got chosen. I only got called on once in all of my life to do this task. I only got picked one time to carry the lunch report to the office, but it was alright because I could always take care of myself. I was always strong.

I had to carry in wood and draw water from the well plenty of times. I drew up dead rats, old shoes, and hurt birds. We would just place these items and animals to the side. It hurt me so bad to see the hurt animals; they were not alive. My family had to keep drinking water. We used to get water from the white people's house where my mother worked, but we did not get to do it all of the time. I did not want my children to go through what I have already gone through. It made my siblings and me strong and honest. We stayed in prayer for a better day. Some children at these current times do not even know how to respect their elders or their parents, only a few children. I never had any trouble with my children respecting the elders or no one else for that matter.

I had to put all of my life in theirs and their father. He has had it harder than me. He told me that he never had enough to eat growing up. I used to give him some of my parents' hog meat out of our freezer. I did not want him to starve. He did not have decent clothes when he was in the early grades just like me. His mother brought him a pair of overalls. He cried all the time at school; He did not want to wear these overalls. We would always exchange stories; I thought about all of this.

I always go back to Heaven in my mind. I will never forget going to Heaven. I will think about this until I get back there, walking around Heaven all day. Minutes after you die you will see Jesus; I saw Him sitting on that rock. It is so wonderful and beautiful. I did not know that I had lived on earth. I did not have any remembrance of here on earth, but I saw my mother and my aunties. I know for sure that those three women are in Heaven having a good time sitting in the glory of God. Oh, what a wonderful place to look forward to! Do not put all of your time in the material things of life or try to live any type of kind way all of your life thinking you will get to Heaven. You have to repent and keep on repenting all day, every day!

Heaven is a place for prepared people; do not lose your soul over stuff, give your life to Christ early! He will forgive sin; we are all sinners. When we finish down here, we are going to Heaven or Hell; it is just that simple. Live your life according to the Bible. We have all sin and fell short, but my God showed me favor. I had nothing to do with it. I just live a life trying to please Him and not man. I want to please God and He said well-done, but you have to go back; when Father

God looked at me, I know I had to do something else because He looked at me with so much love. I never have seen that kind of love and compassion for a person here on earth. I tell a lot of people about Heaven; I got to tell the world that there is a Heaven. God knows our hearts. God knows my heart. We must talk to God. We are not whole until Jesus Christ is with us, in us. Just step out in glory only a few minutes of you closing your eyes you will know where you are; it is not about being here on earth, but in glory, that a whole different ball game. Luke 5-24: says "But that ye may know that the Son of man hath power upon earth to forgive sins, (he said unto the sick of the Palsy,) I say unto thee, Arise, and take up thy couch, and go into thine house."

I had to learn to just stand at this time; I am very weak, but making progress in my mental, physical, and Spiritual body. I am not worried about nothing; I know God got me just like He has me all of those other times. Every breath we all take belongs to God! He gives life and He takes life away; it is all in his hands. This is scripture, Job 1:21. I remember when I awoke about the third day; I believe my blood pressure was so high over two hundred at the top and about 100 at the bottom, the nurses worked with me, and they worked with me. Oh, my God! I am so sick sicker than sick! I did not know a human could get this sick. My daughter played gospel music around my bed, and she massaged my neck; the nurses were working on me as well.

Oh, Lord! What have I done in my life to be suffering like this? He said, "Nothing, my glory has to come through you, your family and a lot of others need to see a miracle." So, I got so quiet in my Spirit. I listen to God speaking to me. He told, "Me, I let you see Heaven. You will be better than ever before just fight on and lean on Me. I will not let you fall." I know that He never lets me fall because He is always on my mind; I got a hiding place in my mind so no one here on earth can get in there. My blood pressure is up and down all of the time. The doctor said they did not understand it, but it did just like it wanted to. Me, I am still alive. I died, but I am back with my right mind. People came around my bed and they asked me to say their names. I told them the only one that I got mixed up was Pastor Pitts because he told me who he was, and I looked at Him again I said, "Oh, yes!" He prayed for me.

You cannot take life for granted; it may be your last time at any given second. None of us has any control over it, we got to lay down everything and go home, whether it is with Jesus, or with the devil. The Lord is coming; no one knows when or where or how, but He is coming. You do not have to fear death just live the life that is pleasing to the Lord and keep on pressing toward Him. You will spend longer moments in eternality than you will spend here on earth.

Sitting there on the sofa before the EMS came, I was almost gone. I cannot breathe at all; I always pray a long prayer in the morning, because I have to pray for the whole family, all of my friends, enemies, everyone I can think of; I pray for them! I have listened to the Bible study with Shepard Chapel every morning for the past 38 years and I also watch T.D. Jakes and Joyce Meyers about an hour or so every day, but this morning; all I could say is "Lord, you know I love you and I have served you and I am in your hands." There always will come a time in your life where you always have to put it in God's hands, because at times there is no other option. We must always put stuff in God's hands and leave it there, but as humans, we try everything else, but God. He is the only source that can help you especially in a case like mines, no one else. I could not call on anyone, but Him. I could not say anything; I left this world in a few seconds.

I am still here at the Select Specialty Hospital praying because I still got joy and peace. I am glad my God test me so deeply. I have no regrets. I belong to the Lord, one thing about life is that no one can pluck His children out of His hands. I never have been the kind of person who pretends! I tell it as I see it! No one has to agree with me! I always seek the Lord no matter what decision I am trying to make, life is tough! This is one of the hardest battles I have ever had to fight, but I had one simple thing to do. I will tell you about that a little later on.

There is a whole world on the other side of Jordan, and I have seen it. The old folks use to sing about it, but I have seen it; I cannot wait to tell the world about what I saw in Heaven. I tell some folks about it; they look at me so strange. I was over there young-looking about 30 years old; I saw my reflection in the shiny, blue river when I laid in it, I did not sink either. I laid in the river on my back and looked up at the beautiful sky. It was very bluish.

Why did He choose me to work a miracle? I am not popular? I do not want to be with that crowd. I want to stay on that narrow road. I love everybody, but I do not expect everybody to love me. I can stand beside a person for a few seconds; I can tell how they feel about me, but that is okay. Before I got sick; I always told them to pray, and I reached a lot of people that the church had counted out; they are nice. Some are the children I taught when I was working in the school system. I never meet a child who did not like me, or I did not like them, all of the white and black children loved me. I never had to send a child to the office when I looked in their eyes; they knew I loved them even until this day when I see some of my students come and hug me.

But I am going to pray on; I love to talk to the Lord. I love Him so much. I always think about when Mary sat at Jesus' feet and poured the oil on His feet and wiped it with her hair. I always think about that, and I think about the centurion man who had the sick servant; he told Jesus to just speak the word, you did not have to come to my house just speak the word and my servant will be healed. The lady with her son at the grave. She had to bury her only son. Jesus came by and stopped the funeral. The lady with the issue of blood, she tugged at the hem of Jesus' garment and was healed immediately. Also, I think a lot about the man who was paralyzed on the stretcher; his four friends carried Him to Jesus, all four of them had a corner. They let Him down through the roof of this shack. Jesus forgave Him of his sins, and he was healed. I also think about the man lying on side of the road, the preachers passed Him by, and the deacons passed Him by, but nobody came by and put Him on his horse and carried Him to the end.

I remember these verses in the Bible; we must take God back to His word. I always tried to keep my mind on things of God and not evil things or trying to find a way to hurt people. I always want to help, but that does not mean agreeing with everything another person says just to fit in. I am not about all of that, because without God there is no hope. I always pray while things are going well for me, when trouble comes there may not be time to pray so send up some prayers while things are well for you, pray to the Father God through His son, Jesus Christ. Psalm 150:6 says "Let everything that hath breath praise the Lord. Praise ye the Lord." I will continue to praise the Lord every day, every hour!

Plant your life on good soil and God will always take care of you. He is all-knowing and all-seeing. As I look around people are not moving when they brought me in here at 10 p.m., nothing was moving. I looked in some of the rooms and it looked so sad, no one was moving. You do not need any fancy words to talk to God, because He knows your heart, but I try to be completely honest with Him. I come to Jesus as a child and He is my Father, God. Every breath I take, He is in charge of it; my sickness is in His hands. I called on Him when they put me in my room. I looked around; I was sick as any human being could be. I was sicker than sick. I know God is with me, so I will pass this test because of Roman 10: 9 says, "That if thou shalt confess with thy mouth the Lord Jesus, and shalt believed in thine heart that God hath raised Him from the dead, thou shalt be saved."

You must fill yourself with the words of God. He will guide you through your whole life and you will be happy and when trouble comes it will not be so hard on you. Pray consistently, study your Bible, go to church, listen to the words of God on television. I play sermons and songs of joy in my car every day. Whatever happens to you, you will have the strength to withstand your burdens, because they are coming. No one will escape! I mean, no one. Treat people as you want to be treated. Plenty of days I laid there, the devil told me, "You are going to die anyway."

I laughed aloud to myself! "No, I am not!" I have been to Heaven and if God wanted me to die; He would have never let me come back. I know God is real, Heaven is real! I believe Hell is real.

Sitting here writing this book, my mind goes back to a poem I wrote a few years ago, it is titled "My Heart". It says—

My heart longs for God's presence, so full of the past thought, Seeking through my days. Remembering my dreams of yester years, On a roller coaster for God. My Spirit only knows my glory, the only peace in my heart is blocked, Beyond the deep valleys. Ease of my heart fades away, Like a flowing feather. No one knows the pain that that surrounds my body. It is only in the shadow of my heart; My feelings are all on the other side. I am just a passenger leaning toward the other home, far beyond the deep blue skies.

I wrote this poem a few years back looking at my husband on his sick days for the last 13 years. I was going through a heavy burden when he got sick so sick, I felt so alone, all of the children were gone. It was just me and Him; praying and hoping, but now I am writing about one of my testimonies. I have another one to tell about later on. I still had to fight with my eternal Spirit; I went to Heaven every day. I just felt my healing coming back; I felt my strength coming back each day. I had to put for effort. The Lord sent me on a vacation to Heaven my whole being was refresh. Laying here thinking about before I got sick, I did feel exhausted for a few days, but nothing out of the usual.

Thanking Father God for taking time out of his busy schedule to come and see about little old me, a nobody—but somebody to Father God. He sits high and looks low; he never slumbers or sleeps, He is always looking at His children; He loves us all. He has not a particular person that he will hear, just try Him, and see what He will do; you do not have to go through no one else, but God. We must meet Him on a personal basis. No matter what the world thinks about you, just keep on praying, keep your hands to the gospel plow and keep rowing! I sent four children to college on "three fishes and two loads of bread" and Father God multiplied that and all of them finished college. No one told me about children going to college, but the Lord. I brought them four into this world and I am their mother; it was my responsibility to make sure they knew Father God. I had to put that in them early before they could walk; I had to lay hands on them and pray to the Father to keep each one of them on the straight and narrow. It was not easy, but I had to play my motherhood role to the very end. I had to give all of them the same chance. They have been right by my side all the way; those four are the best.

The doctors did not see any hope for me! My sons told me that is what the doctors said, but they will tell you about that part because I heard nothing. I was in Heaven looking around! Oh, my God what a sight to see! I walk around looking at those mansions on the hillside. It is so beautiful there! I saw animals pulling those wooden carts. It was amazing! I had no remembrance of this world. I saw my mother and her two sisters. My mother wore glasses here on earth; she had no glasses on in Heaven. My mother and sisters glowed in Heaven. At this time, my sitting balance is getting better; I mean fair. I can sit up; I am almost too sick to sit up, but I have to try to sit. I get dizzy when I sit up but being in the moving bed is getting next to me. I can pull by the side rail and pull myself up at this time.

It is about June 15, 2017. At first, I tried to pull myself up. I got burning in my arms trying to pull. I scrub too hard on my arms. I left bruises on them. Sometimes my blood pressure looked like this 91/53, 77/42, 83/53, and 94/45. It has gotten so low then this; that is when I had to have more blood. Every time, I try to do some exercise with the therapist my blood pressure would go up so high. I got so tired of calling the nurses, but I had to me was glad when my family was there; they would give the nurses a little break, but the nurses still came in to do what they had to do. Lord, Have Mercy! I would always say that when I finished physical therapy.

I thank Father God for His many blessings; we must always thank Father God for what He has already done because He does not have to do anything for us. We cannot be so proud and think that we have some strength on our own; we cannot blink our eyes if he did not say so. We cannot do anything without Him whether you believe it or not; we are no more than a bubble on the waters. We might give out any given second. Never think you have a lot of time left; we do not know. I just had learned to stand up. I could not stand up, but a little while. I do not sleep well at all at this time. I look out my window; I am up high because I can see the top of the trees.

I kept my mind on Heaven where I was and the scriptures in my mind. I always learned scriptures. I say them all of the time to myself. Listening to Rev. Luther Barnes' song, "God's Grace." I played this song all of the time sitting here writing my book. I have to stop and praise the Lord for bringing me this far. It was not anybody, but the Lord. He already had my team of people set up for me. I had to go through all of this; it was predestined with God already, but by the Grace of God I have made it this far. I was God's Grace. I am still standing.

My mind running back over my life. Why God used me to do a miracle? Father God can use anyone he chooses to because He knows how much we all can bare. This was almost the hardest battle I ever had to fight. I got another battle I had to fight, and I went to different parts of Heaven, but I will tell you about that on later on. There are no tears in Heaven. Heaven is a place for prepared people. You cannot get there any type of way. You have to go through the door with the Lord and Savior Jesus Christ. I often thought of Job. I could reason with his sickness because I was sicker than sick. Your flesh was hanging my bones just like Job. When I came through, I did not know what was wrong or that I was sick. I did not know why the doctors did not tell me about my sickness after I woke up. I found out some days later. I guess they thought I knew, but I did not. My daughter explained to me later on.

Laying here thinking about Job remembering scripture—

Oh Lord, though he slays me, yet will I trust in Him. But I will maintain mine own ways before Him. Man, that is born of a woman is of few days and full of trouble. He cometh like a flower and is cut down: he fleeth also as a shadow, and continueth not. Seeing his days are determined, the number of his months are with thee, thou hast appointed his bounds, that cannot pass (Job 13:15; 14: 1-2; 5).

The second day after I awoke, I was sicker than sick. I almost swallowed my tongue. I had to cough my tongue back up out of my throat when I woke up. I was too weak to sit up in a chair or to lay down, so many wires. I looked so pitiful, and I was sicker than sick. We must always remember Colossians 3:1-3—

> If ye then be risen with Christ, seek those things which are above, where Christ sitteth on the right hand of God. Set your affection on things above, not on things on the earth. For ye are dead, and your life, shall appear, then shall ye also appear with Him in glory.

When I awoke, I was holding Pastor Pitt's hand and I said Psalm 23. I always say this Psalm several times a day—

> The Lord is my shepherd. I shall not want. He maketh me to lie down in green pastures: he leadeth me beside the still waters. He restoreth my soul; he leadeth me in the paths of righteousness for his name's sake. yes, though I walk through the valley of the shadow of death, I will fear no evil: for thou are with me. Thou preparest a table before me in the presence of mine enemies; thou anointest my head with oil my cup runneth over. Surely goodness and

mercy shall follow me all the days of my life: and I will dwell in the house of the Lord forever.

And I said the Lord's prayer also I remember every word because I say the Lord's prayer all through the day for God glory and to get help for my life, I give God the glory for letting my mind focus on Him. Matthew 6:9—

After this manner, therefore, pray ye: Our Father which art in Heaven, Hallowed be thy name. Thy kingdom come, Thy will be done in earth, as it is in Heaven. Give us this day our daily bread. And forgive us our debts, as we forgive our debtors. And lead us not into temptation, but deliver us from evil: For thine is the kingdom and the power, and the glory, forever. Amen.

I say these two prayers every day several times a day for as long as I can remember, these are my prayer that I live by. I know my husband and my four children were carrying a heavy load over me because I am the cornerstone in the Chennault family. We are a close-knit family. You should make sure your family is saved and our children. I told them a lot of things so many little things. They had to learn from their mother, but their father taught my boys how to be a man, which was my husband's job. And I stepped back because I wanted them to be strong men. I had to teach my daughter how to be a woman; she always watches me she told me one day, "Mama, I look at everything you do. I even watch how you blink your eyes!" I look at her and smile.

My medical functional abilities rating and goals at Select Specialty Hospital are the following:

Eating (6) and oral hygiene (5), Toileting hygiene (1), Wash upper body (5), Roll left to right (4), Sit to Lying (4), Lying to sitting on side of bed (2), Chair/bed/transfer (1), Ability to express ideas and wants (consider both verbal & non-verbal expression, excluding language barriers) (4), Expresses complex messages without difficulty and with speech that is clear and easy to understand. Ability to understand verbal content (hearing aid or device is used, excluding language barriers), Understand Clear comprehension without cues or repetitions (4)

It is my goal to get to a (6) in every area to be discharged to go to a rehabilitation hospital.

My wounds are healing well. My wounds were awful at first; I had to use cream from the burn unit. Doctors came to see me and took pictures of my wounds; my wounds are healing in my mouth. Lord had to use me! Glory! Hallelujah! Oh, Lord Jesus oh what a test I have been through. No words can explain what I have been through. It is amazing! Lord gave

me a vacation in Heaven; I had a ball in Heaven so peaceful.
Believe me! Heaven is real! I will never be the same until I get
back there, but Father God got something else for me to do.
All of the things people do at church; they put more time on
the furniture and decor and who is in charge at church than
saving souls from a burning Hell. We all should make sure that
our soul is anchored in Lord and Savior Jesus Christ.

Who would want to miss Heaven? The Holy Spirit said to
me before I left, "You will come back one day to this place,
and you will have eternal life here." I got to tell the world
about Heaven. I tell everyone who wants to know and who will
listen. I told the doctors, nurses, and other patients; whoever
would listen to me about Heaven. I was there in that sick body.
I left in a second. I want plenty of Jesus. I just do not pray
when I am in trouble, or I need something from God. I pray all
day long, every day and at night when I awake, I am not trying
to be popular.

I want to be more and more like Jesus every day of my
life. You must be and that means the world will not like that if
you are different; they will look at you more harshly, but you
must hang on to God's hand and stay close to God. He will
stay close to you. My husband told me one when sitting here at
home, the more they prayed the worst I got. It is like that; it
makes me think about Lazarus, Martha and Mary's brother that
had died. Mary told Jesus that had you had been here our

brother would not have died. You cannot hurry God. He is always on time. He even though Lazarus had been dead four days and I know he was smelling, that did not bother Jesus, because he stopped at Jairus' house and healed his daughter on the way to Lazarus' house. He took Peter, James, and John in there with Him, and the little girl woke up and Jesus told them to give her some meat.

I am sitting here writing this book about to shout; when I think about how good Father God is and how His only Son Jesus, which is God walking around in the flesh, healed people of all kinds of sickness. He took time out of his busy schedule and came to see me. He sent me a ticket to Heaven, and I visited Heaven and I am very glad I did; I saw things I have never seen before. My eyes were cracked, but now they are wide open. There is no time to waste. I was just laying here thinking; my room is quiet.

Every second counted on that morning of May 19, 2017. About ten seconds went by and then I was leaving this world. I told the Lord I was in His hands, and I have served Him, and you know my heart, Lord. I could not pray anymore, because I was on my way to Augusta, Georgia in the flesh, but my Spirit was gone before the EMS could turn around in the yard. I remembered nothing; I saw the doors shut on the EMS and that was that until I awoke 10 days later from a coma. I never knew I was sick. I was not sick in Heaven. I was young, strong, and pretty. I look like I looked when I was 33 years old; the picture is in this book, the last chapter, the one picture with my husband and me in a glass.

There is a glow about the people in Heaven; they look so bright; my mother and aunties' skin colors were the same; they looked light in body mass. None of us is excused from the deep valleys; they are coming especially when you put on Christ. You cannot do anything in the flesh. No one can help you, no matter how many friends you have. There is a connecting line, just you and God. No one else.

I do not care how good you think you are; troubles are coming. Just prepare yourself, how can our Spiritual man grow? We cannot get the big head and think that we got it all together? No, you will not ever have it all together down here. Our mission for each one of us is to praise the Lord and live according to the Bible. Every tribulation, every test you pass you will become stronger and stronger for the next test, stronger and stronger. Father God knew each one of us before we entered our mother's womb. So, nothing about us is a surprise to Him. He knows each one of our haters; they are there for a reason. Every person that comes around me. I can tell where their Spirits are, I can feel if they like me or hate me.

Back to my health, everything in my body was out of place. I mean everything, my red blood cells, platelets, sodium serum, potassium serum, protein total serum, albumin serum, bilirubin total, calcium serum, alkaline Phosphatase, and my hemoglobin. I cannot tell you everything, but everything in my body was going zipper, zipper. I always study the word of God daily. I study my Bible and I always pray everywhere I go, because I learned at an early age I had to pray. If I want to change, prayer is the key. God had brought me through so much.

In the year of 2015, my husband and I had a head-on collision in Atlanta, Georgia. We were going I know 40 miles per hour and the other vehicle was going 45 miles per hour. We hit head-on; I did not stay in the hospital, but my husband stayed in there one night. I walked away when that truck hit us. It knocked our car over into two lanes of traffic, both vehicles were a total loss. God has been with me lying here in this hospital bed. I give all of the glory to God. He has brought me over the years, and I am laying here thanking Him for all of His blessings. Everything that he does in my life is for my good. It will work out for the good and this sickness will too. When I saw that truck coming at us, I could not pray, all I said, "Lord, are you going to take both of us together?

He said, "No!"

I said, "Lord, I have served you.

And he brought us out with no broken bone just a little shaken up.

We had three children in college at the same time. They were good children; they knew how to pray. I was worried about them, but I had to lay it all at Jesus' feet. I learn to cry out to God in a very loud voice with tears running down my face, drinking my tears for water.

I often prayed Psalm 86:

Bow down thine ear, O Lord, hear me: for I am poor and needy. Preserve my soul; for I am holy: O thou my God save thy Servant that trusted in thee, Be merciful unto me, O Lord for I cry unto thee daily. Give ear, O Lord, unto my prayer; and attend to the voice of my supplications, For thou art great, and doest wondrous things: thou art God alone. Teach me thy way, O Lord: I will walk in thy truth: unite my heart to fear thy name.

All while I was in the hospital when I woke up, I told my daughter to bring my Bible and It has been open to Psalm 23 all the while I am here in the hospital. I woke up praying and looking around I did not know where I was, I was just looked at all those people. My two sisters, Alberta and Barbara looked at me and laughed at the way I was talking, but I did not mind, because I was alright in my Spirit. I had been to Heaven; if they had known where I had been, Oh, my God, what a beautiful place! Who would not want to go there; you do not have to have any title? No human being or no church can put you in Heaven. We must hear and learn God for ourselves. A personal relationship with God is what it is going to take. No one will stand with you in front of Jesus. It is not about being nice; we should be nice, but being nice and goodwill does not get you into Heaven.

"You must be born again" as Nicodemus was talking about in the Bible days; he was a great teacher and he went to Jesus by night, because he was so confused with Him and his faith. He went to Jesus. You got to have a Spiritual birth. We must get to Jesus any way we can, and we must hurry because any day could be your last. God has set dates for each one of us, every minute, second and hour. We just got to meet those dates. Whether it is sickness or death, we got to meet those dates. Remember Father God while you are young and strong; give Him all of your praises while you are strong. Do not just wait until you get old and weak to send up prayers so if there is a time when you cannot pray; prayers will already be stored up. Do not spend all of your time talking badly about other human beings. The same thing that you measure unto your friends with be added back to you, every word, every deed will be added back unto you.

I thought about a lot of things laying here trying to get my physical body back together again. My Spiritual body was in Father God's hands because He let me saw a glimpse of

229

Heaven. I went on one long vacation, and it will be with me for the rest of my life. There is no time in Heaven, time does not exist there. There is no sorrow there if some of your loved ones or friends are not there; you will not feel sorrowful for them, because you will have no memory of them. If you had remembrance of them then you would be worried about them and there are no worries in Heaven. Who would not want to go? Oh, what a beautiful place! I just looked at the grass and the barks on the trees; they were so shiny and thick. I looked at the ground; It was majestic in many ways and the water there is crystal clear? Oh, the air, I did not have to breathe.

Chapter 7

NOAH

I was just exploring Heaven. There were all races and nationalities of children over in Heaven. One boy just stopped and looked at me. He was bigger than the rest of them. I believed this was Noah, who I lost as a stillborn baby 41 years ago. I will tell you a little about this story in a moment. I told my family and friends about this story of Noah about 41 years ago. This was the first time I went to Heaven.

I am still at the Select Specialty Hospital. I am going to tell you about the first time I went to Heaven and then I will come back to the second time I went to Heaven a year ago. Forty years ago, to this year would be the year of 1978 and it was a bad year for me, my husband and my first son, Lazarus Jr. Lazarus Jr. was the only child I had at this time, and he was born in 1975. The second son was born in 1978; his name is Noah. In the year of 1978, I had been married for three years, both my husband and I was about 22 years old. At this point in my life, I was not what you would call happy, but I was content; I was with the man I loved and still do. I did not work at this time. I never worked up until this point due to having a child, who was two years old and is pregnant with another one. My husband was working at the service station making $40 a week. Later on, he began working with a man up the road from us digging trees and planting them. He made $100 a week. We lived with my husband's parents most of the time and with my parents. His parents lived in Tignall, Georgia and my parents lived in Washington, Georgia. So, we would always go back and forth. We did not know much about how to live. We only knew what we had seen our parents do, but we knew one thing; we loved each other. I cried most of the time, but I never let anyone see me cry. I prayed for better days.

We were having revival at Gibson Grove Baptist Church in Washington, Georgia. I am nine months pregnant, almost ready to deliver my baby. I am very big. I mean big in the stomach area. I am young at this time. We had a 1966 Chevrolet Impala that what we drove; my husband's father gave us this car. We had no running water at this time or a bathroom. The bathroom was outside. But I always prayed and thanked God for His goodness. I asked Him to help us and bless us. I prayed that one day my children can go to college and be a good citizen. I knew the Lord. I always prayed; I said the Psalm 23and the Lord's prayer. My husband did not make enough money, so we qualified for WIC and food stamps. This assistance truly helped us out a lot.

I did not know much about life. I was trusting God; the one that I met in the plum brushes. That was all I had to trust in God. In the last week of my pregnancy, I had a vision that Wednesday night before the daybreak. I looked to the left side of my window. An angel was holding my baby's bottle. He looked at me straight in my eyes and vanished away. This was very upsetting to me. I knew then something was going wrong. I went back to sleep for a few minutes, and I saw blood running from my hospital bed. I saw this happening as plain as day. When I saw that angel at my window, I kept blinking my eyes to see if the angel were real. I made sure that I looked into his eyes and then he went away. I know I said this once, but I will never forget that after 40 years; it is still very clear to me. The angel's hair was very yellowish. Ge had on a white gown with a glow around Him. The bottle he had in his hands did not have anything in it. I had to make eye contact with this angel before he went away.

God has always been with me. No matter what I had to go through, I had to fight with the whole armor of God. Before the angel left, I knew one of us had to die—my son, Noah, or me. I felt that and I knew that, but I did not know which one of us was going to be. When the angles left my window, I am sure he went up back towards the sky. So, when my husband awoke, I told Him about the angel and the baby bottle he had in his hand. My husband looked at me in shocked and amazement. That what was he was supposed to do, look at me in a weird matter. The angel came to me not my husband. The next day, that Thursday morning I got dressed and I got my 2-year-old son ready. We spent the day in Washington with my mother and my husband went to work. He worked at the water plant on Thomson Road with my brother, Joseph. He saw that I was a little shaken up by what I had seen the night before. I did not realize whether my child inside of me moved or not this day. I told my husband that I brought our clothes so we could go to revival tonight; this was a Thursday night 41 years ago; remember I am pregnant with my second child.

I am laying thinking about the time when I was seven months pregnant with my first son, Lazarus Jr. My husband and I was leaving my parents' house late one night in Washington, Georgia to head back to Tignall, Georgia. I was pretty big. We took a back road to Tignall for whatever reason. Soon after we entered this dark road with no lights to be found and no houses to be seen for miles. Our back tire blew out.

My husband got out of the car. He told me we had flat tire. He went looking for a flashlight but realize that he took it out earlier. It was nowhere to be found in this car, a 1967 Chevrolet. I started to pray and pray for someone to come along and help us. We sat and we sat there in the pitch, black dark. Many moments later, we saw a light pull up behind us. The light was so bright. I told my husband not to get out. The individual got out and knocked on my husband's window. He asked my husband where the spare tire was. The gentlemen got the tire out of the back of car, changed out the flat and quickly drove off. We could not see this man's face or anything. We just knew he was a man. I believe and know this was God. We were shocked and full of thanks to the Lord. We drove home safely.

Back to the story of Noah. The vision from the angel was with me all day long. So, I told my mother about my vision. She looked shocked, but she did not say anything; she changed the subject. That afternoon my husband came on down to my mother's house after work and I had his dinner ready on the table. He asked me how I was doing, and I did not answer him. I just kept on fixing his food. I got ready for the revival and everyone else got ready for revival that evening. We went to church at 7:30 p.m. for revival and we left about 9:30 p.m. We were in Washington, Georgia at the Gibson Grove Baptist church. My husband and I went home to Tignall, Georgia, which is about 10 miles from Washington, but we lived on broad road at this time. We were about five more miles down the road from downtown Tignall. So, we got back home in Tignall—me, my husband and my son, Lazarus Jr. who was two years old at this time. I got home and tried to relax. I got ready for bed, and I put my son to bed. About two hours later a sharp pain hit me, I was laying in the bed. I laid back down and a second pain hit me. I told my husband to get up and let us go, its time. I was nine months pregnant with my second child. I already had my bag packed, but he had to find the keys to the car. He put his clothes on and he then put our two-year-old son in the car. It was time to head to the hospital.

We were on our way to the Medical College of Georgia, which is a long way from us, about 80 miles one way. We were on our way. I had pains after pains. I got doing my breathing exercises, blowing, and blowing air in and out of my mouth. I tried to relax. The date is August 14, 1978. My parents lived in Anonia a few miles outside of Washington, Georgia. My sister, Racheal, met me at the end of the road to get my 2-year-old son. We dropped him off to her. We continued on our way to the hospital in Augusta, Georgia. I was in a lot of pain all the way there, but we got there safely. I am thinking back to that day; I do not remember if I felt the baby move all day. I am not sure, but I think so. I knew something was wrong, but I did not know exactly what was going on. The pain was so strong. I could hardly bear those pains. I have had one child, but his birth was very smooth. He came in a few minutes. I had no epidural. I never heard this word until my grandchildren were born. I never had an epidural with any of my children. I had all of my children, naturally. I endured nothing but pain with this second baby. It was more than I could bear. I never knew a human could hurt like this. I did not have a lot of money or insurance at this time. I am just a poor woman having a baby. The good Lord is on my side, because I have already prayed, and I am laying here praying right now.

I told my husband to wait in the waiting room. I did not want him in here with me. It was just me and the good Lord. I had to be strong. All of these pains! How I felt it was unfair for a human being to hurt like this! I was passing blood clots. They were huge. I was only 22 years old, but I knew I had to hang on. I felt like the mother of Jabez. I now know what she is talking about when she bore her son in so much sorrow. All of this is a real-life event that happened to me. It is still on my mind, every day I think about Noah; He comes across my mind so strong. I went through the fire in birth with Noah. He was too good for this world. He went back to Heaven.

I am telling this story along with my current story that happened to me on May 19, 2017, because this is the first time I went to Heaven, but the second time I went to Heaven was on this date and I stayed over there for several days. I did not know anything about time over there, because one day over there is a thousand years and a thousand years is one day, so there is nothing about time over there. Back to my story, laying there in the hospital bed at the Medical College of Georgia 40 years ago. The nurse called me back to the back. My husband stayed in the waiting room. I did not want to see him at this time. Husbands did not have to go with you back there. This was back in the 1970s. Now dads are always in the delivery room.

The nurse started some IVs in my hand, and she left me there for a while. I laid there, and I groaned and groaned. I was in so much distress, pain, and hurt. I was at a loss for words.

All I want is to stop hurting! Please, someone, help me! I had no insurance. I just laid there, but I have the best care. The nurses prepped me. They did everything to me for a woman who is about to have a baby, but I was in so much pain. I was just about to pass out! I was praying to the Lord! Help me, please Lord! Help me to bear these pains! Oh, Lord! Please! The Lord was there. I could feel His Spirit in the room. The nurse said that the doctor would be here in a few minutes. I could not take it anymore. I just went numb, but those pains were still coming, faster and faster.

I had my son Noah. He came out and he is not breathing. He had no life in his body. I said, "Oh, Lord! Lord, have mercy on me! Lord, my son's Spirit is not in his body! The angel had told me that one of us was going to not live. When the angels came to my window, and he went up towards the sky. He made sure I gave him eye contact before he went up into the sky. The doctors and nurses tried to resituate him, but he was gone; when he delivered him, the cord was around his neck. The nurse wrapped him in a blanket, and they brought him to me. I held him for a while; he looked just like my two-year-old son, Lazarus Jr. Oh, my heart was torn into two pieces! There were no words to explain how I was feeling. My husband is in a panic. He is hurting as well. Tears are flowing from both of our faces. Noah weighed about 7 ½ pounds.

After a while, the nurses took Noah away, the nurses then carried me to the recovery room. My husband went out. I do not know where he went, but I was alone. I think they asked him to go out. I laid there for a few minutes. I looked down at my feet and blood was pouring out of my body by the cups. Blood was all around me; I was sitting in blood. I was about gone. I mean gone. The last thing I heard the doctor say was to flip her bed so a cup full of blood can stay on her brain. And I felt the doctor and nurses packing something up in my stomach and then I left this world. I came up from my body into the sky looking down on the doctors working on my body. I was in my hospital grown and I went up to Heaven. I saw the big bright light shining on me and I saw windows. It was amazing! I felt so light! I did not have any more pain! I left out of my body. I stay in the hospital from August 14 through the 24th of August. I did not have a remembrance of what had happened to me until I woke up several days later. I came back to myself wondering what had happened. It was in a blink of an eye of how fast you can get to Heaven. I was just floating in the Heavenly realm before I came back into my body. I saw the stars. I floated up and up. I woke up from a coma. I saw blood running into my body. I had packs of blood running into my body. The nurses gave me blood day after day. My husband told me, they almost lost me. I was in a wonderful place, but I came back.

Forty-one years have passed by, and I still remember the loss of my son, Noah, like it was yesterday. My son, Noah will always have a special place in my heart. When I was able to sit up the doctors told me if this happens again, I will surely not live next time. He wanted me to sign a paper so I could not have any more children and I said, "No, no!" My husband was just torn into two pieces. He looked as if he knew I could not go through that again, but I told him that I will trust God—the One that has brought me through all of this. My son, Noah, was too good for this world. He went back to Heaven. The nurses told me I would die if this happened again as well. We barely saved your life this time. So, the doctors looked at my husband and he shook his head. My husband did not agree with me signing those papers as well for tubulation. My parents called and told me to sign the papers. I said, "No, I am going to trust God!"

No one knows your prayer life, but you! It is a personal relationship with God that you need, and I do not care how much you pray or how righteousness you may think you are, things will happen. I felt at peace!

I think about my son, Noah, all of the time. My heart was in pain. I can blame myself for this or that. I am all right now! I will continue to trust God like I always do! No cross, no crown! We all have a test to take, pass or fail it; but with the mercy and the grace of God, He will let me pass this test in time! It will get a little easier and it did. While I was still in the hospital, my husband and my father-in-law buried Noah. My husband got him from the hospital. He told me later on that he drove with Noah in his arms back to Tignall, Georgia for him to be buried at Thankful Baptist Church. My husband went to the funnel home and got some papers on our son so he could bring Him home to his church, Thankful Baptist Church. He told me today that he drove all the way from Augusta, Georgia to Lincoln, Georgia to the Thankful Baptist Church holding our son in his arm while he drove all the way from Augusta to the place of burial. I asked him, "How did you do that? He told me that he did not turn him a loose until he put him in the casket that his father had built. His father, Hosie Chennault was a great man of God, so he and my husband buried him, and my father-in-law Hosie prayed at the funeral. My heart still burns, but a part of me will always have an empty spot for him, my son Noah. My husband said he did not have his face covered and that he talked to him all the way from Augusta to Lincoln, Georgia and that was over a two-hour drive.

My mother-in-law, Corene, and my father-in-law, Hosie Dee, had a coffin for Him. I did see none of this. I was not at the funeral. This crushed my heart to not be able to attend his funeral. I was in so many tears and my heart were broken. I was still in the hospital from this painful childbirth. I had to suffer. I am not complaining about anything. I am just trusting

God. I am like Job from the Bible days. I went through a lot of pain just like Job, but I am still trusting God. My husband told me about the funeral. I was unaware of what was going on because I was in a coma. I was in Heaven. I was laying in the sky with a light a bright light shining. I was in a majestic world, but this time in 2017 I was on a long vacation in Heaven. I cannot describe Heaven; it is so peaceful there. My husband described Noah's funeral to me. My husband took pictures of the funeral and Noah, but none of them developed. I have remembrance of Noah, and his face will always be with me. He was buried at the Thankful Baptist church about 40 years ago.

The pain of this childbirth was so knife-cutting, deep, and devasting. There will always be a space in my heart and that space belongs to Noah. I believe I saw Noah when I went to Heaven on May 19, 2017. This child was with all of the rest of the children playing on the hillside and he stopped and looked at me for a moment. The rest of the children looked for a little and then went back to playing. I will always say that was Noah. I saw all of this that morning before this day. Father God will not let much slip upon you if you stay close to Him. He will always give you some kind of warning. This was a deep wound in my life. I could hardly bear it, but with the help of Father God, all things are possible. He knows how to carry broken pieces.

Sitting here typing this story, I am getting very emotional. Just thinking back to this moment, I got up and I looked at myself in the mirror. My skin was very dark. My body was too weak. I was wondering why all of this happened to me, but I could not give up, I am only 22 years old at this time. I could not get myself back together alone. I got on my knees, and I told the Lord to help me and make me strong. God eased my pain little by little. I do not know why I went through all of this, but I always can connect with Jabez's mother. She did not lose her son as I did, but she bore Him in so much pain and sorrow. God knows best! I give my life to Him all of my days. I always tell Father God to use me as He sees fit. He has to use you when you ask God to use you. We do not know how He is going to use us. We do not have to be in the spotlight for God to use us.

I had to tell this story along with many others in this book. The doctor told me I would not make it if this happened to me again. Two years later, in the year of 1980, I was expecting another child, my son, Otis. I went to a different hospital to a specialist. I was a little nervous, but I gave it all to Father God. I went to the Doctors Hospital, and I had another child there in the year of 1983, my daughter, Dr. June and in 1984, my son, Pastor Henra. I had more children, and all of these childbirths were smooth. Hard labor, but nothing like Noah's birth. All of my children are healthy and strong. I thank God!

No matter who we are, we all are born into tribulations in this life.

No one will escape, but that is not the issue anyway! The real issue is how we react to the issues of life. The trials we face in this world will either break us or make us stronger. The key to life is to be very sure that your heart is grounded in the Lord and Savior Jesus Christ. I had to stop for a moment and tell you this story of my life where I had so much pain and sorrow, a different kind of pain, but pain. I went into another dimension of Heaven. I stepped out of my body. I could not stay there. It was too much going on to be in my body. At this time while at Doctors Hospital, I left my body for ten days. I was a vacation in Heaven.

Chapter 8

THE LORD AND I

It is the middle of June 2017, and I am still at Select Specialty Hospital. My wounds are clearing up. It feels like it. I know the skin still has not developed back on my buttocks, because it feels so slick. I am still very weak at this time; I still cannot walk. I cannot get to the bathroom, but I use the pot by my bed. I can wipe myself a little, but not much. My arms are very weak, and my leg is nervous and weak. I cannot stand up, but a little. God let people see me suffer. I am talking about suffering. I did not know a human being could suffer like this. I always tell Father God to use me any way he wants to, because I told Him. I am your Lord try me and see. I do not mind suffering for the cost of Jesus Christ; he cried out and asked his father was there any other way to Calvary? He said, "No, I want this cup to pass." I cry out, "Oh, Lord when I awake." I was so sick too sick to breathe. A thousand tubes were hanging from me; I did not know I was sick. I knew when I first got sick, but ten minutes after that I left my body. I did not feel any pain until I came back into my body.

Everyone that looked in on me when I was in a coma saw God working a miracle. My husband said to me the more they prayed about my illness the worse It seems to get, but God is turning things around. He did! I am laying here get stronger and stronger. My mind going back thinking about that man sitting on the rock in the field. His eyes are like the ocean. He turned his head towards me, and He looked at me! I will never forget that look. I just walked up on Him; there is so much to see in Heaven. Oh, what a beautiful place! It is so colorful; every living thing is colorful and bright. I saw oxen and cows pulling the wooden wagons in the field. I walked among all kinds of people; they looked at me! All races of people are over there! They were just looking; I kept walking and smiling.

I had no remembrance of this world; they looked on me as I was suffering. People were coming to visit me from near and far while I laid in my coma at Doctors Hospital. My children asked me if I heard any of my family members' voices or saw them? I never heard a thing that was going on down here on earth; I was not there in that hospital room. We are all going to have our share of trouble. When we can grow in grace and mercy, trouble makes us humble. There is no time to think that you are better than your neighbor. You do not have time to judge people, just stay humble. Do not be prideful! Stay like a little child before a mighty God, because we brought nothing here and we will not take anything away from this world. It is all about Father God and living a life pleasing to Him because we are no more than a bubble on the water. It might be over in a second. Those people who are low and unpopular; God loves those people! He can use anyone He wants to use, and I know He has been using me all of my life. After every round, I get stronger and stronger in my faith in God. I cry out loud and I feel angry at times. I ask, why? However, through it all, I am blessed and highly favored by the Lord Jesus Christ! What He does for you, He will do for me! He loves us all. It is about the favor He shows each one of us! It is up to you as to how much you want of Him. It is all up to you.

I am still here in the Select Specialty Hospital. I see people walking by my room. Most of them are people that work here, nurses or doctors, but you never see patients walking up and down the hallway too much. I guess this is that kind of hospital. I lay here day after day wishing I could walk. I am a grown woman! I am, but I cannot walk or go to the bathroom on my own. I am back to a small baby again, but I tell myself every day I am going to get out of here and I will! It is just a matter of time. God did not bring me this far to leave me now. I am headed home, back to my family. I am reading more scripture.

For I reckon that the sufferings of this present time are not worthy to be compared with the glory which shall be revealed in us. For we are saved by hope: but hope that is seen is not hope: for what, a man seeth, why doth he yet hope for? But if we hope for what we see not, then do we with patience wait for it. Likewise, the Spirit also helpeth our infirmities for we know not what we should pray for as we ought: but the Spirit itself maketh intercession for us with groanings which cannot be uttered. And he that searcheth the hearts knoweth what is the mind of the Spirit because he maketh intercession for the saints according to the will of God (Romans 8:18; 24-27).

Laying here still in Select Specialty Hospital, thinking about how good God is to me! I am also thinking about how good my children are to me. They are standing by their ill mother, because they know I have stood by them. I made sure that all four of them earned a college degree. It was very hard on their father and me, but God answered my prayers. If you do not brag on your children, no one else will brag on them! I thank God for them. When they came by to see they always prayed for me and move my lame body, because I could not help myself. I got all kinds of bruises on my body trying to turn myself over plenty of nights. I just stayed down to the bottom of the bed. There is a purpose for everything that happens to you in life. We were all born for a purpose and God knows that purpose. We are not going to die until we get that purpose done.

No one, even the doctors thought I would get this far! I can tell that in the way that they are looking at me. They are puzzled! You never know what 24 hours may bring; it best to stay prayed up so when trouble does come it will not be such a surprise. Each day, I pray I think God what he has already done. I tell the Lord to hold my hand and cover us with his blood. I ask Him to walk with me and my family as I take a journey through this world. I tell Him every day to keep my family, and friends and my enemy covered in the blood. There is nothing to brag about, but the goodness of the Lord. The Lord is the only one who really understands you; he knows your heart.

Going back to my childhood, thinking about how I use to walk in the mud barefooted. I would stop on the side of the road and pick some plums; plums tress was everywhere in the country road. I was so happy! I did not know what life would hold for me; we did not have a television or phone or electricity, so we played in the woods all the time and we looked for food. No one bothered little children back then. I never did hear about anything happening to small children at this time. We walked the road all hours of the night. We never got bit by a snake or step on glass or anything. I think Father God for bringing me this far. He will bring me back home again.

God does the healing. He healed me. He gave the doctors knowledge about my illness. He had everything in place that I needed. I think God for my husband, my children, family members and friends walking along with the doctors. They gave up a little, but they keep on hoping for their wife, mother, sister, cousin, aunt, and friend to come back. no one really thought I would make it. It was Father God who had the final word over me, and he let me come back to this world. I am glad to be here with my family. You can always plant a seed, but Father God is the one who makes it grow. Whenever my blood pressure goes up so high after I awake, my daughter would play some of my favorite gospel songs and massage my neck. We were praying also. My blood pressure would go up and drop low; back up and then drop low again. This went on for a long time.

I was a little confused when I first awoke. I was thinking about where I had been and the things I had seen. People were just looking at me kind of crazy. I did not know why, because I remember the EMS coming and picking me up, but five minutes after that I remember nothing, because I was in Heaven. It is beautiful over there. I cannot really describe it. I had no thoughts about here. All the while I was at Select Specialty Hospital, my daughter would bring me water from home jars after jars. I drink my own water from the well I got at home. I live in the country, and I have well for house water. I could not use my cell phone as my hands shook so badly. My phone would ring in my room, but I did attempt to answer it. My voice sounded like I was 120 years old. I live a quiet life.

I put most of my time in my church work. I taught Sunday school for years. I put most of my time in my garden every year. I planted all kinds of vegetables. I put my time in my children. I got to make sure that my children get a good start in life. I did not want them to be so poor. They would have never survived the life that I had to endure; every thought it was the best time of my life back in my childhood. My children told me that the doctors told them that I had been sick for three weeks; that is hard to believe. I had done a lot of things in the last three weeks of May 2017. Every time I saw the Physical Therapist at my door, I know I had a day's work ahead of me. They did not pull me, but I know I had to try to try to stand up and this is the hardest thing to do is to try to stand up after being a coma. I did not have to walk, just to stand up for a few seconds. My heart rate and my blood pressure would go up each time, but with every effort I made it got better.

Select Specialty Hospital's physical therapists always praised me! They always told me that I was doing good. I try hard so I could go home. I cannot wait to get home, but at this time I have a long way to go. The lady in the room beside is gone. I do not know where she went, but I have been praying for her. She was praying to die. It was a really loud cry. I was like Job. I am not rich, and I do not have 10 children, but the pain that he had, the physical part; I know about. Job 4:14: "If a man die, shall he live again?"

All the days of my appointed time will I wait, till my change come. There was no sleep-in sight when I first awoke from my coma. I get a little, but not much! I am still very sick, sicker than sick. I never knew a human being could get this sick. I had to put my mind on a lot of other things. I am walking around in Heaven. I found peace thinking of my family, me going home and scriptures. I found some peace in my childhood days. I say Psalm 23 throughout the day and the Lord's Prayer. Praise God! I am thinking back over all of the scriptures that I think about especially the healing ones! I am not worried about anything! One thing about me is that I never know when my body is tired! I do not ever feel tired of my body. I am just breaking down because I never really got any rest. I never got any rest in my childhood. I never got any rest, because in my early years it was so many of us in a small house. I slept in between my two oldest sisters and they always smush me to death. I never got any rest until some of the older children left my parents' house and that was not until I was in high school. The mattress was awful. I never got much rest in my life, so I do not know when my body is tried. I had to sit up lots of nights with my children when they were sick or had a big test to study for, but it is all good. I am still here and got my mind! I am in full recovery.

I was healing while I was in Heaven, but my physical body had to go through the process of healing. I was thinking about my mother. I am laying there thinking about how she looked in Heaven; she was much younger in Heaven. When she died at

254

the age of 82, she was a hard-working lady. She had 13 children, but only ten of them lived. They had midwives back then and they had nothing for the pain. She told me that she had all 13 children with no pain medications. I had nothing for pain either in my childbirths. My mother, I saw in Heaven; I did not see my father in Heaven, but I am sure he was there. My father was a strong man about 6 feet 6 inches tall. He has large bones like my oldest son, Lazarus Jr. My father told me about a story of how he found one handful of peas in the garden and his mother made some pea soup to feed Him and his siblings and it was only water and a hand full of peas, nothing else! He told me how hungry he got in his 30s. He says it snowed once and he did not have any shoes to put on his feet. So, he saw an old tire in the ditch and got that tire out of the ditch, cut it up and made Him some shoes. He called them "Car Tire shoes!" He walked in the snow with his new shoes.

He asked me one day before he passed on to glory, "Wonder how it feels to die?"

I told Him, "The Bible says if you die in Jesus, you will be alright!"

Why me? God knows my heart. No one knows me as God does. I am the apple of His eye. I am just not finished with what God has for me to do! When each of us has completed our task down here on earth then we can leave this place. I got to lay my hands on the sick and they will be healed. I got to tell everyone who wants to know about Heaven. I know my father is in Heaven. The Lord Jesus did not choose to let me see Him. I was closer to Him than the other siblings. I lived next door to my parents after I got married. My father did not have any time to go to school. He never did learn to read or write. He could barely sign his name, but he knew all of the old school gospel songs. Every morning he would get up singing! You could hear Him miles away. My mother told me that she went as far as the 6th grade. Even though my parents were not educated, they are the smartest two people that I will ever know! I miss them! Live for Jesus, every day all day! Do the right things and think the right things. I thank God for my parents being in my life, living beside me and seeing them every day as I grew up over the years. Now they live in my heart and in heaven!

My dad died in my arms in front of the home house, which is my parents' home off of Metasville road. My father died in five minutes from a heart attack. My mother died in my arms as well in the same house. She suffered and died from pancreatic cancer. "One day at a time, sweet Jesus, which is all I ask of you!" My older brother, Charlie called me when he was dying; he told me that he loved me over the phone from the Medical College of Georgia in Augusta, Georgia. He died from a broken heart right after my mother died. He stressed himself out over her death. My brother, Jessie, died from complications of an immunodeficiency disease. He died in the New York

Community Hospital. He moved from New York after he finished Job Corp. He left at the house at an early age. From time to time, I think about them! I know they knew I was sick, my mother, my father and my brothers, Charlie, and Jessie. I saw her face in Heaven, my mother, along with my two aunties, Aunt Lue, and Aunt Nee.

Your feet do not touch the ground like here on earth. I hit the ground in Heaven so light. There is no bodyweight like here; you are very light in Heaven. There is nothing heavy about walking around. It was so much joy! I was just exploring. I saw all of these mansions on the hill that the Bible talks about. Why not take the chance? What do you have to lose with Christ? Give your life to Jesus Christ while you still have breath in your body! Do not go another second without making Lord Jesus the savior of your life. It only up to you! Ask Him to forgive you for all of your sins! Believe in your heart that Christ rose from the dead in three days! Study His words and give your life to Christ! Study and study His words! Just talk to Him, He will hear you! You do not have to go to anyone else! You can go right to Him! Just knock at the door and see that He will let you in; you do not need to know any fancy words.

Years go by in the blink of an eye! Praise Him so you can get home to Heaven safely! You do not have to follow the crowds! Follow God! You do not need anyone's approval, but

God. There is no other way to the Father but through His Son Jesus Christ! He is our mediator between us and God. I am reading my scripture again while laying here in the hospital bed: For there is no respect of persons with God.

> For as many as have sinned without law shall also perish without law: and as many as have sinned in the law shall be judged by the law. As it is written, there is none righteous, no, not one: For all have sinned and come short of the glory of God; So then because thou art lukewarm, and neither cold nor hot, I will spue thee out of my mouth (Romans 2:11-12; 3:10; 3:23; Revelations 3:16).

We should love to be in the body of Christ because we are all messed up in some kind of way, but through Jesus Christ— we can lean towards God and His righteousness. Do not waste your time being fake Christians, be real!

It is around June 17, 2017. I am still at the Select Specialty Hospital where my blood pressure readings look like this 121/66, 119/71, and 122/67. My wounds are healing very well. My temperature is 98.9°F at this time. I can drag myself out of bed to the pot that is beside my bed. All of my family members are gone at this time. I told them to go home. My husband is looking worn out, totally worn out. He is not alone. He is at home with my granddaughter, Hannah. She is with him. It is about 1 hour and 30 minutes from where I live in Washington,

Georgia to the hospital. My daughter goes to the farmer's market and to get her some fresh fruit every day and she always brings me some peaches back to eat. They were so sweet and good. She is getting ready to go back to work; she has to leave, and she is going to five different states teaching at colleges around the United States. I will miss her because she has been the rock during my sickness. Because she is a female, she did things for me that my sons could not do, but they help to turn me over because I cannot turn over myself. Oh, how they pulled me from side to side trying to put the bedpan under me. They pulled me like a rag doll. They have pulled me and turn me over a thousand times a day to let me use the pot because I was drinking a lot of water. Laying on the bedpan is no joke, but now I can drag myself on to the pot every day! The nurses give me stool softeners and it is a big hassle for the nurses to clean me like a newborn baby. I do not want them to clean me this way, but I have to be cleaned. I have already gone back to be a child; I feel like it!

We never know what 24 hours will bring us! Live for today, for today has enough troubles of its own troubles as found in Matthew 6:34. When you take on Christ, there is longsuffering! Thinking over these words by Thomas Shepherd— "Must Jesus bear the cross alone, and all the world go free? No, there's a cross for everyone, and there's a cross for me" I am still at the Select Specialty Hospital, my mobility level is a five, but it will be a six before I leave this hospital. I can sit up in the recliner. I can use my hands. I can hold on to my bed rails and pull myself up to the head of my bed by myself. I can turn over my body. I can walk a few feet with my walker. This is one of the hardest things I will ever do at this point!

Learning to walk again is so hard! Not being able to walk is hard to describe, but I will try. I could not move. It felt like being in a hole with cement all around you. I wanted to get up and walk in my mind, but my body would not let me. This is so emotional. I was like a baby learning to walk. I had to will my body to want to move. I had to make my legs move in my mind. I cried and prayed my way back to walking again. I thought about my husband, children, and grandchildren. My arms are still weak, and legs are just like tree limbs dangling in the wind when it is blowing hard. If I am not holding on to my walker, I will fall over. I have a high level of being at risk of falling as indicated on my arm hospital bands. I am not supposed to get out of bed, but I do get out of bed to use the pot. It is right beside me. I drag myself to the pot right beside my bed, but I can hardly wipe myself off. I tried, but I was not good at wiping myself yet. I get tired of calling the nurses. I know they get tired of me calling them. My activity tolerance is fair, my sitting tolerance is fair, my standing tolerance is fair; I going to have to have more rehab! I am not there yet, and I am trying very hard to get out of here! It has been a long journey, but I would not take anything for this journey.

I have been on a vacation to Heaven; the price was very high, but the cost was already paid by our Lord and Savior Jesus Christ. I just stepped on board. I got to have a therapeutic approach to my rehabilitation to include Gait Training Neuromuscular Re-education, therapeutic exercises for the lower body, endurance building, and therapeutic activities for balance and coordination. My mind goes back to the day when I never heard the word "stress." I remember when all of us, my siblings and me, would be headed to church in a black pick-up truck. My father would put a bench in the back of the truck and the older children would sit on the bench. The younger children would sit down in the body of the truck.

I would have on a can-can dress. The dress is heavily layered with many ruffles. The colors of the dresses were so bright. My aunt would send it to us from the city. My siblings and I were glad to get a box of clothes from the city because she had ten children also. My aunt had five boys and five girls just like my parents. She lived in Washington, DC. We would head to church simply happy as we could be because we did not know anything about being poor. We never live in a neighbor. We would always live in a shack type house; it belonged to the white folks up the road. We worked for them.

We picked blackberries all day and we made 50 cents for picking them; it was a lot of money to us.

I was a happy child. I played, and I played in the woods. Children were safe back then during my childhood. Everyone knew everyone's child; we were always safe! Our main goal was to hunt for food. I had beautiful parents; they worked hard. My mom would iron with this heavily piece of steel iron. She would heat it on the heater, the wood heater. Plenty of days when we ran to meet her, she would always have a piece of bread or some leftover that the white folks gave her she would always bring us some food some days she did not have anything. We were so happy! We did not know any other way to be, this was in the early 1960s.

Life was so simple back then! My mind went back to my childhood days. We had church back then! God blessed us when we needed money or food, so we knew how to serve Him! When we washed, we washed out of the wash pan. We did not have cell phones or even a landline telephone in the early 1960s, but the white folks had one, the landline telephone. Cell phones came out much later. I used to call some of my friends at school and tell them I had a phone. I did not have anything! I wanted to look big to show that my parents had a little bit of money. We did not have anything. We did not get a phone until I got in the 10th grade. I was so happy when we got a telephone because I could call my boyfriend who is now my husband, but I never did court him until I got to the end of my 11th grade year. I only courted my husband and that was that. I only wanted and needed him!

I am laying here in this bed wondering how I got here. I heard the angels singing around my bed with white gowns on, just clapping. I was laying there listening to the song. They would just clap, and clap and they would say, "Lord, Lord!" just clapping and clapping. They sang around my bed for a long time. There is another world over there! I hope everyone who reads my book believes that there is a God, because I saw Jesus Christ our Lord sitting on that rock. I know in my heart that that was Him. I think about Him every day, throughout the day! I will never forget how he looked at me. There is no compassionate look like that in all of the earth, all the days of my life that I have ever seen. I love Psalm 9: 1-3 and Psalm 18: 1-3—

I will praise thee, O Lord, with my whole heart; I will shew forth all thy marvelous works. I will be glad and rejoice in thee: I will sing praise to thy name, O thou most High. I will love thee. O Lord, my strength. The Lord is my rock, and my fortress, and my deliverer; my God, my strength, in whom I will trust; my buckler, and the horn of my salvation, and my high tower. I will call upon the Lord, who is worthy to be praised: so, shall I be saved from mine enemies.

Praise God! He is a personal savior! I can go right to Him. We all can just pray an honest prayer because He already knows our hearts! We cannot fool Him! We can fool each other, but not our God! He knows our thoughts even before we speak them out of our mouths. I am glad! He knows each one of us, our motives. Just talk to Him! You do not have to use any fancy words! You do not even have to speak good grammar, because He feels your heart; He has every heartbeat in His hand. He started your heart to beating and He knows when to stop your heart from beating. He is an "all-knowing God" and "all-seeing God." He revealed Himself to me through Jesus Christ. I met Him sitting on that rock. My whole body just trembles when I think about Him sitting on the rock. I just walked upon Him! Oh, what a mighty God! He can do just what He wants to do! He does not need any permission from anyone! He can use who He wants to. I hope everyone goes to Heaven, that place is too peaceful to miss. That place is shining with bright, vibrate colors. You do not have any worries over there.

You will have no remembrance of this world! All memories of this world are cleared from your memory, but you will recognize your loved ones in Heaven. Your body is different from it is here on earth. You will be much younger and lighter in weight, and you are happier so much happier. I did not look like I do now; I was so much younger. I say again, "Who wants to miss Heaven?" I have to tell everyone who wants to listen, there is a Heaven! I believe there is a place called Hell too! Just like in Noah's days from the Bible, when he said it was going to rain, it rained. Do not wait until it is too late! The window of your life will shut! Make sure you get in the boat while there is yet time!

Give your whole life to Jesus Christ—singing the hymn written by Joseph M. Scriven in the 1800s, "Oh, what needless pain we bear, all because we do not carry everything to God in prayer!" When you put on the armor of Christ; you are putting on long-suffering. Every day, we must grow closer to the Lord, and it is very dangerous to get so close to the Lord. I always tell Father God to use me anyway you want to. That does not mean standing in the front of a church every Sunday; He can use you in a way that you have no idea. It is not the easy way out. You do never know how the Lord is coming. He comes in ways we will never imagine, so be always ready! Build yourself in Him and put on the truth and the armor of God so you will be able to stand at judgment day! I lay here in this bed fighting the hardest to live for my family. I would say one of my hardest battles, but I got peace and I got joy. I am not going to cry any sorrowful tears; all of my tears are tears of joy, unspeakable joy.

Just like you turn off the television switch, that is how fast I left this world. Very fast, but I was not worried! I have always prayed, and I knew that God had me whether I lived, or I died! I know Father God has me. I had no idea what was wrong. When I awoke, I still did not know what was wrong. I did not have a clue. I do not care how strong you think you are mentally, physically, or spiritually; you can be broken into many pieces! So, I can tell the world to be careful how you walk through this world because in five minutes or less you can be in Heaven or Hell! Choose this day where you will spend eternity, because you will be spent it in one of these places. No matter what you are doing in life; the devil will always show up. I told Satan to get behind me. "I am already saved, flee from me!"

The devil would tell me, "You will be in this hospital forever!" I said, "No way, I am going home, and I am going to walk in my front door."
You have to talk back to the devil when he comes to you. He always tries to get in your prayers and confuse your thoughts, but your mind must be strong and on Father God. Keep on praying to the Lord until you feel a breakthrough, even if you just say "Lord, Have Mercy on me!" The Lord will hear you

because He knows what we need before we ask Him. I ask that His will be done. I always say, "Lord let your will be done in my life." I ask the Lord to just speak the words over me and it will be done. Sometimes you do not know what you need or how to pray. I just thank the Lord for what He has already done, and He will do it. The Lord will give us the desires of our heart if we keep Him first.

All sickness is not unto death even, so I died and came back. I went on a vacation to Heaven. I will tell the world if you do not know Father God in the free parts of your sins you need to get acquainted with Him while you are still breathing. I am thinking about many things laying here. The janitor come in every day to clean my room and they are nice to me; one young man came in talking to me. He was an African American young man. He said he had three jobs. I told him how young he was in age. I told him to take a few classes in something you love to do so you can come to this hospital with a different uniform on. You can make a difference. I told him no matter what your job title is you just do it with perfection and God will let you multiply. He did not understand when I mentioned God, but I gave him something to think about. He left my room with a puzzling look on his face.

I also saw this other lady standing at my door. She looks at me every day real hard. She was cleaning. She has the sweetish Spirit. She always wore green and one day she came in my room, and I told her how God has blessed me and how I went to Heaven. She just shouted with the joy of the Lord. I will never forget this lady. She told me that she had two jobs. We talked about the Lord, and she said people talked about her because she worked so much. I told her as long as you are doing honest work; pray to God. He will let your little money expand and go farther than you think. I will always remember this lady; she just looks at me every day, it was as if she drew strength from me at this time. I am still a mess, but I am making progress.

I am trying hard to bounce back. I always been a woman on the move because I had four children and I did not want them to be poor and that was that. They are not rich, but they work very hard every day. The work their dad and I had to do to make a positive impact on them is indescribable. They had to be productive citizen to make a positive impact on the world. We were always so busy, all of my children played sports throughout elementary, middle, and high school even college, sports like football and basketball in college. My daughter played high school basketball. My sons were so busy and everywhere they went from the beginning to college; we tried to be there. Whenever I get to the ball field or college field, no matter what state; I had to let them know that their father and myself were there and that went on for I know 26 years or more. We went to every game here in Washington, Georgia and away. We had to train our children so they can help the next generation of Chennault's. I did not want my children to go through the poverty impact, but I want them to get the other parts of the morals and values of life. I had to make sure that they all know Father God. They had to have a Bible in their hands, finding scriptures in a time of need like when I got sick

Chapter 9

THE STORM PASSED INTO GLORY

As always, my mind went back to my childhood, I stood in a cold kitchen at times watching my mother make a fire in the woodstove to warm the room up. It took a while for the house to heat up, because there were a lot of cracks in that old house. I stood there looking at her. I look a lot like her. She stood there making this firewood using lighter wood that we got out of the woods. If you use this lighter wood, it will start a fire fast. It was still so cold in the room because of all the cracks in the house. We never had night clothes at this time in the early 1960s. My mother kept us so clean.

She always made do with what she had; I never heard her complain. She would be in the kitchen cooking breakfast. She would always cook two pans of biscuits. There were about 20 biscuits in one pan and about 10 biscuits in the other pan. My mom and dad would always buy a 50 pounds bag of flour and a large bucket of Lard, which was grease used to put in the bread. She put can milk or dry milk in the bread. In this large bread bowl, she mixed the bread up. Those biscuits looked so pretty in the pan. My mom would fry enough chicken to feed the 12 of us and she made lots of chicken gravy. She cooked a pot of rice or grits. We were all full for a while.

My father always ate the chicken backs and the ribs. Then my mother ate the chicken necks and for the rest of us; she divided chicken between ten children. I was always hungry for plenty of days. I got nothing, but scraps. I ate through the scraps. There was a struggle for food, but always on Sunday after church, we would have a good dinner. On Monday, back to the struggle for food. My father would always bring some food from the butcher. He brought back parts of the cow and hog. My siblings and I had to clean all of these parts of the animals like the cow's feet, cow's head, hog chitlins, and hog feet. We had to clean all of these parts of the animals. We would be so tired. My father made us work. He did not believe in resting.

We had to work all of the time. We had no television until the late 1960s. My brother, Jessie, went to the job corps and he brought us a television when he came home that summer. The television was small, black, and white. I remember watching soap operas with my mother during the summertime, "Days of Our lives, As the World Turns, and General Hospital." I was about six years old. I saw the live news feeds of where the black people were marching in Atlanta, Georgia. This was during the Civil Rights Movement. I remember seeing the black people being sprayed by the water hoses and the vicious dogs attacking them. I did not understand. I had seen a television at the white folk's house. I did not know anything else about anything that went on in the world until we got a television.

Life was so simple then. I never heard the word cancer, disease, or stress. I never heard these words; we live deep in the county of Wilkes country. We barely went to town. I went to school, and we only had black folks in our school there no white folks; everybody was black. All the bus drivers, lunchroom workers, and teachers when I started school. Those were the days. Life was simple. My mind would always go back to these days we read Ted and Sally books and added numbers like 2+2 =4 and so on. The black children did better back then when it came to discipline; the black teacher did not play. Back then in schools, the teachers had access to belt straps and wooden paddles to spank the students with when they acted up in the classroom. None of the students were out of order in the classroom. The teachers knew our parents, so the students did what they had to do; the students all obeyed the teachers. Days back then were simple. That is where my mind would always drift off while I was here in the hospital.

I have been through a lot in my life. I married the first boy who told me I was pretty and that was okay. We are still married about almost 44 years, and we are still happy. We are getting older, but I would not take anything for my journey. I do not want to go back even if I could go back. I had fun in my childhood. I got to tell my story. There is a Heaven for people who are prepared to know Jesus! Jesus knows your heart! You can go to church and go to church and still have any change on the inside. It is who you are on the inside that matters, who you are in your heart. This face tells the story.

There is nothing, but peace over there. A part of me will always be in Heaven. Even now a part of me is still left there and a piece of me is here on earth. I will go back there one day. The Spirit told me before I left when I will come back. I will come back! My son, Pastor Henra told me, "Mother, I know you got to go, but you got to come back!" I was just smiling at Pastor Henra; he was at my gravesite.

I said, "Okay" and I went through the ground like a roller coaster in a few minutes.

After I died, I went through the ground, and I saw dirt on both sides of me. The dirt was like a real highway, and I was smiling all the way through. I went through the ground so fast, and I stepped out in Heaven. Oh, my Lord, it was so amazing! I could not help to stand there for a while. I had a young body. I looked about 33 years old. I do not care how old you are when you die! You will be the same age as Christ Jesus if you lived past childhood. I looked in the river and I saw myself as I looked at 33 years old. I was young and pretty! I felt more alive than I ever! I was happy! I felt happy all the time; nothing is sad over there in Heaven.

I look to my right and I saw streets of gold, a long walk. I saw all of those mansions; the building was high. They were eggshell in color with gold shining on the sides of these buildings. Oh, what a cross I have to carry thinking about it now. I was not in any pain over there, but when I came back in my body; I felt the pain. Oh, Lord have mercy! I never have been this sick in all of my life, but I did not care; I was too sick to move. I could not turn over or sit up or nothing. All I could be move my eyes. I did not know what was wrong, but I thought about the EMTs coming through my door and a few minutes after that I left this world.

It is now around the date of June 17, 2017; my daughter has left me some clothes in the closet. She went out and brought me some from the dollar store, which is right near Select Specialty Hospital. She would have gone to the mall, but she did not want to waste time there when I was sick in here. I have not had on real clothes on for a long time. My daughter is going back to work, and I miss her so much. She had been right beside me ever since I woke up. I cannot even imagine what she went through when I was away from my body. She has been right here sleeping beside me for a long time. It is time for her to go and she has been gone for a few days, but she left me some clothes. The doctor came in and asked me, which hospital rehabilitation center did I want to go to, Walter's Way or Doctors Hospital? I told the doctor, "Doctors Hospital Rehabilitation Center!" I was about to finish here! My mobility is about six. I cannot walk! I am still very weak; I am improving.

I have improved a lot. This was a few days before I left Select Specialty Hospital. The doctors came to see me often. I had no acute distress at this time; I could not go to the bathroom on my own. I cannot explain not being able to walk or take care of my hygiene. It is something else we take for granted. I know what it is to just lay in bed wishing if I could just walk and just get up out of this bed and look out of the door. It would be good! I got legs and feet, but I am too weak to walk. My muscle is so weak! I cannot stand up put a minute alone and I am straining to do that, but I always see myself walking out of here; this is no way for anyone to live like this! No one! I got to get out of here and get home! I am so tired of this bed moving; my bed is like a waterbed. I cannot stand the movement anymore. This bed keeps my muscles from getting cramps and helps with blood flow. I asked the nurse to help me get in the recliner chair and they always do.

I remember the first time that I sat in the recliner chair. I was feeling so bad, but the nurse told me if you do not try you will be here that much longer. You got to learn to sit up before you can do anything else. I got so shaky and week when she helped me to the recliner for the first time. I tried it. I got so sick. I had to get back in the bed after about 30 minutes of sitting in the recliner. I had to lay down. Oh, my Lord! I was so sick! Everyone was gone at this time it was just me and the Lord. Sometimes in life, it is just up to you and your God. You just got to hold on to your faith just like Job when he was sitting in the ash pile. I always through about Job laying there so sick. When you ask God to use you; you do not know how he is coming. I always pray this prayer. I tell the Lord, "I am yours; Lord use me anyway you want, try me and see!" Many people look in on me and saw God work a miracle through me. Why? I do not know! I am not popular to the world. God loves unpopular people and things in his own way.

I always love God and I want to please Him. I do all that I can to please God, your Lord. We have to bring God's glory through. I belong to the Lord. I always have told the Lord this with tears running down my face. I am so glad that I can talk to the Lord, and no one can tell me to be quiet. I do not try to please the world. I want to please the Lord, because he is the one who will have the last words over me. It does not matter how you die; how you are buried, whether you are cremated or put in the ground; you are safe with the Lord! You are going to Heaven like I did, or you will go to a place called Hell. Who wants to miss that beautiful place, Heaven? The time is now while there is breathe in your body, give your life to Jesus Christ! Do it now; do not let another day go by.

I am sitting here in the recliner it is the early morning of June 19, 2017. I am trying to sit up more. I sit there long hours now, because I can hardly stand for my bed to move. The physical therapist is in here; my mobility level is about 6 that means I can wash my self-off in the pan with a washcloth and some soap. I can hit the main spots, but I cannot stand up at the sink to bathe. I sit down in the recliner to bath. I cannot stand up in the bathroom yet or walk yet. I have a lot of barriers to overcome! Yes, I do! I have to get my endurance back and more strength. I have come so far; it is unbelievable how far I have come at this time. I can hold on to the side of the recliner to lift myself up. I can stand holding on to the walker. I have to just rest. I do arm and legs exercises at this time. I walk as far as to the door from the bed; that is a few steps. I am trying; I am laying down thinking about how I got here. I guess my body just shut down, because I have been busy all of my life. I never had much time to rest when the children were home. On Saturdays, the children and I would go shopping and clean out book bags. On Sundays, we got ready for church and was there at church all day.

Laying here thinking about my childhood again. I remember one day I asked my mother how much money she makes a week. She told me 20 dollars. I said, 20 dollars that is all you make?

She said, "Yes!"

She always had money in her bosom in a rag. I just looked at her and I shook my head, but you could buy a lot of things with 20 dollars in the 1960s. My mother made me a dress one day this was about the year of 1963. I never will forget this dress. I went in kitchen, and I saw a brown sack laying on the floor and I brought it to my mother. She told me to go look in the drawer in her room and bring me the scissors. I did! She made me a dress out of a meal feed sack; it did not take her long to sew that dress. I like it and I will never forget that dress I thought about that dress laying here and how I dance around in the yard looking at my new dress.

I also thought about how I helped my mother make up fire around the pot to boil clothes. She would get a tin tub and a washboard. She put some water in the pot to boil the white pieces of clothes. She would draw water and I would draw water. She made her soap out of old grease that she had cooked with; she had cans and cans of that old grease lard from the hogs that my father cleaned for food. We made up fire around the iron black pot. First, we propped it up on bricks. There were bricks under each leg of the pot. We had three legs; we set the pot on those bricks, and we made a fire so the water in the pot could boil.

We scrubbed the clothes with the soap we made some weeks ago. I was a small girl, but I remember her. My mother worked so hard with ten children. I saw her in Heaven; she made it. I did not see my father, but I know he was there also. Those days were simple. I did not know one day I would have to grow up to be a lady. At this time in my life, life was so easy and free. I thought I would stay a little girl for years and years, but I grew up. We would hang the clothes on the bob wire. We did not a clothesline at this time. This bob wire held the white people's cows in the pasture. I remember I would sometimes find a penny on the ground. I would save it until I get to the store so I could buy me three cookies for a penny. They were the best cookies I have ever ate.

When I was a child in the 1960s, you never seen a penny on the ground like you do today. Children these days would never pick up a penny. I thought about how I chewed bubble gum; my siblings and I chewed that gum three whole days before we throw it away. We would always sick it on the bed frame. Sometimes my father would buy a watermelon and it would just sit there in the house; we would be so hungry, but he would not cut it until he got ready. We could never talk loud in the house. We hardly said a word to each other. You could hear a mouse run in that house. Our father would not cut that watermelon for anything. We watched his every move in the evening time. The watermelon just sits there in the corner. We were like soldiers in the army, my siblings and me. We did everything in order. Sooner or later my dad had to cut that watermelon, so about that Thursday I would be peeping in the kitchen standing. I saw him get that big, long, and black knife out of the closet. He would pick up that watermelon and he would slice in about 12 pieces and all of us came to get a slice.

My siblings and I ate it up in seconds. We almost ate the rim up out of the watermelon.

My oldest son, Lazarus Sr., came by the hospital. He was telling me how many people came by to see me. He told me a whole lot of people came by; some ministers came by to pray for me and he told me, "Mother, if I could have taken your place; I would have." I told Him that was for me and only me. This was a test for me! God is using me to get His glory, for those who looked upon me saw a miracle.

I told my son that I had a vacation to Heaven, and I would not have taken anything for this journey, because I got a chance to see God; I saw Jesus sitting on a rock. I took a look at his face. I saw his robe and I look at his sandals and saw the rag on his head. I saw the belt around his waist, and I saw his eyes. I saw his long leg bone and his feet; the same feet that Mary poured the oil and wiped it off with her hair. I would not take anything for my journey. My life is renewed. God has given me a whole new body. I know I saw God. He looked at me. I never see a human being look at neither human being in that way.

I do not know why God choose me, but I am glad he did. I will tell this story forever to anyone who wants to listen. Glory! I get excited just to thinking about my Lord and your God sitting on that rock. A part of me will always be in Heaven even though I am living here on earth. Glory, hallelujah! Oh, what a beautiful place! So much peace, you do not have to breathe there. I just walked around Heaven, standing there, and watching all of those people. All of the races are in the field gathering wheat, tying it up putting in the wooded wagons; there is no one color there. I stood there just looking and smiling I never knew that I was living on earth. I had no remembrance of earth, but I recognized my family over there. There is a whole other world, it not like this world, it is so calm with beautiful colors. The water is beautiful, the trees and the flowers are beautiful. The children are happy, and I was so happy; I met some of the children. They told me who they were. I saw my grandson who died a year earlier, he had on the same clothes that he was buried in. He asked me, "Can I help you, grandma?" I told him, "I was okay!" and then he went away. He looked at me in my eyes. It was amazing. I got to tell the world! Somebody might believe me and come to repentance.

God had it fixed for me. I never felt any pain. I never have seen anyone around by my bed. I heard nothing. I was in Heaven. I did not hear anything until I awoke, and I was shocked to see all of those people around my bed. I said, "What in the world is going on?" I have not seen some of these people in a long time and I look around a few more minutes. My immediate family and my children tried to explain what has happened to me.

I remember two other times I have had to learn how to walk, but I walk quicker than this time. I was working at the elementary school in Washington, Georgia about 23 years ago, and one day I was over in the room where you have to make copies for the teachers. I was a paraprofessional. One morning, I was feeling very tired. I was taking two college classes at night, trying to study to be a teacher and I was doing good. I made good grades. I rushed home after work. I made sure my children were okay and I already had dinner cooked, because I always cooked their dinner before I went to school. All they had to do was warm it up and eat it; they knew how take a bath and do their homework. They would always leave their homework on the table for me to check when I got home. They were all good about doing what I told them to do. We live in the country about eight minutes from town, but it was in the country. Our neighbor was my parents and another lady live up on top of the hill, we lived in the back; we were in calling distance, I would say.

I went to high school where the classes were. I enjoyed going back to school; it was hard work, but I kept up I made good grades. If I felt my body getting very tried, I always put my tape-recorded under my pillow because I recorded the class as the professors taught the courses. I recorded every word, and I took notes also. So, one morning I went by the teacher's room, whom I was working with: Mrs. Robin Booker. I was her aid at the time, so she gave me some papers to make copies for that morning. I walked out of the building to the copier room to run the papers that she had given me. I was tired. I had four children to see about; they knew about how I felt about during homework. It had to be right, so I always check it to make sure it was right. I told them to leave the assignment directions along with their work on the table and they always did just that!

So, I got Mrs. Robin Booker's papers that she wanted me to run off. It was raining outside. When I walked through the hallway and when I begin to run the paper off, I was feeling tired; I had been at school that night before, but I always bounce right back. I was praying to the Lord to help me and to give me the strength to continue on my journey and I told the Lord I was so tired. Oh, Lord! I told Him to have mercy on me and I thank Him what he has already done for me. I have one child in college at this time and three in the elementary school. I was just praying to the Lord I said the Lord's prayer and Psalm 23. I cried out to the Lord for help.

After I ran off all of the paper for Mrs. Robin Booker; I headed back down the hall. It had rain in the hallway, water had run down the hall. I did not see this water; I was headed back to Mrs. Robin Bookers' class to give her the class paper copies. Next, thing I knew I slipped and fall flat on my back. I caught myself with my elbow on my right side or I would have fallen on my head. All of those children were in the hallway laughing at me; they said Mrs. Chennault fall so hard. I looked down the hall. I sat there for a while trying to get up.

Oh, how this changes my life forever! A life of pain! I went to the office and reported it to the principle, Reverend Ben K. Willis. Mrs. Vanilla Clark, the secretary, wrote the report up. I went to the hospital for x-rays, and it was a long battle in the year of 1995. I had back surgery and it came through well, but that same year; one of my sons, Otis, tore his ACL in his knee from playing basketball at his high school, Washington Wilkes Comprehensive High School. I had to be at the hospital with him. My husband had to work. My son's knee was gone. I had to take him to physical therapy three times a week for six weeks. I did not want him to walk with a limp for the rest of his life. I had barely recovered after my son finished his physical therapy. I was so tired and sick. I had to see about myself at the end of 1998. I had to have another back surgery. I told the doctor I did not want another back surgery and I went home. About three months later I begin to feel numb on my right side. I prayed and I felt all right with the Lord. I filled out all of my papers and I went on with my surgery; the second one.

I thank God that my oldest son was coming home for Christmas for a break from college and he helped me in and out of the chair. He cooked all of the food and he cleaned the house. In late January, he had to go back to school, so my husband and I drove him back to the airport to catch the plane at the Hartsfield-Jackson Atlanta International Airport back to college in Illinois—Carl Sandburg Junior College. My son played college basketball. He was the best basketball player that ever came through Wilkes County. He hung on the goal one day in the gym at practice before he went to college. He tore the whole goal down and glass was everywhere, but he did not have a scratch on him. I gave Father God all of the Glory thinking Him. I always studied my Bible even as a little girl. I just learn how to read. I would read my Bible through and through. I found a very old looking Bible that has lots of pictures in it. I kept it over the years until it just vanished away.

I was laying here thinking back over my life. I often think of Paul in Philippians 3:13-14; 4:4; 6:1:

Brethren, I count not myself to have apprehended: but this one thing I do, forgetting those things which are behind, and reaching forth unto those things which are behind, and reaching forth unto those things, which are before I press toward the mark for the prize of the high calling of God in Christ Jesus. I press toward the mark for the prize of the high calling of God in Jesus Christ. Rejoice in the Lord always and again I say Rejoice. Be careful for nothing: but in everything by prayer and supplication with thanksgiving let your request be made known unto God.

We do not ever know what tomorrow will bring to us. No matter how good you think you are; we never know when we leave our bed will we get back to our bed that night. I left my bed that morning of May 19, 2017. Thirty-nine days went by before I returned to my bed again. Life is like a vapor! You are here and then you are gone tomorrow, but do not live in fear. Give your life to Christ and live as every day could be your last, because it could be, we know not the moment. When our God almighty called us home, make sure that you have your life deep-rooted in Jesus Christ. I can tell the world it is easy to die if you die in Jesus Christ. I was smiling to Heaven when Pastor Henra was saying the last words over me at the gravesite; I was laughing when Pastor Henra told me I could go to Heaven, but he said, "Mama you got to come right back!" He was using his hands; he meant that, and I was looking at my son laughing all the time. I did not say a word; I stepped out and what I saw. Oh, my God! I had no more memory of my family here on earth. I saw the rivers of gold; on each side of the brooks, the water ran down the stream. I saw mountains; they do not look like they do here. They are in a glorified form. The tree's colors are different. There is no danger in dying if you die in the Lord. And there no fear! Five minutes after you close your eye you are in eternity. You can die at any given second. The night before I picked up my granddaughter, Callie Blue, in Greene County the night before; I have no remembrance of driving on after I left the grocery store. I remember putting my granddaughter in her car seat and I locked the door in the truck. I was driving the Blue F150 Ford truck. I never drove home. Who drove us home? I know that I did not drive. I went into another dimension. An angel drove us home.

It is coming on down to the end of my stay here at Select Specialty Hospital. I remember the ride over here; it was on June 2, 2017, about 10:00 p.m. I was transferred by ambulance services. I was so sick. I never knew a human being could get that sick. I looked in the rooms as the man and the woman pushed me down the hall to my room 201. I was lonely at night. I am alive barely, but I am still breathing. I look in those other rooms as I have pushed down the hall and it frightens me. All of these people looked so old, and no one was moving in the beds. I know I was running a high temperature of 105° F. You are talking about being sick and that was me. I cried out to the Lord as I did when I first got sick. I told the Lord I am was in his hands. I told the nurse to give me some ice and he did. I wrapped the ice up in a towel and I put it around my neck to break the fever.

It was so quiet and sad looking, but I had to fight no matter how difficult the days were; when we have on the armor of Jesus Christ nothing will be so easy; he is going to always use us as He sees fit to do. I always tell my God to use me. I always talk to many people daily at the store. I always tell people about Jesus; if they want to receive or if they do not want to receive a word from God through me, it is okay. I never forced myself on anyone. I always talk to my immediate family; they always receive what I say. I always talk about Christ, but some people will never receive a word of God for you.

I do not force myself on anyone; there is always somebody who wants to hear about Jesus and your testimony. Back to the hospital, I stayed here for 18 days. I came here after I awoke from a coma. I had already been at the Doctors Hospital 14 days before coming here to Select Specialty Hospital. When I got to the Select Specialty Hospital, none of my family was there, but they came early the next morning. I was so sick; I could not even sit up or turn over still. I had joy because half of me is still in Heaven and the other half is here on earth. I knew I was going to be okay, because I woke up; I do not know how long I am going to live, but I know one thing I am going back to Heaven when that day comes. It is a smooth ride from earth to Heaven; there is no fear if you are a believer in the Lord and Savior Jesus Christ.

Have you tried to live according to the Bible? Have you put on the whole armor of Christ? Do you believe in Christ?

My mind went back to my childhood, laying here praising God. He is a healer of all kinds of diseases. He knows your heart; we must not waste time trying to fool each other. We cannot fool Father God; He knows our name one by one, and He knows how many strings of hairs are on each of our heads. He looks at your heart and He search your mind and He see your motives and your intentions. I come low and humble to the stone of Grace so the Lord will carry me through whatever I have to face in my life. I give it all to Father God. My whole life belongs to Him; all of my life has always belonged to God. I came in the knowledge of Him at eleven years old when He touched me in the plum brushes. I was eating plums off the tree near, "My Praying Ground," and I was praying while I was eating plums and Lord touched me and my whole shook and I know it was the hands of the Lord.

Thinking back to childhood, I was sitting on the rock that we stepped on when we walked into the house. We had no steps just a large rock at the front door. My mother was sitting in this old rocking chair, and she told me she only went to the 6th grade in school. My mother could read; she read all of the mail that came in the mailbox. We had to walk two miles to the mailbox every day. My father never could read; he only went to school for one year. My mother told me he could never write his name; he scribbled something, it looked a little like his name, Henry Callaway. I could read it. When my father counted, he made five lines and he crossed a line across the four at a time to make five lines. He never knew how to count out loud. He did not have a chance to learn; he had a hard childhood. He told me one day when he was a child, he would be driving a wagon with the mule if he met a white person he had to pull off to the side of the road and he dare not to look at them in the eyes. My father had a very hard life; all of those stories he told me; my heart just was in pain. I remember when I was a small child my mother use to get our Uncle Frank down the road to carry her to the store when my father was working at the sawmill at the end of the road. I pass by the road. I looked over to the sawmill and I saw my father just working and all of my uncles were over there too.

I heard my parents talking about money one time and my father told my mother, "I only made 40 dollars." That is how much he made a week. It was the early 1960s at this time; I had not started school yet. This is when I first heard about my father's salary. Forty dollars a week with ten children to feed! My mind would always drift back to these days. I remember at Christmas time my sisters and I girls got one ball, one apple, one orange, and a half Baby Ruth candy bar. My brothers got a paper cap pistol and some fruit like I did; sometimes I would get a doll. We enjoyed every Christmas. I do not think we had a Christmas tree in the early years. I do not remember any trees in the 1960s, but we did have one later on.

I just thought about June 4, 2017, while I was in Select Specialty Hospital in Augusta, Georgia.

It was my daughter's birthday and she said, "Mama, it is my birthday today!" I was too sick at this time to ever hear her, but she said it again, "Mama, it is my birthday today!" My mind just flipped from one thing to another thing.
I said very softly to her, "Happy birthday, daughter!" My voice still sounded like I am about 120 years old. She always celebrated her birthday with my daughter-in-law, First Lady Taurika, because she was born on the 3rd of June, but this year in 2017; Dr. June was by my bedside around the clock celebrating her birth with me. I was so sick; they still did not know whether I was going to make it or not, but I did I knew everything would be okay. I had to fight to get well even though I was healed when I laid in the river.

I did not sink. I laid on top of the water; I just stretched out in the river and my mother was on the other side saying, "You can't come with us yet; you got something else to do back there. You can come later! Go back!" My two aunties looked around at me; they had glorified bodies; they looked the same as how they looked when they were here on earth. I got somewhere on the other side of Heaven; I was just smiling and walking along, and I walked upon the Lord.

I know in my heart that was God; He was looking to the right side of the field. I just walked upon Him, and He turned, and He looked at me with those eyes, inside of His eyes was a whole ocean of the water. The waves were washing up on the side of His eyeballs, a whole ocean! Beautiful, blue water was in His eyes moving from side to side. I stood there looking at the Lord even before He turned His head and looked at me. It is dangerous to get so close to the Lord. I discussed this with my sons, and they all agreed; the pastor, my last child is a minister and he agreed with me. We must be careful when we tell the Lord to use us, it not only about being in the pulpit. He can use anybody to let His glory come through or to work a miracle through. I just wondered, "Why did the Lord show Himself to me?"

We must try God for ourselves not, because your mother or father say so. Trust God! We must seek God on our own; your parents can only carry you so far. No friends, no ministers, no one, but you and God! You must have that personal relationship with God. We need to get to God; it does not have anything to do with church service or who likes you or you agree with you. Keep your mind and heart towards the Lord and His word, because when you walked through that tunnel in glory you will be by yourself. Keep your eyes on God and not people, because we are all flawed; one no one is good one nobody, but the Lord is worth praising no one else! I looked at the Lord's body for a long time in Heaven. I stood there looking like I was when I was 30, I was young and pretty.

My body was slim. I had beautiful teeth, because I saw my teeth when I look in the river. I did not see a shadow. I saw my whole body just like as if I was looking in a mirror in the water. It was amazing; I can hardly stand to think back, but I think about this every day, most of the day. I just stood there looking at our Lord. Why in the world would he let me see all of this? I always think about the Lord.

My son, who is a minister, said—"Mama, you should be careful what you pray for; he told me if you ask God for more faith, for example, he will give you more trials or burdens to bear and then your faith will be increased. God doesn't just increase your faith that easily."

"I know that son," I told Him—"But I told the Lord a long time ago, I don't belong to myself. I told the Lord I am your Lord try me and see I am your Lord use me anyway you see fit, I am not my own." I told my son all of that with tears running down my face and the Spirit of the Lord was upon me.

Chapter 10

SITTING IN MERCY AND GRACE

I have seen the glory of God! More emphasis should be placed on people being saved. Hell is real! Heaven is real! I just stepped out in Heaven in seconds; it was not about a church or a minister. I saw my son at my casket before I left this world; he told me, "Mama you can go to Heaven, but you got to come back, you come back now!" Pastor Henra said I was smiling looking back at him. Pastor Henra was moving his finger. I went through the ground in seconds, and I step out in this beautiful place. I cannot describe it in words. I saw my folks, my mama.

She said, "You can't come with us yet, but one day you will return here." I wanted to get across that river so bad.

I always hunger and thirst for my God. His Spirit is always with me. I praise him all through the day, every day since I was 11 years old. I am going to praise him until I see his face again and then I will be at home, at last. I hope whoever is reading this book give your life to Christ while you have time because at any second you can be in eternal Heaven or Hell choose which one you will enter. I up to every human on this earth choose while you are still breathing.

The Grace of God will guide us, and his mercy will have carried us through. My husband is the head of our family, but the children call me, "The praying rock of the family." My sons go to their father if they want to know something, man things, but for other things, they come to me. Even when they were smaller, they did the same thing, because a man knows a man and a woman knows a woman especially when it comes to raising them.

Back to the hospital, I am still very weak but somewhat getting better every day, but I still cannot walk. I can wash myself off, but my arms and my hands are still very weak. I am getting ready in a few days to head back to the Doctors Hospital for full physical therapy; they do not have a therapy room here at the Select Specialty Hospital. The physical therapist come to your room and do therapy. I believe it is a place to take newborn baby steps until you reach the steps when you get to the steps then you can go, farther. So, I am almost to the steps. Before I got sick, I was tired of being stressed out dealing with my husband sickness and myself. I had busy issues; I was always busy. I never got any rest. I as always doing something or talking to someone about their problems. I speak to people, and I tell them about Jesus. I tell them to hold on and to hope because without hope, what do you have? A lot of people do not have hope, they are just living.

I am laying here thinking about going home, but I have a long way to go. I have come a long way, but I still have a long way to go. I cannot take care of myself; the people come in my room, and they ask me who live with me, and I tell them just my husband. They always ask me how many steps are going into my house. I do not know why they ask me that, but I am going to walk to my house, just like I see myself walking in there. I am going to do just that. One night, I was laying here look out of my window it was pouring down rain. I could see the rain sliding down on my windowpane. I had the light half dim, and I heard a coin hit the floor; it sounded like a quarter hit the floor and I was looking at the rain falling beside the window. I was thinking about my dad, and I know that he was in my room, because I smelled his chewing tobacco. I know that was Him who dropped that coin in my room. He said, "I have come to see about you, and I saw the back side of Him leaving out of my hospital room." It was a warm strange feeling in the room; he knows I was sick also.

On the day that I went back to the Doctors Hospital. It was kind of sad because I had been through a lot at this Select Specialty Hospital. I was on a journey only God could walk with me. I had to hold on because I have seen the glory of God. I stood beside the almighty God. I see Him in his beautiful gown, his saddles and his head piece were the same colors as his robe. It was the color of cloud white like cotton. It was so beautiful. I am getting happy sitting here writing this book. I go in a crying mood, and I think about the glory of

God. I can walk around and dance like David in the Bible.

It is after lunch; I am leaving. I have put my clothes on, and my daughter went out and brought me, but I still cannot walk at this time. I am critically ill, still very weak, but it about time to go back to the Doctors Hospital. I had a very good meal at lunchtime, and I told my nurses goodbye and God bless each one of you. I had so many nurses! All kinds of specialty wound doctors and every other kind of doctor, but I was improving every day. Every day I just felt my strength returning but real slowly real. I always sit on my bed, and I would cry. The nurse just looks at me and asked me, "If I was, I ok." I told her these were tears of joy. I am reading scripture turning through my Bible because it is right here beside my bed. I told my daughter to bring me my Bible as soon as I awake. I continued to read. I always study God's words.

Looking at John 9:31;10: 27-28—

Now we know that God heareth not sinners: but if any man be a   worshipper of God, and doeth his will, Him he heareth.

My sheep hear my voice, and I know them, and they follow me; And I give unto them eternal life: and they shall never perish, neither shall any man pluck them out of my hand.

I thought about Lazarus who was raised from the dead along with Job because I suffered so much, but I would not take anything for this journey. I thank God for all the pain I endured and still at this time in pain. I had a chance to go to Heaven and I got to tell the world about Heaven. It is a beautiful peaceful place. No one is in charge, but Jesus. Keep your eyes on Jesus! Serve Jesus Christ! Do not make anyone on earth your god, because God is a jealous God. He is the only one that is worth praising! People nowadays are praising just their pastor when they are flawed and need much prayer as well. This is a very serious matter! Your soul will spend eternity somewhere, Heaven or hell? You choose this day. I laid there for several days. My skin tore from my body. I had flesh sores and sickness was all in my body. I was in bad shape! Sores all over my buttocks where I laid there lifeless in the hospital bed, but I was not there I never felt a thing until I returned to my body.

I was so happy exploring Heaven. Can you imagine what it is like exploring Heaven? No, you cannot. Just wait until you go! No one can fully describe Heaven! Why would a person spent all of their lives putting all you have in this fleshly life and leave Father God out! What a very foolish mistake! Death will soon overtake each one of us, whether you live a few years or long life. Death is the final reward in this human body. There are very few people, I believe, who are on the narrow road, but that broad road you will find many travelers even the church members who confess Christ. They plant a seed, but they love their flesh so much. They are not satisfied with the Spirit of God.

I would never take a chance with my soul. I always have taken that very serious. I am not a follower of the world. My inner Spirit lives: no one can reach it, but me and the Lord. I want a lot of Jesus and if I draw close to Him, he will draw close to me. It is all about how much of Him you want. I am afraid to mistreat anyone. I never did try to do that, because whatever I add unto my neighbor will be added back to me. I read Malachi 3:18—Then shall ye return, and discern between the righteous and the wicked, between Him that serveth God and Him that serveth Him not.

Back at the Select Specialty Hospital laying here, no one is in the room. I am the only patient in the room. I can look to my right and I see the top of the trees, because I figured I am up high. I lay here thinking about lots of things. God has really blessed me; he had everything already set up, even the right EMS people came to pick me up. I got sick; I got sick so quickly in a blink of an eye. Every second counted that quick! My husband though I was joking when I said call 9-1-1, because the EMS has never picked me up before; they always came to get Him, and he looked so surprised. I told Him to call 9ll and at first, I told Him to take me to the doctor to Augusta where all of my records were. He just was standing there looking at me. I saw Callie Blue standing there at the door, but I though Hannah was there, but she was not. It happened so quickly.

I never in my life though anything like this would happen to me. I always been strong, an on the go, a super woman. I took care of my parents before they died. I took care of several of my older friends and my sick husband, but I was not seeing about myself. I exercised and tried to eat right, but sometimes I did eat too much at night, sometime especially ice cream and cookies. I was always busy taking care of my grandchildren.

My grandchildren do not live here in Washington, Georgia. I saw them on occasion, and they would come down to see me when they had a school break, but that husband of mines kept me on my feet at night and day; he gets up every morning coughing up and spitting up all morning. He stopped sleeping in the room with me, because he cannot lay down flat due to all of the mucus. He does get any sleep; he would have all of the machines going all night. He would get up all through the night taking breathing treatments, and this had been going on for years even before the children left; they are all gone now.

We had three children in college all at the same time. They are so close in age. They were all in high school at the same time. We had one at the University of Tennessee, one in Kennesaw State University and one in Georgia Southern

University. My husband got very sick in 2005; they cut his back open to do a biopsy on a piece of his lung. I did not know that at this time he had some bad stuff going on in his lungs. The doctor could not do anything about the issue. The doctor came to the waiting room and told me and the children what was going on. I told Him to just sew Him back up; the doctor could not do what they wanted to do. It has been many years since my husband's diagnosis of lung disease. By the grace of God and putting together the herds that the Holy Spirit told me to put together, he is doing fine at this time in his life. He is very busy with his hobbies around the house. He is active. One doctor told me to put Him on hospice, but that was out of the question.

My children and I will fight and pray for Him. He is doing well with his breathing; it almost 50 percent at this time. It has not been easy for me, but I always hit the floor running. I had to train my children to be productive citizens. I had to be strong to raise three wonderful boys and one daughter. They love me. I know and they know I love them, because I tell them every day. I always made it a habit in my life and their father to do the same thing; it is a must! We told our children we love them. When your children know that you love them; they will always want to please you. They will make mistakes at times, but they will never let you down to this day. I tell all of my children, my grandchildren, and my daughters-in-law. I love them! I do this every time I finish talking to them. I hug my sons and my daughter every time I see them, and their father do the same. I hug all my daughters-in-law. All the time, I tell them love them and this alone will keep the family close-knitted.

Live life so they all can see the love in you, especially the love of God. Let them feel love in your heart for God and that alone will take the next generation in a very long way. Trust God and always cry out for help! I cry out for help. I have no pride when it comes to serving the Lord. I do not want to force my testimonies on anyone, because lots of folks will never receive you, so go on! Everyone did not receive the Lord and he is the Savior of this whole world. It was hard kind of to have three children in college, but they did the hardest part. I just had to pray, and it worked! My husband and I pulled together and everything else fell right into place; they studied hard! The Lord kept them out of trouble, because I asked Him to do so! We were poor! I had to prepare for this early in their lives so they would be college material, but they were willing to do as I told them when they were a baby.

I told them that they would be somebody and that they would wear a suit to their jobs. I told my daughter you were going to be a professor. I was dreaming, but it all came to light! I trusted in the good Lord, because my husband and I were so poor! I did not want my children to be poor; they are not rich, but they all have a chance; they are all college graduates. Every one of them said that they would make it. Their father and I followed them all the way. We made sure that they had all the things in their childhood that they needed while God was placed at the focal point of each one of their lives.

My family, we prayed together, we studied the Bible together, we cried together, we danced and planted a garden together and we still do! We sang gospel songs together and we still do. We all ate at the table together and we still do. Their children will catch on to that same training that I gave my children and let it go one to the next generation. My husband and I figured if we could help our children with a good education. They will help their children with a good education. They will have morals and values for their lives.

I just cannot stand being so poor that when you go by the store, and you are hungry not have enough money to buy food. I was poor when my children were in college, but I did not buy myself anything. I went to thrift stores to get my clothes. You are talking about being happy and praising the Lord for all of my children. I brought them into this world to make a difference and to be productive citizens not to chase this world. Nothing to love and be loved in the name of Father God. One day, I was sitting on the porch thinking how in the world would my oldest son go to college; he was the best basketball player ever to come through Wilkes County. He was about 6'5 tall and strong. I have three other children at this time, Otis, June, and Pastor Henra.

So, one day I was sitting on the porch looking in this sports magazine and I came across this article. It said fill out this article on your child if you want a scholarship, so I sat there and read. I filled out everything that my son has done; I got a pen and I started writing and I look I put my glasses on my eyes to make sure I wrote everything correctly. I did not say anything to no one about this not even, his coach. They did not care whether he goes to college or not because they saw how eager me, and their father was for Him to go to college. Sometimes this makes other folk mad when they see you putting so much in your children. I was the same way about their lesson in the classroom. My children could not bring any Cs and Ds in this house, even in kindergarten. They had to make to the top of the class. I would go over their homework every day. I made sure that they learn what was required of them I just had to put that part in there because it was not easy at all; my mother told me if they do not make it would not be that you did not try. She lived up the road from me and she would see me every time I went out or come home because I has to pass my parents' house when I left out I my father never did say much; he told me one day that Pastor Henra would be a preacher. I never thought anything more about that. Pastor Henra was about three years old playing in the dirt; he would walk up his grandparents' house in the afternoon while I would be going over the other children's homework and when I went up there to get Him.

One afternoon my father told me you just watch Pastor Henra he will preach the gospel; he said you will see. I know Pastor Henra was always singing and praying he led the songs in the choir. In Elementary school, the chorus teacher played the piano. Pastor Henra would walk down the aisle just singing, oh, how he was singing that song!

I go, Lord, if I have to go by myself. I will go! If my mother does not go, if my father does not go, if my brother does not go, if my sister does not go. Lord I will go by myself! Just sent me, Lord I go!

I was so busy, until this day. Pastor Henra went one day when he first went to college in Tennessee—Carson Newman College. He got the call to preach on a hot morning. I cannot remember the month, but it was in that first year. I was on the back deck hanging out some blue jean pants, because it was too hot to turn the dryer on. The phone rang! Guess who was on the other end of the phone; it was my baby, my last child, Pastor Henra. He told me to guess, "What mama!"

I told Him, "I am not going to guess."

I had no idea what that boy was going to tell me. I asked Him was he in any trouble. He told me no. His voice was so different. I say what is it then? He told me that he had a vision with the Lord and that he should preach the Lord's word. That changed my whole life, because my mind went back to my father what he had told me about Pastor Henra preaching the gospel. He told me about the vision. I shouted and praise God! All I could say was Lord have mercy! After Pastor Henra finish his bachelor's degree and graduated and he told me that he was not finished with school. He told me that he has to go to theology school. I told Him to go as well. He graduated later from the Mercer School of Theology. That boy preached like nobody business, Lord! I wish my dad and my mother would have lived to see their grandson preach the true gospel of the Lord. He was only 18 when the Lord called Him to go in the season and out of season.

I always treated my boys as gentlemen. I treated my daughter like a princess. My children treat me with respect, because I would have them treat me and their dad with the highest respect. It was not easy raising them, but the love and joy they brought me, and their father is amazing. We are so proud to this day! We corrected our children and we punished them when they did wrong. Back to the part, when my son was in the 11th grade; he was the oldest. So, I filled out all of the information that was there in the article; they wanted to know everything that Lazarus Jr. had ever did. I looked at all of his accomplishment that he had done in school as an athlete. He was best as an athlete and that he had so many honors from the six grades up until the 11th grade. I could not put of his accomplishments on the paper, so I had to write on another sheet of paper.

Lazarus Jr. could dunk the basketball so hard in the goal; it was impressive. The crowd would just yell and scream for Him. I felt so proud; and his father and I never missed a game. I filled out all the scholarship paper and I told the truth, because all he had to do was to call the school. It said, "Send a 40 dollars fee with this scholarship" So I did! Believe me this was all the money I had at the time, but something was pulling at me so hard. I had to send this letter and 40 dollars off to Carl Sandburg, Illinois. I mailed off the letter; I did not tell a soul. I was depending on God to do the rest, because if you do not take responsibly for your own children no one else will and if you do not brag on your children when they do well no one else will. I would always tell my children how great they were when they were in school.

I told them about life, and I told them what I had experiences throughout life. I told them you are going to be somebody someday! I told them every day that you have to try to live and look respectable, because life is going to be hard for you three if you do not get the proper training. I also told them I got dreams for you four, and it will come true. We just got to push through no matter how hard it may get mentally, physically, and financially. "You all will win!" As for respect, I have told my four children not to talk while the teacher was talking in the classroom. One time, my son Otis had an accident with a science project. I had to go to the high school. I was told by Otis it was an accident. The teacher insisted that he did it on purpose. I assured that I raised all my children right and be respectful of their elders. Otis apologized and it was an accident. However, you know how some people can be when they your child will be successful or they are troublemaker, but all of my children made it through college.

I give God all of the Glory, because I was that little child standing in the crowd with two fishes and five loaves of bread. I had a wonderful set of parents, and I will always be thankful to God for letting me be born to Henry and Mamie Callaway. I thank you, Jesus. I did not have a choice. God already knows what you need, and he lets you be born in his time. He chooses your parents. God is "all-knowing and all-seeing." The letter I found in the magazine on a Sunday afternoon while I was sitting in church; I asked the Lord to help me talk to coach at the school. He said, "Lazarus Jr., you are not good enough." I knew how good my son was in basketball. He was great and everyone in the school system knew who he was. I knew this because I would always hang out around the school, because I had to see about my children.

I had to make sure that they were in the right classes, and I had to make sure that they took the right college classes. I had to do all of this from start to finish. I had to go to PTA meetings at every school at one time and I made sure that I spoke to every one of my children's teachers before I left that school. They had to see my face and they had to know what I stood for. I never missed a PTA meeting. I could not let my children live in this world uneducated and broke. My parents told me what they knew, and I could use it but at that time when my children came along, their father and I had to compare a lot of that stuff. I helped my friends with light housework sometimes, but I did not want my daughter to do any housework for anyone or my sons in a factory job. It was all right for us, me, and my husband, but I wanted them to be better, do better and do more. I saw my mother do that. I told them every day that they had to do more.

We got a plan to follow out with the Lord's leading and he will help us. Just wait and see! Back to the letter, I sent it off on Monday morning. I got a stamp from my mother on my way to the mailbox. I was in a hurry, because the mailman came early sometimes. I stopped at my mama's porch. I saw her in the kitchen window washing dishes and I called to ask her how she was doing today, she said, "Fine." I told her that I needed a stamp because she kept stamps, and she said she would bring me one in a minute. She brought me one stamp to the porch, and I walked as fast as I could to the mailbox. My mailbox was next to my parents' mailbox. I got the stamp and put it on the letter very carefully to make sure it stuck. I put it in tight and I put the letter in the mailbox. I said, "Lord, you know me! Please let this be a start! Lord, you know my heart. Please, Lord you know my intentions!" I put it in the mailbox, and I walked back home thinking about the letter.

I had so many other things to attend to. I just went on about my business. I had two other young, black sons and a daughter to attend to; about two weeks later I was sitting there, and I was not thinking about the letter that I had sent off. I was so busy doing work around the house. Early one morning the house phone rung. It was the old-time phone, a rotary phone. It rung like a horse driving on the church ground for a funeral.

I wondered who in the world was on the other end of the phone calling me. It could have been anyone, but who was this caller? I picked up the phone and a voice said, "Hello, is this Mrs. Willie Agnes Chennault?

I said, "Yes!"

He asked, "Did you send some information in on your son?"

I said, "Yes, sir, I did!"

He said, "Him and his staff was very impressed!" I was shaking, but I did not act so country like I am, but I listened to everything he had to say while almost bursting open like a sweet watermelon in the hot summertime. I was joyful, because

I knew he had good news. I thought about this laying here in my hospital bed especially when my son came to see me in the hospital. I am still listening to this man on the phone; two weeks had passed, this call came from Carl Sandburg, Illinois and he was the basketball coach. He told me on the phone that they would be proud to give my son a basketball scholarship and would you all be willing to let Him come up here. I had to sit down and catch my breath. I said, "Could you repeated that sir?" He said it again. He said that they would be willing to give Him a scholarship. He said this was a two-year school, but when he finishes here, we promise we would get Him into a university so he will be able to finish his four-year college degree.

I told everyone about this over dinner that same evening. He was coming up to his last year of high school and I had to get on the ball. So, when were all sitting down at the dinner table this same afternoon, I danced around the house praying and cooking dinner; this was in the early 1990s. I cooked a good meal and I waited for everyone to take a bath and come to the dinner table? My husband knew something was up, but I did not tell Him a thing. We all sat down to the table. Everyone filled their plates up with food. I cooked their favorite food that day, turnip greens with rutabagas bottoms. I also cooked squash, fresh boil corn, and a big meatloaf. For dessert, I made a real apple pie; my apple pie tasted just like my mother's did. I put the apples in a crust after I piled them; I added sugar, cinnamon and butter and a little flour. It was so delicious. We sat looking at each other; they knew something was up, because I was too happy. After we all got our plates, we prayed, and I prayed. I told the Lord. I thank you, Lord for what he has already done for me ever since I was a little girl walking in the mud. I thanked Him for my children and my husband. I thanked Him for this day and the wonderful phone call that I had receive knowing that no one knew, but me and the good Lord. I thanked the Lord for answering the letter I sent off a few weeks ago. I thanked Him for the knowledge of my mind. I thanked Him from day to day and I thanked Him for this wonderful meal we were about to receive. We said, "Amen!"

They were all looking at me, my four children and their father trying to figure out what was going on with me. So, they began to eat, they were so hungry. I asked them, "did they each lunch today at school?"

They all said, "Yes!" No one knows about the letter that I sent off, but the Lord Jesus and my mother; she did not know anything about what was in the letter, but she gave me the stamp for the letter. I said, "Guess what man called from Illinois today?"

My husband said, "What man?" The children just stop eating

looking at me with their mouth full of food. I told them my son had no idea what I was talking about. I told them what Coach Shearer had told me. My husband was just amazed, and all the children were also. I said Lazarus Jr., "Boy, you got a free ride to college! All need to do is pray, shoot that basketball in the goal, study and keep your eyes open!" He was so happy!

I told my mother the next day about it and she said, "You know you are not going to let Him go that far!

I said mama, "This is a blessing from the Lord!" We do not even have gas money to put in the car to get to the college. How in the world will we send a child to college? "Somehow mama every one of them will finish, you watch and see."

I walked back down the hill to my house thinking about how far the college was away from here, but I do not want my children to live from hand to mouth. They will not survive as I did. It is a whole new day. Lazarus Jr went on to college; he was in the newspaper every week for two years playing ball all over the United States. I remembered I told the coach who was his basketball coach at the high school, about it a week later. I told Him what I had done, and he told me with an ugly voice, "Look at me!" As if I had done something wrong. I told him that I got my son a scholarship for college. He looked at me as if I was crazy, so later on that last year of high school the scholarship came in the mail, and I took it over to the high school. We called the Washington News Reporter; my husband

and I along with the principle took a picture with Lazarus Jr. signing that scholarship. That is how my first son went to college; he played all over the world; he played for Mexico Professional Basketball team and the Harlem Globe Trotters. He is a great coach, and he is in the Hall of Fame in Washington, Georgia. I never paid one dime for him to go to college. He graduates from Western Carolina University in 1998.   God   will   do   it.

Chapter 11

SEEING HIS FACE

I am just sitting here in this chair thinking about a lot of things, ready to leave this hospital. This is day I am leaving this hospital. It has been a long journey, but as I was thinking of my vacation to Heaven and how my body was so light over there. In Heaven, there is no flesh is over. It is a majestic place where my mother and two aunties are; there is nothing on earth that I can compare it to. My two aunties were on the hillside sitting while my mother was standing at the river telling me to go back and that I could not stay there. There was something else for me to do. I was just smiling at her and my aunties who were looking at me. When I looked to my right, I saw the streets of gold leading to all of those houses on my right.

I stood there and I got transported to the other side of the hillside and who did I see? I saw all the races of people gathering up food. It was wheat. I saw tied bundles. I saw Jesus! I know that was Him that I walked upon. Your body is light over there, really light. I looked at Jesus' feet. He wore about a 10 ½ size shoe. He has long leg bones, from his knees to his feet; it was amazing! His sandals were made of old leather, but they were in good condition. He turned his head and looked at me. I am always thinking about this man, this Heavenly being. I saw Jesus. Why did He reveal Himself to me? Why?

There was something about His feet; I kept on looking at His feet and His sandals. I looked and I looked! While I was looking at Jesus, He was looking towards the right side of the rock, but there was something about his feet—there was a nail imprint on the top of His feet where His sandal straps went across His foot. These had to be the imprints from His hanging on the cross! I walked upon Jesus. He looked at me. I wish I could explain Him looking at me, but I cannot! Oh, His eyes, His belt around His waist, His robe! I am getting happy just thinking about this! His nose was pointed and His beautiful cheekbones in His face. Why me, Lord? Why did you show this to me? I cannot explain. I am sitting here all of the time thinking about this.

It is almost time for me to go back to the Doctors Hospital. I have been in the hospital for about 31 days so far; I have not had a shower yet. I cannot stand up, but for a few seconds. I just do sponge baths. I have not washed my hair yet. My daughter got me some kind of bonnet to put on my head. My hair feels like twigs. It is so hard and dry, but I am alive. I am living and getting better every day. There are no words to explain my suffering, but I look to Job, Joseph, and Jesus Christ. I place myself with these three people. Remember you do not have to do any sin to suffer. I am suffering, because I always told my God to use me for His glory so that someone my cry out of their sins and come to know Jesus Christ as their Savior.

We must be very careful what we pray for and what we ask Father God. He is always listening to every prayer; he never sleeps or slumbers. He never takes a nap. His eyes are always on each one of us at the same time, because he is all-knowing and all-seeing. It is very important what we think about and how we act on what we think about Father God look at the heart we can talk all we want to just. check out the person's action. We must also watch our motives and the way we judge others the same way that you judge another it will somehow creep; back to you whether it is good or bad it will return. I am sitting up in this chair; I cannot give up now I come too far. I must fight on. I still have a way to go, because I cannot walk at this point a time. I am listening to that old song my husband sings all the time by the Suwannee Quintet sing "I have had my share of Up and Downs." I know someday it will be over because I am going back home and get my gown. My kid always thought of me as a superwoman mother. I have never really been sick, so many nights I did not get any sleep. I was up all night with my husband now I am so sick. He is trying to wait on me; he is still sick Himself, but he is trying. He is waiting on me looking at me strange, very strange. I sound like a 100-year-old woman talking. I always study the Bible with

Shepherd Chapel on the television for over 40 years and I have learned a lot about Father God.

I study my Bible every day. We must stay prayed up because any given second could be your last. It was time for my husband to pay bills and he was lost. My husband had to call my daughter to come home for a while; she had to leave me and go help her dad pay bills, because he never did anything like that; he was in a mess. I paid some of them through the computer. He did not ever learn the password to the computer; he was in a mess. He brought some of the letters to the hospital knowing I could not even hold a letter in my hands, because I shook like I was 100 years old and I looked it too, but I am still alive.

Every morning I would watch Bishop T.D Jakes and Joyce Meyers on television; this was every day while I was cleaning up the house. I turn my computer on the old-time gospel music channel to Dr. C. J Johnson. I listened to Him a while my husband would sing right along with Him and then I would join in, and we had church every morning and that was every day. I prayed for my enemies, my neighbors, my family members, and my friends. I do not have too many close friends. My best friends both died—Ms. Betty Fanning and Mrs. Annie Josephine Gartrell. My closest friends are my immediate family members—my children and their wives. I am a person who knows people, but I do not hang with the crowds. My church family and I hang out; I love them. I have an entire world that I live in; I do not let many people enter in it.

I went back to my childhood; it was peaceful in my mind in the early 1960s. I remember when it had rained half of a day and the drum at the end of the porch was running over with water. It was so hot, and I went around the house and I got this old ten tubs. I pulled it from behind the house and I filled it full of rainwater. I got in there I found me a dress that the white folk up the road had given us, so I took me a good long bath sitting there in the tubs. I did not have any soap. The only soap I had was a small piece of soap that my mother had made. I bathe and I bathe; I had a piece of flour sack for a towel and scrubbed my body good. Oh, how it rained! We always catch water in the drums to bath in, but we did not drink it unless we dipped it in a dishpan. I would just sit there chilling and washing my hair and enjoying life. I was about 6 years old, but I put on my dress after my bath and I had no underclothes to put on, so I did not worry about it. I just put my dress on that my mother got from white folks up the road. I was so happy to get that dress. It was all about survival at this time for food.

So that afternoon my brother and I walked over to our neighbor's house, Beasley, and Lila Booker's house, and all of the sisters were sitting on the porch. It was about four of them. We were playing hopscotch and my dress flew up and they saw my bottom. They laughed at me, and I felt so bad. I went and sat on the porch with them. I told my mother about what had happened and that weekend she went to town, and she brought me some underwear and I was so happy. All of these years, I have not forgotten, but it is all good because everything I went through in my childhood made me the woman that I am today. I am strong, and I stay in prayer because I met Jesus Christ in the plum brushes. I was eating plums. I ate plums because I was so hungry. My mother was at work. She always cooks when she came home. She made biscuits when there was not anything else in the kitchen to eat. We ate sugary biscuits, and they were good if we were lucky. I do not believe in luck; I do not like the word, but I am using it now. We would get a piece of fatback meat and that was a steak it those days. I am eating my last meal here at the Select Specialty Hospital and it was good. I always force myself to eat most of the time they always gave me too much.

I remember the days it was so cold; it was very cold back in the late 1960s. I was on my way to school; I lay here thinking back some 54 years ago and I had a pair of shoes that my mother brought from a tag sell. The shoes only lasted about to days, because I was running trying to catch the bus. Can anyone imagine how hard it was to get ready to go to school with nine siblings and ten including me living in four rooms and no running water or anything? It was hard for me to find clothes every day to wear. My shoes busted open, because I stepped on the shoestring, and I tore the whole top off of my shoe. I had to go back home, and I sat there by the heater all day. I cried, because I did not want to miss school. My mother was on her way to work. I passed her on the way to the white folk's house and she looked at my shoes and she said just go home. She would be back about 4 p.m. that evening. She told me that she did not have money to buy me any new shoes. So, I cried, and I cried, because I did not want to miss school.

I love to learn. I sat there three days without any shoes to wear to school so that Saturday we went uptown to a stores call Blackmon, and I saw a pair of shoes that I wanted, but my father would not buy me those. So, I cried again, but it did not do any good because when my father spoke it was it! He never would change his mind for nothing; I mean for nothing. So, we went to the five cent and dime store for a pair for 1.98 cents. I got those. I missed three days of school for these shoes, but I was very happy to get back to school. My mother was a good woman. She did the best that she knew how to do; we were always cleaning. She saw to that! I mean we cleaned our shoes, and our shoestrings were clean; she would take our strings out of our shoes, and she would wash them in the wash pan and then she would hang them on the porch.

I did not know anything about life. I prayed all of the time beginning in the summer of 1968, but my mother made us say our prayers every night. She was a praying woman and she believed in prayer; she was extraordinarily strong. I laid here in this hospital thinking back over my childhood. I found peace there and in Heaven on my vacation. I was so glad to get back to school. I just looked around the classroom and I sat in the front. I love to sit in the front of the classroom. I never like to sit in the back, because the children who sit in the back did not want to learn and I wanted to learn all that I could.

I got to stop here, and I thank God for my children. They have been by my side. I do not know anything about what happened while I was in a coma. I will let them tell you what happened in the Doctors Hospital because I was not in this world. I went to Heaven, and I went to another dimension. I know it was Heaven, because I was with my mother. She is happy there with my two aunties, Lue and Nee, I recognized them. The other people in the field were of all races. I stood there and I looked at them for a while, gathering wheat. The people were tying it up in bundles. I saw the oxen just standing there hooked to the wood wagon. They looked at me. They were so calm. The women in the field reminded me of Ruth and Naomi. They had beautiful scarfs tied about their heads. All races were out there.

The men had on Bible clothes and the women did too, but my mother and my aunties had on regular clothes. I went to another part of Heaven. When I saw this, I recognized my mother and the clothes that she wore. My Aunt Lue had on a black hat, but my Aunt Nee had her hair plaited and my mother had an Afro; her hair was black and pretty. She told me to go back you got something to do and they need you over there. She said, "You cannot come yet." I was smiling trying to get to her on the other side of the river. I was just smiling, and she was saying in a strong voice—"You cannot stay! You will come back to this place. You got to go back for now!" I dotted to this other place where I saw all of those people just gathering wheat. It was brown grass that had seeds at the top of the bundle.

I saw my mother one more time before I left Heaven. She had a stripped red and blue shirt sleeve shirt and khaki pants that came to her knees that she wore when I was in high school. I was so happy, but when I left my gravesite, it looked like Thankful Baptist Church cemetery on top of the hillside where my mother-in-law and father-in-law is buried. I only saw Pastor Henra, my son, who is a minister. He was the only one that I saw before I went through the ground and that was the best ride I ever took. I went through the ground before I left Pastor Henra. He told me that I had to come back after I left. He told me I was not dead yet. I looked back and Pastor Henra was using his hands tell me to come back and I looked at Pastor Henra and I smiled, and I went through the ground. It was dirt on both sides of me. I was smiling. I was so happy, and, in a few seconds, I stepped out in Heaven. There was mother and my aunties sitting under the tree, looking at all of these children play. My mother was standing at the river; I was on one side, and she was on the other side. She told me that I could not come yet, and I had to go back. Heaven is real! I cannot explain how beautiful it; It is unexplainable to the human eyes.

I am still sitting here in the recliner on my last day at the Select Specialty hospital, thinking back over my life. I was thinking about the tough times that I had growing up, but one thing about my childhood we grew stronger and stronger because we never had junk food. What food we ate was natural food, everyone ate that way. That is why food was so good back in the days. We never had a bathroom or toilet paper. I never had toilet paper until I got in high school and my husband said he never saw toilet paper until his high school days. We used newspapers that we got from the white folks up the road. When we ran out of newspapers, we use leaves from the trees. We would use the bathroom in the woods. We did not have any outdoor toilets until I got in high school. It was a tall, little shack with two holes built in it. It was filthy. I never went in there. I went in the woods in back of my house to use the bathroom. If you look down in those holes in the outhouse through the door then you would throw up from seeing all of those bugs; it was a shame, but we made it grow up was hard, but peaceful and happy and joyful. Most importantly, it made me the women I am today—a strong women that never gave up on life.

I never would think that through the grace of God, I would still be sitting here drafting my book. I got to tell the world my story. The sky over there looks very different from here; it is much closer to you than it seems and so much brighter, nothing in Heaven is dark. Everything is bright, the grass, the trees are glowing. I did see a moon or sun; it was just bright there.

I am still sitting here waiting to be transferred back to the Doctors Hospital. I still cannot walk. I am still very weak, but I have made great improvements. Before I left the Doctors Hospital, the first time coming over here to Select Specialty Hospital they had to put some large shoes on my feet because my feet would just flop over. I had no control of my feet. I was a sick woman. I never knew a person could get that sick, never in a thousand years. God is my healer; he knows me. I met Him or he met me before I entered my mother's womb. He already knew about this day and this day I had to meet this test.

I am remembering back over my childhood because no matter what I was going through I did not know any better. I know all the folks lived like I did; no one that I knew had a bathroom, but the white folks up the road. I did not feel bad at all because everybody else lived the way I was living. We had no shoes; the white folks gave us shoes and we were so glad to get them. One day in the third grade my shoes had a big hole in them before I left home. I cut a piece of cardboard paper and I put a piece in each shoe so my foot would not hit the ground.

I was sitting in the middle of the classroom, and I propped my feet up and the cardboard somehow came out and the children picked at me all day long. We had not integrated at this time, everyone was black. Even the teachers looked at me as if she wanted to laugh. It was so pitiful; I had to fight to find some clothes to wear to school. I had to fight with my inner strength just to grow up. So, I told my mother what has happened, and she got my shoes and she fixed them with some tape. She doubled the cardboard in each shoe, and she said it would last until Saturday and she would try to get me a pair of shoes, but by that week on a Saturday the mailman brought a box of clothes from my aunt in Washington D.C.

My dad's sister-in-law had sent us a box and I got a new pair of shoes. They were new to me. My aunt had 10 children also just like my mother had 10 children. On that Monday morning, I was walking down the hall smiling. I got some shoes, and I am ready to learn; it was the hardest thing for me. Laying and laughing to myself wondering how in the world did I get here. One thing about it plenty of days that I went to school I did not have any breakfast or dinner at Noon. I was too hungry to learn, but I know I had to because I did not want those city children to out learn me so I went some days I would carry a greasy sack to school, it had a biscuit and some cow tripe inside. All of the other children had a beautiful bologna sandwich wrapped in beautiful foil. My sack was so greasy. I had to hide and eat it. When I bit my sandwich one day and some of the other children were looking when I bit it. The cow trip bounced back to the sack like rubber, and they laughed at me all day. I told my mother when I got home. She did not say anything so from then on, I just suffered. Some days the other children would give me a piece of their sandwich and some days they would not.

Lunch in the cafeteria was very cheap about 20 cents, but I did not have that. So later on, in the years free lunch came out and I was so glad; I was so hungry. It is hard to go to bed hungry and get up hungry and go to school hungry. But it was all good I am sitting here drafting my book and I got a way to go, but I will finish soon. I hope my daughter called me today. A country woman like me comes from the little old country town like Wilkes County, but I would not want to live anywhere else in the world. Wilkes county is a peaceful place, very country. Everybody knows everybody's business, but I love it here.

My husband and I have the same kind of childhood that is the reason we hooked up so early. I do not know, but my daughter called me today and I just went to hollering loud, praising God, thanking Him for being God of this universe and praising his Holy name for bringing me this far in my life. I am giving Him all the glory for giving me a mind to even think about Him. He was born in a stable with all of those animals so a person like me could have a chance at life. He had already laid the way when he was beaten up cavalry hill. I just show praise in telling my God, my glory, my way maker, my healer, my breathe, my eyesight, and my inner soul and my burden barrel. I thank Him for letting me see Heaven.

Lord, have mercy! I am praying for all of those people in this world who are on the outside of safety. Lord, please give them the mind to come in before it is too late. Just like Noah when he was building the Ark, they walked by Noah each day laughing and making fun of Him all the time, Noah was following your commands, Father God. When it started to rain it was too late when Father God locked those windows and doors. Please Father God have mercy on your people! Right is called wrong and wrong is called right. My daughter sent me a text of the classes that she was going to be teaching at Yale University, is not God good! A person like me has a daughter, a Doctor of Education. She is going to be teaching at Yale this summer. Sitting here typing this book, I laugh sometimes. I cry sometimes and I stop and dance in the Holy Spirit sometimes. While I was typing this book I have to stop, and I sing old songs like I know. "I got religion! Yes, yes! The world cannot do me any harm!" I say "Amazing grace, how sweet the sound. God saved a wretch like me." I would say "Jesus keep me near the cross and again."

I am singing "Going to Hide Behind the Mountain." I always pray all through the day and that has been all of my life every day because there might come a time in each of our lives that we can't pray it happens to me when I first got sick, I said to the "Lord, I am in your hands fading away fast. Lord, I am in thy hands, Lord, I have served you, Father God." With tears running down my face then I left this world. The EMS said I was talking in the EMS. I do not remember any of that. I remember them asking me what hospital I want to go to, and I said, "University Hospital," but God had another plan for me. It was a stop at the Doctors Hospital where the Lord had my team ready for me. I am still sitting in the recliner at the Select Specialty Hospital, feeling free and at peace.

I cannot walk, but I have joy and I am happy. I got a long way to go but I will make sitting here be about Heaven. I know that was Jesus. I saw sitting on that rock. I saw his feet. They look just like some of the pictures that I had seen Him in. I know in my heart that was Jesus Christ. I always think about Him every day; I think about Him all day long. I always had the Lord Jesus on my mind even when I was a little girl walking in the wood. I heard his voice one day; he was talking to me above the trees. I know it was Jesus because a Spirit came upon me. I am still sitting here in the recliner chair just thinking about the high fever I had when I got over here the first night here at Select Specialty Hospital. My fever was 105°F, and I asked the nurse for some ice in a towel, and I put it around my head. I was so sick, sicker than sick. I never knew a human being could get this sick. This was a test Jesus gave me. I had nothing to do with it was all Jesus. He set all of this up so the world could see all of my doctors and my family could see God working firsthand and he did a great miracle. I am a nobody to the world, because I am not popular. I do not go along with the crowd. I am a pure country woman, living in a small town of 4000 people, born, and raised here in Wilkes County.

Jesus Christ has always been my choice, whoever calls on Him will be saved, keep calling and looking for Him every day and he will not leave you that the way. I do thirst and hunger for my Lord Jesus Christ. He is my peace. I am like the prophet Paul. I am a slave for Christ. It will not take long after a person dies, in a few minutes we are on the other side of Heaven or Hell. I am so glad I stepped out in Heaven; I did not see anything but bright lights. I did not see anything dark only light and brightness. It was so beautiful. I cannot describe it in any words.

Heaven has a whole different time. There is no time over there; you are just there. I saw the people in the Bible days. I walked among them, and they looked at me and I looked at them. I looked at their clothes and their shoes I saw different races of people. I will never forget this as long as I live, I do not fear anything. I am going to pray on until I get back there. There is nothing to fear if you die in the Lord, nothing is dangerous over there. I believed if I had stepped out in Hell; I would have never come back. I feel so sorry for anyone to live their life without Jesus Christ as their Lord and Savior. You will spend more time in heaven than here on earth. One day is a thousand years and a thousand years being as one day.

When we all die, then what? Death? You should make it count while you live, give your all to God by loving one another and serving the almighty God while treating each other as you want to be treated. Praise God every day all through the day! Praise Him! If you praise Him there will not be time to judge other people. I am sitting here thinking about a lot of things. I am still very weak. None of my family are here at this time; they will meet me on tomorrow June 21, 2017. I had to pray. We all want an easy way to Jesus; we do not want any trouble or pain. I just sitting here my last day at Select Specialty Hospital. Everyone is so nice and kind to me, full of compassion, some more than others. One nurse told me that I had no business over here, but she did not explain what she meant about that statement. I did not ask because most of the patients over here do not walk, they just lay still, but who knows what she meant I guess it was because I was moving my body better than the rest of the other patients.

I was alert and ready to get out of the hospital, even though I got a long way to go because I cannot walk, I can barely stand up. I cannot go to the bathroom on my own. So, I just got to continue. I will not give up because I got to get home to see about my husband and my family. All of my children are grown and doing very well. I am just sitting here thanking the good Lord; at least my lips and my mouth is healing. My lips are swollen up so big. All of the skin was wiped off of them. The skin turned inside out, and my gums are sore, and my mouth is sore. Healing wash is placed in my mouth daily, which is given three times a day and then I swallow. I cannot feel sad anymore, because I went to Heaven. I saw my folks and they were happily enjoying themselves. I could start because the Lord Jesus did not want me to stay yet so I had to come back I will know why after a while. I learn to put my socks on using a sock slider. I was good at putting my socks on, but it took a lot of effort. I remind myself of Psalm 119:71— "It was good for me to be afflicted so that I might learn your decrees."

On June 20, 2017—I am scheduled for discharge back to the Doctors Hospital. I am still very weak. I look like a sick cow, but I am alive. The doctors came into my room the day before and ask me, which place I want to go to for therapy. I

334

told her, "I will go back to the Doctors Hospital." On the 6th floor, that is where I am going to learn to walk, learn to take a shower again and learn to put my clothes on again. I am in a small child's state at this time, but I am going to make it back! God did not bring me this far to leave me now. No, he did not! I am sitting here rejoicing in the Lord telling Him what he has already done for me over the years. and I thank Him for hearing my prayers over my lifetime and for blocking danger that was heading towards me, but he blocked so much. Danger as always head towards us, but God stops it and I thank Him for that, seen and unseen danger. I sat up for my bath this morning washing off out of a pan, but I am very weak, but I am alive, I got my right mind. I am coming along. My rehabilitation potential was good. I always keep the Lord on my mind.

I go over scriptures in my mind, I always tell the Lord what he had done in the Bible. I told the Lord to just speak the word; he did not have to come to this hospital, and I will be done soon. Every day I got stronger and stronger. I could just feel my strength coming back, because when I laid in the river, I was already healed. I did not sink like when Peter walked on the water, and I laid on top of the water and I did not sink. I am not the kind of person to live in fear; I gave it to Father God, and I keep on praying, waiting, and watching for my answer to any prayer.

I pray and Father God always answers. I educated all four of my children with good education because I was very poor, and my husband was poor. We both were very poor, but I could not let my children be poor, because the next generation would be poor. That is why I prayed, and I worked hard. I never had time for much socialization in my life. I had to make sure that my children had the right morals and values to make it in life. I had to talk and pray and train up my children in the Lord.

I put it all in God's hands and I look for what I ask Him for. Nothing comes on flowers bed of eve, but I had to make it happen with the Lord leading me along, because I cannot even blink my eyes if he did not say. So, I thank Father God all through the day, and night. That was all of my life, I sat in the woods, and I prayed all during my childhood and my husband told me how he stayed in the woods, and he prayed too. I never slept much in the hospital; I was too sick to go to sleep, cup of pills after pills. IVs after IVs! Lord, have mercy on me, but I am yours Lord use me any way you want me too. I am not my own Lord, try me and see. I always want to please Father God. You cannot please the world and Father God at the same time, but with faith you can treat everybody right.

My June 20, 2017, progress notes and consultation:

Still, critical ill myopathy, Pneumonia and sepsis-complete wean off oxygen as able wound care buttock and sacrum pressure wounds, for now, need for inpatient rehab: based on all the information noted herein, the patient is a candidate for inpatient rehabilitation under the direction of rehab physicians. It was felt that the care could not be supplied in a less intense setting. Assessment: 61-year-old female who was admitted to Doctors Hospital on 5/19/2017 respiratory arrest (intubated in rout) she was found to have pneumonia, sepsis, and cardiogenic shock. Her cause was complicated by rhabdom resulting in AKI requiring CRRT (transitioned to HD, completed), she was discharged to LTAC for IV abx and aggressive pulmonary toilet. Her course there was completed by anemia requiring transfusion, DIC in setting of AKI, her renal function improved, and HD was completed on 6/13. She was continued on O2 via NC (new, was not on before). Abx was completed on 6/18. She improved clinically but continued to have impairments w/ADL's mobility 2/2 deconditioning from rhabdomyolysis and critical illness myopathy. She was admitted to the Doctors Hospital Rehabilitation Unit to increase her functional independence before home-going.

At this time, I have been in the hospital one month and one day, but I still got a long way to go, because I cannot walk or stand. I only can stand up for a few seconds. I am very weak at this time. I am still sitting here in the recliner waiting to be transferred back over to the Doctors Hospital and my husband and my granddaughter, Hannah, will be over this afternoon. It is around noon. I am alone. My children at this time have gone back to work and my daughter had to go to five states for teaching at different colleges. She has done a good job looking after me. I know she is tired, but she got to make a living for herself, because she is not married. She calls me seems like every hour when she gets a break. She is tired; she needs a break. She has been through a lot. I am just like a newborn baby. I would say worst because the work so far has been a lot.

How can human being go through all of this? I am still depending on the Lord and Jesus Christ through faith, and it is a gift that the Lord has given all of us, if we want it! He has no respect of persons; he loves us all every one of us; he made all of us every race of people belongs to the Lord.

I may not talk like anybody in my book, but I tell you one thing, I have a supernatural healing from Father God. He has everything in place for me here on earth and in Heaven. He showed me a lot. I even have seen Jesus Christ; I know it was Him, I looked at his body. I looked at his feet. I cannot explain it. I have told my children and many other folks those who want to listen about Jesus Christ. During my childhood, no one missed me at home because I was kind of the middle child and the older children and the baby children got most of the attention, so I felt somewhat alone and sad. I know deep down in my heart, my parents loved me, but they never told us. No one used that word love, but we felt it, but our parents did not say it to us; it was ten of us. I always prayed and I asked Lord to help us; I asked Him to take care of us so many folks were in a four-room house and one time we had a three-room house with ten children. My mother has five girls and five boys; things got a little better when some of the older children left home.

I just sat in the woods praying hoping for a better day, all I knew was there and then I never knew much, only what I heard my parents talking about. I remember looking at the television in 1968. My second brother dropped out of school, and he went to the job corps and when he came back, he brought us a television. One day I remember I was looking at the television and they were talking about Dr. Martin Luther King Jr. marching.

I remember my mother would always fry two skillets of fried corn every morning in summer and two long pans of biscuits. It took a lot of food for 12 people in the house I never got enough food don't seem like I got a lot to think about the only place I was going to go was back to Heaven, to my childhood and to the scripture for comfort because their three-place brings me comfort mediating on Father God words for a healing and getting strong enough to go home. Medication after medication, vitamins lots of vitamins I take in the hospital. All of my body functions and my blood was all messed up.

Father God is a healer, he knows who loves Him. I have nothing to brag on, but I know the God that I serve can heal me and he will, he already has; when I laid in the river in Heaven I was healed. I looked at the strings that were tied around the bundles of barely. The strings were dark brown. I stood there and I looked at the bundles tied in the field. Those people in the field it looked like Ruth and Boaz who was in the Bible days. I looked at the cows' eye and they had a glow. Everyone has his glow in Heaven. I cannot explain my mother and my aunties. They have this glow just like peace and the glory that passes all understanding. I was in that field; they looked at me as I walked by; I was smiling and happy. You are talking about being happy. I never felt this kind of happiness before. I did not have any remembrance of this world. Heaven was so good. I had no remembrance of this world. I hope everyone who is reading my book get a chance step out in Heaven.

Oh, God! I did not know I was sick. I was not sick in Heaven. I cannot explain it I can hardly describe it; everything was bright and shinning, I have to keep on talking about it because I wondered why the Lord chose me to go on a vacation to Heaven? The road was so rough! I am sitting here one year later writing this book. I have always had that hunger for God, because when I was a child sitting in the woods, he always listened to me. I was a very poor girl, kind of tough on me, but all of my neighbors were the same way. The white folks up the road had everything they wanted, and it looked like they had food, because they had a lot of black cows. The black folks where I lived never had any cows. I call it a neighborhood, but we lived in the deep country.

I am still sitting in the recliner waiting to go back to the Doctors Hospital. My mind takes me back walking the long country dirt road. Sometimes I would cut through the woods to get home, because it was so late sometimes, I went over my aunties house about 3 miles away. At first dark, I made it home walking through the woods at the age of 9 years old. I never saw anyone in the woods, just a creek near the highway and I would run home. I took the woods so I could run all the way. I never saw a snake or got my feet stuck in the sticky briar. The Lord always took care of me. It haven't been easy, but I have learned to hang in there no matter what situation I find myself in; I have to lean on Father God, it is best to learn of Father God in your youth so he will grow in you and you in Him because he knows each one of us by our name and he knows how many strings of hair is on our head.

I always talk to Jesus just like He is sitting right beside me and that has been all of my life. I do not call on Him when trouble comes; I call on Him all through every day of my life. I got sick so quickly. I did not have time to go into no long prayer. I was fading away fast. I mean fast every second counted. I am thinking about that day, and I am sitting here writing my book. I want to tell the whole world to keep your life in order to pray all through the day every day; do not even wait until night. Jesus Christ always went away to pray alone early in the morning; if Jesus had to pray, we should know that we have to pray too. Pray for someone besides yourself too.

I am sitting here praying for different people who are coming across my mind. This young man comes to clean my room and he is telling me how many jobs he has; all the while this lady that stands outside of my door with a cleaning cart. She is always standing there every day and she looks at me all of the time as I pray for her. She always wore green. She came in to see me today and we exchange names and she told me that folks laugh at her, because she got so many jobs. I said to her, "Do you know the Lord in the free parts of your sins? I asked the young man the same question.
He said, "No! I don't know Jesus!"

The lady in green that stood at my door all of the time, she said, "Yes!" and I told her do not give up; keep on working, she was a nice lady. The young man was young too. I told Him to pray to Jesus and read your Bible and ask Him to show Himself in your heart. I told Him you are young; you can take a class here and then one day as time go by; you will be able to get a better job. I told Him you just try. I was so sick. I could not talk long, but both of them got the message. I told them that I had been to Heaven. Oh, look at their eyes and I stopped and prayed for the both of them. I will never forget their faces. They were both janitors; there at the hospital. Never wait until tomorrow, because tomorrow might be too late. I would not want to die and miss Heaven; all of that beautiful glory even in the animals there is glory. Everything is bright, beautiful colors; the colors are much brighter than here on earth.

Oh, Lord! I was just thinking about Job how he has to pray for his three friends. We must all do the same for our friends when they try to put some blame on you, and you cannot explain just to pray for them. All of the people we meet on a daily basis; I pray for them on the way back home or I think about them; before I go to sleep family members, friends, enemies, or neighbor; whoever I meet at the store. A lot of time; I have a brief conversation with people. I always talk about the Lord. You cannot bring up the Lord's name with a lot of people, because the devil always run when they hear the name. They can go to church every Sunday, but if you bring up the name of Jesus Christ; it shows you, their interest.

I am thinking about a lot of things sitting here in the recliner. I have been through a lot since I awoke from the coma. I have not had any visitors. I love encouraging myself. My children are tired, and my husband is exhausted. He is sick Himself when he comes to see me, he has to bring his breathing machine; he always goes down the hall to the waiting room to take his treatments, my granddaughter, Hannah, is always by his side because she is out of school for the summer. My son comes now on the weekend, because they both have your back; newborn babies and my oldest son comes every other afternoon.

They told me that while I was in a coma, they all got motels here in Augusta, Georgia. I do not know anything about that, because I was in Heaven. I heard nothing, and I felt nothing. I tell folks that they look at me crazy, but it is the living truth. I heard nothing. I felt nothing until I awoke up. I could only move my eyes. I could not turn over or feed myself; all I did was suffer. I spit up black mucus and I was sicker than sick my blood was poison and my kidneys have failed, but I still did not know what was wrong with me. No one told me until days later; I had a high fever. I could have died again at any given moment, but I figured if God brought me back from Heaven, I figured he has some work for me to do.

I always told the people about Jesus and what he did for me over my lifetime. It was easy. I sat in the ash pile like Job, and this was one of the hardest times. I have been in the ash pile in life plenty of times. I sit there when I had three children in college at the same time, but God. I worked three jobs and my husband worked two jobs after working at the school as an aid. I cleaned up some of the teachers' houses and some of my old friends every week to get a little extra. I was young and strong. I never got tired, because I never knew when my body was tired. I had to make sure that my children would not be poor; I wanted them to help their children overcome poverty and avoid being poor or being a danger to society.

I am writing this book, because I must tell everyone this story. It is my story of a pleasant woman from a community of 5000 people, and everyone knows everyone here. I am telling it my way and it is the truth, every word of it in my book. I am a person no one would expect to know God. I do not mix well with church folks. I love everyone, but I cannot mix with them because I see people who act like they do not need Jesus in church. They sit on a high horse. The see me as low, but I am humbled like Jesus, because I don't mix with the world, I don't want to be in the crowd; I am just a little countrywoman married who first man who ever told me I was pretty and look at me twice and that was it for me, after 44 years and still hanging.

Now I am still sitting here in this recliner ready to go back to the Doctors hospital. As I am thinking, a lot of things come to my mind, but one is God will help the cast out and the brokenhearted. And those are called nothing, God will be right there for them, and God is here with me. God let me visit heaven, I get happy every time I think about my journey; Why did Jesus let me see this? And when I finish this book, God told me as I was sitting here, the doctors had no hope for me in my room. However, after I awoke, God affirmed to me and my journey. My family prayed all they could for me.

It happens so quickly. I was not feeling sick just a little. I figured it was nothing out of the normal. It happened so fast just like a blink of an eye. I was gone. I did not have time to tell my family anything. I was gone so fast that is why it is best to stay prayed up, because bad things can happen to good people. I am not calling myself good, because there are none good according to the Bible, but I told the Lord, I have served you. I went to sleep. I saw many things, but some of them I cannot reveal, because there were things that I had to pray to against for my grandchildren when they grow up. I cannot reveal those things. I have already met one of them with my sweet grandson Otis Jr., but I have already told his parents and it came to past.

I do not have a big title by my name, but I tell you one thing. I have always leaned on the Lord. I will continue lean on Him more than ever. I always see myself walking with Him in the cool of the morning just like Enoch did in the Bible Days. I walk with Him, and I talk with Him, and I love Him like old lady Anna did; I love the Lord with all of my heart that is why I cannot do certain things. I cannot talk about people so because whatever you do until your neighbor will be done back to you. Have you ever thought of the evil that will be added back to you? So, we must pray for each other, I give God all the glory. I cannot even blink my eyes if he does not say so. Walking up and down the long country road when I was a child, I looked for food, I always found food in the summertime on a fruit tree whether it was a peach tree or an apple tree. It would be on side of the road, especially plums. I would always find plums in the wintertime.

I would eat pecans all day. I went down through the pecan orchard, and I got a lot of old pecans. I filled my pockets full of pecans. The white folks had pecan trees planted in front of our house and we helped ourselves, but they did not want us to bother them, but we got them anyway because we would always watch when their cars leave the yards. We know they were gone so we helped ourselves. I am just sitting here wondering what I have done in my life to be suffering like this I mean suffering just like Job. The no difference is that he was a rich man, and I am a poor woman, but I am rich in grace and mercy from the Lord. I gave my children my life; it was all about them making sure they would be ready for college because my father never read a book in his life. I never saw Him with a book. If a letter came in the mail my mother would have to read it. She read what she could and then she brought it to me to read for them. I live in calling distance, I could stand on my porch and call them.

Chapter 12

I AM FREE NOW!

Sitting here writing this book, I have been talking to my daughter for the past three weeks. She is teaching at Yale University. I cannot believe this little, old peasant woman has a daughter teaching at Yale University. She is teaching for a summer program at Yale. I only have one daughter and she is a blessing to me, and her brothers are a blessing. I thank God for lending me the sweetish bunch of children in the world. I had to be a strong mother at an early age and my husband, a strong man to raise three boys.

I had to speak loud enough for them to hear me. I talk to my children all of the time even before they were born, I never knew what gender they were, but I talk to them. I told each one of them that they were going to be somebody in this world, and I meant that. Each one of them chose their careers. I am proud of all four of them, none of them fell by the wayside. I had to pray and pray, and I had to make sure that they knew Jesus. I was their Sunday school teacher.

It is still June 20, 2017. I have to sign the release letter to go back to the Doctors Hospital's Rehabilitation Center. The release letter that was given to me from the rehabilitation center said:

Willie Agnes Chennault

Dear Chennault and family,

We trust that you have been pleased with the care we have provided during your hospitalization. In anticipation of your further needs and as part of our discharge planning process, the medical team has recommended one or more of the following: home health care services, medical equipment, skilled nursing, or extended care facility. Many agencies are available to meet your current needs It is your right to select the providers of your choice.

Sincerely,
Doctors Hospital

I chose Doctor Hospital's Rehabilitation, but I am still sicker than sick. I meant sick but improving all of the time. I cannot sleep! I am still too sick to go into a deep sleep. My mind is always on Heaven and getting home. My mind runs back to my childhood where there was peace for me. It does not matter what shape I was in the 1960s; there was a peace that passed all understanding. Seem like things were simple then and more love was in the world. Even though there were racial problems. My parents were so afraid. I remember hearing my older brother and sister talking about marching at this time. My mind went back to the early sixties as I was a little girl during this time. I heard my mom tell my dad to go to the jail and bring these children home, because my brothers—Charlie, Jessie, and my sister, Mamie had been locked up due to a march for integrating the schools in my hometown of Washington, Georgia. Everyone began to get afraid, because black people were truly afraid of white people at this time.

I think about being in Heaven, chills just run across my body. I think about Heaven all of the time. I see Jesus in my mind. He looked at me with the most compassionate look. He turned his head to the right and looked at me. Then He turned His head back towards the way He was sitting, looking straight ahead. I never saw this look before. I will never forget that look as long as I live! Why did Jesus show Himself to me? I do not know, but He did. I know that was Him. I stood there looking at Him. He was looking opposite from me. I walked up on this man sitting on a shiny dark brown rock that glowed. He was nicely dressed in an eggshell-colored robe. The robe was a smooth, shiny type fabric that laid to his skin. His sandals were deep brown with thick leather. I could see his scarf on his head and the brown belt around his waist and his shoes. He has long leg bones, and his eyes were like the blue ocean with waves washing up beside of his eyeballs. Why did I have to see all of this?

I will know my purpose when I finish writing this book. I got to tell the world that there is a whole other world over there. I heard my parents sing the song about Heaven in the song "I see over there." I always tell anyone who wants to listen, and the Holy Spirit just come right to me as I am talking; I started crying because the Spirit is so powerful. I cannot control myself from that warm feeling when it comes upon me. I can feel the Holy Spirit very quickly. The Spirit came upon me. I am sitting here still waiting for the ambulance to come and take me back to the Doctors Hospital. No one is in this room with me at the moment, except me and the Lord and a whole lot of memories. I wish I could explain what I am feeling, but I cannot. I am still a very sick woman. I cannot walk or dress myself alone. I am free, happy, and full of joy!

I have been to Heaven and back! When I die again someday, I will not be back. I am going back to Heaven! The Holy Spirit told me before I left that I would return to this same place, Heaven! Pastor Henra told me at my gravesite when he finished preaching my funeral, "I know you got to go mama, but Mama, you got to come on back now!" I was just looking back at Pastor Henra, just smiling. I was feeling no pain. There is no pain over there! Nothing, but joy, peace, and beauty to the eye.

While exploring Heaven, I looked at all of those people in the olden days—like the people in the Bible days. I looked at the cows' eyes; they were happy, and the glory of the Lord was over. All the time you are just filled with God's glory. Oh, God! I will never forget this! It is with me every day, thoughts of Heaven. I mean every day. It will be with me until I get back home again to Heaven. I wish I could explain it better, but there are no words. There will come a time in every person's life, saved or not saved; You will need to know God. Learn to pray and study his word for yourself. I read the Bible over and over when I was, I first learning to read, because I had to have some help.

I had good parents, but I had to have something else in me, because no one understood me. I am the black sheep of the family especially with the women's side of the family. However, one thing that I know is you can get as much of Jesus Christ as you want. You can a little bit if you want or just enough to get by and say you went to church today, but for me all of my life I got too had to have a lot of Jesus and I mean a lot of Him! I am and I have always given the Lord Jesus a lot of my time. I have had to pray and pray while I was with my husband.

I had my mind on the Lord Jesus Christ, praying and giving God the glory! My mind just stayed on the Lord all of the time. I have always been like that because I looked at my parents working many days. My father would come home from cutting pulpwood. His pants' legs would be split apart, and he would be trying to pull his shoes off. He would always to anyone in the room, "Come here and pull my shoes off." I would always pull off my father's shoes, but none of the other children would move. His shoes would have sawdust in them, and his shoes were always untied. I have seen my father cut down plenty of trees. He cut the tree in half on all sides, and he pushed it with his hand and that is the way it fell. I have seen this several times. He never missed the tree and the tree always fell the right way. I said to myself, "There has to be another way to make a living!" My mother worked hard all day at the white folk's house. She did not mind. She was a strong woman of faith and a great mother. She took care of all ten of us and she made sure that we were clean. We did not have any running water or lights in the early part of our life, but we made it by the grace of God. I am writing this book as God inspired me to do.

As I am sitting here typing my book, but I am at the Select Specialty Hospital in the recliner waiting to be transferred back to Doctors Hospital. I was over there for 15 days now I have to go back over there for physical therapy, because I cannot walk; my mobility is a level six. I am very weak; I cannot use my arms very well or bathe myself or put my clothes on or sit up for long, but I am sitting here waiting. While I am lying back in the recliner, my mind goes back to my childhood; it goes to Heaven, and it comes back to the hospital. I know thesc patients over here are so sick, no one moves over here. I guess the doctors felt the same about me when I first got here. I was in bad shape, but I am alive, and I am going to fight to get out of here, and I will! I can feel my strength coming back every day. I feel my body improving. When I woke up—my sons showed me a video of when I woke up. I do not remember waking up. I looked at the video over and over. I still look at the video to this day. I still have it on my phone. I was in shock to see this.

I believe when patients leave here, they are headed to the graveyard if they are sick as I am—I mean sick beyond measure. I am going to leave the Doctors Hospital after my physical therapy. They do not let anyone walk out of the hospital. I am going to ride in a wheelchair when I leave. They had to train me every two hours; I was so sore everywhere. There was blood all over the bedsheets where my skin had pulled away from my body. I never could have imagined being in a shape like this. We never know what shape we might get in so it is good to stay prayed up and let God handle it when you get in a situation where you cannot pray for yourself.

We never know what tomorrow will bring. A split second and your whole life can change. I am free; I went through the process. I would repeat Psalm 23 and the Lord's prayer every day all throughout the day, along with thanking the Lord for his grace and his mercy and thanking God for more time to say my prayers. God knows our heart, that what is a secret part of life. You cannot fool God, and He knows our motives and He looks at our minds. There is always a path each of us must take, even if we do not understand it. It is not for us to understand. I ask God a question, "Why did let me visit Heaven? Who am I to visit Heaven? It was so easy, because I felt no pain. I felt a few pains of not being able to breathe. I was very weak before the EMS got here, but I remember them coming in my house. I was sitting on the sofa with oxygen on my nose, but I still could not breathe before I left home. At that moment, I saw the EMS doors shut very slowly.

I saw my husband and Callie Blue standing there waving at me saying goodbye as if he was happy, but he was not, it was just me trying to see and after that I left this world. As you were reading this book you noticed I repeated myself; I wanted you the read to know you can be gone in a blink of an eye. I was in another dimension. I was young and strong; exploring Heaven it was amazing. I cannot explain, but it is my job to tell the whole world, Heaven is real. I walked around Heaven; however, I did not know anything about time; it is so amazing! Time does not matter over there, no essence of time in Heaven.

One thing about my life, I have always had the Lord on my mind. Even when my husband took me out for dancing, I was always praying even dancing on the floor. I would pray for safety and everywhere I went I always prayed even in the car on my way to different places I prayed for understanding and I prayed for others before I pray for myself. I do not pray for myself like I pray for others all the time. I pray for my sisters, brothers, and neighbors as well as myself. I pray for my children and their children. I pray for my aunties, uncles, cousins, and other family members. I pray for friends and strangers I meet daily. I just have to let my mind stay on Jesus.

My husband asked me one day—"How can you live your life and pray all of the time as you do?" I told Him without the peace of God and talking with Him constantly all through the day, I would be fitting for nothing. Your mind battles between good and evil—always fighting. So, if I keep my mind on the Lord—I will not go wrong. Jesus is where our help comes from for this family and the coming generation. I am sending up prayers now for the next generation to come; when I am dead and gone, I want some prayers to be stored up for them so they will know Father God and so they will not to be poor. I was very poor, and my husband was very poor, but for my children and their children—they will not be poor.

The curse of poverty has to be broken somewhere and it was my job to make sure of this before I leave this world. It was hard on my children when it came to accepting Jesus. I laid the rod, but they had to accept, believe, and trust. It was their father's job and my job to make sure that I laid the foundation for them. It was our job to make sure that each one of them had an education. That was my main goal for them in life. A Bible in one hand and a coin in their pocket if they read the Bible, prayed, and worked hard; they would always have some bread to eat. It was not easy, and it was not that hard, because I had the best children. It was easy raising those four children. They always listen to their father and me.

I am still sitting here, praising God for my health and strength at this time in my recliner. I am now thanking my Father God for this mighty test because I know a test like this is hard, but worth the journey. I always told Father God to use me any way he wants to. I cannot question Father God, because I have no strength of my own. I told Him to use me as he sees fit. I see a lot of people acting like they have some more time, but in a blink of an eye, everything can turn around. All through my growing up; I use to cry all night praying and praying. I pray now always, and I sing myself to sleep.

When I wake up, the first thing I think of is something about the Lord. I have heard people say I did not have time to pray. I do not understand that how can you be so busy in life that you cannot say good morning to the Lord and tell Him I love you and I give you all of myself. And tell Him that I need your glory. Oh, Lord, and help those who do not know how to help themselves! Lord, I ask you to help those who go all day and do not even give you a thought! I cannot and I never will know how an hour feels without praying, because I do not belong to myself. I always ask Father God to help those who are on the outside of safety. Lord, let them come in before it be too late.

My mind has thought about a lot of things since I have been awake from the coma. I had no idea that I lived anywhere else, but Heaven. I want to make this plain. You have no remembrance of this world. Jesus can show Himself to any person in any type of way he wants to—he is God. He can look anyway, but I saw Him as I remembered on the hillside. My soul and my life were in Heaven with my mother and my aunties. I saw lots of children. I stood there to watch all of those children play on the hill.

You are lighter over there just like a ghost's body, not heavy inside your body. The clouds look different. I stood there looking up at the bright sky, there is nothing darkness over there. Everything is beautiful, bright, and shining over there in Heaven. The water is bluer. I laid in the river on my way across the water, but my mother said to me to go back. I could not come with her yet. She told me that that family needed me. I will never forget this! I will go back to Heaven one day! I do not know how long I will live, but I promise God I will continue to praise Him every day all through the day.

I say bits and pieces of prayer. I sing hymns and read God's words as I have always done. Just think about it for a while, what other help would we have if it had not been for the Lord? I am no longer afraid of death! I welcome it next time with a smile. God knows my end. He laid all of my children's education out. We studied, and we prayed; my children went to some of the best colleges. My oldest son leads the group over all the other three who followed. My oldest son graduated from Western Carolina University; he is a teacher and a coach. Tears are running down my face! My next son, Otis, graduated from Georgia Southern University and he went on to get his Master of Science. He is a Network Engineer. The next child, my only daughter, Dr. June, has graduated I know 10 times. She graduated from Kennesaw State University with her bachelor's degree, has a master's degree from Liberty University, and lastly her Doctorate from Nova Southern University. She is a Doctor of Education. The last child, Pastor Henra, is our Spiritual leader in the family. He spent his first year of college at Carson Newman College in Tennessee then and he went on to the University of Tennessee and later he graduated from West Georgia University with a degree in Business Finance. He then went on to Mercer University for his Master's in Divinity degree. The Lord called Him into the ministry when he was 18 years old.

I am reminded by Psalm 16:11—"Thou wilt shew me the path of life in thy presence is fulness of joy at the right hand there is pleasure forevermore." Pastor Henra always took a bigger role than the other three children, but they all played a great role in the country church growing up. My daughter, Dr. June was the Sunday school secretary. Lazarus Jr was the Superintendent of Sunday school; Otis was an usher, and I was the Sunday school teacher of Gibson Grove Baptist Church. And my husband and younger son, Minister Pastor Henra, sung—Oh, how he singed; he always led devotion.

We all were one big happy family, I could just walk in the house, and everyone was in place, but when I left home maybe to go to the grocery store or do some errands; their dad always let them relax, but when I stepped in that house, it was business as usual, and they were good children. They followed the rules of the house. My husband and I were young parents. My husband and I were married at 18 years old. We did not know much, but one thing we knew was that we loved each other, and I know to this day I would not have never found another love like my husband because we wanted most of the same things for our children.

As I sit here alone thinking about how this has been a tough toll on my husband, he looked so dark the past few days since he came to visit me. I told Him to go home and get some rest. He really looks bad. I told Him I was sick enough for the both of us and I told Him that he had to be strong for the rest of the family. My mind went back to our wedding day almost 44 years ago on that Saturday. I had made my wedding dress myself. I only weight 98 pounds and I wore a size four. My husband weighed about 150 pounds; he was a strong man. Many moons ago, he was outside with my father, and I was looking through the windowpane. It was broken at the top; so, I could hear what they were talking about. My husband knew that he had to ask my father for my hand in marriage. As I was looking out of the window, I noticed my husband following my dad. My father was a tall man over 6'5 in height. My dad had on overalls; he always wore his hat. So, my husband was very nervous. I could tell that as I was looking at Him, and my husband finally got up enough nerve to ask for my hand in marriage.

When I saw my father laugh, I knew the answer was yes and my husband stayed out there awhile longer and then he came in the house later on smiling. He told me that my father agreed with us getting married. I already knew what he has said, because I was reading his lips and he said yes. I made my dress; I sowed it myself. I made all of my clothes, because I learned to sew at school. My husband never saw my dress until I had it on. I still have my dress to this day and my husband has his orange suit and his blue shirt and his stacked hill shoes. I remember on that Saturday morning on the day of the wedding; we did not have any rings. He did not have a ring and I did not have any ring, but the wedding was at 2 p.m. and that morning I walked around praying knowing I had ordered both our rings from the Gold Metal catalog; my ring cost 10 dollars and his ring cost 10 dollars. When the mailman ran that Saturday, guess what he put in that box? I was standing on the porch just looking at every car past that morning. I thought it was the mailman, but I heard a car slow down and it was the mailman, praise the Lord, and he had our rings! I prayed all the way to the mailbox and from the mailbox praising God for his goodness. I always prayed; I would be sitting in school praying to God to help my parents and us poor children. Lord help us! Lord I am so glad I had to suffer to get up! I am glad unto this day, because I got a chance to know Jesus Christ.

I would not take anything for my journey right now. I remember my father pulling me up the hallway; he was so tall and strong. A few people on my husband's side of the family came and a few people on my side of the family were there. My father gave me to Reverend C.P. Wright, our pastor who married us. My father gave Him a hog ham for marrying us and this is the same minister that baptized me when I was 11 years old. He was glad to get that hog ham; my mother had the table fixed so pretty—a full table of food. She put a special white tablecloth on the table. The white lady, Mr. Ruth Tutt, who my mother worked for made me my wedding cake and it was beautiful. I still have the man and woman she put on top of my wedding cake. This was the happiest day of my life. I was so young. I think this bothered my father a little, but he told my

mother early that I was too young to get married and my
mother told my father to let me marry if I wanted to and stated
that my husband came from a good family.

That was only the beginning. The hills and deep valleys
that come with marriage after you pull the wedding dress off is
to be a responsible wife and mother, which is the hardest job in
the world, but with much prayer, hope and endurance; you can
do it, you can never think about giving up; just keep pressing
on. Nothing in life comes easy that is worth having. My father
never read a book in his life; my mother reading was very
limited. Look at my children what the Lord has done; I give all
of the glory to God so he can use each one of them with the
knowledge he gives them for his glory. No one has to be
jealous, because most people cannot wear my shoes. They are
only for me. Father God can get the glory, we brought nothing
here and we will take nothing away. What I figured out about
life is that I am going to spend more time in eternality so I
must prepare for it now while the blood is running in my veins.

I see the glory of God. God is real. Jesus is real. The Holy
Spirit is real. We are just a vapor, in a few words just here for a
very short period. We need the Lord every day of our lives. He
does not need any help. He got all the power in his hands. So
why not get prepared for your Heavenly home. It is about
having a church relationship with Father God, but they do not
know anything at all about a personal relationship with Him. It

is about you and the Lord; no one else. This is where you lay your heart and your life out to God, no one else can enter between you and the Lord. No lies are told to God. He knows every secret thing that you have ever done. No one else knows about what you have done. Fall to his feet just like a little child before the "all-mighty, all-knowing." God, this is what you will need to make this journey. You cannot lie to Him, because he sees your heart, motives and he looks at your mind.

On my last day of Select Specialty Hospital, I am still sitting here! All of the nurses that are on duty on this date, June 20, 2017, are telling me bye. This is a very small hospital. No one can move in here. I could not move much when I got here; I could not even turn over. Lord, how did I get here? No matter how good you think you are or no matter how religious you may think you are, anything can happen. I know I have lived the life that I have prayed, and I have served God. I have taken Him with me over my lifetime. I pray all the time. God is using me for his glory just like I always ask Him to. I am not my own. I belong to God. I cannot speak for anybody else. I love to feel God's Spirit moving upon me. His Spirit comes to me quickly now that have been to Heaven. It is like fire shut up in my bones as Jeremiah said. His Spirit comes to me and almost knock me down it hits my body so deep. I just praise the Lord for his Holy Spirit; so many people out there cannot even feel God's Spirit, but he is free, and he has no particular one that he will do more for. It is up to you; how much you want of Him. Father God is always standing there with an outstretched hand. I thank Father God for allowing me to leave here; this hospital feels low in the Spirit it feels like death. I do not think most people that come to Select Specialty Hospital return home it just my feeling everyone here treated me nice. I had most of the same doctors as I did at Doctors Hospital. I am not worried about nothing, because I have been to Heaven. A piece of me, I left over there until I return one day. I got to tell my stories, because someone might come to Jesus Christ. He told me to tell everyone that wants to listen to my story, but lots of people did not receive Jesus. Why would they listen to a person like me? No one can make this journey, but me. You have to pray that God's will be done. When I got so sick, I prayed one line of the prayer. I said, "Oh, Lord, I have served you. I am in your hands."

I live a very low-profile life. I tell a lot of people about my story, a true story that my children then tell people about in the grocery store and everywhere I go it I tell my story to people I know. The people who do not know God will not receive my story, but that is okay. I got to tell someone who will listen. My children and my daughters-in-law always listen. I tell the story to so many people, if they do not listen, I just smile. I never force myself on anyone at any time unless they are my grandchildren, my children, or my husband. I tell everyone who wants to listen. I have improved, but I am still very sick. I cannot walk yet, but it will take tiny pieces of strength to come back to me every day. Physical Therapists come by in the evening. They exercise my legs. I never knew a human being could be this sick; never in my wildest dream would I have thought a human being could feel like this. Hurting up in my chest, but the doctor says my heart has improved, everything is improving and that is a good thing. My strength came back to me supernaturally. Just like a flower begins to bloom, you look at it one day and the next day it almost full bloom and you look at it again it blooms, and it gets pretty with time, but I am still not fit to look at. I had a one-bathroom section with physical therapy. I tried to make it on my walker, feeling so guilty every second. I almost was ready to hit the floor any second, it the hardest thing I ever did was trying to stand up at the bowl and wash my face. I looked so bad, but I am alive, ha, ha. I did not look at the mirror, because I never seen that woman. I was looking at my eyes, they are black instead of brown in the middle. I am very sick looking; my skin is dry. I never had the strength to put lotion on my body. My daughter did it when she was there, I always had to put cream on those sores on my body. I cry a lot, tears of joy. I thank God for my daughter.

My family did it when there were big sores on my buttocks, but my skin has started to tear away from my body, because it was dead. I was in Heaven; I was a young woman looking like I was about 33 just like one of the pictures I have here at home. How do I know how I look? When I looked in the river, I saw myself young and pretty. I did not look like I look now. Everyone was so nice to me; they always came when I called them to use the bathroom, the spot beside my bed. I did not have enough strength to get to the bathroom. I called them a million times, so I just got tired of calling them; I pulled my pot close to my bed. I slid myself toward the bottom of my bed and I use the strength that I had in my arms. I pulled the wires to the bottom of my bed, and I slid on my pot plenty of time. I got very tired of calling the nurse and I know that they got tired of me calling them, but everyone was so nice to me here a Select Specialty Hospital. I know all of my doctors were very surprised to see me improve like I did; they all know I was somewhere, but they did not know where. They had seen plenty of patients like me and most of them did not make it. You are not going to die until you have finished your task that God has for you to do. No matter what you are going through, it not over until God says it is over. I am blessed. My husband is blessed. My children are blessed, and my children's children are blessed, because I have suffered for all of them down through 42 generations and more.

I am sitting here tonight on July 30, 2018, writing my book. You are not going to die until you are finished with the tasks that God has for you to do. If it is just taking someone old to the doctor or helping an elderly person clean their house. Until God says it is over, it is not over! So do not worry about dying—It is not over until God's says it is over. No matter what you go through, it is not over until God says so. I am blessed and my family is blessed I suffered for all of them, all generations. I must tell the world that Heaven is real! There is a whole other world over there, a Holy Spirit feeling world where everything there is in another dimension and Father God's glory is all over the place called Heaven. Oh, God! When I walked up on Jesus, Lord have mercy; I was just walking in this field looking at all of the old prophets of the Bible days. They were looking at me. I saw all the colors of the people there. They were dressed like the people in the Bible days. They had bright colors on, all different colors. I recognized the clothes my mother had on. I saw them in real life and the hat that my Aunt Lue had on; I have seen it before.

My other aunties' voice: she was so happy! Her face was glowing. When she called my name, "Willie Agnes," my mother told me to go back—"You cannot come with us yet." My Auntie Nee hair was plaited and that smile on her face was so beautiful. My mother said, "They need you to go back." I continue to walk and flowing in a glorified form. I was light, very light. I saw Jesus. I know in my heart that it was Him. When I saw Jesus, I was in no human form; I was in another form. I was light as a feather. He looked at me the way I never have seen before. His skin was like ash gray and pink. From his feet to his knees was extra-long, his long arms, his features, his cheekbones, his dark chocolate brown hair. He had a light bread on his oval-shaped face. His eyes have the ocean in them. The waves were running from side to side in his eyeballs. His robe was so beautiful. His robe was an eggshell color with a brown belt around his waist and his sandals were a leather brown. I look at his feet. Lord, when he turned his head and looked at me! Lord Jesus, I am sitting here at this computer getting happy with the Holy Spirit, it is running all over me, thinking about my God, your God, and Lord. Why did Jesus Christ show Himself to me? It is not for me to question this experience. It was a mighty one! I think about this every passing day! I will never be the same again. He does not need no one's permission to do anything. He is God all by Himself. His nose was sharp at the end. His compassion was nothing like I had ever felt in this world.

Who does not want to praise a mighty God like this! Do not give your soul to the devil, try Jesus Christ, while breathing is still in your body. I am reminded by Revelations 21:4—"And God shall wipe away all tears from eyes; and there shall be no more death, neither sorrow, nor crying, neither shall there be any more pain, for former things are passed away." Jesus and Heaven are real! I believe Hell is real! I talk to a lot of people everywhere I go, and they tell me of some experiences that they had as well. Some told me that they went to Hell and somehow, they struggle out!

Now they are living for Christ! When a person shut their eyes, there is no second chance. "For we know that if earthly house of this tabernacle were dissolved, we have a building of God, a house not made with hands, eternal in the Heavens" (2 Corinthians 5:1). I died, and I went to Heaven. I was in Heaven. I saw my son preaching my funeral. I did not see people in the church. I saw was at the graveside. Everyone was gone, but Pastor Henra. He told me mother, "I know you got to go, but you go and come back!" I was looking back at Him smiling. I felt myself going through the ground in a tunnel, dirt was on both sides of me, but I was so happy. It was just like a rollercoaster ride, and I stepped up and out. Oh, what did I see? Beautiful green grass and all types of flowers, buildings and mansions of pure gold, streets of gold, and a shining bright world awake for those who know Father God. Heaven is a glowing place. I knew it was Heaven because I saw my mother and aunties. You can relax with Jesus. You do not have to tell God anything, because he knows you already before you were created.

We got to take that walk alone with God so we must make sure that we all make it into Heaven to see Jesus Christ, because Heaven is real. Why did go to Heaven? I have been working for this moment all of my life! God's grace and mercy will lead you home. It is a gift to all of those who seek Him. He will never cast anyone out, but you must come through his door and go through the process of being a saved soul. Repent if you are a sinner and need saving. Confess and believe in your heart the birth, death, and the resurrection of Jesus Christ, taking on Christ is nothing easy it long-suffering; it no flower bed of eve. Each one of us must travel up Calvary hill for ourselves, no one can stand for no one. It is up to every person, that is why a parent must train their children in knowing Christ. It was a must in my house. The foundation must be laid early even while they are still in the womb and the baby can feel what the mother feels. This is my story; I do not understand it all myself, but I am telling it my way inspired by the Lord Jesus Christ.

I still sitting in the recliner ready to go back to Doctors Hospital where I was there in a coma for several days. Heading back in a few, waiting on the ambulance to carry me back; my daughter brought me a bluebonnet to put on my head. It has been over a month since I combed my head or washed my hair. I rub my hand on the back of my head and I have no hair at all in the back of my head, where I have laid in one place so long. The back of my head is as clean as my hand, no hair at all. I was not worried about that because I am alive and improving. I cannot see my children and my husband and my grandchildren and my daughters-in-law. My immediate family is always around me helping. I am so blessed to have wonderful children and their wives it is a blessing to have good daughters-in-law; it was not about me. It was about my children. All of my life my husband had to make sure that our four children get the right start in life. I did not want them to be poor I had to break the line of poverty.

I prayed the scripture of 2 Peter 3:9—"The Lord is not slack concerning his promise. As some men count slackness; but is longsuffering to upward, not willing that any should perish. Out that all should come to repentance." I know with prayer and hard work poverty can be broken. There were ten of us, my brothers, and sisters. My husband had a large family also. He was raised the same way I was. I never remember having decent clothes to wear to school. My parents did the best that they knew how to do. I had the best parents, but I had to take it a step further. All I know is that I had to make sure all of my children got the best education life had to offer not what I could not afford. All I could do was to get them ready Spiritually, mentally, and physically. Father God would to the rest because I prayed for this every day of my life. There were plenty of dark days, but we had to keep our focus on God and keep pressing forward. Folks were laughing at me when I told them that all of them would finish college; they laughed at me and told me, "What makes your children so special?" I told them, "They were three princes and I got one queen and I will invest in each one of them to break the curse of poverty." My grandchildren and their children will have some kind of chance at a good life. I was just thinking the week before I got sick, I was not feeling that bad when I started throwing up blood; my stomach did not hurt or my chest. I just got so sick all at once; I could not breathe right. I always got my colonoscopy and my check-ups each month as well as my mammograms and my gynecology checkup and my blood work all the time, but this all happened at once. I am talking about the fastest I have ever seen sickness happen to me. Like I said, every second counted. This time, my husband did not believe I was sick; I never get sick that often. I was always working on Him. God uses us when we are most broken, God is doing something with me. I got to tell the world; someone may come to Jesus while there is still time. Jesus knows what each of us will endure and this was already set for me, another test that no human had to take. I did not have time to get nothing ready. I had already taken a shower before I left, but I did not remember taking a shower.

I know I got in the shower, and I vaguely remember getting out my clothes and I was feeling weak and disoriented. I came in the living room, and I sat on the sofa, and I went back in the bathroom, and I spit up blood lots of blood and I told my husband I know I had to move quickly. I told my husband to take me to Augusta to the doctors, because I have never been to Washington Hospital for an emergency. I have always gone to Augusta that is where all my records are. because I had all of my children there. I have been to the Doctors Hospital since my last child was born and that has been 34 years ago but thank God for letting the EMS stop there because my blood type was already on file there.

Chapter 13

MY SOUL WONDERS

I am talking backwards and forward, because that is the way I am thinking at the moment while writing this book. I am broken into many small pieces at the moment this year of 2017 in the month of June. This month has put me back together. The Lord is giving me a new body. I am sitting in the recliner thinking here back at Select Specialty Hospital on my last day here in this place. I was so sick when I first got here. All I do is cry! My family has to leave; my children and my husband both come some evenings to see me and, on the weekends, but I got this! I never let anything get the best of me, but this is a very hard one, no matter how much the doctor or nurse would say to me. I would just look at them and say, Lord you got this! They told me that my blood was not clean, and I said Lord you got this!

He told me that my kidneys are still not working, and I said, "Lord you got this!" Who else could help me at this point; no one at all? I was fading fast; I mean fast. It is just me and the Lord working through the doctors. He is guiding the hands of the doctors and I am praying. I lay myself at Jesus' feet, because I have been to Heaven; I fear nothing whether I live or I die, I know I will be saved because I have seen Heaven when I looked in the oxen eyes; They had the Spirit of the Lord in their eyes. Oh, how they looked at me! The oxen have the Holy Spirit all about them. I looked right into the eyes of the oxen, and I got so happy.

I was so happy in Heaven, but I had to come back! My mother told me to go back, but my Aunt Nee wanted me to stay. The Holy Spirit brought me back to earth. The oxen had brown wooden bow yokes held on their necks. Jesus' hair, it was dark chocolate brown hair. The Lord looked at me a few minutes and He turned His head back towards the right. This was amazing! I saw the Lord! Why did He show Himself to me? Why? I have some kind of power, but I cannot explain it to anyone; I know that I can bring healing to people through Jesus Christ. I have helped some people recover from sicknesses. The Holy Spirit comes right to me all the time because only half of me is here on earth; the other half of me is in Heaven.

Make sure your prayers are stored up because there might come a time where you cannot pray. While you are talking about other people in a bad way, you should use that time to pray for them whether they are your family members or people. Ask God to help those who are on the outside of safety, because when God in the Bible days shut the ark and it began to rain, it was too late. Please, God! Speak the truth and it does not matter who agrees with you; tell the truth, because each of us has to walk through that gate alone. No one else walked with me, but Jesus. I know that was Him sitting there. It looked just like Jesus; He is amazing! Many may say that no one can see Jesus in this life, but I was not in the flesh; I was in my Spiritual body. I saw many things. I saw trees in their natural colors. I saw buildings of gold; gold was all around the windows and doors. The street was paved with gold—pure, thick, shiny, yellow gold. I saw the Bible peoples.

Everyone was so patient with me at Select Specialty Hospital. I am glad I have reached the point of mobility to move on to rehabilitation back to the Doctors Hospital. The EMTs from the Doctors Hospital are coming in the door to get me. I know my husband and my granddaughter, Hannah is here. My husband is helping to gather my belongings. I told my husband to give me my Bible on the table next to my bed. I kept it open to Psalm 23 all the time. When I am not reading it; I recite Psalm 23 all the time. I teach it to my grandchildren all the time and the Lord's prayer. I told them when they get frustrated at school to say the Lord's prayer and before they go to bed at night to repeat Psalm 23 and the Lord's prayers. Everything is in this Psalm and the Lord's Prayer that you need for the rest of your life. I am looking for the room as the two men are putting me on the strength back to the doctor's hospital. I have been over here for 18 days, and I am still very weak as they left me from my hospital bed. I am still very weak I cannot walk.

My legs and hips feel like cedar tree poles and my arms and hands shake. I have not had a full bath yet, but I am living. I am going to Doctors Hospital to learn to walk again and use my muscles in my arms and my leg and my whole body are still very weak. I am a strong woman. I have always been a superwoman! I have always been a workaholic. I have raised four children, my husband and me.

My husband and I saw all of my children through college with the Lord leading us because I did not have any money. I worked and my husband worked. My children worked and they studied. We prayed and we sang hymns. We read the Bible. We went to church, and we worked, and we worked. The Lord educated all of my children as I asked Him. The Lord did it! Family members told me it was impossible to educate four children, but my husband and I made sure they finished college. I have a Doctor of Education, a minister, a coach, and a Network Engineer. One of the daughters-in-law is a lawyer, one is a teacher and the other one is a beautician.

I am so thankful this evening! Please remember when you read this book, I am just a small-town, countrywoman still planting my vegetables, going fishing, and eating wild meats like deer, squirrels, and rabbits. I live back in the woods. I keep to myself. I do not socialize much. I pray and I study God's word. I have always lived like this—I am a person who keeps to herself. All of my children are grown and gone, but we are very close. I mean very close. I love them all with all of my heart. I do not see them as grown men and women at times; I always see them as they were when they were in kindergarten. I am looking in the rooms at Select Specialty Hospital.

The EMTs rolled me down the hall to the ambulance. No one is moving in these rooms. The patients are alive, just no movements. I am so glad to be leaving here, because I have improved, and everyone is happy for me! All of my doctors are happy for me; they have worked with me. They have been so nice to me! I believe God has surprised them all because He is working with me in His way. I call myself Job because I have been in the ash pile with boils all over my body. I know the Lord is with me because I have seen Him. I saw Heaven; it is beautiful over there! There is no sun over there. The sun is Jesus. It is bright and shining everywhere. My cross was heavy, and I carried it. I stood the test of all time. A test that only I could take. I got a lot to look forward to.

I am just riding back to the Doctors Hospital. I am getting into the elevator now. I see the sunlight it is about 2 p.m. Everything looked strange. I looked up at the sky it was dark about 10:30 at night when I got to Select Specialty Hospital; it was daytime when I was leaving, and I am on the outside of the hospital. I see a lot of people walking up the road; my husband told me that this hospital was in the hood. I agreed with Him, but the Good Lord is with me; he will not let me fall, because I do not want to fall. They are checking my blood pressure in the ambulance and my heartbeat. It is a good ride from Select Specialty Hospital to the Doctors Hospital. I guess about 15 minutes after laying there in the ambulance riding along thinking how I got here. It is a test for me and only me! Why is this test so hard? I will not complain never again in my life no matter what I have to go through, because I know God is with me and he brought me back for a purpose.

The sun was shining so bright when I got back to the Doctors Hospital. My room was right in front of the nurse's station; they have to wheel me in my room. I am still very weak, I got on a bluebonnet and some pants, a blouse my daughter went to the dollar store and brought me clothes before she left. She has been gone now for a while; she is gone back to work. She is teaching at the college this summer in Dallas, Texas, and some more places; she calls all day long when she gets a break. She has been with me a long time; she got to go make a living. Lord, I miss her. I got God's Spirit all around my bed. God gave me a wonderful daughter, Dr. June, but the boys are coming in the evening and some weekends too. Two of my sons have very young babies, but I am going to make it on my own, just me and the Lord.

They are getting me to set up in my room! Oh, I have a roommate for the first time. I got a roommate, the sweetest lady in the world; she is so nice to me. We exchange names; I told her my problems and she told me her problems. I tried to get some rest. I am still too weak to sit up long. I am hurting up in my chest area, and my eyes are blurred. I have Glaucoma. I told my doctors, so he got a glaucoma doctor to come and look at my eyes he said they are okay, just continue my drops as has been instructed; I have tubes in both of my eyes. I had this operation in 2014 for drainage tubes and it was very painful, but they are during okay. I got the same doctors I had at Select Specialty Hospital, and that is one good lady and three men. Now I go to physical therapy to learn how to bath first. I very quiet in my room; all the lights are out. I have to call the nurse to help me get to the bathroom, because I am a fall risk. I was late eating tonight because the kitchen was closed and they forgot to save me a plate, but they found me something to eat, cold cuts and some chips. I got a cup full of all kinds of pills and vitamins to take; it is very quiet at night over here. I cry myself to sleep, but I do not let anyone see me cry; sometimes it is just you and the Lord, because no one understands you like the Lord. I do not sing and cry, because I am sad. I am alive doing very well for what I have been through. I am laying here singing, "My storm is passing over, hallelujah oh hallelujah my storm is passing over, Oh, Lord! Sometimes I am up and sometimes, I am down singing, hallelujah! My storm is passing over hallelujah!"

I cry myself to sleep. I did not sleep long, because I cannot sleep. I am too sick to sleep long. They are always doing something to me all of the time. I never thought in a million years that I would be this sick with double pneumonia, who would have thought? Lord, have mercy on me! I always tell the Lord that! I do not know what to say after I tell Him "Thank you" over and over, I tell the Lord to give me a clean heart and a right Spirit so I can please Him. I only want to please the Lord, no humans. I love people, but the Lord is what is going to count; we must treat everyone, we meet in life the way we want to be treated. I always told my children this is the one thing that will carry you through; treat people the way you want to be treated. I drilled this over and over into my children, because what goes around is coming back around. So, do what is right as far as possible. This is my first night here back at the Doctors Hospital. My mind is getting out of here and going home, but I got a very long way to go before that can happen and I know that it will, because God has brought me this far and he will not leave me now.

The Ophthalmologist is coming in looking at my eye tubes; he says the tubes are in place. I told Him that my eyes were sore; he just said continue to put eyes drops in them. I always say that we might plant and water, but God gives the increase. I laid here thinking about the early 1960s when we had some chickens walking around the yard; how hungry we would get while my mother and father were working. We did not have any food to eat so when we heard the chickens holler loudly; we knew that they had laid an egg somewhere. Most of the time it was under the house so my brothers and myself would always find that egg and we would run in the house and cook it on stove, a wood stove we had at this time. We were always hungry most of the time. My brother, Joseph and I would go fishing by ourselves deep in the woods, but God took care of us; we would always see snakes, but we never got snake bit. Oh, what a wonderful childhood, we had to suffer to get up, but life was so easy back then; the only thing we had on our minds was finding food. Things like this just run across my mind as I laid here from day today. Remembering how we use to run and meet my mother, when I saw her coming and walking home from work, she never rode to work. She never learned to drive; I drove her around all of my life until she died, we were so close, and I love her so dearly.

As I stop here, and I read Psalm 139:

O Lord, thou hast searched me, and know me. Thou knowest my down sitting and mine uprising, thou understand my thought afar off. Thou compassest my path and my lying down, and art acquainted with all my ways. For there is not a word in my tongue, but, lo O Lord, thou knowest it altogether

Thou hast beset me behind and before and laid thine hand upon me. Such knowledge is too wonderful for me; it is high, I cannot reach unto it. Whither shall I go from thy Spirit? or whither shall I flee from thy presence? If I ascend into Heaven, thou art there: if I make my bed in hell, behold, thou are there. If I take the wings of the morning and dwell in the uttermost parts of the sea. Even there shall thy hand lead me, and thy right hand shall hold me. If I say, surely the darkness shall cover me; even the night shall be light about me.

As I sit here writing this book my oldest son who called me today with a heavy heart, praising God for letting me live; he said the doctor only gave me a one percent chance of surviving. I just always praised my God as I have always done, because I never had the things that I needed growing up so what I had the best parents, and they did what they knew how to do with ten children. I am glad; I came up the way I did, because it made me strong enough to put the right morals and values in my children to make them strong enough to face this mean old world. I had to teach them and tell them everything I knew whether it was good or bad or ugly, because they were going to face it all in this world. I knew that they were not as strong as me and their father, because we were raised the same way.

At this time, I am at the Doctors Hospital. When I left there on June 2, 2017—I was in bad shape and I was so sick; I never know a human being could get that sick when I first got to Select Specialty Hospital I didn't know whether I would live or die, but I thought about that the Lord would not have brought me this far if he was going to take me right away. My temperature was 105°F and I was so sick, the nurse set my food on the table when I got to Select Specialty Hospital; I could not eat a bit of it. I was so sick thinking back to this date; it was too sad and lonely over there at 10:30 p.m. I felt so bad. I just cried and I just wiped my eyes. I used the bathroom all over my self several times already; the man nurse cleaned me. I did not have any shame and he did not neither. I felt some kind of way, but I did not let it bother me. I felt pitiful, very pitiful, but I been to Heaven, and I have peace and joy in spite of all of it; I got peace and joy. I love the Lord Jesus, because I had to go up cavalry hill; I had to go to the cross.

Here on June 20, 2017, and I am back at the Doctors Hospital. I am writing this book just like it is. I got to tell the whole world my story because it is a sad one, a blessed one and a true one and a blessing for anyone who reads it. Laying here back at the Doctors Hospital, the lady the physical therapist has come in here and put my scheduling of physical therapy on the board for three hours a day of physical therapy. No one in the world thought that I could do it; I am so weak, but I will make it happen, because I am ready to go home, but I know I cannot go home like this, no way. Who would take care of me this sick? My husband is sick; he barely can take care of Himself dealing with me. This will only make Him sicker, but that is my take; the children always tell me how he cried every day for me, because we were tight for so long; we were in the same homeroom in the tenth grade, and we dated in high school. He took me to the prom, and we finished school together and we married at eighteen years of age. We have been together a long time, but it does not seem like all of those years has passed. Part of my physical therapy was learning how to use the bathroom again and learning to put my clothes on again.

I was a mess still this is the first time I looked at myself in the mirror on June 3, 2017. I stood in the bathroom on my walker for a few minutes. I just looked at myself. My eyes were black; It looked as though I had no white inside of them. My skin was so dry and rough, but I am alive; I love my family. I look at myself for a few minutes, because I could not stand up on my walker, but a few seconds. I was at great risk of falling. I am on a whole lot of medications at this time. I do not have any wires in my arm, no IVs running. My blood is finally clean now and my kidneys are working okay. On June 13, 2017, my renal function kicked in good. I know the Lord will make a way. He will! He is making a way for me, and he will make a way for you, he will! There is no way to explain my illness. It was kind of like leprosy in the Bible Days. I am glad I went through this. I am going to live longer.

On June 20, 2017, here are my rehab notes from the nurse:

Rehabilitation Necessity/Diagnosis; Medical impact on function as a result of impaired functional mobility, ambulation; bed mobility, transfers, self-care/ADL's strength, endurance, range of motion/flexibility, coordination, and impaired balance. Treatment plan will include a comprehensive rehabilitation program with intense therapies for three hours/day, 5 days /week. Physical therapy to address bed mobility, car and mat transfer, progressive ambulation with use of least restrictive assistive device, optimization of gait biomechanics, truncal strengthening, lower extremity strengthening, coordination, range of motion/flexibility, wheelchair and cushion evaluation, durable medical equipment evaluation, upper extremity strengthening, range of motion/flexibility, dexterity, coordination and patient and family instruction. Occupational therapy to address feeding, grooming, upper and lower body dressing, and bathing, toileting, tub/toilet/bed transfers, durable medical equipment evaluation, upper extremity strengthening, range of motion/flexibility, dexterity, coordination and patient and family instruction. Rehabilitation nursing 24 hours per day to monitor bowel and bladder functions, work on bowel routine, bladder management per protocol, assess fall risk upon admission and periodically thereafter, implement and revise falls prevention strategies, maintain skin integrity through initial and daily pressure sore risk assessment (Braden scale), implement and revise pressure sore prevention strategies, educate patient and family members regarding medication administration, ADLs transfers, and mobility and continue therapy carryover with ADLs, transfers, and mobility. Social work and case management consult for discharge planning/disposition issues, as well as coordination and communication of patient progress between family and providers. Rehab psychology - as needed for adjustment, coping Goals: Mod 1to 1 w/transfers, self-care, and ambulation w/least assistive device Estimated length of stay: Discharge in 14 days remember I have already been in the hospital over a month now I have to learn how to bath and walk and use my legs and my arms and I am very weak. Rehab potential: was as followed by dr. the patient has an excellent rehabilitation potential and is well motivated. Patient has excellent family support.

The doctor has discussed the above goals with me, and I agree with the plan that they have for me to follow. I still have a lot going on with me, a whole lot, but I am trying to hold on tight and fight this battle; that is before me, I do not mind fighting. I will not give up; I have come too far too quickly now. The Lord has brought me too far to leave me. Sitting here typing this book, my husband and my oldest son were sitting down yesterday, which was Sunday; he told my son.

I do not know why your mother got so sick, because she prays and reads and sing hymns. She listens to gospel throughout every day; she be outside praying and looking up in the sky all of the time. I do not know why she got so sick and no matter how sick I got, she waited on me, and she never complained!

I just looked at Him and I say it was all in God's plan, my sickness was not only for me; it was for all of the people that came around me, everyone even all of the doctors, my whole family and friends who came around. God used me to work a miracle so someone might come to Him and be saved; I always pray for God to use me, and this was tough, but I had a chance to go to Heaven and it was all worth; it every pain, every moment. I laid there and I cried in joy and peace. The Spirit of the Lord was all over me. I would not take anything for my journey. I always told God to use me and try me and see. I live in my own world; there is no crime in my world or no hate. No matter what is going on around me; I pray, and I pray for other people when I know in my heart; they do not like me, but I stay in prayer for them, because we are all comfortable in a way. We must lean on the everlasting God for all of our mind. He got to give us a clean heart and mind that stays on Him. My husband always asked me how to do you live your life and enjoy your life; you always got the gospel going. I always tell Him that I am not my own. I belong to the Lord. We all belong to the Lord; he uses us as his will; I could not do anything.

My God has all of this laid out; he was and is in control of all of our lives. If we want Him to be. Why did Job get sick? I cannot put myself with Job, but the suffering part, because I am not rich nor do I have ten children, but I cannot relate to Him in suffering. I have tried to live a life that is pleasing to the Lord. All of my life, I am just like a brim fish. I am always running trying to get out of the way of my enemies, when you are for God, the enemies are always on your back. You have to pick and choose what you say and who you say what to, because people are so frightened, they will fall out with you, if you do not look at them right. I got to keep pressing on down the road. I mean praying and pressing towards God.

Life is no flower bed of eve, but I had a good one just let God lead you all the way. I had to find some help in my life as a young girl. I had no money, so I tried Jesus and I found out that he works a long time ago. I always prayed for a better day when I was a child. I wanted to go to the armed forces when I finish high school, but I was in love with this boy from Tignall, Georgia and I could not leave him, because I found love when I found this fellow; I was not looking for no love. I knew nothing about love; I never thought about loving a man.

I knew nothing at all. I mean nothing; this is my first day back at the doctors. I got lots of nurses and the doctors come in all the time. I got a walker by my bed; I got a big belt around my waist that the nurse holds me by to keep me from falling, because I am very weak. I always sit at end of my bed and cry. The nurse come, but sometimes and ask me what is wrong. I tell them; I am okay sitting here typing this book. Tears just running down my eyes. It was so hard, but I am going to make it. I have to take so much medication, mostly vitamins, because my body has been stripped of everything. Everything in my body was a mess, a big mess. I did not know that, because I was in Heaven looking good, feeling good and enjoying the view. It was amazing over there. I look in the river and I saw a reflection of myself. I was very young about 30 years old. I was always smiling over there. I cannot say, but those who miss Heaven I feel so sorry for them. Many people have so much fun; they give their soul no attention of where they will spend eternity.

I have met people and they say it is just here and nothing else. I said no there is a Heaven and I believe there is hell according to the Bible, but I went to Heaven. I stepped in Heaven. I got to tell the world that Heaven is real! It is so bright over there nothing is dark about Heaven. I was there; we cannot explain anything about Jesus; we only know a small part, a very small part! Why did he let me go to Heaven? Why did he let me see Him? Why did Jesus look at me like that? I never saw that look in this world. He loves me and he loves all of us, but it was so hard. When I awoke, I looked around at all of those people; they looked at me in shock. I mean shock! When I awoke; I tried to cough, but I could not; I had all of these tubes down my throat. The nurse got something that looked like pliers and she pulled them out of my throat. I looked around at the people in my room. There were all kinds of Spirits in the people in there; I blinked my eyes, and everyone was gone. I never saw anyone else again but my immediate family.

I am repeating myself, because this was a tough test, the toughest test, I will ever take. My granddaughter, Hannah, told me she said, "Grandma when we first got to the hospital. We were riding with Uncle Pastor Henra and when we first got to your room the doctor told us that your liver had failed and Uncle Pastor Henra and all of us cried. That is what the doctor told us. My heart stopped and my kidneys stopped and my whole body just shut completely down. I was on a respirator; it was pulling about 30 percent. My son, Otis, told me what was going on and my blood was poison. I was in Heaven; I never felt a thing until I returned to my body too much was going on for me to stay there.

I was worrying about nothing, even when I first got sick. I was sitting on the sofa in my living room, waiting on the EMS. I was at peace even though I could not breathe at all. Blood was coming from my mouth, lots of blood. My lungs were filling up with blood, but I had no idea at all what was wrong with me. What could have been wrong with me? I could rest in the Lord even though I could not say a long prayer, because I was too sick to pray. I tried in my mind, but I could not.

We are all filthy rags before a mighty God, but I told the Lord that I have served Him. I did not say I have tried to serve; I told the Lord that I have served Him and Him alone. I gave God all I had all in my life, but it was up to the God of Abraham, Isaac, Jacob whether I lived, or I died. It was all in God's hands. We are all going to die one day. We just do not know when or where, but we will all meet that day, and we must prepare for that day. We all will die no matter what you have, want, or own! It does not matter what kind of house you live in; you will only be here for a short period. Life is be enjoyed, but more time will be spent over there than here.

I am reminded by Psalm 9:8-13—

> And he shall judge the world in righteousness, he shall minister judgment to the people in uprightness. The Lord also will be a refuge for the oppressed, a refuge in times of trouble. And they that know thy name will put their trust in thee: for thou, Lord, hast not forsaken them that seek thee. Sing praises to the Lord, which dwelleth in Zion: declare among the people his doings. When he maketh inquisition for blood, he remembered them: he forgetteth not the cry of the humble. Have mercy upon me, O Lord; consider my trouble which I suffer of
>
> them that hate me, thou that liftest me up from the gates of death:

I always just stop writing and I read scripture in the Bible. I need some strength and my strength came from the word of God along with prayer and I would sing hymns to myself and my dog's name, Fuzzy, he always listens to my prayer and my singing. He always wags his tail that lets me know he is happy in the Lord, because the Lord loves his animals. Psalm 14:1-3 says—

> The fool hath said in his heart, there is no God. They are corrupt, they have done abominable works, there is none

that doeth good. The Lord looked down from heaven upon the children of men, to see if there were that did understand, and seek God. They are all gone aside, they are all together become filthy: there is none that doeth good, no not one.

Psalm 16:1 says, "Preserve me, O God: for in thee do I put my trust." Every morning the physical therapy nurse come and put my schedule on the board, and I just look up at it hoping I cannot just get down to the physical therapy room. I had to get there, I cannot not or stand up for a few seconds, how in the world will I get to the physical therapist room. It looked too far away for me to start walking again, but I got to try. I must I never fail at anything I wanted to do; if I try hard enough, I will make it with the help of God. He has brought me this far I got to go on, all my family is gone; the last time I saw my children it was a few days ago and I sent my husband home, because he looks darker than usual. He looks so tired, but he is there for me. I told Him do not come back until I tell Him to do so. He just looks at me with a half-smile. My bed was right in front of the nurses' stations; it was 628 on the rehabilitation floor of Doctors Hospital. I met the nurses for each shift all of them were so nice to me. I should not get up alone, but I tried; I got so tired of calling the nurses when I wanted to use the bathroom.

I had to use the pot over at Select Specialty Hospital, but over here I got a walker to get to the bathroom with assistance from the nurses. So many pills, three times a day, a shot in my stomach and I drink a lot of water. I ate good food, but I did not want to eat, but my children told me, "Mama, if you do not eat you will be in here longer." So, I tried to eat enough to sustain myself. It was nothing easy learning to use my body again. I hope to use the bathroom on my walker with assistance to take a pan bath. Every morning, I am still so weak. I got an older white lady for a roommate it hard for us to use the bathroom, because it took each one of us so long to use it. She was eighty-three and I was 61 so she has to be moved to another room so she could use the bathroom when she got ready, but this was the nicest lady, I had ever met. She always talks to me at therapy.

The first day, I went to therapy they came to get me in a wheelchair. I could hardly get in the chair, but a belt strip was around my waist to hold me up so I could get in the chair, and I tried to put my tennis shoes on to get to the therapy room. The first day was so hard; I say to myself, Lord if you do not help me. I cannot even try, so as I tried to stand up for a few seconds I was just shaking my hands, my legs and my knees were all shaking. I looked like a rag doll that the dogs had been playing with for days. My eyes were so weak; I could hardly blink them. I had to stand up for long as I could; it was about

30 seconds and then I would fall back to the chair that I was sitting in; I looked around the room and we were all trying to learn to walk, all kinds of physical therapy were going around the room. I just looked around the room wondering what in the world, am I doing here; we never know where we will end up in this world. It is best to stay humbled and low profiled and keep your mind on the cross.

I cry everyday out of nowhere! I am writing my book and I think back what I have been through, what the good Lord has brought me through. I can only cry with joy in my heart, a bucket of water runs from my eyes. I think of what my husband and my children went through. They all stayed by my side as each one came to see me. My mind went back to when they were very little. Oh, what a good time we had as they were growing up! The years flew by; all of them played sports and they kept their grades up.

They knew if they did not; they were not going to play any sports. One day I remember when they were very young, I had three in the back of an old yellow station wagon. It was dragging the ground and I laid my baby on the front seat and I was passing by the place where they cooked hamburgers and I did not have enough money to buy all of the burgers, so I did not buy any burger. I remember seeing their eyes looking back at the burger place as I drove by; lots of things ran through my mind as I laid here. I am still so sick; I am back at the Doctors

Hospital trying to get my arms and legs strong and learn to walk. I had a lot of other things going on as well my chest hurting a little bit, but they have run all kinds of test they say my heart is sound.

My hip is very numb on my right side, no feeling in it at all. I touch my hips and I feel nothing. It is just dead. My sores have not healed yet. I still; put my cream on it. I have some terrible sores on my buttocks area. As I looked in my children's eyes as I woke, they looked so tired and relieved; I am still with them. I am so glad to see them. I pray to God for all his mightily blessing, I am so glad to be alive. God has brought me back from Heaven. He let me see Heaven, all of those beautiful shiny buildings made of Gold. The roads paved of gold. Plenty of mansions on the side of the hill. I see the mountain top; I look over the sides of the hills and I stood there smiling. I always have a smile on my face when I walk upon the Lord Jesus Christ. I just stop in my track, and he turns his head, and he looks at me. I look in his eyes and it was an ocean in his eyes with the water running upside of his eyeballs. He looked at me with the most compassionate look. I have ever seen. I will never forget this look! I was young and pretty! I was just like a ghost; no blood was in my body. I was light. I looked at the ground. It looked so much different; it was brown, but a different kind of brown. I am a miracle, the doctors called me a "miracle." This was an act of nature. This was the mighty works of God that He performed on me! God worked many miracles in the books of Exodus, Kings, Daniel, Matthew, and Acts—just to name a few!

I am still sitting here typing thanking God for letting me be able to get out of bed; I have seen the time that I could not even turn over. I was just lying here hoping that I was able to turn myself over. I am standing here in my front door looking at this cool morning. It looks like we will have an early fall. Praising God that he spared my life and restored me better than I was. I was thinking back about this particularly; I am back at the Doctors Hospital for therapy, so I can learn how to use myself again. I have nice people here taking care of my every need that is all so nice to me just like those at Select Specialty Hospital. Those people over at Select Specialty Hospital are so sick.

We never know when our time is out, when God says it over, it is over no matter what doctor or hospital you are, but my time is not over yet. I do not know how long I am going to live after all of this, but I do know one thing I am in Jesus' hands and when he said it is over, I will go back to Heaven! Heaven is so real; the preacher does not preach much about Heaven, but I have been there, it is real and one day I will go back!

I was sitting here thinking about how I was standing there looking at the Savior's feet and looking at those brown sandals he had on his feet, thick leather sandals. I looked at his long leg bones. I looked into his eyes, and I looked at his cheekbone in his face and looked at his hair—beautiful, chocolate brown hair. He looked at me. Why did he let me see all of this? A little countrywoman who keeps to myself. I will repeat myself lots of times while I am writing this book, because I have to stop, and cry and I pray. My eyes get so full of tears; I cannot see. So, I have to stop and dry my eyes to catch my breath, because the glory of God's Spirit of the Lord be upon me all the time when I get in deep meditation about Heaven.

My children and I always talk about this; I always start crying, because I never thought in a million years, I would get a chance to visit Heaven until I died for good, but I was dead. I came back! I was raised from the dead! My body had begun to rot and had all kinds of deep sores on my body. All I went through, people thought I would have brain damage, but I still remember when I was five years old before I started to school. I went to school plenty of days very hungry and when I got back home from school my mother always had some pinto beans cook with fatback meat and a little apple or peach pie. She had all our plates fixed on the table, a small wooden looking table just plain wood with no shine on it, just a homemade table. She had about 10 plates fixed and each one of us would get one. We mostly had two biscuits a piece and fatback meat with molasses. We were full until the next day;

about this time, we had no snacks like the children these days have after school. Life was hard during the hot summer. We had no shoes to wear. It was hard! I always wondered why a person would have 10 children and it would be so hard to feed them. My father would go by the butcher pin and get the parts of the animal that they threw away. He would always bring it home to be processed.

We would have to stay up half of the night cleaning these animal parts that my dad brought home. We cleaned cow feet, hog chitterlings, and cow heads. It was all about survival for food. Lunch money was about 20 cents, but I never had money for lunch. I carried a greasy sack of a cow tripe meat sandwich in it. Somedays, I had to hide and eat it because I did not want the children to laugh at me. They always picked at my shoes. I did not care, because I always knew who I was in Christ. Whether they played with me or not it was okay. I stood on the wall plenty of days while some of my classmates thought that they were big stuff. My mother and my father were very smart folks. They knew what their parents had taught them so they could only pass on to me what they knew. They told me a lot of things that I passed on to my children. A lot of things they did not know that I found out about life as I grew with the Lord talking to me every day.

I knew deep down in my heart that it had to be another way out. I read every book that I could get my hands on. I mean every book. They are seen to be no hope at times. It would rain for weeks, and my father could not work. My father worked in the woods cutting pulpwood and that looked like the hardest job in the world. I never have seen lotion. I always grease my legs with lard from the hog that we had killed over the winter. This is what my mother used to cook with, lard from the hog fat. I think everyone did it back then. Lard fried good food and made good biscuits. If we did not have anything else to eat, we had a biscuit! My mother went into that kitchen and made two pans of biscuits. We always had little molasses with the biscuits.

My husband came the first day back at the Doctors Hospital and he brought me some clothes for me to do physical therapy in; he brought the simplest thing that he could find. I just needed some exercise clothes and a pair of tennis shoes. Oh, this was the hardest time, just trying to get dress the therapists would always tie my shoes. I barely got to the bathroom. I always wiped myself off. I glanced at myself in the mirror. I did not know the person that I saw in the mirror. I have been through the deep valleys and Heaven and back to life in the hospital. Oh, my God! Lord have mercy on me! I have tears of joy running down my face. I am weak still very weak.

This is the second day back at the Doctors Hospital. I told my husband to go home, and I told my children do not come back.

I got to do this on my own. So, I laid for days and night thinking that I am going to get out of here. Praying and thinking back over my life thanking God for all His many blessings and thanking Him for my family. Praising God for my wonderful husband, my children, and my daughters-in-law. They all stuck by me, but now it is my time with the Lord. The nurses, physical therapists, housekeepers, and I always had church. We always take about the Lord. Most of the people here know the Lord; they told me their stories and I told them stories of what I have been through. The people in physical therapy exchanged stories as well. We talked about the Lord has blessed us. He kept us and healed us.

Willie Agnes Chennault

Chapter 14

COMFORT

Thinking back to when I went to Heaven; I was just there in a blink of an eye. I just flew out of my lifeless body. We all have a soul that is going to fly out of this body, whether we believe it or not! Your Spirit will leave this body and spend eternality somewhere, Heaven or hell. We must choose the place ourselves. God gives us free will. My Spirit flew out of my sick body. I was too sick for my Spirit to stay there; my daughter told me that the respirator that I was on was breathing for me. I never know that. My children tell me things in bits and pieces, because my sickness opens their eyes. They saw a miracle upfront.

My daughter told me yesterday that she always held my hands while in was in a coma and there was no life in them, they were like dead meat and very white inside. I know I looked at my hands when I awake, and I saw no blood in them they were still white inside, but God is God, and he can do anything he chooses to do. He does not have to explain anything to no one, because he knows the heart. I always loved Peter among all the disciples. I love Peter. He loved Jesus. He loved Him so much that he died upside down on the cross. He did not want to die head up on the cross. I sit here day after day typing. I have been typing for a while it took me about six months after I got home to get a part of my strength back.

back at the Doctors Hospital, I am trying to get my strength back the first day I went to physical therapy. I had to try to stand up beside the table. I only could stand a few seconds before I drop back down in the chair, I always had supervision, because I was at risk of falling. I try to stand for at least a minute, but I could not.

Lord this was so hard test. A person cannot even imagine until you have been in these shoes. My legs were so weak, but I wanted to give up. All my family is gone, I told them not to come back, my immediate family gave me all of their support. I never saw anyone else at this time. After I tried to stand a few seconds. I sat down at the table, and I picked beans out of some hard pieces of dough, and this was a hard job. It was to get strength back in my hands and arms. This was no easy task, but I wanted to give up and I went to the other side of the room to lay down and do leg raises and quiz the rubble ball. Ever since I got back to the Doctors Hospital, one of my doctors would come in and feel my legs to make sure that they were not swelling and he did this three times every day even when I was in physical therapy there; then he would come in and feel my legs to make sure they weren't swelling; this has something to do with my heart I know that.

About two days later, I got another roommate; she was an older lady, a retired schoolteacher from Harlem; she has a lovely family. They always spoke to me, and we talked about a lot of different things. She has six girls and two boys. She was old school, but a very nice lady. I will never forget her. She told me that she had fallen in her bathroom and her granddaughter climbed through the window to rescue her; she had been lying there for days. She was in bad shape. She did not want to eat so I told her to just drink Ensure if you did not feel like eating. It was so hard to stand up holding on to the rails doing sidekicks with my legs. I have a wheelchair right side me and the therapist were standing there beside me counting the leg kicks if I could just do five on each leg.

I was so weak; they were always checking my blood pressure all the time while at physical therapy. Sometimes my blood pressure would shoot up and my heart rate would go up and my chest would start hurting. The nurse checked it and it would be okay; they gave me medication. At this time, I do not have an IV going into me. I have had a million IVs, and all kinds of vitamins. I am still on different kinds of vitamins. Somedays I sit there in therapy, and I cry and cry, just like I am doing now. Lord, have Mercy! Why am I going through so much? I always try to live my life for Jesus. I told Him that before I left home when I was spitting up blood sitting in my living room, I could not pray at all. I told the Lord I have to live my life for Him, and I am in your hands. I always cried with tears running down my face. Life is no joke; you never know what you will have to endure, or your children will have to endure or your spouse.

It is better to stay prayed up. Most people do not have that personal relationship with Christ, but you are going to need it. Just going to church on Sunday is not nearly enough; you must give Him praises and learn of Him all through the week, everyday bits, and pieces of prayer, studying mediation, singing hymns, and holding up your hands to Him and crying out to Him.

I know God was preparing me for my illness because I felt like I was getting ready to die, but I did not know what was wrong. I went on about my regular living. I always prayed a lot. I learned this as a small child when I had learned how poor I was; I did not want my children to have to go through the things their father and I went through as a child.

There must be another way and the Lord did for us as we asked of Him. He educated all of our children, because we work harder. When we met each other, we were both virgins and we stayed that way all through high school. We talked about that after a few times we met; there was some kind of force pulling us tighter. I never had a chance to date other people. I think about that sometimes; I wish I had but it too late now I love Jesus too much to go outside my marriage. I have headed to Heaven again, but I know the Lord did not bring me through all of this to take me right back. I got some work to do, I must tell everyone Heaven is real! I will continue to pray with hands lifted like 1 Timothy 2:8 says, "I will therefore that men pray everywhere, lifting holy hands, without wrath and doubting."

I always read my Bible and I listened to Bible study on the television all the time I go to sleep Look at the Bible study with Shephard chapel every night. I listen to them for the last 35 years. I love the Lord if you talk about the Lord's people, they will think you are crazy, but I do not! I was a great miracle because every minute counted in getting me to the hospital, but God had me all of those who were standing around looking at me when I awoke, still cannot believe I am alive.

Back at the Doctors Hospital, on this second day, my goal is learning to stand up and walk. The nice, old lady that is in the room with me is going to another room. I guess she cannot get the bathroom, because it takes me a long time to drag myself to the bathroom. I do not have to use the bedpan anymore. I can drag myself to the bathroom with the help of a nurse because I still cannot stand up good. I am on my walker at this time lots of medication in cup vitamins and more vitamins plenty of victims every day my food is good here my appetite is coming back, but my mouth has healed my gums feel better my lips still sore, but I look terrible I peak in the bathroom mirror at a miracle. My doctor calls me Mrs. miracles and I just look at her and I smile knowing that God got me. He has always had me because we have a personal relationship.

411

You must have a personal relationship with Jesus Christ.

I am just a countrywoman who believes in Jesus Christ. He is my breath, my whole being belongs to Him ever since I was a small barefooted girl. I fell in love with the Lord, and I would always go in the woods and sit by a tree, and I wondered about life. I thought about those white folks on top of the hill and them having a better life than us. I said to myself there has to be more to life than being so poor, my family was always looking for food. Lord, why do not we have enough food and clothes? Why do we live like this? I was happy because I knew somehow someday things would change for me, but after I got grown, I married exceedingly early, and it was work; raising children was more work and more work. I had no time for nothing else, but to take care of my family.

I always had to pray everywhere I went. I prayed in my mind some time. My husband would take me out dancing. I would be on the dance floor saying the Lord prayers. I had to find another way to live. My parents worked hard so hard, and they prayed. We went to church, but their minds were on so much hard work. I had to find another way; that is why I read every book that I could get my hands on, and I prayed, and I trusted the Lord.

At this time, I am in the room alone. I am still sicker than sick thinking back, my father would never let us drag our feet. He told my siblings and I to walk straight and keep your head up! You cannot see up high looking down unless you are picking up something. Laying here in the evening of the second day back at Doctors Hospital no one is here. My family is gone. It was just me and the Lord real with all of the hospital staff. I am on the 6-floor physical therapy floor everyone up here is up here to learn how to do something the young and middle age and the old. we are all up here struggling like the frog I saw in the can of water on the back yard.

I stood there for a long time on my walker until my leg got so weak. I sat on the bench in the back yard, but as long as I stood there I look down on the big drum of water. The frog hatched in this drum of water; it was half full of water and just the frog struggling and trying to get to the top of the barrow. It is a she because I stood there hold on to my walker looking therein with all force she has climbed up and slid back down again struggling with all forces in her body. I stood there and I stood there just like the frog. She made it to the top of the barrel, and she looked around afraid to jump, but after all that struggling and struggling; I made it home. I struggled with trying to walk at this time. I am here alone, no one is here. My children had to go, my husband is sick Himself and he cannot overload Himself, because he has to take breathing treatments every four hours.

I am laying down feel like I got indigestion in my chest. I told the nurse that my chest is hurting. So, they ran in my room, and they put all of the wires to my feet's and my chest, and they brought that large machine, and they took pictures of my heart, but everything came back clean. As my children grew up in life, I told them everything I knew and everything my parents wanted me to see, and their father told them everything that he knew and what his father had told he told the children. We must talk to our children while we sit at the dinner table, while we drive along the highways when we are in our homes. We must always guide them so when they go out onto the world, they will know what to expect and tell them about everything you know good or bad tell them to pray while they are small, even before they are born pray with your children. God has been with me all my life, but I had to fight the good fight.

The devil will always come by, but if you talk to the Lord honestly through prayer; He will always show up. I had good parents. I am glad my children got a chance to know their grandparents on both sides of the family that made a big difference in their lives, because they did not let them get away with anything. They had to be in order at all times. They love them because a child loves discipline. The doctors and nurses are in and out of my room all day half of the night looking at me laying there thinking God for his goodness, he did not have to do it, but he did. He healed my body, I got to tell the world. Laying there I get a few pieces of clothes my husband had brought me early from home, he picks the worst things I have ever had to wear. I have to go to physical therapists; the therapist pushes me all the way and I was willing to go also just look at me. I am in the bathroom trying to wash off. I never had a shower, yet maybe soon I will be able to bath all over again. A whole month has passed by, and I really need a bath, my hair is lifeless. It feels like wood and is dry as grass in the fall of the year. I am alive my children my husband and my grandchildren most of all needs me, because I give them a hard time. My grandchildren, they are my breath. I get so much joy just by looking in their eyes, looking at the next generation of Chennault's. It is a blessing to be alive, but I see Heaven and that will always be with me. My leg and arms as well as my whole body is still very weak right after I got in the EMS. I left this world my body was here, but I was gone to a land that I heard my mother and my father talk about nothing, but joy and peace are over there. On the other side of Jordan that is where I was, Heaven is so beautiful. I think about it every day, the things I seen looking at Jesus' feet, His hair and His robe was light gray, real light. He looked at me why me? I never have seen that look or that belt he had around his waist or his sandals. His long arms, I just walked upon Him. I never knew that I live here I had no memory of back here. I did not know what was going or I did not know I was in the hospital sick. I really did not know when I woke and saw all of those people I did not know, what was wrong with me or what I had. No one had told me yet how long I had been in the hospital. I did not know because my Spirit was in Heaven. These earthly bodies that we have now will not go, Heaven.

Our Spirit will fly out our bodies. I had a glorified body. I looked young when I was 30 years old. I felt nothing until I woke, I could only move my eyes, I am repeating myself. I have to I got to make sure that those who are on the outside of safety come in before it is too late. Heaven is awaiting each one of us, but you must come in by the door of Lord and Savior Jesus Christ. Come now before it is too late. It not all about going to church. I love to go to church, but a lot of things that are being taught is not true. it is about a personal relationship with Christ that will pay off just you and Him. Let every man be satisfied with his mind. Ecclesiastes 5:15, "As he came forth of his mother's womb, naked shall he return to go as he came, and shall take nothing of his labor, which he may carry away in his hand."

No matter who you think you are or how good you think you are trouble is coming. If trouble does not come you know the devil already got you, because you are not growing in Christ. Trouble cleans your Spirit for God to use you to help some on else. God has the hardest test for the strongest patients and when you pray always be cautious what you talk to Him about, because he hears every groan, every motive, every thought. He knows even before we enter into our father's seed. He knew us, remember Jeremiah. God chose Him even before he was born to be a prophet. He knows all of us even though he gives us free will to choose to live with Him or the devil. You choose this day, do not go another moment chose to love the Lord and Savior Jesus Christ and to love Him and in all his ways. Pray and repent for our sins daily. Everyday salvation is always there if you accept Christ as your savior, but when we sin, we must always repent. We do not want to drift so far from the boat that we cannot get back to the shore. Stay connected to Christ Jesus that the way If your mind drifts off to a lot of things, He can keep you sound.

Laying here in the Doctors Hospital, I tried to learn to walk again just like a baby learns to walk. This is me again! How did I get here, I was always a superwoman nothing ever stopped me, and have been through chaos but I have been healed through Jesus. I am going to hold onto Jesus, and I am going to get out of here. Soon, I am going home, I got a way to go yet. My hands still shake like a leaf and my body is very weak, still very weak. My doctor always comes in and he touches my legs to see if there is any swelling, three times a day he touches my legs, but he does not say anything. He just looks at me and he just looks. Laying here with my bluebonnet on my head, I must get dress because I have physical therapy three hours a day. They are tough to get out of this bed for, and I try to be ready sometimes before I eat my breakfast down in the physical therapy room. Early in the morning at 6 a.m. My room is always full of all kinds of nurses. I talk to them, and they always tell me to pray for them and their children. They find out what I have been through, they say, "Oh, God! you have been through so much!" They cry sometimes and I cry because the Spirit of the Lord comes to me quickly. I feel his glory all over me and the peace and the joy even though I am very weak.

I am happy in the Lord. We are all going to leave this world in just a matter of time. A few years in your nice house, a few years driving your new car, a few years enjoying life, a few years down here if you live to be 80 or 90, is still a few years compared to eternity. No essence of time is there while I was Heaven. I had nothing to do with time. I only knew time when I woke up. When I went thought the ground it was fun ride, I was light there is no darkness anywhere. I went through looking like I do now, but when I stepped out of the earth. I looked like I was in a whole other form. I was prettier and younger. I was smiling all the time, amazingly happy there Oh, Lord, where am I? How did I get here? When I saw my mother and my aunties I wanted to go across the river where they were; I started across I laid in the water and my mother told me to go back. They need you back there. I was smiling. I stood there looking down to the right of me and to the left of me and then back to the right of me. I saw all of those beautiful mansions shining with the streets of pure gold. The doors looked more brighter than any other part and the windows also. I looked to my left and I saw water running down the side of the streams with gold shining on the sides of the river. I saw trees and mountains.

I looked in front of me; I saw all the children playing. My aunties were sitting down at a table a few feet from my mother. Aunt Nee and Lue were facing each other at the table. My mother's chair was pulled out from the table; it was as though she knew I was coming. It was a square, grey table. My aunties and mother were watching the children play. They all looked at me and my mother was standing on the side of the river directly in front of me.

I know I was in Heaven. I thought I had been there all the time. I know nothing about being back here on earth. Nothing at all, your body and your mind is in a whole another state of life. A new life you will put on. This is about the second time I am back at the Doctors Hospital. I am still very sick, but I am here to learn how to walk, and a lot of things come with learning just how to stand up. I got to stand up before I can walk. If I could just stand up, my body is so weak, but I will not complain. I could not keep my mind on how sick I was, or I that could not walk. I had to go home and see about my husband and be there for my children and my grandchildren because I love to talk to my grandchildren and my children also. I have been through turmoil and trials in the physical realm, but over yonder in Heaven I had no pain at all. I was not sick at all. I had joy and peace. I was so happy, but the Lord brought me back because I was not finish down here. I know my family has been through chaos not knowing whether I would live or die. My immediate family was ready to let me go; I am talking about my husband and my children and their family.

I lay here day after day praying for other folks. I put myself last on my prayer list. I know that is crazy, but I do that most of the time unless I need some help right quickly and God sometimes answer me sometimes quickly before I finish my prayer; he has already answered my cry. My children were in a storm while I was in a coma. Their lives were shattered like broken glass in the middle of the road. I am here learning how to walk. I do not want pity from no one. Do not be sorry for anything that happened to me. I let God fight my battles because I asked Him to; he knows what he is doing with me. I let Him use me any way he pleases to get his Glory. I always tell the Lord that I am not my own and that I belong to the Him. The Lord sent the right EMS out to get me; the Lord, Himself, was driving the EMS, he was in the EMS with me. The Lord never left me alone and when he saw that I could no longer stay in that sick body of mines, he snatched me out of it for a few days and I am glad he did, he let me see Heaven. Glory to God! I will never be the same again, part of me is still in Heaven. I always have talked to the Lord. I like to prepare ahead of time because I always pray my best when things are going well with me, when trouble does come, and it is coming; I will not have to fall apart and call on everyone, but Him, the Lord. I do not have to do too much talking to the Lord, because the line of communication is already open when you talk to God regularly. You do not have to say a whole lot because he knows your voice anyway. He read Nathanael's mind; I came to John 1:48, "Nathanael saith unto Him, Whence knowest thou me? Jesus answered and said unto Him, Before that Philip called thee when thou was under the fig tree, I saw thee."

I thought to myself was Job this sick? If he was as sick as I know the only way, he made it was through the healing of the Lord. The Lord healed me also. Job prayed for his friend when he was so sick. All I can do now is to hold on, my body has begun to decay. I cough up black mucus when I am awake, I vomited when I ate solid foods, a tube sucked it out of my throat. I was in terrible shape, but I have come this far. I looked at my hands when I awake, they were very white inside; there was not enough blood in my body to support my body, but I got to keep on trusting God. I cannot stop now; there is no other help I know. Only Jesus can heal me, and it is only

Him working through these good doctors at the Doctors Hospital and the good folk and doctors at Select Specialty Hospital.

All are working together for the good of God's plan; even the housekeeper and the food service was all in God's plan. John 16:33 says, "These things I have spoken unto you, that in me ye might have peace. In the world ye shall have tribulation: but be of good cheer; I have overcome the world." Psalm 46: 1 says, "God is our refuge and strength, a very present help in trouble." I read Job 14:1: "Man that is born of a woman is of few days, and full of trouble."

Looking back to when I woke up, at first, I did not have my right mind. My daughter told me this, but after a while, it came to me fully. I am glad I had no brain damage or hearing lost. My mind came back to me as it was. I was sicker than sick. I still didn't know whether I would live or not, but I got to thinking I have seen Heaven and the Lord brought me back to my body because the doctor was ready to let me go, but God steps right in and he brought me back from Heaven, because I got something else to do for Him. I had to accept my suffering it is not what I did wrong; I am what I have done right all of my life.

My mind goes back to my childhood for a few minutes. I remember my mother has to go to town and she would leave my younger sister in brother sitting in a chair. She tied a rag around their waist to the chair, I was too small to help but I would sit there until she returned. She could go outside to the garden for a long period of time, but that baby would sit there not saying a word. She would put sugar and butter in a white rag and tie it up and the baby would suck on it until she returned. She tied them to the back of a chair and when she returned the child would still be sitting in the same place where she left them, I remember this. I remember when my dad had an old mule. The mule was old when the white folk gave Him to my dad. I remember seeing my dad plowing in the field up the road. He planted food for us. It was hard to feed 10 children plus my parents had to eat also. He plowed with that old mule. My dad would be falling down on the field; he would be holding on to that plow. The rolls would look so pretty.

I always walked in the cool, red dirt barefooted; I dropped seeds along in the rows. He would always grow a good garden. We had more food in the summertime than the winter, because we lived beside the white folks who had all kinds of fruit and nuts trees, but they always watch their trees. We slipped fruit in our pockets as we passed by the road. I do not call that stealing! We had to survive and survive for food was our biggest thing. One day that old mule was lying beside the house; I knew he had died. My dad got his pick-up truck and pulled him down in a large gully back behind the house, so we could sleep with the window open. We never had a screen in the window just a small crack in the windows and doors. No one was going to bother us. I have to live in a smooth, comfortable world; everyone lived the same mostly all of the black folks were all in the same shape, but there was more love for each other unlike how it is today. My mind took me back to comfort, laying there sick day after day.

I remember my comfort days before I became a woman. I had a lot of tough days, but they built my character. My faith in the Lord was brought out. I always knew to pray, because there was nothing else, I had to hold on to, nothing. I had to find something to hold on to and the Lord stepped into my heart. I was very different from the rest of my sisters. I was a lion. I stayed outside most of the time with my brothers especially the one that is under me, Joseph. We always hung together went fishing. We were so small; we saw plenty of snakes, but none of them bothered us. We always went fishing. My mother and father did not know where we were, because children had survivor sense back in those days. Parents did not have to watch us every second. We went fishing; we never caught anything much but what we caught, we cooked, and we ate the fish that were too tiny to turn over in the skillet, but we ate them anyway. We went to pick blackberries and we sold them to the white folks up the road for 50 cents a gallon. Some time we did not have any shoes to put on our feet, but we made it. It was hot but we never paid that any attention. We never had a fan; I do not know how we made it. I never seen a fan. I know when we went in the white folk's house where my mother worked, it was cool. I never knew what it was to have running water; we had to walk a long way to get water to use. I never knew what it felt like to take a shower. I never heard of the word, "shower" until I got grown.

Life was simple back then; my children never will experience that "Little House on the Prairie Life" Every day was just so simple, no television and no radio until later on in the late 1960s. We got electricity and television, but no running water. I went all through high school never having running water or a bathroom toilet, it was outdoors, or we used the bathroom in the woods. We bathe in a wash pan or a tin tub. We got clean bathing in rainwater that my sweet mother caught outside the back door. She washed her greens in it, but she did not cook with it; we would always go to the spring down the hill after the well dries up. During my high school years, my siblings and I had a hard life, but we had many moments of laughter. We only knew what we saw in person. I remember all of those chickens that my father had brought home from Bud Holloway Chicken Farm. Bud raised chickens and when the chickens laid eggs my dad would go get some eggs and chickens. We had to slaughter the chickens, clean the insides out of the chickens, and pick the feathers from them. It took us all evening. My father would ride out somewhere into town.

We had to pick all of those sick looking chickens. I was just disgusted when my mom cooked them. The chickens had to cook a very long time. We did this on a regular basis. My dad did all he could to raise ten kids not knowing the cost. He only knew how he was raised and that is what he went by, but like I say I had to seek more for my family. I always think about that little Bible that I found in the old shack, the second house we moved to during my high school career. I found this little old Bible. It was full of pictures of the Bible Day people. I kept this Bible and I read it daily. Life had to be better than what was happening around me, but I had peace. It has is not about material things; it about the love of Jesus Christ our hearts. Lord, have Mercy! We made it! Life was simple back then, but how could these children today survive those days. I am glad I had a chance to live as I did.

I have nothing to complain about at this point in my life. I am trying to learn how to use my body again; it is about my third day back at the Doctors Hospital and my mind takes me back. Oh, how I suffered, or I am suffering. I do not know why, but God got a plan for me. I just laid here a lot of days looking out of the door wishing that I was strong, and I could walk. I got some dirty clothes from going to the physical therapists three days already and I need a washing room, it is right across the hall from me beside the nurses' station, but I cannot stand up long enough even on my walker; I cannot make it over there so a nurse offers to wash my clothes for me. I need these clothes for physical therapy.

I do not want anyone coming to see me, my family, my children, and my husband are worn out completely; they call on the hour every hour. I am okay; I never complain to them. I am so glad to be alive, glory to God! I have a new room with a retired schoolteacher from Harlem, Georgia and she is a doll. She fell in her bathroom, but she could not get up at this time, so I got the bathroom all to myself, it takes me a long time to get in and out of the bathroom. I always have to have help at this time, but a few more sessions with the physical therapists. I will be out of here, that is my plan.

It is so very hard; I have to try to walk around the nurse's station it is a circle around it. I am on my walker weak as a newborn chicken trying to walk around. The nurses are right behind me with the wheelchair. I am tired and weak, but I am it making a step by step. I feel like I have been remade. I cannot explain, but it is a whole other world over there. I hope everyone is saved, but I know that is not going to be true. I cannot tell you what they will be missing. It is so beautiful there! Lord, have mercy! Why did the Lord let me see Him? I looked at the Lord Jesus Christ. I just stood there looking at Him. He turned his head and looked at me with the most compassionate look I have ever seen. I never seen a look like that in this whole world. Never!

I am at the Doctors Hospital. My patient care records stated:

> Lung fields clear and free of signs of respiratory distress.
> Patient needs help to aid in getting on or off the toilet for
> toilet transfer patient requires raised toilet seat grab bars.
> Patient needs help getting in or out of bed., chair or
> wheelchair patient walks 150 feet without a rest break no
> walks minimum of 50 ft. w/o rest break and no assistance
> from help No for walking patient needs : rolling walker
> patient on the 6/21/2017 patient goes up and down stairs
> 4 to all steps without rest break yes patient requires helper,
> the extra time has mild difficulty yes cooperates,
> participates a demonstrates appropriate behavior w/o
> assist.

Yes, I am still being seen for a nonhealing pressure ulcer
wound. I am on a Javen drink and Ensure clear with every
meal. Javen helps advanced wound healings, still on my
buttock area. There is so much going on with me. I cannot tell
it all each day. I have to walk around the nurses' station for
part of my physical therapy. It will be so hard to do, but I must
do. I get on the exercise bike in the physical therapy room, and
I just sit there looking around at all of the sick people trying to
improve themselves. I never thought in a million years that I
would be sitting among these good folks all who are trying to
help themselves. There are nice physical therapists here; they

are really good in what they do. They come to get me after breakfast. I got my bag headed to the place where you take a bath at.

We had to go a good way down the hall, and I was on my walker; the physical therapist carried my bag, and I was just trying to get there. I have been wiping off in the pan and then I roll my walker into the bathroom in my room, but this bathroom was down the hallway. When I got there, I tried to pull my clothes off; I was very weak and sick, but somewhat better but I still very weak. I pull my blue bonnet off my head. I have not seen my hair in over a month. My hair felt like straw, and I pulled my bluebonnet off and the physical therapists said, "Mrs. Chennault you are going to take a shower." I was so happy to hear this. I have not taken a shower since the morning of May 19, 2017, and I barely remember even getting in the shower that morning my mind was leaving me fast.

Willie Agnes Chennault

Chapter 15

A NEW BEGINNING FOR ME!

It is June 23, 2017. The nurse is helping me undress. I use my walker to help me get around my hospital room. When I take a shower, I have to sit in a chair to bathe. I sit there and the nurse left out. She stood out in the next room; she did not hurry me at all. I poured some shampoo soap in my hair, and I rubbed it in. It felt so good to wash my hair. I had no hair in the back of my head from laying in the bed in my coma. I lost a patch of hair in the back of my head, but that did not bother me at all! I am alive and on my way home! I am making improvements every day. The Lord is healing me. His Holy Spirit comes over my body every day and the Holy Spirit is healing my body daily. Oh! This water feels so good on my body. I sat there. I prayed and I repeated Psalm 23 and I said the Lord's Prayer. I cried, thanking Him for letting me live so I could be with my family.

I know that they have been through a great tribulation dealing with the fact of not knowing whether I was going to live or die. My youngest son, Pastor Henra told me one day a few days ago that the Lord told Him that I was not going to die. I sat in the chair a long time thanking the Lord for His goodness and for sparing my life and for letting me see Heaven! I will never be the same again, long as I live; I will never be the same. Sitting here in the chair with water running all over my head. My head is clean, but my buttocks is still sore. My wounds still hurt on my buttocks, but they are healing. I am sitting in the bathroom thinking about how I got here. One thing about life we never know what a day may hold. Each day has enough trouble of its own.

We must take one day at a time. We must live one second at a time! I say these things to myself. I know I changed! My hair is in bad shape, but that is the least of my worries. I have no worries because I have been to Heaven! I saw the Lord and He looked at me! I saw His clothes. I looked at His feet and His sandals. I looked in His eyes. I looked at his hair. I saw His whole face. I looked at the belt around His waist and I saw all of those people in the Bible days. I saw all of those children. I saw my mother and my two aunties. I saw the oxen pulling the wooden wagons; they were looking at me and I saw the glory in the animals' eyes, all around them. Isaiah 11:6-8 says—

> The wolf also shall dwell with the lamb, and the leopard shall lie down with the kid; and the calf and the young lion and the fatling together; and a little child shall lead them. And the cow and the bear shall feed; their young ones shall lie down together: and the lion shall eat straw like the ox. And the sucking child shall play on the hole of the asp, and the weaned child shall put his hand on the cockatrice' den.

Their eyes and I felt the glory of God all over Heaven! Heaven is real! I hope that all of you out there who are not save come to Christ while there is time. While breath is still in your body, come now you cannot clean yourself up. Come now before it is too late. Come now! I am still sitting here in the shower. The water is running over my head. I am scrubbing my body. I do not need oxygen anymore. I am sitting here relaxing; my family is not here. I told everybody to go home, I got this. The Lord is with me, and he is always with each one of us if we want Him to be, he does not force Himself on anyone; his hands are always stretched out if you want Him. there is no other way to the father, but through his son. Sitting here thinking about how good God has been to me. Lord you did not have to save and heal my body, but you did Lord. You know no other help, I know.

When I was a little girl sitting in the woods. I had to pray to be in the middle of the group; my sibling I mean I never got much attention. I was like the slave running around the house making everyone else comfortable; getting most of the wood and walking a long way to the white folk's house to get water with my brother. I was a tomboy; what did I expect. I worked along with my brother the one who is next to me, Joseph. I did the major work outside, but it was okay. I loved the outdoors. I was just thinking while laying here knowing I got to learn how to walk again it is one of the hardest things I ever had to do that is to walk again. Grown women like me are always super women and look at me now. My bones and my body are weak as a worm, but my mind is stronger than usual, because I have seen the other side of Heaven.

I am free! I mean free! I have been with the Lord, I seen Him for myself, I am free. His gown was on top of his knees. I saw his knees and his legs. His skin color was gray and pink. I looked at his sandals, a while. I looked at his feet in the middle; it was amazing! Lord, have mercy! I will never forget this as long as I live. I see the Lord I got to tell the whole world that I see the Lord in his robe. It was so beautiful. His belt and his sandals and I see something around his head; I cannot explain it, it was so beautiful, dark brown. It was unexplainable, to die in the Lord is so beautiful. I no longer have a fear dying; none, nothing to be afraid of. If you die in the Lord, believing in Him, he will carry you through safely to the other side. It was amazing going through the ground, being spit out into Heaven. My children were calling me on my cell phone, but my hands were still shaking like a leaf on the tree. I told them I got this, I told them to stay home I got this. I had to do this on my own. I need my clothes washed at this time, so I am going to try and go across the hall and put my clothes in the washer. I got my clothes in a bag, I can see the laundry room door from my bed as I sat on the edge of my bed wondering if I could make it over there on my walker. I cannot stand up, but only for a few moments. I thought if I could just get over there and just drop them in the washer. I will be doing good. So, I tried, I got halfway, and I just gave out. The nurse saw me, and she helped me back to my room. She took my clothes that I use to wear to physical therapy, and she washed them for me. I was so tired, but it will get better.

My body is still upside, down! Everything in my body was all tied in a knot, but things are looking up. I still have hypertension, hyperlipidemia, Critical illness myopathy, Rhabdomyolysis, physical deconditioning, Impaired mobility and ADLs, impaired gait, decreased strength, endurance, and mobility, Kidney injury, Hx of bacterial pneumonia, Hx sepsis, COPD, Anemia, Thrombocytopenia, Hx of respiratory failure and Systolic CHF. I am still sicker than sick, but I will hold on because if I was going to die the Lord would have kept me in Heaven, but the Lord, brought me back to tell my story; that someone might believe and come to Him while there is still breath in their body. All of those who looked upon my sick body at the hospital will now that God is a miracle worker. God is still in the business of working miracles.

At this time, I am back at the doctors. The date is June 23, 2017. I am on the following medications: Dextrose 15 gram ASDIR PRN, Dextrose/Water 25-50ML, Glucagon 1mg aspirin, Atorvastatin Calcium 20mg bedtime, Preservision 2 per day, Potassium Chloride 20MEQ,vitamin B Complex,

Prednisone 20 mg, Levothyroxine Sodium 50 mcg, Hydralazine
HCI 50 mg Q8 HPO, Docusate Sodium 100 mg Q12HR,
insulin Human, Lumigan 0.01, Timolol, Metoprolol Tartrate 25
mg Q12 ,Pantoprazole 40 mg bedtime, Silver Sulfadiazine l
Applic Q12 Topical, Albuterol/Ipratropium 3ML
0600,1200,1800neb, Clonidine HCL0.1 , Lactobacillus
Acidophilus 2 ea, Magnesium Oxide 400 mg, Sodium
Bicarbonate 650mg, Hydralazine 25 mg, Al Hydrox/mg
Hydrox/Simethicone 30 ML, Acetaminophen 650mg,
Bisacodyl 10 mg, daily rectal Polyethylene Glycol l packet daily
on my skin.

I am always busy now that the doctors come in and out all
day and night. The doctor always touched my legs to see if any
swelling is taking place, but the doctor never says anything. He
never says anything; he looks serious when he touches my legs
though. I can be in physical therapy and the doctor comes by
and he would touch my legs on top and he never says anything.
Today in physical therapy my chest starts hurting as I was on
the exercise bike. The nurse just told me to slow down a little
each day, I felt my strength coming back to me; I was amazed
how my strength was returning but I am still sicker than sick. I
mean sick, I am too sick for a visitor. When I went to physical
therapy, I had to put lots of screws and bolts together by
screwing them together. It was a very hard job, putting the
puzzles together. Both tasks were so hard.

I just cried. I did not want anyone to see me cry, but I was crying tears of joy. I was thinking about Heaven; my mind will always be over there until I get back there. I always tell my children about Heaven, they listen because every time we talk, which is every day all through the day, I tell them about Heaven. Part of me will always be over there. It is nothing you can explain; you have no remembrance of earth or the people back here. It is so light, bright, and peaceful over there. How can I explain it? I cannot! The flowers are so bright in colors, and the green is a different green then it is here on earth. It is amazing, and there is always something to see. I was smiling over there, and I was smiling before I got there. I was smiling going through the ground. I was happy, I mean happy!

I have to tell everyone Heaven is real! Oh, the mountains! I stood there looking at all those beautiful mountains over there with beautiful colors. Everything is in the glory of God. God's glory is so peaceful and so shiny, and all of those mansions—sparkling and streaming off the building. God's glory is everywhere. I saw it all around my mother and my aunties and all of those children playing on the hillside. They all looked at me; some of them were kin to me in some type of way. I saw all races of children as I stood there for a while. I looked and there is no time in Heaven, you are just there. How I got there was amazing, it was just like the rubbing of two hands together, and I was there.

I went through another dimension; I was holding on to this chain that was breaking in the sky. I saw Otis saying, "Hold on mother, hold on you are all most there, you got to hold on!" You have no remembrance of this world in Heaven, none at all. If you did, you would not be worried about your family, and I had no thoughts of them. I was just smiling to see my mother. I recognized her and my grandson and my son and my aunties, Lue, and Essie. I saw these people in Heaven, and I saw the people in the Bible days. It was amazing. It is not going to be like a lot of people think; God's glory is all around.

Everything is in his glorified form, even the animals are in their glorified form. I can tell how those two oxen were looking at me. Glory hallelujah, God is real! Heaven is real and I believe Heaven is real.

When you are walking on the ground in Heaven, you make no sound. It is like taking on a ghost form, you move from here and there. Whatever the Lord wanted me to see is what I saw. I stood there, and I looked over at the mountains on my left side; all of those sparks were shining off of those buildings on my right side along with streets paved with gold. I saw it, and it was amazing. I was young, no one I saw there was old. Jesus was amazing why did he shown Himself to me, I always try to do right. Most people agree with me because I love to follow the scripture on how to live, and how to teach my children to live according to the word of God. Lord, I thank you for letting me live, my son told me one day when we were talking, that my heart stopped beating on Blair Road, when I was on the way to the hospital. I did not know; I was so surprised; my children tell me things in bits and pieces because they do not like to talk about it. I want to know what happened while I was in Heaven, but my body was here at the Doctor Hospital of Augusta. I was not there I had no remembrance of what was going on over here. I had no thoughts of the system over here. I was in Heaven, whether I came back or not it was all up to the Lord, not me. I had nothing to do with it I had nothing to do with being born and I will have nothing to do with my death you are minutes always from Heaven it is a bit of an eye. and it is all over who want to take that chance dying without Christ who? Thanking back to what my husband told me, looking at the EMS report also when I arrive at the hospital none of my family was present.

All my children live away from Washington where I live, they all moved away after finishing college two of them live in Smyrna, GA, one in Marietta, GA and one live in Gainesville, GA. So, it would take them a while to get to the Doctors Hospital about 3 hours; it was just me and the Lord I was already in Heaven by the time they got there. I will let them tell you about that in their part of the book. My husband got there. My last son told me he has to get all of his oxygen and his breathing machine before he could come a long way. My husband has one of the grandchildren with Him because her mother has had a newborn and I was keeping her for a week, but the night before remembering I just have been 40 miles to Greene County to meet my soon Pastor Henra to pick her up he met me. I was alone in the F150 ford pickup truck my husband was going with me, but he was up a friend's house telling Him how to fix his faucets.

The date is June 24, 2017—I got to tell the world about how quick up and get sick I have been really busy this week before me getting sick. I drove to Green County and how I got home have no idea my memory started to leave me in and out I was feeling live. It was so hard to learn how to walk; my arms, my whole body was so weak. I could barely stand the Spirit of the Lord was with me. I always prayed; I found out early, very early that I had nothing else to help me so I always would go sit in the wood and I prayed, and I prayed I just talk to the Lord like he was standing right beside me and still do I talk to Him about anything and everything. I always engage myself. I never had any friends much. I do not guess I have time. I had to raise my children a certain way and I had to make sure that they are saved and that they know how to pray. I did not want them to be poor because it was hard growing up poor. I learned how to survive whatever state. I learn how-to lean-to God; I always have a hiding place and I went there laying there in the hospital. I got to learn how to use my body again. I was so weak; my eyes look like sick animal eyes.

I suffered; Lord, I asked Him what have I done to suffer like this? Lord have mercy on me with tears of joy running down my face. My nurses have compassion for me; they always took good care of me. my children were right there with me the whole time as well as my husband. They know me; they know what I believe. They know how I pray, sing hymns, and listen to gospel music, listen to sermons and how I talk about the Lord. I always gave them hope. I told them to always stay prayed up and stand strong in the Lord. I told them I did not care what their friend believed in; I told them to pray, because there will be a tough spot in life.

I try to prepare them for that. Laying here in my bed, the doctor put a sign over my bed, and it said, "Go home date will be June 29,2017". This would make 39 days for me in the hospital and about two weeks in a coma. I always look up at that sign saying to myself how in the world can I go home this sick, but I work even harder trying to be ready. I went in the physical therapy room one day and I had forgot that I did not have any hair in the back of my head. I felt really bad. I did not think about it long, because I got a long way to go. My hair was like dry grass, and it was dry as my hands; did not realize it until I took a shower. I was sitting in the shower in the hospital and I rubbed some soap all over my head, but I had no hair in the back of my head; I am glad to be alive praising God thanking

Him for spearing my life, which no one had any hope, but God worked a miracle through me with all of my family members and my siblings. The doctor had no hope, but they were doing all they could. My children told me that they have done a wonderful job on me, because they were all right there playing and singing hymns and playing my favorite gospel song over me, they say.

I had to stand up for long as I could at the table with my chair beside me. I have to stack some sticks in the high as far as I could reach, I got so tired. I just dropped back down in my chair, but I will continue, and I will make it. I will never give up on anything. I never have and I never will! I must keep pressing on until I get stronger enough to get out of here. I am feeling better overall, but I still got a lot going on with my body. I am still very sick. I meant sick I never knew a human being could get this sick. A lot of folks are in here for therapy; they have all kinds of sickness going on. I am in here for three hours a day. I got to go when the physical therapist come at me. I got to be ready to go; they help me put my shoes on. I walk down the hallway on my walker to the other hall in the hospital; the stairs have about four stairs up and four stairs down. Oh, this is so hard, but I must do this. I walk around the nurses' desk. The physical therapist is right behind me. I get so tired. I stop and I rest all the time and I make it on because I got to get home. Every day it gets a little easy. I feel my strength coming back to me. God has brought me too far to leave me he will bring me on. One of my main scriptures about the Lord is Roman 8: 26-27—

> Likewise, the Spirit also helpeth our infirmities; for we know not what we should pray for as we ought: but the Spirit itself maketh intercession for us with groanings which cannot be uttered. And he that searcheth the hearts knoweth what is the mind of the Spirit because he maketh intercession for the saints according to the will of God.

These two verses say a lot about Father God. He can do anything. He wants to, whether we agree or not. He is our Father with all powers in His hand; He gives life, and he takes away the life. We are not our own; we all belong to Father God. He created all of us, whether you server Him or not that is our choice. One day you will wish you had, just as simply as that.

I am repeating myself, but I am talking to all of you all who will be reading my book. This is a true real-life book; it was so hard for me when I awoke. I was so sick; I am glad Father God took me to Heaven for a while, because I was too sick to stay in that body. I never felt a thing all of those days. I was in a coma, because I was there. I was so happy in Heaven; why I did not say Father God only knows the answer to that, but I am glad he brought me back for a while longer. I will never be the same as long as I live, I will never be the same and

I am so glad I want I see life better, and I am stronger.

Getting back to physical therapy, the Doctors Hospital trying to learn how to walk. I am very weak thinking about how far I have come. Doctors come in here about three times of day. It looks like the nurse stays in here all the time. Well, I do not have to have any more dialysis or oxygen. I am breathing good on my own and my kidneys are working well. I am improving, but just like boot camp. I have to be ready for the physical therapy; they come early, sometimes I eat breakfast in the therapy room. Lord, have mercy! I always say to myself; feeling very blessed the Lord has won again, not me. He has won again, because he worked a miracle through me.

I have my right mind! I never needed a psychiatrist. I have my God to talk to; this was all in the works for me before I was born. Father God knows I would have to take this test. It is all good. Learning how to walk is so hard; my left hips are numb. I have no feeling in my left hip and part of my right hip is numb. The sores on my buttocks where I laid for so long are healing. I have big sores all over my backside, but the burn unit is already in the Doctors Hospital; they always come to see me. They took a picture of all of my sores weeks ago, but it is all good! Glory to God. Laying here thinking about how good my children have been to me. Each one of them knows that I gave them my last. I had to make sure that they get the right start in life. That was my biggest goal in my life. I had to make sure that they do not be poor. It is no fun needing things life like food or clothes. The little things like toilet paper, soap, or toothbrush. We never had those things growing up as a child in the early 1960s; we suffered our way up. I did, but I was always praying to the Holy Spirit to put into my children's mind that they could be anything that they wanted to be, and I had to follow up on the putting my trust in God and working toward Father God. My husband and myself married at 18 years old, but we had to hit the floor running.

When my oldest son turned two years old, I went looking for a job. I got a job folding men thermals at the factory. I saved my money and the first thing I brought was some land. I never told my husband until I had paid for it, and I told Him this is where we are going to live. On this piece of land where I am at today on Metasville road, which is up the road where I grew up. I asked the Lord if it was His will let me live on this road when I am grown. I am still living on this road to this day. The first time I tried to get to the washer and dryer. I could not make it, but I know all my clothes are dirty. I need clean clothes for physical therapy tomorrow. This time I do not want to ask for help, so I am going to get my walker and I will get across that hall somehow; it is only about 10 steps across the hall beside the nurses' station. I am very weak, but I got to wash my clothes. I am tired and my body is shaking, but I am going to make it to the nurses at the desk. They are looking at me. When I got in the washroom, I just fell on top of the washer, but I found enough strength to put my clothes in there. I am so blessed. I have nothing to brag about, but Father God, because he knows our heart, that is one thing for sure. Father God is all-seeing and all-knowing. We can hide from each other, but not Him. I always try to meet Father God early, because he knows all about every one of us.

I look back over my journey. It is June 24, 2017, a few days before I get to go home. I am laying there thinking to myself. I am too sick to go home, but when the doctor says I got to go; I got to go. I will never forget that look that Jesus had in his eyes. His robe was so beautiful. His eyes. He looked at me and I stood still. I was about 30 years old; young and pretty. I stood there looking at Jesus even before he turned his head and looked at me. I walked upon Him. I say to myself, "Oh!" I stopped and I looked at his feet. I saw his knees, his sandals, his robe with the belt around his waist, his hair, dark brown, his skin ashy pink or grayish pink, his feet, the leather brown sandals. It was amazing. I have told everyone who wanted to listen to me.

A lot of people will not receive my journey, but that is ok. It will be with me until I get back to Heaven. I am free. So free! I do not fear anything, not even death! When your soul leaves your body, you are immediately in one or two places. I saw nothing dark; everything I saw was so bright. The light was beaning off the building on my right side and my mother was standing in front of me on the other side of the river. My auntie was sitting under the beautiful trees and all of those children were playing on the hillside.

Praise the Lord! I get happy in the Spirit just thinking about my journey. I have told my children and my husband a hundred times over and over. I tell my daughters-in-law and my grandchildren. I tell them all the time about Heaven and all those who come in contact with me, whoever wants or needs to listen. Those who do not want to listen to me, that is okay. It is fine with me. I am going to tell everyone who wants to hear, but I will never force myself anyone. Life has knocked me hard, but I count it all joy. I cannot have a pity party. I always got to fight the good fight of faith and hold on and out. Once we die and our body goes in the ground or the cement; we will not need our bodies anymore, because the new you will step out into eternity very quickly. You have no memory of what you left behind; it is all a new beginning.

Every day I had a smile on my face, because I saw myself when I was looking in the water. I saw all of those people who were in the Bible days. I walked among them they look at me; they just looked, and I was so happy. I just enjoyed walking around Heaven. I walked; I did not know anything about time. Everything is the Spirit of the Lord. I looked at the bundle of wheat tied in the field. I looked at the string that was tied around the bundle. It was amazing just to see. Oh, what we all have a chance to see over there! In Heaven, it cannot be explained what I went through; but I would not take anything for my journey.

Chapter 16

I CAN AND I WILL!

At this moment, sitting here writing this book—I thank God that I am in my right mind. Glory to God! I remember how hard my mother worked; I never heard her complain about raising her children. She raised my siblings and I the best way she knew how to. She loved all of us in her own way. I look more like her for some reason. My mother would always keep a needle and thread in her clothes because if she saw one of us with a torn place on our clothes, she would sew it up. She was always sewing something. Those were the days growing up, my childhood!

We never locked the door. There was no screen on the window. Lord, it was hard, but we made it! Glory to God! We should not be so worried about how a person looks in the casket. We should be concerned as to whether they gave their lives to Christ. When we finish with these old organic matter bodies, we will step out of these bodies fast. The time between life and death is a matter of seconds. I am here to tell you this. A few seconds after death you are in a whole new world. I know God can do anything He wants to do, and He can show each one of us whatever He wants us to see. I have to tell the world there is a Heaven and it is a beautiful place! There is no hate there, nothing but God's glory is there! We do not know what the Lord will reveal to us. I always read that you cannot see the Lord with the natural eye, but I am here to tell you that I had to die to see Jesus. I was not in my natural body. I stepped out for a few days. I did not know anything about time. I was just there. I do not know how long I was in a coma or how long I was going to be in a coma. My husband, my children, other family members, and friends prayed and singed over my body while I was in a coma, but I did not hear anything. I saw Heaven, I was in Heaven! I never knew that I lived here on earth. I had no remembrance of the earth until I awoke. I saw all of those people around my bed. I did not know what was wrong. My mind was still in Heaven. I could not tell anyone. I was too sick to talk. I was a sick woman. Why did God bring me back? I know, but I will not say anything about it yet.

One thing about it, I have to write this book. It is now June 24, 2017, and I am laying there thinking about my father, Henry Callaway. He never read a book in his life, yet he was the smartest man that I have ever known. He could only scribble his name. It was recognizable, but just a little bit. He always told me to pray, and he told me his mother whipped him many times, but this one time she whipped him with a car tire strip. He never forgot that whipping. When he became an old man, he still remembers that whipping. I asked him what he did he do to deserve such a whipping; he never answered me. He died in 1991. He was born in 1919. My father worked and he worked; he told me that after working for the sawmill and only making 40 dollars a week; he would never work for anyone else again! And he did not! He brought himself a pulpwood truck and a tractor. He started his own business and for years he cut pulpwood with his motor saw, and he loaded the wood on the truck by his own hands. Years went by and he brought another truck with the loader on the back, but by this time my dad had worked himself to death. He was a strong man. He stood 6 feet 6 inches tall. He was a dark skin good looking black man. He died of a heart attack in my arms. My mother also died in my arms in the year 2003. She had pancreatic cancer.

My husband and I moved next door to my parents in 1980. My dad brought some land, and I brought a plot from him for 1100 dollars. It was hard, but I trust God. My father would cut a tree down with a saw by himself. I saw him do it; he would cut a tree on both sides and the way he wanted the tree to fall, it always went that way. My husband and I never want my children to work that hard in the woods. It was too hot, the weather. My brother told me one day that my father was beginning to cut down a tree and he saw a big black snake. My father did not kill the snake. He picked the snake up by the head and he threw the snake out of his way. My dad was fearless and strong. My dad worked so fast! Everything he did was fast. He killed hogs so we could have food to eat, and He skinned them so fast. I would be standing there looking at his work. I was always looking and watching my parents. I learn, and I learn! Everything that I saw my parents do, I did for the most part.

I watched my mother daily. She would read her Bible. Every day she prayed with my siblings and me. She loved her children. She did the best she could with what she had, and she never complained. She was with me in Heaven. She told me, "To go back you can't come yet. They need you." I know that was the Lord talking through her. I saw the Lord Jesus. He just looked at me. I was smiling! I stood there looking at Him even before He turned His head towards me. I know who that was the time I saw Him. I looked at His feet first. I looked at His legs. His robe was hanging to His knees. I saw His feet. His feet looked close to a size of 10 ½ inches. His robe was so beautiful. I keep repeating myself, but it is amazing. I have told my children and my husband as well as some people who want to hear about this experience. Most people do not want to hear about Heaven, but a lot of them do. I have told a lot of people about Heaven.

I am going to try to take a nap, because early in the morning; I have another day of physical therapy. I am excited. I am alive, here praising God for His blessings! He has healed my sick body. I am still alive. The doctors just strangely look at me. I know none of them had any hope for me, but I know the chief of staff and his name is Jesus. He knows our hearts. When I saw the EMTs coming in my door, I only saw their legs coming in and I was almost gone. I was too sick to look up. I was fading away fast. I told the Lord with the few seconds that I had before I left my body that "Lord, I am in your hands, and I have served you!" I could say another word and then I left this world believing that I would make it back home to my husband because he is sick. He has been sick for a long time. I put everything in the Lord's hands. We never know that when we get out of our beds in the morning whether we will return to them again.

At this time, I can now walk to physical therapy. I can put puzzles together. I can do my legs exercise and ride on the exercise bike. I can go a little longer maybe about 25 minutes now. I am getting stronger each day! My blood pressure is still up and down, but somewhat stable. My kidneys are working well, and my heart is beating steady. I have been in the hospital for 35 days already. I can get up at night and use the bathroom with my walker. I am praising God as I have always done all of my life. You must send up prayers every day throughout the day whether things are good or bad, still pray. Therefore, when trouble comes, you do not have to panic!

Always pray for others when you hear that other people are in trouble. Start praying for them right away! You do not have to know what is going on with them, just pray for the individuals. Those who you come in contact with daily. I am still very weak. I do not have my voice back completely; it is still very weak, but I can talk. I talked when I woke up from my coma. It took a little bit of time for me to get my mind back in order, back here on earth. My eyes are weak. There is a sweet old lady in the room with me; she is a retired schoolteacher from Harlem, Georgia. She is a nice, sweet lady. She does not eat most of the time. I tell her to try to eat so she can be strong. I could use the bathroom whenever I wanted to because she had to use a bedpan and it took me a long time to get in and out of the bathroom on my walker. When the other lady, another roommate, was in my room with us we had to wait on each other to use the bathroom. This lady was put in another room, because we all took so long to use the bathroom. It was hard to do. So, now I have the bathroom to myself.

The retired schoolteacher is a wonderful lady in spirit. She was so sick! I had to beg her to drink her Ensure, because she did not eat. It was hard for her to get her food open, so I tried to help her. She did not have the strength to call the nurse for help. My husband would help her too when he was in there. I talked to her about the goodness of God. She is an older African American lady in the room with me here in rehab at Doctors Hospital. She also shared her testimony, and I told her mines. I told mc her about going to Heaven and she started to cry. I did too! It is so amazing! I will never forget our conversation. I told her, "It is a place!"

She said, "What it is all about?

I said, "Your inner Spirit."

She asked, "Are you prepared to go back to Heaven?

The question caught me off guard in the spare of the moment. I said, "Yes!" I spoke on and told her, "It was so quick. I could not do anything. I mean nothing. I went just that fast. It was faster than your mind can even imagine! It is quick, in a blink of an eye, you are in another dimension, a whole other world. The only way to get there is through the Spirit. I went through the ground in a tunnel. I did not go down too far into the ground. I slid through the ground just like I was on a roller coaster. The tunnel was shining bright. I never saw anything dark; it was a five-minute ride. I saw the light from the time I began in this tunnel until after I left my grave. I told my son, Pastor Henra goodbye with smiles, but Pastor Henra was talking to me, and he told me to come back even though he knew I had to go. I saw the light and I stepped out! Oh, my God! I never knew I had lived on earth, but I recognized my loved ones and I saw Jesus and all of those folks in the Bible days. They just looked at me.

I tried to fall asleep, all the lights are out, but I still can hardly go to sleep. I am thinking back to the old house that I lived in when I was in high school. It had nothing conventional. It was a big, old, cold house, but we are alive! My father never let us watch television or talk on the telephone when he was home. When we left to go to the store, we could watch television for a little while. I remember watching, "Good Times." It just premiered on television. I loved to look at *Good Times, Gun Smoke,* and *Sandford and Sons* during this time and I still do. We had a small black and white television. We never talked loud in the house. My father would have a fit if we talked loudly; we had to walk around the house in silence like zombies. My siblings and I did not understand why he did not want us to talk loud in the house? My mother did not say anything. She was just like us; she did not talk loudly.

I love my father. He did the best he knew how to do. He never repeated himself once. When did he tell us something to do that was it! He always had a "switch' somewhere laying in the corner to whip us with if we got loud or out of order. My mind always runs back to Heaven, to my childhood and being there at the hospital. I always drink Ensure and Juven every day. These drinks help me get stronger than ever. I never thought this could happen to me. I have always been a busy woman all of my life. I am a superwoman. I am always on the go; I never knew what it felt like to rest. I never had any rest until now; sick as sick could be, how sick is that? I do not know, but I would not want anyone even my enemies to be this sick.

If I know there is a Heaven, I know there is a placed called "Hell" as well. Glory to God! He knows our hearts. He took care of me. As I read my children's part of my book, they were saying they were just getting ready to unplug my wires and let me go, but I awoke, and God took care of me. God, He has won again. It was so much fun in the glorified body, no worries. I felt good just exploring Heaven. It is hard to believe! I talk to a lot of folks, and they tell me that they know some folks that say they have been to Hell, but never anyone that said that they have been to Heaven. I told my doctor about my experience, and she told me that out of all of her patients she has one more person that has been to Heaven that she knows. I see things in a whole new light, clear very clear. We waste too much time on things that are not important in life. We must concentrate on the Lord and His will for our lives and stop trying to out-do each other. We all have a task to finish and when our task is done, we are going home.

Back at the hospital a few days before I go home, the date is up over my bed, it is June 29, 2017. That is my going home date. My doctor put the date up there a few days ago. I am so weak. I say to myself, "How in the world am I going to make it this sick back home?" I cannot say a word. I got to go home on that date and that is it! I have not seen my children or my

husband for a few days. I told all of them to go home! I got
this! I told them to not come back down here until I called
them. I am not worried! I am free! God got me! I was in
Heaven! I am going to press on! I am praising God for all He
has done for me over the years. He never failed me! He has
been good to all of us, whether we believe it or not. How can a
person live in this world and not give their whole heart to Lord
Jesus? He is the one who will meet us if we have lived for Him!
It is sad; I am thinking if a person does not die in the Lord
Jesus, what will happen to them? He is always standing out
with a hand stretched take his hand. Some folks think you have
to go through them, but no you can go directly to the Lord. To
have a personal relationship with the Lord; just talk to Him. I
have no one else to go to in my life, but the Lord. Growing up
so poor, my husband and I were raised the same way. We had
to suffer to get what we wanted in life.

I am sitting here writing my book. I have been writing for
a whole year. It took me about eight months to get strong
again. I wake up every morning thanking the Lord for another
chance to praise Him! All we know is this second, not a minute
or hours or days just this second, because things can change in
a second. Stay in prayer and tell everyone to read their Bible.
Love those who you know hate you and pray for them daily.
Do not try to get even, let God handle it. Just pray every
moment you get to talk to God; He will take care of you. Give

Him all you got when you are young and able. Give Him your best do not wait until you are old and sick and can hardly pray or read, meditated on God day and night, do not hate anyone, it is not worth it, just pray God to be the glory.

We all are going to leave this earth from our bodies, it is just a matter of time. No one will escape! I saw all those people in the Bible days who have died; flesh and blood cannot enter Heaven, I stepped out of my body. I left my body here for the doctor to work on it, but God still had my physical body; He had angels around me while I was in Heaven with Him. I had a lot of machines hooked up to me. My children say, I never seen them, but a few of them when I awoke. My son, Otis, says they took one by one away. I got my tests to take, and you got your test to take. I got a chance to go to Heaven. I would not have traded a thing for this journey; it was all good for me to see Heaven. It was hard when I woke up sicker than sick. I never knew a human being could get that sick. My body was deteriorating fast and bed sores were everywhere on my backside and sores were in my mouth, but I fought my way back to God. He stayed with me all the way from earth to Heaven from Heaven back to earth, glory to God.

I cry all the time while I am writing this book, thinking back; it is hard to write. I get so happy in the Spirit. I have to get up and walk around the house. My husband has gotten use to me now. I tell them the Spirit of the Lord is upon me most of the time. He does not say a word; he just sits there looking at the television. He says most times; he was a mess. Why did you go through all of that? I told him, God used me for a miracle for those who looked in on me said, "There is no way she was going to make it!" I looked at their faces when I woke up; they were all in a daze. I just looked around the room. Folks, mostly family that I had not spoken to me in years were standing around my bed.

Back to the hospital, it is about 6 a.m. Every morning when the nurse hears me waking up, they all rush in my room. They give me this one pill that I have to take on an empty stomach and they check my sugar and my blood pressure. I always ask for apple juice. I always get two little containers of apple juice. I put it on ice in my cup and I drink all of the juice. The nurse always told me that she had to check my blood sugar first. It always is normal. She brings me the juice each day to get stronger and stronger. I am still trying to walk. I walk around the nurses' station on my walker, and I got into physical therapy where all the other people are, they are trying to get stronger. I look around the room each day and I wonder how I got here. Never think it cannot happen to you! Anything can happen to anyone. We never know what tomorrow holds for us; just stay prayed up and the Lord Jesus will take care of you.

It is good just to be able to be alive. I look terrible, but when I was in Heaven; I was pretty, because I looked in the water and I saw myself. I was about 33 years old. I got a picture of how I looked here in this book. I was in paradise where Lazarus and Abraham were; it is no different between Heaven and paradise. This is where the man who was hanging on the cross beside Jesus; I was there. I saw all of those buildings with the beautiful colors gleaming with the bright lights and the streets of gold. I stood there watching that road that leads to those buildings. I was just looking at all of those children playing on the hillside.

I still have my blue bonnet on my daughter bought me. I wore my hair out one day, but I do not have any hair in the back of my head, so I put my blue bonnet back on. I had no idea; I did not have any hair in the back of my head until I took a bath a month later. Sitting there in the bathroom was part of my therapy; I had to learn how to bathe again and put my clothes on again. I did not have any emotions about hair; I knew it would grow back.

I was thinking about my children and my grandchildren and my poor husband. He was a mess when I woke up; he was so dark and worn completely out. That is why I had to send him home, he could not take it anymore; he stayed with me a few more days after I woke up. I had to have help around the clock. I had to be turned every two hours. I could not wipe myself. I have been on a long journey in my physical body and with the Lord. I am taking my time writing this book; I get so tired, but I have to write. I want the world to know that there is a Heaven and the Lord showed it to me. I do know this is not for me to keep to myself; I must tell the world. Heaven is waiting on those who love the Lord Jesus Christ. It is no danger in dying, if you die in the Lord.

When my father died in my arms, he smiled. I know he saw Jesus and someone he recognizes is in room 628 on the sixth floor at the Doctors Hospital. Everyone on this floor has physical therapy and I am up here too. I never got any rest in my whole life, none; I was a busy lady working three jobs in the early 1980s and 1990s. I worked at school as an aid going to school at night. I have four children that I must make sure that they know Jesus. A good friend of mines got me the job at school when her husband got sick. She went into the superintendent of the school and told them to hire me in her place. She told them if you all want to hire her; I will quit my job, so they hired me in her place as an aid at the school. I was already working there as a substitute teacher.

The superintendent asked her who she was; he did not know. She told him she is the one who cleaned your house; he never did see me when I cleaned their house, they left the keys, and I cleaned the house before they got off from work. I worked and I worked; my husband and myself had a job as well as the children, but they all played sports in school, and they had so much homework to do. I had to check homework all the time. It was hard and long, but I made it. I never knew what rest was; I did not get to rest in my childhood. It was so cold in the wintertime. I had to sleep in my hat and clothes. We never had any night clothes. It was hard, but everyone lived like that except the white folks up the road. They were good to us back in the 1960s; they had all kinds of fruits trees and pecans trees, and we ate and ate off of the apple trees, muscadines and scuppernong vines.

If it had not been for God on our side, oh, Lord, what would we have done. My mind we through a lot of things laying thereafter I work up. Lord, I wonder what I have done in my life to go through all of this? I still cannot believe I been through this every day of my life. I am with Jesus. I think about Heaven sitting in church. I think about Heaven in bed every day, all through the day. My mind is back in Heaven; part of me will always be over there in Heaven until I get back there. I am still at the hospital; they bring me a lot of food. I never eat all of it; my body is very weak. I eat enough to please the nurses. They bring me Ensure and Juven drink with every meal, all kinds of vitamins and medication.

I have no IVs running in me at this time. I am doing okay. I just get too tired when I try to wash myself off, get to the bathroom or try to put my shoes on. I have to have help with my shoes most of the time. I will try to make it to physical therapy again. I got to put this puzzle together, which I hate; the pieces are so small. None of them fits and finding these buttons is a chore. I got to find all of these buttons; it is hard to pull the string apart to find a one, but I will pull it apart until I find every one of them. I am going to do this. I got to get out of here and get home. I do my legs stretches and my arm exercises.

Today, I do my walking around the nurses' stations. I try not to stop today. I am walking with my walker today and I am not going to take a break not today. I told myself not today. I always have to take a rest break and then walk some more, but today I am going to try to walk around the nurses' station and try not to stop. It is going to be slow, but by God's strength I will make it around it at least one more time without stopping.

I am just sitting here typing my book. It is one thing that happened to me that took me out of this world. We think we are somebody. We do not have any power. We little humans are sinful, filthy rags before a mighty God. We are nothing, but a few days of a vapor down here. It is only a few days in God's eyes even if we live to see 100 years old. It is still just a few days three scores and ten, which is 70 years. We are still going to spend eternity somewhere so live your life with truth, honesty, and humble yourself like a little child when it comes to God. He will understand; come to Him with pride! We are nothing, no more than a bubble on the water. We never know what will happen to us. We never know what tomorrow will bring us; so, we must beyond all else stay prayed up so when the hard days do come, they come stacked up against some prayers.

Be honest with yourself; it does not matter whose family you are born in; we all have the same chance when it comes to the Lord. He has no respectable person. Look at me, I tried to do it all right, just look at me. I tried to be the perfect Christian. I studied my Bible all the time. I prayed mostly all day. I pray myself to sleep; I leave the television on the gospel channel. When I awake, I have the television on gospel playing early. I love the Lord with all of my heart because when I was a child, I did not have anyone much to talk too.

I found the Lord. He already knew me from the foundation of the world. This test was in me before I entered my father's seed; it was as easy one, but Father God had this test for me; it was mines. We all have a test or tests to take; this one broke me in half. It helped me. I cannot explain it all, but I am free. I saw Heaven. This world does not exist in Heaven. The real you will pop out of that soul and your Spirit will fly out anew. I cannot come up with another way to explain how this happened to me, but Father God had some reason to bring me back? He can do anything he wants to. We need to be told more about Heaven. Heaven is not spoken about enough in our churches now a days. I wonder do they really believe in Heaven? Heaven is real as day and night. Everything in Heaven is so bright. There is nothing dark over there. I can see myself standing there looking at Jesus' feet. I looked at his toenails. I was a young woman in Heaven; it was amazing, no stress over there! It is so calm over there. Nothing is painful over there.

When you step over there a whole new world awaits you. There is no lying or jealousy over there in the spiritual body. You will have a light body. My aunties, especially Essie was smiling. I remember that smile. She was in her glorified body. She said to me, "Is that you, "Willie Agnes?" Aunt Nee always called me that. My other auntie just turned her head and she just looked at me when I stepped out of the ground. I went straight out, not down. My mother was already standing at the other side of the river. She told me to go back and that I could come with them yet. They were sitting on the hillside looking at all of those children play. I stood there looking at all of those children; they are looking back at me. They were at peace in their glorified bodies. The side of the hill was so beautiful. I saw some green pretty flowers downside the meadows. The trees over there do not look like the trees here on earth. They are much simpler, greener and the bark on the trees are thick and dark brown.

I can hardly tell this story. I think about Heaven all the time. It is always on my mind. I sit in church, and I am thinking about Heaven. I look at different individuals in the church; they think that they have more religion than someone else, but if they only knew. No words to explain my experience. I am doing the best that I can through this book. I hope this book helps someone realize that Heaven is real! I just stepped out of my body so fast. I must tell the world, Heaven is real! Father God is real! Just praise Him! A personal relationship with Father God is what we all need, and I need it!

I am still here at Doctors Hospital. I am very weak. I am much better, but still very weak. I look terrible, but somewhat better compared to what my children told me how I looked in a coma. I was swelling up bad. My daughter told me that my hands were colder than ice. I am still here not by my doing, but by the mercy of God. I have a few more days here at Doctors Hospital. When I went to Select Specialty Hospital, it felt like death over there, but they were good to me! I guess the doctor who sent me there had no hope that I would recover, because no one moved in that hospital at all. I looked out of the door all the time. I never have seen patients walking down the hallway. I could walk down the hallway over there, but I only learned to walk to the door. I was so sick! My heart rate and my blood pressure would go up and down. I felt so sick! I would never give up!

Ever since the Lord brought me back from Heaven, he wants me to live a while longer before he calls me home for good. I must tell the world Heaven is very real! There is no more trouble over there. You do not need any more medication over there nor will you be misunderstood over there or overlooked by church folks. In Heaven, every day is bright and full of so much joy and peace. The glory of God's Spirit and His joy was so high in Heaven. I was always smiling all the time. I had a smile on my face. I never been happier in my life; just to be able to walk around Heaven in so much glory. The oxen I saw were so happy. They looked at me and I was happy just to look in their eyes.

It is so hard for me to believe that I went through all of this; my daughter just told me this the other day. She told me that something was eating up all of my blood in my body. I was in disbelief. I know when I went to Select Specialty Hospital about the third day over there, I had to receive more and more blood, but it all good; I had to bear my burden just like Jesus had to up cavalry cross. We all have a cross to carry. So, get yourself ready to carry your cross up Calvary hill. I do not sit here and say why me Lord? It has wondered through my mind, why me? I had a vacation to Heaven.

I am so glad I had a chance to go to Heaven and come back to tell the world about my experience. There is nothing to fear if you have accepted the Lord and Savior as your Lord. There is no danger in leaving this world. I know what that means now; it is just as easy as rubbing your hands together in getting to Heaven. Once you die and you are in the Lord's presence; where you chose to go depends on how you live, it is up to you! Listen at yourself, God will warn you of your sins and He gives all of us a chance to repent and repent and ask for forgiveness over and over again. We must ask Him daily all through the day, because every idle word or deed will be remembered by Father God. Do your best! You cannot please people and God. So, I live my life to please God and love people the best I can, because everyone wants to let you love them.

Father God has the last word; He had it over me. I laid there in coma for nearly three weeks; the doctor was ready to unplug all my wires. I told my children that I was in Heaven, and I had a ball! I saw King Jesus! I will never be the same. I thank of Him all through the ever-passing day. My Lord is very real. I have tried to live my life for Him. We are all sinners, but I always have to try to live for Father God.

I am happy with Lazarus after 44 years. I am still holding on to my vows and my contract that I made with Father God. Father God will always stand in the middle of me and my husband if God did not; maybe one of us would be dead. My husband has always been my best friend. I have not had many friends, that is how I chose to live. I made Jesus my close friend when I got sad or lonely, because he is the only one that understood me. It has not been easy, but through it all I am thankful. Joy will always come in the morning, but one thing about that morning; we never know how long that morning will be. A lot of things have gone across my mind since I have been sick. I laid there for days and days thinking my children had to leave for a while, because I know all four of my children, deep down in their souls, prayed for me deeply. They went on a fast and they did not eat at all until I made a change at Doctors Hospital. They just prayed; they just told me that. I look at each one of them. I know they will never forget this journey I had to go through; they had to try Jesus. I know they tried Him, and they found peace. My son, Pastor Henra, who is a Pastor told me that he knew I was not going to die. He said mama, "No matter what the doctors told us; We were never going to give up on you, mother!" I was glad.

I had to fight after I woke up, I did not have to fight in Heaven, because I had no remembrance of this world. I did not know I was sick over there. I was younger, and I was very pretty. I did not have pain in my body. I mean, no pain! I saw what was in Heaven. I saw my aunties and my mother. They are having fun in Heaven. We do not have to worry about dying if we die in the Lord. Man cannot put you anywhere! No matter how many people are at your funeral or how many times we try to put someone in Heaven or hell; God has the last word and that is that! The transition from life to death is so

470

easy. When a person gets so sick, they do not be in their body, so their Spirit and the soul takes over.

I did not suffer! I felt nothing. A few minutes after sitting there on the sofa before EMS got there; I was lost my breath fast and a few seconds after that I was gone. I did not stay in that sick body. The Lord had it fixed for me so I would not feel a thing. All of these days laying there in a coma, I felt nothing, and I heard nothing. I was there in my body, but my spirit was gone away to a place. This place called, Heaven, is full of peace. God gives all of us peace. I am still here at Doctors Hospital sitting on the side of my bed thinking how far the Lord has brought me. I have seen so many doctors. Some of them had no hope for me. One of them told me so! The others just waited and had to see whether I was coming back or not. I am back! I saw this lady doctor. Her name is Amy Spruge. She would come to see me three times a day at the Select Specialty Hospital and she would come to the Doctors Hospital to see about me. She called me, "Mrs. Miracle!" She did not call me, Mrs. Chennault anymore. She told me that I was a miracle for making it through all of that. She would hug me. She always looks at me with a smile. I had some of the best doctors in the world on my team and most of all my Heavenly Father was leading the whole team even the EMS who came to pick me up. It was all in God's plan.

Sitting here on my bed with tears rolling down my face. I have two more days here today. It is June 27, 2017. I am somewhat better, but very weak. I am still holding my blood in my body and my hands are not as white as they once were. I can see some blood running through them now. I am just praising God for his goodness. I am free! The Lord showed me Heaven and when I died for good, I will be going back to that same place; the Spirit told me before I left.

No matter what illness you go through, you will not go until Father God is finished with you! No one cannot make that call, but Him! We all must be a strong soldier for the Lord. You cannot let every wind that blows by you move you from side to side. You must hold on! We must raise our children to be a strong solder for Christ so they can endure hardships of the world. When my children's father and myself raised them, we always had to speak loud and clear so they would understand what we mean. We had to make sure that they were going to be good citizens.

I can walk up and down the steps during physical therapy. I am pushing myself so I can be strong again. I have never been a weak person. I had to what was always right. We all have made mistakes, but I tried not to make so many that it would cost me great storms in life. When I woke up, I saw all of these people around my bed. Some looked at me in utter shock, their hair was standing up on their heads. The Lord brought me back from my vacation. I was so sick; it felt like I was going to die again for good.

I was in bad shape! I wondered was Lazarus in bad shape when the Lord raised Him from the dead? The Lord raised me from the dead like Lazarus. I know Lazarus' body was broken like mines. My blood was all over my bed from the sores on my backside, but they are healing very well. I have to hold on, because I got one grandson, Otis Jr. who needs my prayers so he will know how to conduct himself in life. I have to teach my granddaughters how to look pretty and be strong. I got to show my grandchildren how to eat greens and cornbread with their hands. I am still very weak. I have to use my walker to use the bathroom or to try to take a bath. I can dress myself, but I am getting strength back in my body every passing day. I can breathe fresh air for the first time. I do not have to have oxygen anymore. I am finished with that! No more breathing treatments! Praise God, I give my whole life to God. I tell the Lord all of the time. I am yours, Lord! Try me and see! I have no strength of my own only what you allowed me to have.

They always give me a lot of food to eat, but I never do eat it all. Even though I am a big-boned woman, I always watch what I ate; I grew most of my food. I believed 90 percent of what we eat must come from the ground. I work in a garden, but something told me that I will not work one this year. I went down to the garden spot, and I looked at it. I told

Lazarus, my husband, that we would not have a garden this year. He was unsure why I told him that. He told me he will just plan some peas. I felt that was a great idea. I always think of the Lord every day. What He has already done for me! He brought all of four of my children through college and I will always thank Him every passing day. I asked Father God to give me a clean heart and renew in me a right spirit. I come with no pride.

I come humbly as I can like Zacchaeus, who was up in the tree when Jesus was passing by. Jesus spends the night with Him. He was a little man. He was but he knew in his heart something has to change with Him. I always tell father to just speak the word and it will be done. I am so glad I can do right to Father God. I do not have to let no one else know what I ask God for because if I did, they would tell me, no, but I pray to Him directly. I need Jesus every second of every day. He loves all of us. I have to tell the truth. Lord knows my intentions. I am glad I was afflicted. I cry a lot here in the hospital; the nurse asks me what is wrong. I cannot explain, they are a tear of joy and happy tears, glad that I saw my mother she is happy in Heaven. The Lord let me see who he wanted me to see. I am glad he did it! It is almost time to go home for a long journey from the other world. Back to Heaven, to the hospital, and to home.

On June 28, 2017, the last day before I go home, I am just thanking God, for being with me through it all. I am all happy my organs are working well. I met a lot of people, doctors, physical therapist, housekeeping, and food service workers—all kinds of people that work at the hospital. I am so glad to be alive; I can go back home again and be with my family, my children my husband, and their wives. On my last day, everyone was excited the day before I was to go home. They just looked at me, I looked at them. The sign up above my bed said, "Go home on June 29, 2017". I did not think I was well enough to go home. I am still very sick. I cannot stand up but a minute or two, but the doctor say it is time to go, it's time to go. After 39 days; I hope, I will be ok at home; I am thinking this is my last night here, oh what a test, I have taken! It is all good, I got a chance to see heaven. I will never, never, forget Heaven until I get back there. Heaven is a place in the spiritual realm. There is no trouble in Heaven; there is nothing, but the peace. I lay there in my room thinking about my mother and all the things I have seen. Some I cannot mention, because it had something to do with the future. I am still writing my book, because I got to tell the world about Heaven. Heaven is real, believe me or not. I hope you do; whoever is reading my book. Please do not wait; come on the Lord's side. Do it now for tomorrow may be too late. Come to Jesus now while there is still breathe in your body. No one can change God's words.

The world is trying to change it, but it will not work. I have seen events that will happen in the future. I cannot tell anyone. I had to block it and fix them in front of my family, my children, and my other family members in the spiritual realm.

On day twenty-eight, I am telling my roommate goodbye. I will always remember her. She is a retired schoolteacher from Harlem. She is a good-hearted woman, and her children come to visit her. They always speak to me; I tell them my stories of Heaven and they standstill in their shoes. I tell them I am going to write a book, on what I have been through, and they told me to let them know. They want to read my book. This lady came in to ask me how many steps went up the porch into my house, because I cannot climb up long stairs. She wanted to know, was my house on one level. At this time, I cannot stand, and I got to have a caretaker when I get home. I told them my husband and my granddaughter will take care of me. My granddaughter is out for the summer so she will spend the time with us in the country. She comes every summer; she always helps me in the garden, and we go fishing; she is best fisherwoman. She catches more fish than we do; she uses a reel-in-rod, no pole for her. I show her one time how to use a rod and she get the first time. The doctor is getting all of my prescriptions ready to go, so I am going home after a long stay in the hospital, without double pneumonia and sepsis. I know the doctor sees me getting better. I am going home in a few.

I am writing my book; today is October 22, 2018. I have been writing ever sent I was able to sit up after I got home from the hospital. Sitting here remembering a few months ago, my husband and I were on our way to Atlanta to visit our children on a busy Friday afternoon and the traffic was heavy as usual. On a Friday evening, we were just riding along. We are on I-285 around 5:00 p.m. in the evening traffic was heavy so we were in the lane close to the left the fast lane. So, I told my husband that you should start getting over as soon as you could, he did that, because we were coming up to our exit. So, a minute passed, and he goes over to the next lane; the traffic was so heavy. He got over, and then it seemed like he hit a bump in the road and a few seconds later the truck just cut completely shut off. He said, "Willie the truck has cut off." I say, "Oh no, we are still running just as fast as before." I started to pray to Jesus, and I held up my hands to Heaven. I told my husband to try to relax. God got us, and we never lost speed. The truck was still running about 65 miles an hour just as fast as the rest of the traffic. We got over in time and we ran about a half of mile with the truck cut off. It was still running going down the hill, and back up the hill. It was still running; it never slowed down, not one bit.

Oh! The Lord took care of us; I was praying. My husband was sitting over there frozen, but he was holding on to the steering wheel. Oh, I prayed to save your children! Oh, Lord

guide us to safety! There was a spot on the road right before
you get to the Dr. Martin Luther Jr. sign. Be careful how you
pray, and what you are asking for. He hears your every word;
everything that you say. We have to come to Jesus as a child,
because no matter how old we get, we are still his child. I thank
the person for the parking space that was there for us to take; I
just went over there by myself; my husband did not turn the
steering wheel. The Holy Spirit carried us over there to safety.
This is another miracle just knowing God will take care of you
in the smallest of ways. Just live for Him, I always live my life
for Christ always because when trouble does come, I will be
able to handle it through Christ.

We were sitting there, while cars are just passing us by. We
are sitting right on the curve of the road, trying to get the truck
started. We tried and we tried, and then my phone rang; it was
my nephew, Dominic. He called, and asked "Auntie is that you
all on side of the road?"

I said, "Yes, boy!"

God just works so many miracles, and he saved me again.
In about five minutes, my nephew is pulling up right behind us.
They tried and tried to start the truck, but they could not get it
started. My other two sons came, and they were riding
together. They tried to get the truck started but could not
neither. They called a Recker truck, and it was about dark
before the Recker came with the police, to try and help. The

next day, we found out what was wrong with the truck. One wire had popped off and needed to be fixed. That was that a tense situation, but God save us again. I just had to add this story here, because it could have been so much worst, but God always looks out for his children.

Praise God from which all our blessings come from. Storms can and will come, but God will allow the storms to pass over you. These storms will keep coming all of your life until you die. I am sitting here writing my book. I do not know anything that has happened to me. I was sleeping in a coma, and my children told me bits and pieces of what had happened. They did not want to tell me much, because they cannot stand to talk about it. My daughter told me more than my sons, because her and I talked more, each day. When I read my children's and my daughters-in-law's parts of the book, I will be reading this information mostly for the first time.

My children are all writing their part of the book. My part is the longest, and I am sure of that. My husband has a part in the book that he is writing. My granddaughters, Hannah and Semira, has a part of the book. This entire experience has changed my whole life for the good. I thank God for choosing His strongest soldiers, for the hardest test. I have been using faith all of my life, because God will give you double for your trouble. Even all the years that the worms ate up; He will give them back to you. Just like Job, the Lord gave Job double for his troubles. That was 140 years more of life, because of the blessing of double. My suffering was hard after I woke up. I never felt so much discomfort before I went to Heaven. I was so sick in my body; I never felt anything, and I cannot even remember the ride to Augusta, Georgia. It was about an hour and a half ride from my house to Doctor Hospital. I was in bad shape by the time they began working on my body, but my Spirit had already stepped out. I got sick so quickly, and everything happened in 15 minutes of me first getting sick. I was gone!

I am so glad God has restored me. I am not rich like Job, nor do I have oxen or goat or sheep. God will give me double for my trouble; I believe that. There is something much higher than this life for all of those who love the Lord, and for those who live for Him. I do not know how much Job suffered, but I know he had boils all over his body, and he sat in the ash bile. If job was any sicker than I was when I woke up, how could he stand it?

I had so many wires hooked up to me, and I mean all types of wires. My children told me, that by the time I had woke up, the doctor had taken some of them away. It is a good thing that I got the best four children in the whole world, because each one of them know I would not give them an inch. I made sure that they were ready for this world, spiritually, physically, and mentally. I tried to get them ready to meet this world of people. Education was a must, to ensure they could live a good life, as well as their children. I know one day, I will be leaving this earth for good, and someone needed to break the poverty curse that existed. I had to do that through Christ, I had to start when they were in my lap. I told the four of them what their father and I expected of each one of them. They followed our rules, and they are all success by the grace of God. He sent them to college, and it cost so much to send four children to college. My three sons received scholarships that I applied for. This is how they went to college, I applied all by myself by, and with the help of the good Lord they all finished.

I am sitting here writing my book, praising the Lord for His goodness, and for letting me have a mind to praise Him. I do not have to call anyone else up to ask them to pray for me, God hears my request Himself. I am so glad because, I see people all the time that control other people's lives. They cannot do anything, unless they ask someone else, and that is very sad. There is a personal relationship between God and me. I love to go to church. We have forgotten our first love, and that is the Lord and Savior Jesus Christ. It only takes a few who want to serve the Lord. It is not about being in the church! It is about serving Him, every day that you have breath in your body.

I do not have to wait until Sunday morning to get my praise on. I praise my God all through every passing day. I mean every day! The first thing on my mind in the morning, is the Lord Jesus Christ. I praise Him, and ask Him, to take care of my children, and my grandchildren. How can anyone say that they forgot to pray today? How can a person get into their minds that they forget to pray? When you leave your bed in the morning, there is no guarantee that you will return. Who knows? I was gone from my bed for 39 days. I was in Atlanta, at my daughter-in-law's graduation on May 12, 2017. I walked about three blocks to Georgia State Law school, where she was graduating from, on May 14, 2017; I was in the church in Atlanta, with the rest of my family.

On May 19, 2017, I took on sickness and death in a matter of minutes. I was gone out of my body, because I was too sick to stay in there. I will never be the same, because I saw the Lord Jesus Christ. I was in my Spirit body; I saw the Lord. His robe was so unique and beautiful. He looked at me he turned his head and looked at me. I was so close to Him, I did not touch Him, but I was so close to Lord Jesus.

I am sitting here typing with tears running down my face, every time I think about Him sitting there and I am standing only a few inches away from Him Oh, Lord! I hope that the people, who do not have hope, and who are on the outside of safety, come in before it is too late. I know everyone wants to go to Heaven, but there is a way through Lord Jesus we all have to go. This way, God looks at your heart, He, knows each one of our hearts, we cannot fool the Lord. It is best to be honest and truthful, with the Lord, no matter whether someone agrees with us or not. There is a separation line, we all will meet sooner or later, and it is just you and the Lord. A person can have power, and all the influence in the world, but that will soon end. Get sick, and stay sick for a while, and you will see, what I mean.

That is why I am, so blessed. I am favored by almighty God. He let me see Heavens, and the water over there. It was so blue, and it just shined, and sparkled, with total brightness. I saw all of those mansions over there, and you cannot get there, unless you go through the Spirit, one step at a time. I always cry a lot, because of the glory of God, and the way comes upon me. I feel sorry for anyone who cannot feel the Holy Spirit. There is no other way to Heaven. You cannot fly there. You cannot pay your way there. You must be born again. So many people, do not know what that is, and everyone needs that in their life. It is our guide for living our lives, to live again. My husband told me that he cried for me 30 days straight. He said he would not eat anything. I told Him; I was in God's hands. The God that, he always saw me praying to. All through the day, my husband would ask me "So how did you get sick as much as you pray and sing and listen to gospel sermon and sing all day every day?" He said he did not understand, I told

Him that, Father God has been using me all of my life, and the tougher battles are for the tougher soldiers.

Back at my room, it is almost time to go home as the doctor comes in. I thanked Him, for all they all have done for me. I shook, their hands, and one of them said to me

"I did not do anything."

I do not know what he meant by that, but he said it and looked at me strangely. I hugged my lady doctor. She called me "Mrs. Miracles."

I am still very weak, I am going home, but I cannot stand long. I am still a sick woman; I will be a while before I get my strength back. The physical therapy lady told me, I will have to have more therapy in my hometown, and she made arrangements so I cannot get one more month at the hospital in Washington. That is what she suggested, and I agreed. The other doctor, told me, he will be getting all of my prescriptions ready for me to go home. I nodded my head, I have so much to be thankful for, knowing that the blood is warm, and remains in my body. My mind is good, I have no brain damage, all of my wounds are healing. I can wash myself off in the sink, I looked at myself in the mirror, I looked at my eyes, they were black. They were supposed to be brown, but I was thankful, I was able to see.

I was asleep all of that time in a coma. I have glaucoma and eye drops were put in my eyes while I was slept in a coma.

I asked my daughter where my eye are drops when I wake up. I could not say a word until those tubes were pulled out of my throat. I remember that everyone was just looking at me. My mind was in Heaven looking at all of those children play over. There are children looking at me when I stepped out. I went there through the ground. I was smiling all the time. It was amazing how things are set up in the other world. It is no danger in dying, just die in the Lord. We all need a Savior, and we all need God that is why Father God chose me to see Heaven. I got to tell the whole world.

Chapter 17

OVER NOW

There is a Heaven and there is nothing scary about death. People cry over death! It is a wonderful thing to walk around Heaven. I was just there, and it was time for me to go back to earth, because Father God did not let the doctor unplug all of those wires that kept my organs going. There is a Heaven and there is nothing scary about death. People cry over death! It is a wonderful thing to walk around Heaven. All of my organs just stopped my heart, liver, kidneys, and blood was poison. All of my organs just stop working, but I was in Heaven though. I told a lady that I saw in front of CVS whom I knew that she had not seen me in a while because I had been sick. I told her that I had been might of been sick, but I am doing well. She told me that there is something different about me. I told her that I had been to Heaven; she had a tear in her eye, and I got a little shaken up. I cried! Everyone was looking that was sitting in their cars parked out front. She told me that she has talked to many folks that were sick and they say that they went to hell, but never met anyone to say that they went to Heaven. I told her that you have met someone like that now. I saw Heaven.

Well, this is my last day here, June 29, 2017. I have been at both hospitals, Doctors Hospital, and Select Specialty Hospital all together for 39 days and my whole life will never be the same again and that is so good. I am free now. I saw Heaven. All I have been through; I would not change a thing. All the suffering I went through when I came back from Heaven, I never felt a thing all those days I spend in a coma. I had no pain, but when I awoke from the coma; I was in a mess! I thought I was going to die again for good, but I had to put my fighting shoes on. I had to press on like the lady with the issue of blood in the Bible. I was like the Hebrew boys in the fire! I was like Job! I was sick! I was sitting in the ash pile with sores all over my body. No one thought I would make it! I do not take anything away from my journey! I had to vacate this world for a while. Jesus told me the morning of May 29, 2017—

Willie, you are so tired! Come on with me for a while! I am going to take you to rest until your body is anew! There is no danger in going with me! Willie come on my child! I love you!

My Aunt Clifford, my mother's younger sister, called me on my hospital phone and told me over and over how I was a strong woman. She said, "I was so sick, and I was not going to die!" She knew that! My Aunt Clifford Samuel is still living! Her older sister and baby sister is still living. All of her brothers are deceased! My Aunt Clifford is my prayer warrior. She loves Jesus Christ! We talk about Jesus and His goodness every day!

She calls me or I call her every day. She makes my soul happy! Her baby sister who is a wonderful, name is Mildred Randall, she lives in Washington, Georgia too like Aunt Clifford. The oldest one under my mother is still alive and she lives in New York City; her name is Elizabeth Walton.

I received my discharge to go home; I was so thankful because my discharge could have said something else. "If God is for you then who can be against you?" I am still and still very sick, but I am going home to finish getting my strength back. I am still very weak, but somewhat better. On this day, it is the 29th of June—before each patient leaves, there is gathering for the patient. The physical therapists and nurses line up on side of the hall to clap and congratulate the patient for completing rehabilitation. I am waiting for my husband and my granddaughter, Hannah, to come so they are the ones who will be at my leaving party with the rehabilitation staff. I will never forget how the rehabilitation staff worked on me and helped me become whole again. I looked at each one of them even the patients that are in here with me. I talked with of them each day. I never thought I would have to go through this, but you never know what life will put you through. I suffered; I am glad I went through this ordeal, and I made it! My God has won again! Not me, but God won! I am just one of God's servants. We are all just vapor here on earth for a few seconds and then we are gone. I looked at all of those people in the Bible days;

they lived a long time in the Bible, yet all of them are now in Heaven and they are living again in paradise. I saw these people; they are enjoying themselves.

My husband and my granddaughter are finally here. The nurse has brought my paper to sign, and she brought me my last dinner. It is about noon, and I have to get my prescriptions about 15 of them; I have to get them filled; most of them are vitamins, but I got to get 15 filled. I told my husband; we will go by CVS in Thomson, Georgia so I will not have to wait so long, because I need to go lay down in my bed when I get home. I am sitting here eating and waiting on my nurse to come back with my medications for today and they are checking my vitals before I will be released. This will go down in history, in my children's lives. All the people in the therapy room are lined up on each side of the hallway and music is playing. I see my main physical therapist, Beverly, she is crying, and I am sitting in the wheelchair crying. My husband is crying, and my granddaughter is carrying my bag. The music is playing. Guess who is in that wheelchair? I am! Mrs. Miracle Chennault! I am going home. I am strolling down the hall. The nurses are passing by me, clapping. Everyone is clapping. Some are holding Tambourines. I am in the elevator smiling going home for a long journey. I have not seen outside in a long time. I have not felt the earth in 39 days and have really have not breathed the air from outside in a while. Here I come!

I am waiting in the front of Doctors Hospital. My husband has left me to get the truck; I got out of the wheelchair with my walker and my husband helped me get in the truck. I was so glad to be on my way home. I am still very weak, but I am on my way home riding in our blue Ford truck. My husband looks so tried. I have not seen my home in 39 days. It is a good ride home. I am looking at the cars on the road and the trees; everything seems so new to me. I am sick, but excited.

Just to be alive, I lived in Heaven! I had a chance to visit Heaven. It was the Lord's will that I return to earth. I had nothing to do with it! It was in the Lord's hands. This is about an hour and a half ride home and I am weak; hoping things will be okay at home! I will not do anything much, because I cannot! I am too weak at the moment. I thank God with all of my whole heart for letting me return home. I am still riding home going by CVS to get these prescriptions filled and I know that will take a while because I have 15 of them to get filled. I am still very sick, but the doctors say it is time to go home. I know my hospital bill is about a million dollars or more, but I have good insurance. The Lord already had all of this in order just like the colt that was in place for Him to ride into Jerusalem. The Lord will take care of you. He will stop trouble before it gets to you, but he did not choose to block this trouble from me, this sickness. This is one test I had to take, and I had to pass it! I had nothing to do with it! It was just a path that I had to pass through. I am glad I did! I had a chance to visit Heaven. It is very real! People are enjoying material things and enjoying the flesh of this world, but Heaven is much better than here on earth.

Death comes so quickly; I died, and I went to Heaven. I saw Lord Jesus! I will never forget how he looked; his toenails and his feet, the brown going around his toes. His skin was gray and pink mix together to make that color. I stood there just looking at the Lord's robe; his belt around his waist, his dark chocolate brown hair, he turned his head and he looked at me with so much love. I was a younger woman about 33-years-old.

I am sitting in the truck while my husband is getting all of my prescriptions in CVS in Thomson, Georgia. My granddaughter, Hannah is in the truck with me; she has been with me even at the hospital. She is right there with her mother and grandpapa. Her mother, Dr. June, has to go back to work so Hannah will spend the rest of the summer with me and her papa. I am just sitting here at CVS in Thomson, Georgia waiting on Lazarus to get me medications; most of these are vitamins. This is all Father God's doing. It had nothing do with me. It was not my time to stay in Heaven. I must tell the world get your house in order, because Heaven is a beautiful place to live forever. I am sitting here in the truck just looking at the cars and the people go in and out of the store. It seems like I have been gone for a while, but it seems like a short time also. I had to fight so hard to even get to this point. I had to fight with my mind and my body.

l am still a very sick woman, but my strength is about 60 percent back. I have long ways to go. I am looking around; I still have my blue bonnet on my daughter brought me, and I am weak. My husband is coming out of CVS with a whole bag of medication. My mind is on Heaven. I get peace and joy when I put my mind back in Heaven. It is just not about going to church or having friends or anyone else, but you and the Lord God. God knows the life that you live; he does not need anyone to tell Him anything, because he knows your heart. We can fool each other but not the Lord. It is all about the personal relationship between you and the Lord. I am so glad I have that personal relationship with the Lord. I always talk to the Lord.

This is an evening on June 29, 2017; I am on my way home after a test that has completely changed my life. I will never be the same I am free. I am free! A part of me will remain in Heaven until I get back there again. I do not know how long I am going to live, but I will never fear death. I have nothing to fear. The moment your soul leaves your body, you are in the presence of the Lord. I did not see anything dark in Heaven, everything was so bright! There are beautiful colors. The grass, flowers, and buildings are shiny. Bright gold is everywhere. The bluish water laid still. I laid in the bluish water with tears running down my face. No matter who you are, if I was you, I would never waste any second without Christ; he is real! I saw the Lord and I can tell the world that God is real! I have told everyone. I know some people cry and go to shaking when I tell my story, some walk-off from me with fear. Some people do not want to hear anything from me, but it is okay. I tell the others about my test who wants to hear. I never force myself on one, but I hope this will enlighten someone's faith.

This was a hard test for me! My doctors, I do not believe; the doctors had hope for me. The doctors they worked a miracle! One of children told me this. I got the best husband and four children and daughters-in-law in the whole world. They were all there for me and is still there; whatever I need, they are here for me. Bless the name of the Lord; I love the Lord. I always tell the Lord that all throughout the day, all my life. I always prayed, because I had no other help in my life. I came through very hard times and very hard living with my siblings. We did not have a lot growing up, but we had what we needed growing up and this made me the woman I am today. I would not trade my childhood with anyone else; it was hard to survive, but it made me strong.

I had no other help, but the Lord. Riding along in the truck, my husband looks real tried and Hannah do to. I am not saying now a word. I am crying thanks to the lord for loving me so much. He is letting me go home again. I did not know I was sick when I woke up. No one told me what was wrong with me. I am still crying and riding along with Hannah and my husband. He is excused, because he is sick Himself. For years, I have been waiting on Him. He has had a lung disease for 13 years. He waited on at the hospital me ever since I woke up. Crying on my way home, we are about 35 minutes from Thomas, Georgia. It is a nice summer day.

I have been through so much. There are no words to explain. Every organ in my body just stops working. I left this world. I stepped out of my sick body, and I went into the Spirit realm. My son, Pastor Henra, was part of that Spirit realm. He told me, "I know you got to go!" standing at my gravesite. He said, "But you got to come back!" He was just using his hands to say, "Come back!" I was looking back at Pastor Henra smiling and he was so serious looking at me. Then, I went into the ground. I went through the ground. There is no danger! It was fun and all the bright lights were with me the whole all the time! I saw no darkness even in the ground was light going through the tunnel, bright and light! So amazing!

One thing about all of this crying, you cannot explain all of your tears of joy and peace. No one will understand, but the Lord. I am so glad the Lord gave me a mind to praise Him. The Lord loves all of us. Love Him back by living a life that pleases Him. I have fought so many hard battles in my life. Almost home, no one is saying a thing. I am looking around with tears running down my face, feeling very weak. I only can stand up for a little while, we do not have very far to go. We are turning on the road, Metasville road, where I live a few blocks down in the country. This is I see my mailbox turning in to my driveway. I am in my house again after 39 days. I am in my driveway look looking around I saw my dog coming up to the truck; he wants to greet me.

Praising God! Lord have mercy, Jesus almighty God! You have to hold me in your hands. Lord you are so powerful. Lord Jesus thank you Lord! Glory to your name! Praise the Lord! My husband getting my walker out of the back of the truck. Hannah come around my side to help. I put one foot out of the truck and Lazarus put the other one out. he put my walker in front of me and I got hold of it. I told my husband and Hannah to go on in the house. I went to stand in the yard for a while. I cannot stand so I made it around to the backyard and I sat in the swinger. I looked around, nobody but I and the dog were around there. I told my husband when I get ready to come to the house, I will call him. he said OKAY, because he saw that I was a little worn out. I cannot tell you what is going across my mind.

God will answer prayer just stay with Him and trust Him above all else. God loves us all unconditionally. We may tell God that we want this or that; His hands are always stretched out. Pray and ask Him for what you want or need. I am sitting in the swing out in the back yard. Everything looks strange to me; I have been gone for 39 days. I am looking at this can of water that I always catch from the rain to water my plants. I have a lot of house plants and a lot of flowers outside my house. I am just looking around and I look in this can of water. In this large can and there is frog trying to get to the top of the can. I stood there looking. I am looking at how she is struggling to get to the top. When she gets to the top, I take a picture, my hands are shaking, but I got to take this picture of this frog because the Holy Spirit came to me and told me to put this picture on the front of my book. I will not say too much about this frog, because I have already told the story behind the frog. I am looking around the yard and looking at the trees. I thank God for letting me come back home.

I am still very weak, but the doctors said it was time for me to go home and I am here on June 29, 2017. God is so good to me. I have seen the Lord Jesus Christ why he let me see Him I do not know I saw the Lord and I am back here to tell everyone who wants to listen. God is real; He is nothing to play with, He knows each one of us by our heart and our name. He knows everything. For just knowing Him, oh, Praise His Holy name. This was a test I had to take, and I am glad I did. My children tell me the more they prayed the sicker, I got! It is "not unto death on this side," but I know I died because I was in Heaven. I was over there with my family and the people of the Bible days. I lookcd at them. I saw oxen over there they were happy; all of God's glory is all over there.

God gave me the best of the best—my husband, my children, my grandchildren, daughters-in-laws, and other family members. They love me and I know they stuck by me. They have always done that even when they were little. They got to know me; they always had a love for their parents even when I disciple them. I always told them it was for their best interest. I call to my husband; he had the back door open, and he looked at me and he asked me why I was crying? I told him that the Spirit of the Lord was present, and I was crying, because I was so happy. It is great just to be able to feel the Spirit of the Lord upon me. The Spirit of the Lord is so powerful; it will make you feel like fire shut up in your bones. I told Lazarus that I am ready to come in the house and I got my walker. I am coming in the house for the first time in 39 days. I have only three steps to get on the pouch. I got my walker; my husband is helping me up to the steps. Next thing you know, I am on the pouch and into the house. I stop in the doorway looking into my granddaughter's eyes with tear in my eyes. I saw a lot of love in Hannah eyes. She has been with me ever since I woke up. She looked and she looked at me. My sickness has been tough. There is something in Hannah; she always told me that she was going to be a brain surgeon and she will be, because her mother is a Doctor of Education, and she will be a Doctor of Medicine.

I am looking around in my house with tears running down my face. I have my blue bonnet on my head, my gray pants, and a blouse that my daughter brought me to the dollar store. I am in the house sitting down it about 8 p.m. in the afternoon, but it very lights in the summertime. My husband is in the kitchen fixing some supper. No one else is here at the moment. My husband looked really tried. I walk back to my bedroom where my room looked so beautiful. The whole house has been clean by my oldest son, Lazarus Jr., and his wife, Skirkea have come and cleaned the house. It is very clean. My husband told me that my house is always clean. I love a clean house. I feel better to be clean than dirty, but I am so glad to be home I do not care how it looks. So, I got ready for bed, and I have not slept very well since I woke up from the coma, but I am alive, and I love God, Jesus Christ, the Lord. I talk to Him a lot. I mean a lot. He is my only friend. I can leave everything with Him.

I got so happy in the Spirit. I thought about David and how he dances when he was full of the Spirit of the Lord. I always dance like David. He dances until he got naked in the street. I can dance like David did, because I always love the Lord ever since I came in the knowledge of Him. I love Him. I hid in the Lord. I push myself into Him. I hid from this world that is why I have a hiding place to go to when trouble comes. I know how to hide in Him. I can explain what I am saying, but if you been born again, you know what I am saying. I am so free no one can hurt me, by talking about me or not liking me! I am free from all of that I am so free. I love folks. There is no hate in me. I am so free. I do not fear death. I welcome death whenever God get ready for me to go home again. I am sitting here on the foot of my bed. I am sick still sicker than sick, but I am alive. I am free in my spirit. I can read people and their spirit.

I am so glad I am real. I cannot be a fake person. I got to be me, because God wants us to be ourselves and never let anyone rule your mind but the Lord Jesus. Sitting here on side of my bed thinking about how good God has been to me. A little old country woman like me. I have been through a hard test, but one thing for sure; God, it was all worth it. I had been to Heaven! How many people can say that they have been to Heaven? And then came back to tell about it? I can tell the world about Heaven. I have been through the process of life.

I know what Job from the Bible days felt. I was pulled apart and my God and put me back together. Why Lord was the test was so hard? Lord have mercy! The test was so hard on me. Lord have mercy me! I had everything in place for me, but it was so hard when I woke up. "It was easy over there, but God when you brought me back to that Doctors Hospital in room 16 in intense care unit!" You are talking about one sick woman!

I have no idea a human could get that sick and still live to tell about it. I hope I can help someone. I got to tell you that everything is in God's hands. Whatever tests that He has for you; It is your test to take. It is for no one else, but you. I am so glad that I had to take this test. It had my name on it; it was all for me! I am glad for this test!

Oh, Lord! You are so real! I want everyone to know that God is real! Please pray and live according to the Bible! God is real! He lives in each one or us so please let Him manifest all over your body. My home is long in feet so I can be on one side of my house and my husband can be on the other side of the house looking at his sports. Everything still seems so familiar in the house. I think back over some of my hardest points while being in the hospital when I am awake. I thought about how the nurses turned me so much every day.

Praise the Lord! I am so blessed to be alive, glory to God! I am coughing all day every day. I coughed up black mucus. Everything was out of order; I mean everything was doom. I had to have every kind of vitamin and other medicines that I cannot pronounce. God had everything in order, because he allowed me to go through this. He wanted me to go through this because everyone who saw this and heard about this knows this was a great miracle. No one believes that I was going to survive. No one deep down, but God. My son who is a minister told me and reassured that God told him that I was not going to dic, and he rested on that, and he told those doctors what to do for his mother and the other three children went right along with him. I had the best staff of doctors and nurses in the world.

The Lord already had everyone in line even the EMS from Wilkes County who took me to Augusta. God sent them here to get me. I do not care how good you thank you are; you cannot do anything without the Lord. The Lord is in control of everything. I mean everything. This was another hard task for me when I tried to turn over so many wires after I work up, but I did not see those wires. When I work up, I saw a lot of wires attached to me and I could not turn myself over in my bed, so I just laid there until the nurse came to untangle these many wires. The nurses are always in my room; they are working on me every passing minute all day every day. The nurses and doctors are always busy with me.

Oh, Jesus, I cried all the time. I did not want to see anyone, because it comes a time in each of our lives, it just you and the Lord. Another hard task was when I had to go to another hospital that was Select Specialty Hospital. On June 2, 2017, I was transported to this hospital at nighttime around 10:30 at night. I was so sick. I had a fever 105 °F. My blood pressure was so high. I was a sick woman. I had to go through the process, and I did with the Lord holding my hand. Another hard task was when I had to learn how to bathe and walk again.

I had to learn to feed myself and how to stand. It was all so hard, but I made it. I give my life to the Lord. I always did! I love the lord! I always told Him that even before I got sick! I always love the Lord, because he always looks out for my children. He educated all four of them with the best education, because I ask Him to do that for me, please. He did! They worked hard and accomplish their dreams. I did not want, them to be so poor. I did not want my grandchildren to be so poor. My children will make sure that their children know God and be educated. Someone had to break the path of poverty. I had to do it for my children. Life is hard enough, being so poor that it is double hard. I remember when no one was working, but my husband. I had two babies in two years, and I had two more older children. I had to rap what few pennies that I could find in the house to make it to the clinic for check-ups for my children. My husband and I drove around with children in the old station wagon dragging to the ground. I never was the one to quit and say that is it! I always came up with another way, but God will take care of you, if you let Him.

One the next day after I got home on June 30, 2017—I did not sleep well on the night before the night that I got home. I am still a sick woman. It is going to take a while before I get my strength back. So that next morning the lady called me from Thomson, Georgia. The lady from the dialysis called and told me that I was scheduled to have dialysis three times a week Monday, Wednesday, and Friday. I told her I did not need it. My kidneys are working fine! She was so shocked. She was in disbelief. She kept on saying and asking me was I sure. When I first work up my kidneys were not working, and my body was eliminating the poison from my blood. I was in a mess in my body, but in my spiritual mind. I was okay, because the Spirit of the Lord was upon me. She just we on and on about my kidneys. They have started back working full force. I praise the Lord and she said it was not anything, but a miracle and I told her how the Lord's hands are upon me, and he is a healer. I am not worried about nothing. God got me and he has all of us. If we want Him to hold us. She was so happy for me, and she took my name of the dialysis list. She was still in shock. I am still very weak at this time. I cannot stand up very long at all. I sit down and rest for a while. This is a Monday, my first day back at home after 39 days in the at the hospital with double Pneumonia.

I am looking around; my husband is so tired. He looks exhausted, but with his sickness; he is holding up good. My whole life has changed. I will never be the same again. I see life clearer, and I see people in a different light. I always think about seeing Jesus. I looked at his leg; they are long from his knees to his feet. His feet are a little long. I looked at his toes nails they had a brown line around each one of his toes; his toenails look like fish scales and his skin was mix of gray and pink, a beautiful, bright paleness. His skin was smooth and flawless. It was amazing! why did the Lord let me see Him? There has to be a reason! I know it will come to me soon! I got to tell everyone I know and who wants to listen. Some people will listen to me, and some will not, but it is okay, because I saw the Lord. I hope everyone will be able to read my book. It is unbelievable! Who do not believe in the Lord? I hope they will come to Christ over my testimonies.

God be the glory! I just was a test for others to witness. The Lord always knows what is going on with all of us at the same time, because our little minds cannot even utter his mind. He can do what he pleases when he wants! This test had my name on it, and it was for me! God be the glory! Some are so shocked that I survived; they stop breathing, I am sure. I had nothing to do with it this; God working through me. He showed all of you all a miracle upfront. This was not only for me; it was for everyone who played a part in it even the doubter. God's hands showed me it is not your time.

Chapter 18

A NEW

God brought me back from the dead just like he did Lazarus and Jairus' daughter. I went to Heaven in one second. I had no remembrance of this world, so it all what you do for the Lord that will pay off in this world. Live a life according to the will of the Lord! We all make mistakes, but we must learn from them. God is so real! We should care more about what God thinks, than our friends, but at the end of the day that is your life! It only matters what God thinks. I am so glad! I love the Lord! I love Him! I have loved Him from the time of being a little girl sitting in the woods. I always sat praying in the woods all throughout my life! I still sat in the woods, and I talked to Father God, because he is my friend. Sometimes no one else understands you, but the Lord. I always told Him how I felt, about every situation that surrounded my life. I still tell Him to this day; he knows all of my thoughts afar off. I tell Him anyway; I cry to Him daily. I always did; he understands. Also, if Jesus had to pray; what about us? We must always pray for others. What good are we if we love those who we know love us. Love those who mistreat us. Do good wherever and whenever you can; with everything we do it does not have to be so someone can see it. Do good in secret and God will reward you openly!

I became a young mother very early in my life. The first boy I fell in love with was the one that I married after 44 years. I am still married to Him, and he is a part of me. We are not perfect, but we were raised the same way. We wanted more for our children, so they will help the next generation from poverty! God is always first in our lives. I cry all the time and the Spirit of the Lord come upon me. Thinking back every passing day, about my illness and in Heaven; It was the best part of this whole task. We have no memory of this world that we have left behind when death comes so fast on your eyes; they are closed in a few seconds. You are in another dimension, and no one can help you or hurt you, because God's glory is everywhere in Heaven. I mean his glory is in everything over there! Even the animals and their eyes are full of glory; the oxen's that I saw had glory in their eyes! The grass, the trees, the water, and the clouds. I look up at the clouds; it very different, the sky is closer to ground. Everything is just so bright over there and shinning bright! Who would not want to go to Heaven?

My mother was busy telling me to go back and that I could not come with her and my aunties yet. I was busy trying to get where she was on the other side of the gulf. My aunties were just looking and sitting under the trees; they were looking at all of those children playing on top of the hill. All the races of children were playing as I stood there looking towards the hill.

I was smiling. I was so amazed. I knew I was in heaven, because I walked all around, and I walk upon the whole world. I walked upon Jesus Christ. He turned his head, and he looked at me; I cannot explain that look. I told my sons and my daughter and my daughters-in-law. They were amazed, I have told a lot of people in my hometown about my experience in Heaven. I never seen that look before, but his eyes had the ocean in them; bluish water running from side to side in both of his eyes.

Glory Hallelujah, I was amazing! I was young and pretty! I did not look like I do now. His deep dark brown hair, it is about the first week of July. The physical therapy from Washington called and told me that I have three more weeks of physical therapy to go. I had to go three days a week to try to get my strength back. I can walk on my walker, that is what I came home on, and I walked through my house, on my walker. If I tried to walk without my walker, I just fall upside the wall and I have to hold up by the furniture even I hold up by the door. Until I got where I needed to be. One day my husband was sick, I had to try to fix myself some breakfast. I was just struggling to get to the kitchen, and I almost did not make it to the kitchen, but I struggled around the kitchen trying to fix me some food. It was hard, but I never gave up.

I always say to myself, "I must press on and on and I will

get back stronger one day soon; it is coming, and it is coming."
I always tell myself that every single day, and I picture it in my
mind. I will be walking strong again! I was in the kitchen, while
the phone rang, and it was my best friend, Betty Fanning. She
has been sick for a long time, but we always talked about life
situations, our illness, and we always talked about the Lord, for
hours. We never complained about our situations, but we
always gave the Lord thanks. Our good days outweighed all of
our bad days. She told me that she has heard that I was sick,
and I told her this is my first week back home, and it is kind of
tough. I am still very fragile. I told her I was in the kitchen
fixing me some breakfast, and she said she was doing so to.
She said that she was very weak, also I told her that I was
falling around in my kitchen, even she said the same too. She
said we just have to give it to God and all his glory. Betty and I
praised the Lord all the time, because she was my best friend
from the first grade.

After 47 years, she is still my best friend after high school.
You do not keep, but a couple of friends. All the rest just speak
friendly whenever you see them. This is the kind of friend that
you never run out of words with; we can chat forever about the
Lord, and we never get tired. We talk about how our children
are doing whenever we talk. Even we always, praise the Lord
together whenever we are together; we trade testimonies and
get happy in the Lord. There is no one like her and she has

gone home the be with the Lord now. I know she made it home safe, with the Lord.

Three weeks of physical Therapy, here now, in my hometown, Washington Georgia. I have to go three days a week, trying to get my legs and my upper body stronger, but I am still weak. I not able to socialize with anyone, only my children come by to see me. My Aunt Clifford came by one day. I enjoyed her! And her son, George Jr. He is the one who told my Aunt Clifford that I will not die! He said, "She is critical, but she will be back!" I cannot stand up very long, I walk in the hospital, on my walker get to the physical therapy each day for three weeks.

One day the physical therapist checked me, and he said that my blood pressure was too high, so my husband took me back to Augusta to the emergency room to the University Hospital, because I knew that my heart doctor was there. They checked me and they put me back in the hospital. At the heart center, I went through all kinds of heart tests and the after two days, they let me go home again. Everything looked well, so I went home to continue my physical therapy. Here in Washington, Georgia, I have already gone through my biggest part of physical therapy at the Doctors Hospital. I am trying to learn how to walk better! I learned to stand up again after the coma at Select Specialty Hospital, where I was a very sick woman. Too sick to sleep! I still do not sleep well! It seems like

everything is backwards here at home, back here on earth. I
have not been here in so long! One day on up in that week I
got mighty sick and seemed like I was dying. I thought to
myself, if I was going to die, my Lord Jesus would not have
brought me from Heaven. I am going to live.

I told my daughter-in-law, Kianna, how sick I felt. She was
here that weekend; she said, "You are going to live and get
stronger and stronger every day!" My children and everyone
else, who has looked in on me has seen me beat death, Hell,
and the grave. The nurse teases me about coming back from
the dead. I told them I had nothing to do with it! My life is in
God's hands, whatever he wants me to do is fine with me. It
does not matter what I want, I want to do God's will for my
life. I am in God's hands not the doctor, but God; he worked
through the doctor, he put me in the hands of the best doctor.
I look at myself in the mirror, I look so tough and pale, and I
had no hair in the back of my head and my eye looks like a sick
animal, but I am alive.

My family, my children are coming in and out on the
weekend. My husband is worn completely out. He is taking
good care of me; I am still alive. I am praising God like I
always have done. Everyday all through the day; I always praise
Him no matter what I am going through. I always talk to God;
I still set a peaceful tone in my house. I love to talk to the
Lord, in the woods. I live in the country, so I always go sit on

the bench up from my house. I always pray and sing hymns to myself. I pray for other folks more than I do for myself; I always put myself last, I have to always pray; I never let up. If Jesus had to pray, what about us?! I am going back home to Heaven again one day! That I will see Jesus again face to face again. I will never be the same again. I have seen the Lord; I have seen his glory, everything in Heaven is full with the Lord's glory. Even those oxen, seems to be full of God's glory. Heaven is like nothing I would never thought of or dreamed about! Heaven is a majestic world; who would not want to go there? You cannot drive there, you cannot fly there, you cannot walk there, you sure cannot buy your way there! You can only get there through the Spiritual realm.

Every day I am getting stronger, I cannot drive yet! It will be a long while before I drive again. I ride up the road with my husband in our blue ford truck. Oh, how people be looking because we are the only ones in Washington who have a deep, ice blue truck. Everyone knows that we drive a blue truck. I sit in the truck while my husband go get groceries; all eyes be on that truck because no one really believes that I am still alive, but I am still here!

Another day to serve the Lord, I feel so sorry when for a person when they only serve the Lord on Sunday; everyone must serve the Lord and pray more during the weekdays, two hours on a Sunday. It had never been enough for me. I will never be the same, the Lord had to use me for miracles to come through. He has ever thing ready for me, he is so loving and caring for all of his children. Jesus loves us but, he will not force any one to praise to Him. He has His hands reached out, come to Jesus while there is yet time.

Grandfathers and grandmothers please help your children! Grandchildren come to Jesus while there is yet time! Teach your children while they are young, on your lap by taking them to Sunday school and to church on Sunday. It was mandatory in my house every Sunday. We praised the Lord all through the years, all through the week. I told them about the Lord, with tapes and sermons and reading the Bible. I had to tell the first hand and their father had to tell them and live the life. No one is perfect but we tried.

Being home after 39 days in the hospital, the phone never rang; my children always called, and my auntie called too. A couple of other people called, I love people, but I keep to myself a lot, because I do not like saying bad things about people, I rather be praying for them. When you love Jesus, deep down in your soul, you will not have many friends. I have a great friend, Mrs. Gladys Pinkston. I talked about her mother earlier in the book, Mrs. Annie Josephine Gartrell. We talk about life and our children all of the time. She is an awesome friend!

Whatever you add to other folks' children, good or bad it

will come back to your children. When my children come home, I can be sitting in a chair and I get up to go to the bathroom or go to the kitchen they look at me real strange, they have seen me as still laying there in that bed and with no movement; their eyes are just wide open. The Lord can use simple things to get his point across to us. He is still God, just like he uses rocks, his spit and dirt; he can use just what he wants to. He does not have to ask anyone's opinion. He needs to get no one's permission. He is the same. He changes not; he never sleeps nor takes a nap. He looks low and he looks high. He sees what we are all doing at the same time. He is a mighty God.

All sickness is not unto death; my children say the more they prayed the sicker I became in the hospital. I felt nothing until I work up. I was a sick woman, sicker that sick. I never knew a person could become that sick. I had an unspecified bacterium in my body with double pneumonia in both lungs, but the God that I have been serving all of my life is the Lord that met me one day in the plum brushes. He is the same God that healed my body, and I can tell the world. God is real. I do not have to go through no one at church. I can go right to my Lord whom I love, a true child of God.

I cannot do any and everything. I always want the Lord to hear me, and I always tried to do what is right, not in my sight but according to the Holy words of the Lord. If I stand up too long during the day, my feet would swell, and I stayed off my feet. I was still very weak. My husband and my granddaughter Hannah are here with me, and my other children come on the weekend and help out praising God each day. One thing about Heaven every day of my life. I got back to Heaven in my mind, remembering the things that I had saw most of all. I think about seeing Jesus; I know that was Him. I know that I will with all of my heart; why did he let me see Him? I can barely stand up. I get in the shower, weak and holding up by a chair. My granddaughter is helping me. I cannot do any housework or cook at this time, but I try to make me some oatmeal in the morning.

I have to get up; my husband does not be feeling good in the early morning, he has to take breathing treatments. He be all choked up in the morning, so I struggle to the kitchen, which is a pretty long way from my bedroom with tears in my eyes. Praising God! God is the first and last thing that is on my mind in the morning and at night before going to bed. Praising God, for all he has done, and I praise Him for helping other folks who I do not even know. I pray for whoever I met or think about during the day. It is about praying for someone else, that will help you.

Well, the first week has gone by. I am at home heading into the second week it is about July 8, 2017. I am resting and thinking about my time in Heaven. There is no time there. I saw the Lord and I saw the beautiful robe that he has on; every time I think about the Lord I start to cry, and I still do! I can hardly stand to think about all of his glory that comes to me in a good way. I get so happy just thinking about the Lord and all he has done for me. My soul just cries out, "Lord have mercy on me, and I thank you Lord!" I asked my son, who is a minister, why the Lord showed me, Heaven, why? He just looks at me strange. I tell all of my children about Heaven, and it is a beautiful place; there are no words to explain Heaven; it is just like the Bible says.

I saw half of the Lord's hands, because he had them kind of inside of his robe, but I saw his feet better. I will never forget how his feet looked and his sandals and his legs. It was so amazing! You would never believe this, but it is so true. I explained it the best way I know. I talked about the mountains, the trees, the ground, the grass, the oxen, and the people I saw in Heaven. I saw all the races, the Bible folks; they were dressed just like the clothes in the Bible days, but my mother has on some of the clothes that I recognize. She had on a red, white, and blue blouse and pants that came to her knees. The same pants that she wore all the time when she was here on earth. She was in the glory of God and my aunties had on some of the same clothes I recognized; my two aunties were sitting down under a tree where the children of all races were playing on the hill. I was going across the river until my mother told to go back. I was not sick. I was pretty about 33 years old. I know I am repeating myself, but Heaven is real! I feel so sorry for anyone who does not know the Lord and savior Jesus Christ.

Heaven is so real, and you go into eternity in a few seconds! No one can go with you! Jesus, has it planned out for the born-again believer! It is so simple to get to Heaven. One blink of an eye, you are there it doest not matter how you be put away after you die; the body that is buried will not go into Heaven, but the soul that is inside of you will spring out just like a squash plant. You plant it, it dies, and it comes up a new something. I died and I saw Heaven and the Lord showed me part of Heaven. I saw all of those mansions and I walked among the people in the Bible days they just looked at me as I walk among them. I walked up to Jesus; can you imagine walking upon Jesus? I am about to shout at this miraculous event that happened to me!

I am sitting here writing this book. I always get happy in the Spirit while I am writing. The glory of the Lord come upon me all times of the day; the glory of the Lord is upon me as I sit here and write this book. My soul is happy in the Lord. I have prayed to the Lord Jesus all of my life. I mean all of my life; my mother always prayed with my siblings and me, and my father sung hymns all of his life. You could hear Him singing hymns all over the neighbor; everyone knew who he was, we never lived close to anyone, but you could hear Him for miles, singing hymns. My second week home and I am surrounded by my children and my grandchildren. When I look at them in their sweet eyes; I know they needed me, so I had to fight the good fight of faith. I used all of the body strength that I had with all of my might to learn how to walk again; this was one of the hardest things. I ever had to try to do is to learn how to walk; I have to learn to stand up first and I did; I had to try very hard.

The second week, I am at home, and I am still very weak, doctor appointments after doctor appointments. I was still very weak but trying to see about myself at this time is hard. My husband has gotten very sick, and I had to call EMS to pick Him up and they did; he has to stay in the hospital. I could not drive at this time. I am too weak, two weeks after I got home my husband is so sick, he cannot breathe; he has lung disease. I told Him to hurry back. I have my granddaughter, Hannah here with me and she is my hands. She asks me all the time, "Grandma, why were you so sick and I told her it was one of the tests that I had to take!" I saw, Heavenly Hannah, and I would not trade that for moment, not even my life back here. I saw the Lord; I do not know, why he showed Himself to me, but I have to tell the world that I have seen the Lord in his glory. I will never forget looking at my mother and my aunties and the people in the Bible days. It was amazing! Five seconds, you are in the presence of the Lord after you die, not one else can help you! Who would not want to see Heaven? Heaven is so real! No talking about any one over there but Jesus Christ, no gossiping or hate or jealousy or envy is found in Heaven. It is all about God's glory and excitement, walking around Heaven. I never know that I had lived here until I work up.

I just fated back in the world from Heaven, no one expected me to wake up, but it was in God's plans for me to tell people that Heaven is real! It is time for all of those who have doubts to get their house in order to meet the Lord. The time is now! Do not wait another day without accepting the Lord. It is time to get right now before it be too late; it's time for the ministers to tell people about the Lord and Heaven. I hope all of you who are reading this book seek Jesus while there is, yet time and you are still in your right mind tell your children. Get your grandchildren on board and tell them every day about the Lord Jesus.

My husband is in the hospital, and I cannot go to visit Him, because I cannot drive at the moment. I am too weak, and I am calling Him to see how he is doing, and he is better, but he has to stay about three days before he returns home. My oldest son is coming home to pick Him up from the hospital to bring Him back home. He looks bright like he always does after he comes home from the hospital. I am still weak looking, very pail but I put cocoa butter on my face and my legs.

I have no hair in the back of my head. I remember the

first day I took a bath in the hospital this was for physical therapy. I took a bath for the first time and after I took my bath for the first time in a whole month; I was crying so much just to be alive able to see my husband and my children and my grandchildren. I was so happy, the therapist stood on the outside of the room while I sit in a chair to take a bath. I wash my hair for the first time in a month and I rubbed my hand in the back of my head. I had no hair; I had none in the back of my head. I dried off good; it took me a long time to bathe; I could use my hands, but they were so weak. She stood there helping me put my clothes on and we went into the therapy room. I felt so bad I forgot to put my little bonnet hat on that my daughter has brought me and I felt so bad! I had no hair in the back of my head, I mean none.

I had hair in the front, but none in the back and when I washed my hair more fell out in bundles, but I said to myself I am alive, and I am going home! I know the Lord is with me, because he let me see Heaven! I do not know how long I am going to live, but I am going to tell everyone who wants to listen about Heaven.

Three weeks has passed, and my hair is growing back little by little. My eyes are not like they should be I went to the eye doctor; the Eye Guys is where I always go, and I told them I have been to Heaven. I told some of the nurses there; they got so happy listening to talking about it. My eyes were so red when the doctor came in; I have had glaucoma for years and years and it is a struggle, but my God. My mother had the same thing and one of my sons has the same thing, Glaucoma.

I put everything in God hands, because he is a healer. I know the Lord as a mind regulator and a heart fixer, as a friend that will be closer than a sibling, a mother, or a father. I know Him as a lawyer in courtroom. I know Him as my only friend who will always understand me when everyone else fails you. He has always been there for me; it not easy to struggle up toward life. My five-year-old granddaughter told me how she has cried for me, and she ask me why you were sick grandmother. There is a reason for everything, but only God knows, and I try not to question Father God because he always knows best for each one of us. We have no strength of our own no matter how good you may think you are; things happen. I have been praying and serving Father God as long as I can remember. I never let up from praising Him, whether my life is going good or bad. I pray the same always. We can never let up, pray continuously. Keep on praying and keep on talking to the Lord; sometimes you be to be trying to pray, but I always pray anyway nothing in this world has no meaning me.

I will and I have always talked to the Lord in my wildest times, when me and my husband use to go out to the club and dance, I had my mind on the Lord out there on the floor dancing. I always pray because I wanted to get back to my children safely and the Lord always let me, and my husband get back home safe. We did not get a chance to go out much, but I enjoyed myself when we did go out. I would not take anything for my journey. I love the Lord with all of my heart. I would not trade a thing. I love the Lord and I love people. I do not have many friends. I speak to people.

As time went on—I noticed weeks, days, and months went by fast. After two months, I am still weak; my children are coming and going back and forth from Atlanta to Washington to see how we are doing. Two months passed by my husband's blue truck goes up and down the road; my husband is driving. I am still too week to drive. I did not want to run over anyone so I will wait until I get stronger before driving anywhere. My husband go he asked me if I wanted to ride to the store. I told him I would. He waited patiently for me to get ready, and I walked really slow. When my husband rode out to the store people stop and stare at me like I did not suppose to be here. One day our blue truck broke down in front the Mary Willis library and I had to get out.

I stood on side of the road waiting for the wrecker truck to pick our truck up. While I was standing there with my husband waiting for the wrecker truck to come, people were passing by and many of them almost ran out of the road looking at me, because everyone knows that blue truck. Some of the people who was passing by came by several times to see was that me standing there. They could not believe I was able to stand and that I was looking well. They slowed up and then they would speed up. Some of them spoke and some did not speak to me. I was still alive after all that they have heard about my illness. Each day I got a little stronger and a little stronger it is going to take a while. I can see that before I am able to drive or do any heavy housework like vacuuming or moping, but I do small things around the house.

I am always praising the Lord. I do not know what happened while I was in a coma. My children always tell me a bit and pieces. I am questioning them about what was going on when I was in a coma; they tell me maybe two sentences. I always ask my husband questions about what happened to me when I was in a coma in the hospital; all he told me was that I was a mess. He cannot stand to talk about it, but I wanted to know. I was in Heaven having a ball; I was in my glorified body. God can do anything he wants to do! We must believe it is possible to know what all God can do; I went to Heaven I believe there is a Hell. I talk to two people; they told me they went to Hell. I listen to their story, and they listen to my story of Heaven. I feel so sad for people who are going to miss Heaven. Heaven is real nothing, but peace there. Everything is in God glory.

I rested at home week after week. I had a lot of doctor's appointments for the first three weeks. It was very hard to rest when I got home; I was still so weak very weak. I prayed and I listen to sermons as usual, I walked outside up from the house my house is in the woods. I thank the Lord like I do all the time. I tell Him how good he is, and I take Him back to his word because he cannot lie. He cannot. I always take Him back to Him word. If I do this, he will do this, and he always brings me out no matter what kind of problem or what kind of sickness; he always brings me out. He always does the same for my children; he always helps them.

I must love the Lord with all of my heart, mind, strength, and soul. With all of being, I just love the Lord. I always tell the Lord that I love Him, because I know he loves me. He loves all of us; he wants everyone to be saved; most of the people do not want to be saved; they put everything before the Lord. If you bring up the Lord to most folk, they look at you like you are crazy. The Lord wants us to live and enjoy the fruits of our labor and be happy and be in the good health as our soul prospers. I get so happy in the Spirit of the Lord; he comes up on me and I have to get up and move around the house. The Spirit of the Lord is like burning fire shut up in my bones. I become light as a fellow. When the Spirit of the Lord come up me as I sit here, and I type, and I type. I tell my story, a true story. Someone might come to Christ while there is still breath in their bodies.

On this day Dec 21, 2018, it is my wedding anniversary of 44 years. He was the first boy that told me I was so pretty, and he became my husband, and we are still tighter after 44 years of marriage. We have three boys and one daughter. I lost one son early due to a stillborn birth. I am so glad I made it back to my husband; he cannot make it without me, and he always tells me that. It is so sad. He told me that he always depends on me. He never paid a bill. I always took care of all the bills and all of the other financial parts of our lives. He always worked and brought his money home to me. He did not know how to manage when I got sick. He had to call our daughter for help, and she took care of all the bills. We never think about this part of life until it happens in a blow of a moment. Not that he did not know how to take care of the bills; he did not know the password to our bank account online.

My husband is a good man; he always took good care of me, and we loved some of the same things. We were raised alike. We went through some of the same hardships coming up as a child, but it made both of us strong so we could see to it that our children had a better and a good mind also. I never dated other boys. I do not think he ever dated other girls, because when we fell in love, we were enough for each other. The years has passed by, and all of our children are successful; it just me and Him again! This is the best part of my life; my husband and I give each other a little space throughout the day, he got his television and I have my television. We look at different shows on television sometimes. He can be at one end of the house, and I can be on the other end of the house as long as I know he is in the house; I am okay. Marriage is not easy, but it is up to you what you want to do in your marriage. If you do not want to be treated a certain way, do not treat your spouse like that.

It is now about September 2017, and I got to go the doctors; he took me off most of medications that I took after I got out of the hospital. The doctor told me that you do not need those medicines anymore. All of my test came back, great. My kidneys, my heart, all came back to normal. Remember I stop breathing on the way to the hospital it was over an hour ride. My liver stopped and my heart stopped beating and all of my organs failed, but God has me in his powerful hands. When God got you, no devil in Hell can do anything. God is real! It does not matter how rich you are, how poor you are; whether you are saved or not, God has the last word, and we should live accordingly to his word, because only what you do for the Lord will pay off in this world. We are to live and praise the Lord so we can get home safely. We will all die at some point in our lives. Heaven is real. I have seen the Lord. Why did he show Himself to me? I do not know! I got to tell everyone who wants to listen. Heaven is real! Get prepared people for God.

You must be born again of the Holy Spirit, because blood and water cannot get to Heaven.

It is a glory filled place. God's glory is everywhere. I knew I was in Heaven when I saw my mother and aunties. I know they were in their glorified bodies; they were together, three sisters enjoying Heaven looking at the children playing; there were all races of children. When I stepped over, my mother recognized me and my aunties also. I got to tell God's people about Him and his glory. You need to love God and believe in Him and live your life according to his word. What are you afraid of? God has a test for me to take. All of those who were standing around my bed saw God work a great miracle through me.

I am a living testimony and a living miracle. God had everything in place for me. I always told Father God to use me any way he wants to. These are powerful words to tell the Lord. He gets the glory. I have to bring people to Him. I always told the Lord. I have not found anything in this world that I would trade my journey for; I did not care who likes me or hate me. I am free. I have been through the fire, and I came out like pure gold. I had nothing to do with it; it was all in the Lord's hands. The Lord picked out all of my doctors. He knows everything.

What people do not understand; the Father God knows everything. He sees all we do and knows all that what we say.

Every word will be brought up again! We must ask for forgiveness throughout the day, that is every day! I always tell Father God to give me a clean heart and renew in me a right Spirit. We are going to Heaven or hell? Who would want to miss that beautiful place! It is so bright and so free! God knows your heart. I always want to be right with God no matter what, if I fitted in with the church family or not. I always want to be right, because everyone at church does not love you. Everyone in your family does not love you. Listen to your heart and love them anyway, but you have to love some people sometimes from a distance.

It almost October of the year of 2017. I am still here, but I can manage myself better. It is Sunday and my husband, and I are going to Atlanta to hear my son, Pastor Henra, preach. This is the first time I have been out walking in public. My son told the congregation that his mother is back, and this is her first time back to church since her illness. Everyone welcomed me back, but a few people stood still and watched me. They looked at me with shock and deep wonder. I looked back at them. I smiled! I am still weak, remember my whole body was torn down. I mean nothing was in place. I mean nothing. I was not there. I was in a place where trouble does not exist, no crying over there. Nothing, but joy and glory! It is Hallelujah, every day all day!

It is amazing! The Lord brought me back to write this
book and it may help someone come to know Him. He just
used me. He uses some of his strongest soldiers for the hardest
tests. This was a test so hard for my physical body, but not for
my spiritual body. The Lord gave me triple back in strength to
my physical and spiritual body. The Lord gave me a better
body than what I had prior my illness. I am much stronger
now; I am better now. I can look at people with more
compassion and I do not judge anyone no matter what they are
doing. I feel for people even more and I pray for them, because
God is love. I see all people as people, and they are God's
creation. We must love one another.

I see life clearer now. I understand death! It is nothing to
fear! I am reminded by 1 Corinthians 13:12— "For now we see
through a glass, darkly; but then face to face: now I know in
part; but then shall I know even as also I am known." If you
die in the Lord, in just a blink of an eye you are in eternity
without test and pain. Where would I be? I am so glad my
Father God chose to test me so I can help others! I am so glad;
I am free! Lord Jesus! I have been made over! I am free and
healed! I have been remaded! Lord, I am free! Thank you,
Lord, for this journey! Lord, I am free now! Thank you, Lord,
for this affliction! I am flowing with a mind of freedom. I
would not take anything for my journey at this moment in my
life. Money is good to have, but good health is even better to

have, but we never know when it will go bad. I was not sick at all. I just had a physical weeks before I got sick; my physical results were good. My doctor checked my blood sugar and cholesterol. It was all good. I exercised and ate a good diet and took my vitamins.

I still had this big test to take, and I am glad I did; I suffered, and I suffered just like Job. I had to suffer; my body was broken with bed sores. I suffered after I came back from Heaven. I suffered; I never knew a human could so sick. I was a sick woman. I mean sick, but I am a living witness that God is really a healer. We all will suffer in some way at some point in our lives. No one will escape it! Keep your spirit clean; you will see life so differently. I will walk that same journey of sickness again just to see Jesus Christ in glory. Hopefully, next time I die; I will be very old and sleep away. It just a very quick transition over there; no pain in Heaven. We will never understand the power of God. In Heaven, you just dot here and there. It is very different than walking on earth. It is like you are walking through the clouds. I cannot explain it. If you are all born again believers. You will experience it one day!

Five months have passed by, and my hair is growing back nicely. My skin is glowing. I am going for walks, and I pray while I am walking. I say the Lord's prayer and Psalm 23 while I walk all the time. I love to walk with my granddaughter, Hannah. She is always in front of me. I always have and I pray for my family. We all need prayer. I feel so sorry for folk who do not know the Lord. The Lord is real. He is an awesome, God! He is so compassionate to all of us; he loves all of us. He will help us. He knows our record; he never sleeps or take a nap. Sometimes the more you pray the worth things do get, but joy will come, just keep on praying and believing it will come to pass and it will. I am still moving slow, but it is all good I am building muscles and moving better than the first day since I have been out of the hospital.

I went to Bilo, and I drove the Blue Ford F150 truck. I got out feeling kind of weak and I went into the store. I walked over to the fruit area, and I felt so weak. I had to walk out of the store very slowly and I got in the truck. I did not buy anything. I was still so weak. I could barely get home. I said, "Lord help me to get home in one peace!" He did! I waited a while longer because I had to get stronger before I drive. And I did wait, but the Lord is my strength, and He will supply everything that I need in His timing. I still cannot believe I been to Heaven. Just as sure as my life is back, I went to Heaven. I will never forget the beautiful trees and the branches on the trees. I was standing close to the "Almighty." I was standing next to "Breath of life." I was standing next to Jesus Christ Himself in the Spirit. I was so close to Him; I could reach out and touch Him. This was a supernatural experience. Most people will not believe that this happened to me, but this is the truth; this happened to me! I cannot tell anyone why a miracle came through me. Everything was in place for me, everything! Stay prayed up because this could happen to anyone; I had no time to pray. I left this world so quickly. I am glad I was at the store or driving. I usually go to the grocery store in the morning.

I was feeling bad when I got up the morning I fell into a coma. My husband was cutting my hair and life started fading away. I was talking to my daughter. Life will start to fade away; we have no idea how fast one can die. We take life for granted. I never will again. I am guaranteed nothing when it comes to living or being alive. No one knows the minute or the second or the day they are going to die, all we know is it is coming. So, it best to be ready whether you are young or old or middle aged. Death is going to hit you like a ton of bricks and there will be no coming back, but the Lord brought me back, because I got something else to finish before I go back home.

Every day the Lord tell me to finish my book. It is not easy sitting here going back over a few hard moments, but my mind stays in Heaven most of the time. It is my safe place. I tell my husband all the time about Heaven. I always lived in the corner. I never dealt with many people. I always keep to myself. I talk to people, but I got to have my quiet time in the corner of my life. I just cannot talk about things that do not mean anything. I always talk about things to help not hurt. My four children are the best; they are always calling and texting me and visiting to see how I am doing. I got to the gym and exercise. I feel so much better exercising; it good for me. I exercise alone. I pray while I am in the gym. I thank God for giving me the mind to think about Him, because if I did not have the mind to think about Him; how can I praise Him and tell Him things?

I will never be the same the same person I was, before I got sick; I always prayed. I tried to do the best I could with what I was given in my life. I made the best and a lot of hard work from my husband and me. If I do fall, he would catch me. People still are looking at me very shockingly after a year passed and they are still looking at my strength they wonder how I made it through that sickness.

A lot of people are still wondering how I made it through all of that. I told them that the Lord will have to be done. I never would have lived long in the body that I was in before I got sick. The Lord, Jesus Christ gave me a new body and a new mind. I see things clearer now. I am free. I have been through the fire. I mean a fire ten times hotter than it should have been. The Lord was in there with me; he let me see Heaven and I got to tell the whole world whether anyone receives it or not. I must tell who all who wants to listen. It is your soul that is a stake. All of those who are outside of the safety of God must get on board as soon as possible. Do not let another second or day or minute go by, come on in before it is too late. I am going to live longer now. I had to take this test. I cannot explain the test, but God allowed me to pass this test.

I went to a church down the road where I use to go when I was very young and I still go, but I have not been since I was sick. When I walked in this church everyone just stopped and looked at me as I walked in ready to serve the Lord. I got this look from the congregation and when the services were over this young lady came up to me and she said, "I know God is real now! He has brought you from a long way.
I told her, "Yes."
She said, "Just by looking at you, my faith in the Lord has increased."
I told her that I was glad. I have been through this sickness, double pneumonia with severe sepsis, all of my organs failed me. God took me on a vacation to Heaven. I am here to tell the whole world that Heaven is real; it has taken me a long time to get my strength back, but I am still here! I will never be the same and I do not want to be.

I am a new inside and out. I am stronger. I see things more in a humble way. I am glad. The Lord has used in a way to get all the glory. I am free. Heaven is bright. Heaven is real. I eat differently now. I do not eat junk food. I try eating a lot of green food and I pray all through the day, but now my prayers are so direct to the Father God. I saw the Lord in his glory; he is amazing. The Lord had me on my mind.

I cannot explain all that happens to me and everything that I saw in Heaven. I can never put into words what I saw in Heaven. It was so real; it is a quick step out of one's body. There is nothing you can do after you die. God got it all handled from there. Do not worry about what you did not do or did do, just make sure you give it all to the Lord because the Lord will forgive sins. He looks at our motives and our hearts. I do not have to be depressed about nothing. I am too busy living a new life; the old life has passed away. I got a new life and I sleep better. I will be so glad just to wake up in the morning and be able to get out of my bed and wash myself and be thankful to the Lord for letting me live. He gave me a second chance at life, and I will receive it to the fullest no complaining on my part, about anything.

I laid in my bed at the hospital. I could not move anything, but I wish I could walk. God raised me from my affliction, and he healed my sick body. I will always be so thankful. I do not worry about fitting in with anything because at the end of each our lives; it is just you and the Lord. Only what you do for the Lord will pay off at the end of your journey. One of these days; I do not know when, but my name will be called again just like Lazarus who died and was stinking; he was raised from the dead just like I was risen from the dead.

I was in Heaven just like Lazarus and the Lord called Lazarus back and the Lord called me back. I was in a coma for a while, but I did not know it because I had no memory of this world. None! I live in a corner of my life. I always have; even in high school I live in a corner. I prayed and I prayed; I got so close to the Lord. In my lifetime, he spoke to me, and I always told Him to keep me so I can pray. I do not want anything to take my mind off the Lord. I hunger and I thirst after Him most of the day every day. I love the Lord Jesus. I always take the Lord back to his word; the more you pray the closer you get to the Lord, the more you will be tried. He will use you more. He has no respect of person. It does not matter you can be in great shape and all of a sudden, boom! It is all over and then a great sickness has taken over your entire body, so it is best to stay prayed up and trust God.

I am ending it here. I took sick on May 19, 2017, and here it is, December 25, 2018. I am writing at the end of my book. I hope my story will open blinded eyes, helped the sick, and bring those who do not know the Lord to Him. Heaven is real. I believe Hell is real as well. So chose this day to serve the Lord, the rest of your life! I am sitting here on Christmas day. My husband was taking about our first plan ride to Connecticut. We stayed there for 14 days visiting my daughter, who is a Doctor of Education. Our first plane ride was great! My husband never rode on an airplane before! I was sitting at the window looking down at all the water when I could see it. I was not afraid. The Lord can take you anywhere He pleases. I mean anywhere in any way; he has complete control over all our lives.

On this Christmas day, I am sitting here with a stronger my mind. I think better! I do not worry about anything. I am very thankful for being alive and enjoining my children and my grandchildren. I am praising the Lord more than I ever did; I can say that I love everyone. It does not matter whether they love me or not; if they know what I did to praise the Lord, it would be so easy to love; let love flow and live and let us live. You should treat everyone that comes in your path the same way you want to be treated, that is how you should treat others! I am free. I do not take much medication now. I feel great waking up every morning ready to meet a brand-new day; Feeling good just to get up and meet a new day. It is another day to serve the Lord. It is another day to praise the Lord and another day to see who I can help along my path. It is another day to enjoy the natural and the beauty of the Lord earth. It is another day to sing hymns unto the Lord and another day to pray for other people.

I always thanking God for raising me off my bed of affliction. I will always give Him glory and all the praise in all my life more than ever. I do not force my testimony on no one. I never get tired of talking my experience in Heaven. One day,

I do not know when, but I will die again, but the next time I go to Heaven I will not be back. So, I am telling all who read this book to take your next home seriously, you will spend eternity somewhere; you soul will either go Heaven or hell. Heaven is like standing on the beach with the wind blowing straight from the ocean in your face. It is breathe-taking. It is a wonder, just standing there looking at the view of Heaven. Why me, Lord? Why did you let me see Heaven? Nothing, but peace! The trees and the mountains were full of the Lord's glory, even the ground was full of glory! There is nothing about Heaven that is dark. I saw nothing dark. I saw all the races of peoples, but they were dressed like Bible Day people. I walked among them. I tell everyone I mostly meet about Heaven. A lot of them will receive my story and some do not, but it is ok.

The Lord will not force Himself on anyone. He loves us all, but we must come to Him full of humility like a little child because we do not have any strength on our own. It does not matter how poor you are or how rich; we are all going to die in a matter of time, no one who is born will escape death and death is the only way to get to Heaven. It was so joyful just to walk through the tunnel. I have suffered enough for the next 42 generations from me on down to my children and their children and their children and on and on.

I am thanking Lord for his angels being on each corner of my bed watching over me the second time I died. I will be praising the Lord in my mind thanking Him for letting me be able to walk around in the store all by myself again. I praise Him in the grocery store walking down through the aisle in the store. I prayed a lot before my sickness, but I pray a lot more than I used to. These days my life is full with the glory of the Lord. Just to get out of bed each morning to face a new happy day. Lord thank you for a good night's sleep and I look forward to the day just to hear from my children and my grandchildren and my daughters-in-laws send me pictures all of the time and that makes a grandma feel good, just to see their faces.

Each morning God sets a new bowl of grace and mercy out every morning. There is no fear in death if you die in the Lord. I went to Heaven. I have seen the Lord's face; it was oval shape, and his face has a light beard. I looked at the Lord. I walked up on the Lord and Savior Jesus Christ. How was it possible to be standing so close to the Lord? Why me? His robe was eggshell color, very beautiful and his sandals were made of old leather, his arms were long. His robe did not cover all of his arms they were folded inwardly. I saw a piece of his hand. He would not show me all of his fingers or hand. His fingernails were square-shaped; his nail was fish-scaly like as well. I saw the white meat of his fingernails. I saw his whole feet; I saw his toenail, Lord have mercy. Why did I see all of this? I have seen the death and I got to tell the world do not be afraid to die; it not hard! It is so easy after you die; just in a blink of an eye you are in Heaven.

God is real! I cannot praise Him enough! I always have been thirsty for Him and me long for Him; I am a slave for the Lord. I am a slave for my Lord. I am going to live longer now. The Lord gave me new organs and an improved mind. I always try to see the good in everyone. I look at everyone the same. I hope everyone is saved. It will be a shame for a person to miss this beautiful Heaven. I can live a better life in every aspect of my being. I always pray for people. I got to pray for my family and all the people that I hear and see that are in trouble. I live in the corner of my mind. I do not let a lot of people in that corner. I do not get angry; I stay calm no matter the situation. I just stay calm because it will pass; no matter how bad a storm is, it will pass. I have been to Heaven and back.

I was so beautiful over there. I was exploring looking around Heaven. God delivered the "Three Hebrew boys!" He delivered me! The same God that open blinded eyes and the same God that turned water into wine. Delivered me! The same God that raised the dead! Delivered me from my sick bed; it was a great test. I always told the Lord to use me any way he pleases to get his glory. I am not my own. I have no strength only what the Lord gives me, and I am thankful for all he has done for me. The same Jesus that walks along the dusty road and preached. The same God that went up cavalry for all mankind. I was standing beside "The Living Water."

My children will not ever be the same; they are better. They see a miracle work through their mother. My husband is still so blown away. He cannot believe that I am still alive. I can hardly get Him to talk about it; he told me; I look just like an old dead cow laying by the roadside ready for the buzzards to eat up. He said there was no life in my body none at all. My husband will tell his part later on in my book along with my children, grandchildren, and daughters-in-law. My daughter told me her faith in the Lord has increased. This will never be forgotten for many generations to come, my children and their children and their children will remember their mother and grandmother, Willie Agnes Chennault.

The test was so hard. I cannot explain it; not even in a million years could I explain fully how I suffered, but it was all worth it; I would do it again. Going to Heaven was a gift from the Lord, from God. He uses the smallest thing to get his glory across to us. His mind and his ways are not our minds and ways. He is all-mighty, all-knowing, and all-seeing. I do not belong to myself. I belong to the Lord. Live for the Lord, trouble will not last so long; he will help you and deliver you all the time! He will not let you fall. I was in the hospital 39 days just as Christ was beaten with 39 lashes. I am sitting here on Jan 3, 2019, feeling well praising the Lord. I am a better person. I do not worry. I just pray and try to live a life pleasing to my

Lord. I will always thank the Lord for my trip to Heaven.

As I sit here feeling pretty good on this Saturday afternoon, January 6, 2019, typing up my book and coming down to the end of my book. God is so powerful. He looks at everyone's heart. I wonder what did he see in me? I am still alive; my husband and I are still here at home. All of my children are gone, none of them live here in Washington. I am glad; I took this test. I will never be the same again! Each day is new to me. I am glad to have taken this journey. I know it was hard for my husband and my children to watch, but they were strong. I had the best doctors in the world, and they did what the Lord told them to do. The Lord is going to bless my latter end more than the beginning. I believe this with my whole heart; I give all I got to the Lord when I pray, and when I am hurting, I lay my hand on that part of my body and the pain is gone. The Lord can do above and beyond all we can ever ask or think (Ephesians 3:20). This was a journey on one else could travel alone! God has washed me in the river of Heaven, and I saw the Lord sitting there! I was so close to Jesus Christ! I just looked at Him with joy and unspeakable peace. I was standing so close to the "Breath of Life." I was standing there filled with the Holy Spirit. I belong to the Lord! I know that nothing can kill me until it is my time to go back home again! I was standing beside the Lord Almighty. I was so close to Him. I could reach out and touch Him. When He turned around, He breathed on me! When I walked up on Him, and He turned his head; he looked at me a few seconds with the most compassionate look I have ever seen. He was so full of glory! It was amazing! I knew who He was; you will know Jesus when you see Him!

The glory of the Lord is full in Heaven! It is everywhere over there! My family is over there: my mother, Mamie Lue Callaway and my aunties, Lucinda Cullars and Essie Mae Wooten, had the full glory of the Lord. I hope I have explained how Heaven is to the world, but I cannot perfectly! I have tried in my book, but this is not explainable. I was glad that I was afflicted, because whatever happened to me; God allowed it. It was okay with me, because I had no control over it! It was one of the tests that I had to take. Nothing is too hard for God. I am a stronger person! Flesh and blood cannot enter Heaven only through the Spiritual realm, no one can enter in the physical bodily form! All I can say is God! This is my true story called "The Next Time I Go To Heaven I Will Not Be Back!

Chapter 19

THEIR STORIES

My Husband, Lazarus Sr.'s Account

I was at home with my wife, and she had been to Greene County to pick up our granddaughter, Callie Blue the night before, which was a Thursday night. My youngest son's wife has had a baby. My wife and myself was going to keep Callie Blue a few more days so my wife drove our F150 Ford truck to Greene County to meet our son, Pastor Henra. I was going with her, but I had an errand to run. I missed her so she called me, and she told me that she was going on to pick up Callie Blue, because our son was meeting her in Greene County at 8 o'clock at night. She went on alone. It was getting late in the night, and she still have not came back home from picking up Callie Blue. I asked her why it took you all so long to get back. She did not say anything. I told her that I called her three times and she said nothing. When she got home, I notice that she had been by the store; the bags said Ingle's food store. She cooked some cheese and eggs for Callie Blue and then she said she was going to bed. Callie Blue and I stayed up and watched television. I gave Callie Blue a bath. Callie Blue and I ate scrambled cheese eggs. My wife went to bed.

I heard nothing else from her until morning. Callie Blue and I fell asleep in the den of my house. My wife slept in our bedroom. I did not go check on her, because I know she was okay. She is always okay. She never is sick. She is too busy doing things to get sick! She cleans, cooks and she goes to see about her older friends who cannot help themselves. She is always trying to help someone. We go fishing. We do our hobbies together. We plant a garden together. She is a super woman always has been. I do not know why it took her so long to get home, our grandbaby Callie Blue was in there with her. Our son was just calling me see were they home yet; I told Him no, but they okay. She is a good driver. She be here in a little while.

So, that next morning chaos begin to happen! At first everything was going as normal. When my wife woke up, she was combing her hair, she told me to cut the ends of her hair and I did. She was not looking anything out of the normal. Our daughter called my wife talk to her like she usually does every morning. We were in the bathroom when my wife was talking to our daughter, Dr. June. My wife looked normal when she came out of the bathroom, and she sat on the sofa. I looked at her with her head down a little and I passed by her. I went in the bathroom, and I asked her where did all of that blood come from? She was not able to answer, and she went in the bathroom again. She said she could hardly breath. She asked me to take her to the doctor. I told her I would not make it; I was too nervous and in shock that she asked me such a thing. She said, "Call 9-1-1!"

I did! My granddaughter, Callie Blue was standing there looking at grandma.

She asked me, "Papa what is wrong with grandma?"

I said, "She is okay!" So, I called 911 and they were there amazingly fast, extremely fast! They came in and got her. I knew she was very sick. She was always a super woman, a good wife. She is always busy. she is never the one who sits around; she does not ever know how to rest! She is always busy doing something, so I know she is good. My granddaughter and I was standing in the yard as the ambulance drove off. I just took my time getting to Augusta, Georgia, because I know I was not anything serious, but I called our children. I called all four of our children; three lived in Atlanta and one lived in Gainesville, Georgia so it was going to take a while before they would get to Augusta. I could not tell them nothing about her condition, because I did not know anything! I mean nothing at all! So, I told Callie Blue that I would finish cooking our breakfast and then we are going to see grandma. Callie Blue did not say anything. She just looked sad, because she never seen grandma sick before. Callie Blue did want any breakfast that I cooked so Callie Blue and I went to the store to get some dog food.

I went by McDonald's, and I got her a biscuit. We carried the dog food back home and I packed my medications. I took my breathing machine in my red bag, and I locked up the house. I just know that my wife just has a little cold or something, but I thought about all that blood she has thrown up before she left, and a cold feeling came over me. I started to cry. I also prayed to the Lord to have mercy on my wife. "Lord, hold her in Your hands! Lord, she is a good person and good wife! Lord save my wife!" I still do not know anything on her condition as of yet. I start to cry again. I cried all the way to Augusta and it as about an hour and half drive to the hospital from Washington, Georgia. My granddaughter didn't understand why I was crying, and she start singing, "Papa is a cry baby! Papa is a cry baby!" She started to laugh; I cried, and she laughed. I cried more while praying for her to be ok! I met her at an early age; she is my whole being!

I was driving hope everything would be okay, but I did not know about her condition. I went to the wrong hospital. I went to University Hospital looking for her, but when I got in there; the front desk told me that she was not there. So, I called my son and he told me where she was, somehow, he found out, I do not know! I left University Hospital and I went to the Doctors Hospital. I was feeling tired at this time. I need to do a breathing treatment. I do one every four hours for the last 13 years, because I have a lung disease; I feel exhausted a lot. I got to get to my wife to see if she okay.

When I walked get in the Doctors Hospital, I asked the front desk where is Willie Agnes Chennault? She was in the emergency room, so me and my Callie Blue went up there; they had taken her upstairs. I went up there I saw my son Otis sitting in the hallway when I look at my son, I saw my sons face and I knew something was wrong. I could feel the pain just by looking at Him, because my children love their mother! The hurt in my son face told me everything, Otis said, "Do not go in there yet, dad!" I went on in any way. Otis was holding me up as we walked in there together. I started to feel weak in my legs. I cried loud. My son held me up; I looked at her for ten seconds. I had to leave the room, because my heart start pulling extra beats. I cried and I prayed every second of day and every day! I prayed that my wife would be okay. My other three children have not got there yet. Callie Blue did not go in to see she stayed in the waiting room with Otis' wife, Kianna. I prayed—

> Lord is there any way, if possible, Lord please spare her life, please! Raise her up to get stronger than she was; please, Lord please help her! I met her very young, and she has been a praying woman. Lord I know she has she prayed all the time. Lord, I see her praying! Lord when I do not see things or believe, she tells me all the time that

God got it and she always be right! Lord, I know you got this! Lord, please help her children and grandchildren! They need her and I need her most of all! I went in the bathroom in the stall, and I cried, and I prayed until the Spirit of the Lord bumped me. I told the Lord that she has waited on me all of these years and she never said a hurtful word to me all while I have been sick. She always helps me any time of night when I am sick. She is right there so how am I going to go on without her! I am drinking tears for water. I cannot eat or sleep! my wife is in a coma. She is sleeping now look at her with a thousand tubes pulling her body! Lord, have mercy! Help her! I do not know whether I can live without her.

Days has passed by; I have been here for a while. I go to the bathroom and take a sponge bath. I have no clean clothes to put on, but I am holding on the best I can. I know I cannot make it without her. I have been with this woman all my life; we met in high school she is my light to life. Why is she so sick? Why did not she tell me? I thought this to myself. She cannot be sick! We just came from Atlanta, Georgia. My daughter-in-law's graduation from law school. She been busy around the house all week and helping her friend who is sick. She took her friend to the physical therapist on Wednesday and Thursday. She went to Greene country to pick up our granddaughter, Callie Blue. How in the world could she be this sick? And, in a coma? "Please wake her up, please Lord! Wake her up!" The Lord knows I need her, it is just me and her! All of our children are grown and gone. We do not have any children or grandchildren here in Washington, Georgia. I said more prayers—"Please, Lord have mercy on my wife and let her wake up; she is not breathing on her own. She is on a ventilator it is breathing for her! Lord, please help us!"

I looked at our four children; our three sons and our daughter are so messed up. I do not know! Lord have mercy! I looked at our children's face. They love their mother so much. They are looking with hurt in their faces, but they all know how to pray because my wife taught them to pray, and they know who to lean on. My children went to the store and brought me some clothes. I am sick myself, but I got to be strong for them. All I can do is cry and pray, weeks have gone by, seem like months and she is still sleep. She is hard and cold laying there like a frozen dead animal. She is not there; her body is there, but I do not believe her Spirit is in that body.

A lot of people are coming in and out; our family members and many ministers are coming and praying over my wife. My children are praying and playing gospel music over her; they know what she likes, because they heard her gospel music play all the time when they were growing up. I question God. "Why is she so sick? I have been married to this woman over 44 years and plus known her through the high school years; I know her Spirit." This woman gives God her fullness everyday of her life. I watch her walking in the yard looking up to Heaven, praying. I hear her in the bathtub praying for the condition of the world and she is sick?

She does not even know I pay attention to all that she does. I watch this woman listen to gospel music every night, it put her to sleep. Every morning the first thing she do is pray, pray for our children safety to work. She prays for her siblings, her nephews, cousins, aunties, distance relatives, friends and who ever she meets running errands. She always read her Bible; she is so close to the Lord. She told me all the time that she thirsty for the Lord. She longs for the Lord. She breathes the Lord every day! I told her one day, how can you live your life? You are so close to the Lord. You give Him all of your time. How can you live your own life? She told me that she has no life; she said her life was the Lord's and he can use me any way he please, because he gave me this life. I belong to the Lord. So, I just looked at her. This woman has been so busy over her lifetime she does not know what rest issue never got any she is always busy doing something.

She grows all her food, vegetables. I always help her in the garden; we love to work in the garden together and she love to fish. I look at her and I can hardly stand looking at her like this. I prayed again—

Oh, Lord please hear our prayers and restore my wife back to health. Please, Lord, she knows you! Lord, she is a born-again mother and a good wife to me. Lord, please restore her and help me to whole out give me the strength to be strong and help her on Lord please. Lord take care of our children they are so hurt their mother is so sick. My sons got a motel here in Augusta near the hospital and I had to get some rest for a few minutes. When I am so sick when my lungs get infected, I always have to go to the hospital, but time has gone by, and I have not had to go to the hospital. My wife prayed over me for a healing, and she always say, "Lord, heal Him" while touching me with oil.

She says, Lord, just speak the word and my husband will be healed! You do not have to come to our house! Lord, just speak the word." She always thanks the Lord before she prays for all of the blessings that she has already done. She cries a loud over me! "Lord just speak the word and my husband will be healed"

So, I say, "Lord speak the word while laying my hands on my sick wife." She will be healed with the same oil that she used on me. My daughter went home and got the oil. I prayed over my wife as she did for me all of these years. My daughter spoke the word over her mother, putting oil on her lifeless body!

She said, "Lord is there any way possible Lord to send my mother back to us? Lord just speak the word and my mother will be healed.

As I sit here today on Jan 22, 2019, I look at my wife she is whole again! She awakes every day never complaining about nothing. She got a new walk and a new talk! She thanks God more than ever before for raising her off her bed of affliction. She is bright looking. She always has something good to say. She sees the good in people and she trusts God! She tells me every day of her vacation to Heaven. She tells me how good it is to die and how easy it is to die. She goes through every detail about going in the ground and how quickly the Spirit leave the body. It is all brightness over in Heaven. I just listen; she will never be the same. She tells me a part of her is still in Heaven.

My children are so happy. They love their mother. She is their heart. My wife is stronger than ever before. She told me this was already predestinated before she was born because she has suffered enough for the next 42 generations to come after my children's generation. She has suffered! She always tells me that. She tells me that when she was in Heaven, she was not sick; she was young and pretty. She was so free, and she told me where she saw Jesus sitting and that she was so close to Him that she could reach out and touch Him, but she did not touch Him. She describes Him in full detail. It was a hard journey, but Jesus was right by my wife's side. He made her over again! She always played the song, "Lord make me over again." She played this song all the time. I do not know how long we are going to live, but I thank God for every second with my wife. She is my first love and my last love. God gave us a special kind of love. We married so young right out of high school; we both had no doubt even though we never dated other folks; we both was enough for each other. I always look at her very closely. Now she tries to be strong! She does not want to be a bother to no one, but I keep my eyes on her because her illness sneaked up on us like a brick wall crushing down; there was no warning signs none I mean none.

Nothing does not bother her. She always tells me that she defeated death hell and the grave. She always tells me folks look at her strange, because they know in their Hearts God has worked a miracle through her body. She is a living witness to that! I see my wife struggle to walk and struggle to turn over in the bed. She struggled when she came home. She was still very weak, but she struggled, and she held onto her life, and she fought like hell to get stronger and stronger each passing day. She could not drive for a long time, and she could not cook. She only made her some oatmeal and I had to do the rest until she got better; her strength came back to her little by little. I would ride her out around the block just to get her out of the house after two months of being in the hospital. We cannot question God! He can do whatever he pleases to do; he is the boss of the entire world. I thank Him every passing day for restoring my wife to good health. "The Lord is my shepherd I shall not want...." that is all I can say!

My Oldest Son, Lazarus Jr.'s Account

During one morning on May 19, 2017, my dear sweet mother became very ill. Before I heard of it, I was sitting in a meeting at work, feeling as if something had come upon my emotions—something dealing with a family member. I could not put my finger on it. I just figured out why I was feeling this type of way. Around 9:30 a.m. on May 19, 2017—I received a group text from my siblings that said, "She is being rushed to the hospital and it doesn't seem good." After glancing over the text, I realized the "she" that was being said was to be my mother, Willie Agnes Chennault.

After being shocked and is disbelief from looking at the text, my mind became blank, and my thoughts were over the place five minutes after I regrouped; I at once informed my boss I had to leave. While driving back to my apartment to get prepared to travel to see my mom at Doctors Hospital, I asked God to keep in good Spirits and let your will be done and also how sweet she is and how lost I would be without her. While talking to Him, I became very teary eyed and kept praying.

When my wife and I arrived at the hospital, I asked the receptionist where my mother was found. My adrenaline was at an all time high during this time. About 10 minutes after speaking with the receptionist on the first floor of Doctors Hospital, I finally approached my mother's room in the ICU. When I entered, I stared at her before I could really grasp what was going on. I also continued to pray to our higher power asking for restoration and guidance through this, knowing this illness my mother has, has a survival rate of 1%.

During her first week in ICU, I traveled back and forth from North Georgia each day thinking about if she was going to survive this terrible illness. As the weeks went by, she started to get a little better each day, by taking different types on antibiotics with repeated dialysis treatments. Also, during this time, doctors kept on reminding the family about the survival rate of this illness. I listened to what he said, but I was still in denial, hoping for a miracle. Immediately, the family had a long group prayer for healing and restoration. A few more weeks went by with drastic improvements with her vital signs. A couple of days went by, and her facial features were starting to become normal, but there is still much work and prayers to be heard. Family members and friends gave her comfort during this critical time.

My trips back and forth to North Georgia became more emotional knowing how hard she is fighting to stay in this world. Being in the ICU for a few weeks, she began to show some movements with her arms and legs--And this is when I knew that there was hope that she could pull through this and make it to read-which happened a week after she showed us how tough she was. During rehab, I watched her stand up, talk normal and feed herself with confidence. My mother really adapted better than I thought. By observing her, I notice it was a little hard at first, but I knew she had the fight in her to get back to a normal lifestyle. In conclusion, this made me realize, (God) has all power in His hand and no mankind is smarter than Him)

My Second Son, Otis' Account

It was May 19th, 2017, when I got the call from dad about mom. My wife and I was at Campbell middle school at my daughter's end of the year award ceremony. My daughter was an "A" student but did not get an award that day and she was so upset. During the ceremony, I was getting call after call from dad, so, I finally picked up and left the award ceremony area. I answered the phone and dad told me mom had been taken to the hospital. I did not take it too seriously, because mom has never really been sick. So, I was not panicked. She goes to the doctor for checkups more than anybody I know, so in my head I thought she was fine and that I did not have to rush to get home to Washington, Georgia. However. something came over me once we left the ceremony and went home to pack some overnight bags. I suddenly told my wife that we needed to leave *right now* to see what is going on with mom. During the ride, I called dad to see if he had found out anything and he told me what happened leading up to Him calling 9-1-1. He said that he was cutting her hair in the bathroom, when she began to cough up blood and complain that she could not breathe. Dad told me she was being taken to a hospital in Augusta, Georgia; so, we rode to Augusta instead of Washington.

My wife and I finally got to the hospital. We were the first to arrive. We told the front receptionist we were there to see Ms. Willie Agnes Chennault. She told her the room number and we proceeded. When we got to the room door, there were approximately 3 to 5 doctors standing over the top of mom and at that point I almost fainted and hit to the ground. In fact, my wife had to grab my arm. I was in total shock to see mother like that. The doctors were scrambling to attempt to put tubes inside of mom, but she was completely swollen. It was unbelievable to see my mother in that condition. I then called dad and my brothers and sister and said you all need to get here as soon as possible. Hours later, we were all finally able to come back to the room and see her. She was unresponsive and full of tubes. I cried and cried and prayed and prayed, we all cried. During this whole ordeal, I learned how to really pray and trust God 100%. The entire weekend is a blur to me. The doctors were not saying too much. I guess because their primary objective for the weekend was to keep mom alive.

On the following Monday, the doctor explained to me what was going on, and they did not give mom much of a chance. The doctor was giving to me straight, but I thought he was being a little pessimistic. I honestly did not like Him too much. So, Day One, Monday, was a wait and see what happen. I wrote a day-by-day account for the first five days of my mother's condition.

Day 1: We were full of prayer; extended family were present, and my brother Pastor Henra prayed a powerful prayer while we all held hands in the room. I could not hold my tears back; I felt something was about to move in the Spirit on my mother's behalf.

Day 2: Tuesday was much of the same; her blood pressure up and down. Day 2 they explained that her organs were failing; at that point, she had a bad heart, kidney, liver, sugar was high, and her blood was full of poison (septic). I just could not believe it; I was thinking what causes the blood to be poison, but the doctor later explained that she had a type of double pneumonia that was airborne. After all that, somewhere in my heart, I was still believing and that somehow, some way, she was going to come of this alive. Tuesday evening, the doctor mentioned that she would need to go on dialysis, putting her on dialysis was risky but necessary. It was a chance she would not make it through the procedures according to the doctor. I told the doctor to do EVERYTHING he could do. The doctor understood and said he would "throw the kitchen sink at her."

Day 3: It is Wednesday. The dialysis machine came, and the kidney doctor performed dialysis on mom. Afterwards, the doctor told us that everything had gone well, and mom had made it through the procedure. I said, "Thank you God! We made it across one river." However, throughout the day, the doctors continued to check mom's blood and they found that it was still poisonous. I just shook my head in disbelief. You know us, we are Baptist country people that happen to live in the big city. So, we did what we know best: we took out our cell phones and played all the good ole Baptist hymns and sermons we could find. I know the doctors and nurses thought we were crazy, but we did not care, nor were we ashamed. We know that God can do, and we have seen Him move so many times before in our lives. My friend James called and asked how my mom was doing. I told Him "Man, not too good at the moment, but she is hanging on." Now, James has always been a big believer of laying on hands, and he instructed me on how to do so. Heeding his advice, I went back in the room and laid hands on my mommy's stomach and begin to pray with tears in my eyes. Later that night, the doctor started to talk about hospice because my mother was not responding to anything. I could not believe it.

Day 4: On Thursday, it looked like all hope was gone. My mother was still not responding to anything. She had little movement; her mouth was beginning to decay. That evening, my brother and I got the final report for this day, and it was not encouraging at all. The doctors told us mom needed to respond to something the next day or she would be taken to hospice where she would likely die. She needs to respond to something, or she was going to hospice to likely die. I looked at my brother and my brother looked at me, we prayed one last prayer that night and then I said, "let's go man." We headed back to our hotel and we both gave it over the Lord; we felt hopeless. But during the hopelessness that night I still felt she would come out. My mother is a strong woman physically and strong in the Lord. My dad was a mess during the entire time, crying, sad, mad, more crying and more crying. It was hard to see my dad like that, I could only imagine what he was going through, seeing his wife laying in the hospital bed in that condition. They have been married since they were 18 years old. They love them some each other. They love making dollars together and coming up with ideas.

Day 5: On Friday, my brother, and I got up went back to the hospital and Lord have Mercy, my mother started responding! Her eyes opened but they were glazed over, she started pointing at the wall and talking to someone in the corner of the wall. She was saying "NOT YET! NOT YET!" with her finger waving. We were in total shock and full of happiness at the same time. My mother blood pressure was still up and down but she was responding and that gave the doctors more hope to do more and do more with encouragement. I can truly say with confidence that if the doctors did not see me, my brothers, sister, and extended family at the hospital 24/7 witnessing and praying, my mother probably would not been here today. She was saved through the power of prayer and the talent of the doctors and nurses. Most of the nurses were great; they genuinely cared for my mother. I always say, if I ever get rich, I will go back a pay them for the attention they gave my mother. The nurses' names whom I can remember are Amy, Rosa, Christina, Allison, and Andre. They all did an excellent job, and I am eternally grateful.

"The Floor" My Daughter, Dr. June's Account

It is cold, damp, and lonely down on this hard hospital room floor. My eyes are crusted over from all of the tears that have ran down my face for the past month and a half. I am here at Select Specialty Hospital watching my mother try to rest and sleep in this bed that moves all the time. She is restless. I have driven back and forth from Augusta to Atlanta about 10 times, because when I first got the call that my mother had taken sick; I was packing my loft apartment in Smyrna, Georgia to move to another two-bedroom apartment in the area. I often asked myself, "How did my mother end up here? How did I end up on the floor?" Even though my back is stiff, and my legs are numb from trying to cover them from the cold floor; I am unbothered by this pain. I am praying and reading over Psalm 91. This is one of my favorite Psalms. There is healing in this Psalm as well as protection. This Psalm has saved my life many of times. I have to get ready to go teach soon. I got a great position running several STEM camps around the United States. I am headed to the New College of New Jersey, then to the University of Dallas in Texas then finally to Wake Forest University in Winston-Salem, North Carolina. I did not want to leave my mother. I have been here with her through her whole sickness. I had to will her back to health while she has been here at Select Specialty Hospital. Her blood pressure was extremely high; she was looking so pale when I arrived back in Augusta, Georgia from Atlanta, Georgia.

I have been to the farmer's market every day for the past month grabbing her fresh fruits and vegetables so that she can gain some of the key vitamins that she lost during her sickness. I am always studying up on the best herbs, fruits, and vegetables for various types of healing. I drink garlic and lemon water for weight loss and blood pressure maintenance. So, I brought my mom lots of fresh garlic and lemons from the market to make her a fresh tonic. As soon as she drunk this tonic, she told me she felt so much better. The paleness in her skin went away and her blood pressure went down! I was thanking God for giving me these instructions to make her this tonic. I was still hurting so much inside. I had to change my mother's pad under her buttocks for her when the nurses were not around. I did not ever think I would be wiping my mother's backside when she used the bathroom so soon! I did it with no complaints, because she did it for me when I was an infant.

I am sadly thinking back to the day I got the call that my mother took ill. I was packing my loft apartment in Smyrna, Georgia. I was listening to gospel music, and I was excited about my new apartment. I was deciding on whether or not to go stay with my mom and dad for the summer along with Hannah since I did not think I was going to do any summer camps this year. I held out on applying to any summer camp positions.

My current job title at this time was a Learning Director of a charter school program. I was excited to have my summer free for a while. I called my mother on the morning of May 19, 2017, as I did every morning to ask her how she was doing and what were her and dad's plans for the day. She said dad was cutting her hair and that she was cutting up collard greens for lunch. I love my mother's cooking; she is the best cook ever! I told her I was packing up my apartment and that it is getting hot, so I wanted to finish before the temperature increased outside. It gets so hot in Atlanta during the summer months. I hung up and told my mother I would call her right back. I told her that I just wanted to finish packing this last load in the car and I would call her right back. The time was a little after 10 a.m. A few minutes later I called her back; it was close to 11 a.m. Dad answered her cell phone and said mom cannot breathe; she cannot talk right now. I was shocked. I had just got off the phone with my mother. I was confused. My dad did not hang up right away. He just put the phone down. I heard Him telling her, "To breathe, please breathe, Willie." I hung up and prayed right away that all was well with my mom.

I texted my brothers and said mom was not feeling well. Otis said he would call to see what was going on as well as Pastor Henra. Lazarus Jr. said the same thing. A few moments later, after I sat in my empty apartment waiting; Pastor Henra called me back and said he was leaving work, mom is very sick. She is headed to Doctor's University. He arrived at my apartment a few hours later and by that time Hannah was getting off the school bus. It was early release day for her. He had to work until someone relieved Him at work. We did not think it was that serious with mom. On the way to Augusta, Otis called and said he had gotten there, and it was so serious. He did not tell us over phone any details; he just said she was not moving. We drove in the car in silence for a while, Pastor Henra, Hannah and me. I broke down in tears, tears just started to stream down my face; the tears did not stop.

About two hours and twenty minutes later we arrived at Doctors Hospital. When we entered the emergency room; dad, Otis and his wife, Kianna, and Lazarus Jr. and his wife, Shirkea were in waiting room. All of their heads were down. Their eyes were so red from what I noticed, uncontrollable crying. Henra and I began to walk into the ER room. What I saw I could not believe? Nurses were all around. There were at 20 different tubes coming from my mother, out of her mouth, nose, she had IVs running everywhere. The wires looked like long plastic straws, but much longer. There was a suction tube for her lungs. I could see mucus, pink and frothy being sucked out of her lungs. I pulled a chair close up to my mom's bed. I touched her hands, I yelled out and cried uncontrollably for about five minutes. I heard a still voice say, "Stop crying and pray!" It was like I stopped my cry in mid-cry. I prayed to the Lord; I took Him back to His word. I repeated every healing scripture I knew while holding my mother's cold hands, she was not moving. Her eyes were closed, she was lifeless. I told the Lord,

By Your stripes, You said we are healed. Heal her, O Lord and she will be healed, restore health to her and heal her wounds, You also said, Lord you will meet all of our needs! Forgive her of any sins, Lord, that may have caused her sickness. Lord, I am calling to you for help! Please heal my mother. Cover and seal her in your precious blood, Lord Jesus. I pleaded your name, Lord Jesus over her sick body. I ask that any demonic or evil forces that is trying to attack her body be sent back to the floors of Hell! Have mercy on her, Lord Jesus. You Lord are my shepherd, I want for nothing, but asking for healing for my mother, she is excellent mother. I talk to her daily; I need her Lord Jesus. She prays for me and with me. Touch her Lord.

I continued to hold my mother's hand. My brother, Pastor Henra had his hands on the forehead the whole time. He was praying as well and quoting scripture. I felt the glory of the Lord in this hospital room. I stayed at the hospital with my dad and Hannah for weeks. We slept in the lobby of the hospital on this floor, the sepsis unit. I slept in a chair for almost two weeks, praying and playing gospel music for my mother. I talked to her. I held her hand at night and prayed for her.

I acted like she could hear me. I knew in my Spirit she could not, but I spoke to her anyway like she could hear me. I left about two weeks later early one morning, because I had to move my car due to my lease being up at my old apartment I was moving from to another apartment across the street. However, I did not leave until the doctors told my family and me that it was time to take the tubes out. Finally, one antibiotic had worked after the doctors tried many antibiotics. My mom had less than a 10 percent chance of living, but I know through prayers and singing of the gospel—she woke up. My brother, Otis, video recorded her waking up after the doctors lower the anesthesia and removed the tube from her throat that went into her lungs to clear out the infection. She woke up not knowing where she was; she wondered why her sisters, brothers, nieces, and nephews, cousins, my dad, and my brothers were standing all around her. I cried tears of joy as I saw this on video.

That same morning, I left; I came back and hugged my mother. I kissed her so many times on her cheeks. My side kick was back! My mother's sickness gave me a new perspective on life; I have had many trials and tribulations. I give it all to God. He heard our prayers; I never imagined what my life would be like without my mother. I call her every day, every hour of the day! I love my mother, she is my hero, Mrs. Willie Agnes Chennault!

"The Call" My Youngest Son, Pastor Henra's Account

There was a call around 9:30 a.m. Dad called and said that he had to call 9-1-1, and the ambulance had to rush mom to the hospital in Augusta Georgia. I asked Him what had happened, and he explained that he was cutting her hair and all of a sudden, she could not breath and that she started to cough up blood. So, he rushed to put oxygen over her nose to help her breath but that did not help, my mother's body was shutting down and at that time nothing would help; my mother was dying, pneumonia was killing her.

And at the time I did not know that she would be fighting for her life, because just the night before I had seen my mother. She was doing fine. She had meet me half-way between Atlanta and our hometown Washington Wilkes to pick up my oldest daughter Callie; my wife had just given birth to our second daughter, Caia and mom was trying to give her a break. So, I could not believe that she was that sick, as I said, I had just seen her, kissed her on her checks, gave her a hug and told her "I'll see you this weekend."

I did not take the call serious, because Mom was the center of our family, a praying woman, a strong woman, a woman, who up to that point I thought was untouchable, a machine, someone that could overcome anything that life had to throw at her; plus, I had never seen her sick. So, of course I thought she would call me later and say that she was ok. But I did not get that call. Instead, I got a call from Dad, he was lost trying to get to Augusta to the hospital. He had taken a wrong turn, so I spent the next hour trying to get Him going in the right direction; but still no call from mom, no worry from me.

I did not take the call seriously. Until dad made it the hospital she was supposed to be at, and she was not there. So, as the worry started to flow; I started to feel the nerves. I called the ambulance service in my hometown of Washington Wilkes, and they told me that we had to drop Mrs. Willie Agnes off at the Doctors hospital because she had gone into Cardiac Arrest.

Now, I had heard this phrase on several movies and shows like ER, Law and Order, but I never quite knew what it meant, so I googled it. And what I found increase my worry and my fear. I found out that Cardiac Arrest happens when you have a sudden loss of blood flow, which tells you that the person's heart is not pumping correctly. One can lose consciousness and stop breathing. And without treatment within minutes, it can lead to death. My heart dropped into my stomach. I told my manager that I had to leave, and I did not know when I would be back. I stopped by my apartment, changed cloths, told my wife that I was leaving and got on the road. I picked up my sister from her apartments, as she was packing getting ready to move into another apartment. My sister cried almost the whole way down to Augusta. She did not understand how mom was sick. She talked about how they had just a phone conversation that morning. The entire drive down to Augusta felt like I was in a bad dream. I played gospel song all the way down to Hospital. And what should have been a 2hr drive turned out to be a 3hr drive. It was in the middle of rush hour and there was a wreck on the I-20, "so it's like God made me wait".

My brother, Otis, who was already there called, and he did not sound hopeful about my mother's state; he sounded scared and in shock to say the least. So, as I drove, I singed, I prayed, I cried, not knowing what was just ahead of me, not knowing if my mother would be alive when I arrived. I talked to God as if God was sitting in the passage site right next to me. Made promises that I knew I could not keep; And as I drove, I asked myself the question, "will I never hear my mother's voice again?"

Will we ever laugh together again? Will she ever hold Caia again or Otis Jr.? Will Caia get to know how amazing of a grandmother she has? None of this can be happening now; it was supposed to be the happiest time for our family. Two new additions had just been added. We were not supposed to be at the hospital. But we were. And when I arrived, everyone had a look on their face that said, "This is it," yeah, they all sound like they were unsure, but I could feel their energy, their Spirit, they all thought it was the end. And I saw why, as I walked into that cold room, the second door on the right, I saw four or five machines hooked up to my mother body. She was swallow as if she was already dead, like how a dead body gets after some time. Her hands where cold, her body just lying there, no movement, no life it seemed. There was a machine monitoring her heart, one helping her breath, one flushing out her kidneys, one doing the work of the liver, and together all of these machines were keeping her alive. And at that point I knew that there was a chance I may never speak to my mother again. But all of my hope was I not gone. Even after the doctor told me that maybe you should start planning for your mother funeral. Your mother has gone septic, and she has a 10 percent chance of making it.

At the time, I did not know was septic shock was at the time, but for some reason the hospital had a sign up that explained it and to be honest it did not sound promising. I never understood why they had the information up on their wall. It stated that most deaths in the ER are from septic shock. It explained that septic shock happens when the body basically is trying to save itself. So, it focuses its efforts on saving the brain and the heart, everything else is damaged, lungs, liver, kidney, etc. It was not comforting information to say the least.

So that is what happen, it was cause by her having "Walking Pneumonia" and it had taken its toll. She was dying and the doctors where sure that she would be a part of the 85-

90 percent of those who had died from the condition, but I was not convinced.

I often have feelings of when something bad is going to happen or how something bad would end. It is the same feeling I had when I was in a bad accident that totaled my car in college. Car was spinning, glass breaking everywhere, my girl at the time, now wife, screaming, and me, calm, and while holding on to the wheel, something told me, "It's not your time"," this want kill you." And something was telling me that again. It was not her time. Just a test. Just a resetting. A wake-up call. A faith building event. But this event was not going to be a fast fix. It was not going to be easy. Then next two weeks would be the hardest two weeks of my life. I had so many emotions. I even had to deliver a sermon in the midst of my mom being on the other side to say the least. (Oh yeah, I am a pastor and the youngest of the four children.)

And even with me being a Pastor, those two weeks almost drove me crazy; but I never felt as if God was not present. And even though that room was cold and sad, I believe till this day that there was something, better yet, someone in that room helping mom to hold on. I felt a presence, I did not know what or who it was, but it is the feeling you get when you feel like someone is watching you. And that presence was God; I believe and know that he kept her alive.

So even when the doctor said she had a 10 percent chance, "I told Him to his face, your numbers don't trump what God can do, because you don't know who is laying in that bed; she is the strongest, praying women that I know, and if God is real then God is here and God will show up and outweigh all of your numbers and statistics. At that point I asked Him to not come into my mom's room again; So, from then on, for the next two weeks; he stood outside of her room and did his observation from her door, I did not want any bad energy in the room. So, for two weeks my family and I went through a Spiritual awakening. It was a test of faith, a test of our belief, a test of patience.

And as the days passed, our emotions were on a roller coaster, just as her blood pressure meter was. It would go up and down, up, and down. She had medical procedure after medical procedure, nurse after nurse coming in and saying what they thought we wanted to hear. I got tired of seeing the same doctors, the kidney doctor, liver doctor, heart doctor, lung doctor, all saying the same thing, we have done all that we can, it is up to her body to respond, it is up to God. So, I prayed and prayed and prayed. Played some of her favorite gospel songs from Lee Williams, Travis Greene, William murphy, believing she could hear the words and it would help her to keep fighting.

And she did. Even when challenges came along the way. At one point, she needed dialysis and there was an issue with her blood pressure and her body's ability to clot. And one of the main issues where the fact that there was a lack of blood available. Patients were basically sharing plasma and everyday a new bag would be flown in from California; And every day that pack of blood and plasma would be one of the deciding factors in my mother living or dying.

And she did. Even when challenges came along the way. At one point she needed dialysis and there was an issue with her blood pressure and her body's ability to clot. The doctors were where afraid that she may bleed to death if they did the incision into her kidney. And they held off as long as they could, until the day came, she had to have the procedure. So, we prayed again, knowing that this procedure could kill her; but once again, the women laying in that bed was tough and she made it through. She stayed on the machine for 48 hours, no problems.

During all of this, I must admit, I was more concerned for my father. He barely came into mothers' room. I do not think I have ever seen anyone, so heart broken. I felt like if she died, then dad would die soon after and then we would have anyone. He kept saying 'I'm the one who is supposed to go first, I'm the one who is always sick" (my father has COPD). For two weeks he was in a shell by himself, could not eat, could talk hardly, he just sat in the chair in the hall and looked down at the floor wondering what his life would be like his wife of 40 years dies.

I could not image losing someone who you have been with since the age of 16 years old. I guess I could blame Him for not wanting to see her that way. I guess to Him, she was superwomen as well; superwomen to all of us. So, the days passed. The doctors would check her through the day, change breathing assisted levels to see if she could breathe on her owe, and with every step forward, the next day would be two steps back.

And then came the day, where she had been on the breathing machine too long and they had to see if her body could live on its own. I remember that night so well. I had gone home for a day or two, I could not afford to stay in the hotels every night, so I traveled back and forth for a couple days. But on the last night, prior to the morning in which she would be unplugged from the breathing machine. My brother called and said you better get here; Mom is not looking right. She is talking to someone in the room, and she keep looking up to the corner of the walls.

So, I rushed back to Augusta. And when I got there, her eyes were open but she for some reason did not see me. I was almost like she was looking through me, to see someone or something else. Her eyes had this film over it that made her eyes look grey. And all she keeps saying was No, No, No, not now. And her head would go from one side of the room to the other with one finger up saying, "No, not now!"

At that point, I knew that her body was here with us, but her Spirit was fighting with someone and letting them know, "It's not my time. I have work left to do. I have children and grandchildren that need me so you can go on back, I am going to stay here." So sat by her bed, my brother Otis was there in the chair, and we just sat and watched as my mother ha this conversation with death, this fight. The same fight she had fought all her life for her children. She was not going to leave without a fight that night.

It got late, and around 2 p.m. after which this for hours, me and my brother decided to get a room and we said, "Two things will happen in the morning, mother will be dead, or if she is alive; she will make it!" We prayed and we both left her life in the hands of God. I left that room and I believe he did to, not knowing how things would turn out, but hopeful that whatever way it went; we were at peace, because we knew mom had fought. She fought and in that moment that was all we could ask of her, that if she kept fighting, then we would keep believing.

We went to bed in peace. And when we woke up, I felt happy to wake up, almost like I knew the hard part was over, and when we got there. She was alive and doing better. She had won the fight. The family had arrived, they were in and out the entire time. Her sisters and brothers. Pastors and friends. Nephews and nieces. And I knew my mom was back, because the first thing she said once she was able to talk was, "What are all of you staring at me for?" and soon after that she asked for her cell phone, mom definitely was back!

My Daughter-in Law, First Lady Taurika's Account

On May 19, 2017, my baby, Caia, was just two weeks old. I was sick. I was trying to get strong again, while working with a newborn baby. Here comes the message, that my mother-in-law is ill. I did not give much attention to it, because I knew it was not anything much. I never knew her to be sick. She always helped us out; she loved to clean our houses and organize things. She always helped. She always cleaned her daughters-in-laws' houses. I appreciate her so much. As hours, seconds and minutes went by; it got really serious. I was exhausted from childbirth. I love my mother-in-law. She has taught me in ways to carry my journey. She is strong, smart, and beautiful. I love her as a person. I will never take knowing her, for granted.

I got so sick, after Caia was born. They wanted to put me in the hospital again, but I could not be from my baby. I was alone and trying to make sure I had the strength to take care of my newborn. My blood pressure kept going up. Nursing and taking care of myself was very hard at this point. Everybody was in Augusta, Georgia at Doctors Hospital. My mother-in-law was in a coma. My husband, Pastor Henra was out of it. He was so pitiful.

Valerie, my niece Semira's mother, Gwen, Pastor Henra's aunt and Dominic, Pastor Henra's cousin helped me. I will never forget how they helped me. I drove all the girls to the grocery store, and I was completely worn out. This stranger helped get everything in the car. Caia was only 2 weeks old. I had her, Callie Blue, and Hannah. It was pouring down rain and I got them in the car. I fell down on my knees in pain, in the Kroger's parking lot. I prayed for my mother-in-law to be healed from her sickness. My pain was a lot to bear; I had no one to help me most of the time. Everything was focused on my mother-in-law.

My husband, Pastor Henra was a poor critter. He loved his mother, no questions about that! I prayed for Pastor Henra to have the strength to stand, for his mother, I needed Him to. He was in and out, seeing about me and the girls. Also, my husband was so lost even being a pastor. This was a hard one for Him. Days and nights were lonely. My husband was so lost, and he did not know what to do. He knows about praying. He had to preach doing this time. I think that my mother-in-law's four children would have died along with their mother. The father would have done so too, if she had passed. They cannot live without their mother. I was so sad, to see four grown children need their mother, so much. I just cried said, "Lord have mercy," because they were not prepared to see their mother die. I never seen anything like this in my life. My husband is out of it. They worship her, they cannot live without her. All four of them know that she keeps them afloat in prayer, in conversation, in love, in hope, in peace and she keeps them pressing on for another day. It seems like they get fluid from her daily; I prayed that she lives. I was not at the hospital, but Pastor Henra, my husband, called me twice a day to update me on her condition. Believe me it was looking good at all!

My sister, Whitney, is an emergency room nurse in Tennessee. She helped Pastor Henra to understand exactly what the medical terms meant when the doctors talked to Him and the family about her condition. Whitney stayed in close contact so they could understand her health. Whitney knew exactly how bad it was looking and she told Pastor Henra what questions to ask the doctors. If it was not for my sister's information, Pastor Henra or anyone else would have known what questions to ask the nurses or doctors.

My cousin also works as ICU nurse gave information to what her levels meant and what they needed to be to survive. My family really came through on my mother-in-law's behalf. My sister and my cousin, Meka helped everyone to understand my mother-in-law's case. They were in constant contact about her case every day and they would call and talk to Pastor Henra. No one in my family ever stop praying for her! We stayed in constant prayer and through each and every day we sang hymns. We cried together and we read scripture to each other for strength.

This woman is the backbone of this family. She has all the answers to all the problems. No matter what was going on, we could always call on her and she be praying for all of us, no matter what we were going through in life. If we had a job interview, she would always get a prayer through. A test we had to take; we would call her. I never met anyone like her; I mean no one! I met this woman at a Carson Newman's football game. This is where my husband went to college for a few years before he transferred to the University of Tennessee with me. I was standing at the gate at one of Pastor Henra's football games. She came up to the gate by the concession stand and this woman spoke to me. I said, "Hello, mama!"

She said, "Hi!" I did not know we would meet again. Later that afternoon Pastor Henra, my boyfriend, has told me that he wanted me to meet his mother and father. They came to all of his football games. They stayed on the road for all of their children. All of the children had equal importance notice to them. When I walked in Pastor Henra's dorm room, I saw this same lady who I had spoken to at the concession stand. I caught my breath.

My cousin who helped out a lot is a nurse at Park West and my sister, Whitney, is at Fort Sanders Hospital in Tennessee. They were so helpful to the family. My sister told me that she has left work plenty of times thinking that her patients would be died over night, but in the morning, they would be very much alive. She told Pastor Henra and the family not to give up yet! Every time I spoke to her, my sister, she spoke life over her. She never spoke over her as she was dead. She said, "I never in my life seen a woman fight so hard to live. All of her organs have failed; she on a ventilator, all of her blood is poison. She in a coma nothing looking good, but she is a fighter."

My husband, Pastor Henra, showed how she laid in her bed in her coma on a video call. I had to fight back all of my many tears. I had to be strong for my husband, Pastor Henra. He loved his mother. If he could have changed places with her, he would have and the rest of the children as well. I never saw so many wires hooked up to one person in my life, but when I got off the phone; I let the tears flow. You are talking about crying. I cried aloud out to the Lord to help us be strong. "Please, Lord help us!" My tears ran like a river. "Lord, please spare my mother-in-law! Please!"

My mother-in-law was cold and had gray looking skin that I have never seen before. She was non-responsive, cold, and portrayed the look of death on her face. She had no response to treatment than all of a sudden, she just came a live—a miracle. What else could it be? A miracle! When I looked at her on video, her eyes were rolling back in her head and tubes were everywhere. I could not stand to see her like this. She was always a super woman nothing bothered her; she fought her battles on her knees in prayer. She was swelling up and cold, completely out of this world. Pastor Henra's voice was shaking with fear; she knew nothing. she never heard us talking around her bed; she was not there! She was gone. I knew she was in Heaven. She looked so dead to me. I see that look before and a few days later she came out fighting for her life. I still never ever seen anything like this. She tried to pull all of those tubes out of her throat at one time in the beginning. I didn't that it was serious until Kianna, my sister-in-law, she said, "This isn't looking good. She can't breathe on her on and all of her color is gone."

"Just pray," I said to her. There was nothing else we could do, just pray and we did!

When I heard that she was on ventilation, I know it was not good! Pastor Henra said that she is not responding to antibiotics and the doctors said the next 24 hours was critical. It looked really bad. They tried three antibiotics before they stared to work any all of her organs, which were shutting down. This is a praying woman of faith. She completely depends on God for everything, no matter how small or big! She lives like she is in total dependence on God! I have been known her for a while now and I am married to her son. I just kept praying for God to bring her back, because her husband and her children is not ready to let her go. Her children are not going to say, "goodbye mom" and that is that. They will follow her to the grave. I hate to say this, but this is the way I see it. I had to help my husband with her illness, his church was a big help, Park Avenue Baptist.

Now every time I see my mother-in-law, she tells everyone see meets and wants to listen; she tells them how she visited Heaven and what she saw in Heaven. Every time I see her, she tells us about how beautiful and how shinning Heaven is, and she tell us about God's glory. She tells us about Jesus Christ and how she walked around Heaven. She tells us that she saw her mother, her two aunties, and all of those children playing on the hill. She always says that she is free now! She says she is better all the way around, body, mind, and Spirit. She has no more fear of nothing. She tells all of us that she has been through the process of human existence, and that she was glad that she was afflicted at the cost of Jesus Christ. She always talks about how happy she is in life now and that nothing can bother her anymore. She is walking more in the glory of God! I am so glad for her. I am proud to know her, and I can use everything that she tells me. She tells me all the time, a part of her will always be in Heaven until she gets back to Heaven again. God Bless you, mother-in-law, Willie Agnes Chennault!

Daughter-in-law, Kianna's Account

On May 19, 2017, my husband Otis and I along with our son Otis Jr., are attending the sixth-grade award ceremony for my stepdaughter, Semira. Towards the end of the ceremony, my husband stepped out to use the phone, and he was gone for a while. After the ceremony ended, we began looking for Him so that we could take pictures. Eventually he reappeared, and, after we took a few pictures, he told me that his mom had fallen ill and that we had to drive to Augusta.

We immediately left the ceremony and stopped by the house to grab a few pampers for the baby. On the way to Augusta, Otis told me that his mom had to be rushed to the hospital via the ambulance. He was visibly worried; but I reassured Him that I was sure she was ok. I was confident that she was ok because she had not been sick, and we had just seen her in Atlanta the week before. She appeared to me to be fine.

The ride to Augusta was unusually long due to a massive amount of traffic. When we finally got to the hospital, we walked in and asked for the location of Willie Agnes

Chennault. We were told that she was in the Intensive Care Unit. I think it was at that moment that I realized she was sicker than I thought. Nothing could prepare us for what we saw when we arrived at my mother-in-law's room. She was laying in the bed, eyes wide open, with her chest heaving up and down. The doctors and nurses were rushing all around her, trying to intervene in some way. Honestly, she looked dead.

My husband and I stood there in shock for a few minutes, which seemed liked forever. Eventually, he said to one of the nurses, "Is she ok?" I do not remember what answer was given; I just know that shortly thereafter the nurse shut the door and we retreated to the waiting area. My husband began to cry as I held his hand. It was all I could do to comfort Him. He then called his dad and said something like, "She's not breathing. Where are you?"

That was the beginning of an excruciating two weeks for us, although I know our experience pales in comparison to what my mother-in-law was going through. For the first few days, we stayed at the hospital 24/7 and had on the same clothes until some family brought us new ones. After we received my mother-in-law's prognosis, we knew we would be there much longer than a few days, so we started to book hotel rooms. My husband and brother-in-law, Pastor Henra, would alternate booking a room for each night. We lived on hospital food and fast food. Our days were filled with going back and forth between my mother-in-law's room and the waiting area. All we could do was wait, and of course pray.

After realizing we would need a miracle, I solicited some of my family to help us pray on my mother-in-law's behalf. My mom, aunt, and I started a liquid only fast, because we knew some things can only be accomplished through prayer and fasting. The fasting was particularly hard for me, because my son was six months old at the time and I was still nursing. Nonetheless, I wanted to do my part in seeing a miracle come to past.

During those weeks, I did not go into my mother-in-law's room much, because I had to care for my son. Also, the doctors explained that her illness was very contagious, and of course I did not want to pass anything on to Him. But when I did go in, I would talk to her about her grandson and let her know how much we loved her and were depending on her to wake up. I would pray, "Lord I believe, but help my unbelief!"

I do not remember the exact date, but I remember almost two weeks had gone by and mothers-in-law was still in a coma like state. The doctors told us that if there was not a substantial change by Friday, which would have been two weeks after her arrival, they would be sending my mother-in-law to hospice, because there was nothing more they could do. The Thursday before the deadline, I remember my husband and brother-in-law were at the hospital very late. The next morning, they told me that they had spent the evening praying to God on behalf of their mother.

Miraculously, the next day, that Friday, my mother-in-law's organs began to work again, 10 days of being in the coma she opened her eyes and began speaking after the nurses took the tube out of her throat. It was like something out of a movie, and we could hardly believe it. It was that day I knew God had worked a miracle through her and that she would be okay.

My Granddaughter, Hannah's Account

My name is Hannah Samore Chennault, the granddaughter of Willie Chennault. I received my name from my grandmother. My grandmother is a very special person to me, she is one of a kind. Grandma is loving, kind, and caring. Grandma is a godly woman, who prayed and taught me how to pray when I was little. Grandma and I would always pray at night whenever I stayed for the summer. We usually say the Psalm 23 and The Lord's prayer. She always made me pray out loud with her, at the track, when we walk. I love to pray with grandma. Grandma is special.

On the morning of May 19, 2017. Grandma got sick. I did not know how grandma got sick, but she was. I asked myself "why is grandma in the hospital." Why is papa not the one in the hospital? It is usually papa that in is the hospital for his lung problems... Why my grandma? I was told by my mom that grandma had gotten sick and needed to be brought to the hospital right away. My heart dropped. I thought that this would be the summer that I would experience six flags and have lots of fun. This was not what to place. I went from extremely happy to extremely sad. It was the last Friday of the school year, I had three days left of school the next week. I did not go to school those days. Only Wednesdays I went to school of those last three days.

I got off of the school bus. The next thing I know Uncle Pastor Henra is picking up us. He was going to drive us all the way to Augusta with Him, to grandma's hospital, where she was. We are in the car driving; my uncle gets a call from one of the family members, that grandma is not doing any better than when she got there. Uncle Pastor Henra hands my mom the phone. Minutes later my mom is crying. My mom is crying. I never liked when anyone cried in my family, because it would always be so depressing to hear them cry. We stopped at a nearby gas station. I got two big bags of BBQ and Honey LAYS potato chips. I wait at the counter while my mom used the bathroom, and while uncle Pastor Henra gets gas. My mom pays for the chips, we walk out, and we are one our way. Two hours or less later, we arrive at the hospital. I could not see grandma, because they did not allow children in the room at the time. I waited at the outside waiting room, outside of the

ICU waiting room where family members could spend the night and things like that. I see some close family's members. My Uncle Nick's wife, Shaquille, I look across from me and see tears running down her face, one by one. I sit in sadness. I remember eating something. I think it was Chick-fa-lay, or something like that.

Callie Blue is there too, and my papa. No one looks sad, it was a different type of sad. They are sad but an unexplainable sad…That night, I see all of grandma's sisters and family members, close family members and I remember, bring all this food. Sandwiches, Krispy crème,' chips and drinks. All kind of food. One of grandma's sister, brought all of that food. I was looking around and like why is not anyone crying. I never cried, because I knew she was going to be okay. It seemed impossible that my grandma would die sometime, at this moment of my life. I told myself, "She has to see my children, when I grow older, even see me, and my cousins get married."

Uncle Pastor Henra got a hotel. Me, Callie Blue, Uncle Otis, Uncle Pastor Henra and Auntie Kiana stayed the first night at the hotel. The next morning, we leave so we can get back to the hospital. I did not remember the next day, but I do remember going with Aunt Gwen and Callie Blue for the night. The next day we are able to go see grandma, she is doing not good still, but she is a little okay.

I walked into the room and walked out a few times. I do not know why I did, but I did! I remember my grandpa crying, I remember Uncle Otis crying, Uncle Pastor Henra, and Uncle nick. I remember sitting right in front of grandma's bed with my black hoodie on, just sitting there. Just sitting and praying for grandma. That was the time I knew she was going to be just more than okay. I walked in again, and the doctors said her kidneys where failing. In shock, I sit saying 'How?!' I walked back into the ICU waiting room, and my mom asked me what the doctors said. I told her and Auntie Kiana that the doctors said that her kidneys were failing. I watched them hug and cry.

After a few weeks, grandma is doing kind of better. They have taken the tube out her throat now. She is kind of talking now. She cannot talk that good, because her teeth are out. Fast forwarding to when she moves to Select hospital, because she is doing more better. Grandma has a big bald spot in the back for her head, because she has been lying in bed so long on the back of her head. Me and my mom had just moved out of our apartment at that time, we were basically staying with my grandma at the hospital that summer. I do not think my mom was working, she had to quit her job to help out grandma that summer. My papa and I used to sit out in the waiting room, and sip coffee 24/7. At night I used to hear this lady next door scream something, and sometimes in the daytime. I do not know what happened to that lady, but I always wondered why she screamed like that. Did she know Jesus?

Grandma has been transferred back to Doctors Hospital, for more therapy. At this time, me and papa are driving back and forth. My mom as went back to Atlanta to fly to different colleges for work, for the rest of the summer; she eventually took a summer job, but until she knew grandma was okay. I never did anything fun that summer, never went to six flags or a water park or just even a regular park, but it was worth the wait. I remember me in papa getting lost in the hospital and getting on the children care side of the hospital. Seeing this kid that had bandages all over his head, it scared me; It left me feeling sorry for Him.

It has been a couple of weeks and grandma is walking and talking again. My grandma, papa and I wait for our truck at the valet parking at the hospital. We road back to the small, quiet place known as Wilkes County. Soon as my grandma got home, she starts cooking okra soup. I knew she was going to be okay.

Willie Agnes Chennault

Chapter 20

MEMORIES

Willie Agnes Chennault

From Left to Right—my parents' old house where my siblings and I were raised, the back door of our house along with the meat house where my father cured the hog meat for us to eat, bedroom where my parents slept, and me by the well where my siblings and I drew water along with other items.

From Left to Right—kitchen of my parents' old house, my bedroom that I shared with my siblings, Mamie and Rachel, Pete Chafin's sawmill where my father worked in the 1960s, me standing in my old bedroom in March 2017 and me standing on the porch of my parents' old house.

From Left to Right—Mr. Cheston Hall's outhouse on the Garrad's place, this is where my brother, Joseph and I found apples to eat, my husband standing outside of my parents' old house, "My Praying Ground" in the back of house, dirt road leading from our house to main street that my siblings and I walked down every day to go to school and back home.

595

The steps on the backside of Mrs. Garrard's house where my mother nursed my siblings.

On the left is my mother, Mamie Lue Callaway. On the right is my father, Henry Callaway.

From Left to Right—My parents' wedding anniversary picture, they were married for 47 years, my grandfather favorite place to rest, his sofa, taken before he died in 1991.

My husband's parents, Corene Chennault and Hosie Dee Chennault. They were married for 49 years.

Willie Agnes Chennault

On the left is Lucinda Cullars, "Aunt Lue" and on the right is Essie Wooten, "Aunt Nee" in the white dress and Aunt Clifford Samuels is in the black and white dress with poky dots.

My siblings and I, from left to right—Joseph (brown suit), Alberta (stripped skirt), myself (scarf around neck), Racheal (blue long sleeve dress), Charlie (bright blue suit), Mamie (silver dress), Barbara (in the back) and James (gray suit jacket with dark pants).

My brother, Daniel (leather hat) and my brother, Jessie, on the right.

From left to right—My best friends, Betty Ruth Graves Fannie, and Mrs. Annie Josephine Gartrell.

Top Left to Bottom Right, Formal Graduation picture (18 years old), Gold Cap and Gown picture (18 years old), red dress (22 years old), 12th grade picture (18 years old), curly hair picture (19 years old), 10th grade picture (6th picture), 22 years old(the year I lost Noah), 23 years old (blue sweater), short curly hair (32 years old), gray dress standing on porch pregnant with second son, Otis (29 years old), striped dress (32 years old), last picture (53 years old)

On Metasville Road, where my parents moved in 1978. My dad's pulp wood truck he used for his pulp wood business, me at the age of 31.

From left to right—my husband's 12th grade picture, our wedding photo (1974), our prom picture (1974), and wedding anniversary picture (33 years old, how I looked in Heaven)

From left to right—My husband and I after I came out of hospital (August 2017), me standing in my yard after my sickness (September 2017), me in my yard by the flower garden (October 2017)

My attendance at Park Avenue Baptist Church after my sickness in September 2017 with all of my grandchildren and my son, Otis.

Family photo, my mother, my husband, and my children (1986)

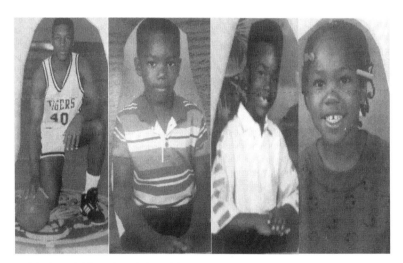

All of my children; from left to right, Lazarus Jr., high school basketball picture,
Otis, second grade, Pastor Henra, Kindergarten, Dr. June in the first grade.

Pastor Henra's family—First Lady Taurika, Caia, and Callie Blue

From left to right—Pastor Henra's family, Hannah, Me, Dr. June, and my husband

My second son, Otis and his wife, Kianna, the lawyer, and grandson, Otis Jr.

My son, Otis' family—Baby Olivia, Semira, Otis Jr. and Kianna, Esq.

My granddaughter, Semira's track award picture

My older son, Lazarus Jr, and his wife, Shirkea

My niece, April Robertson and her husband, Dwayne Robertson.

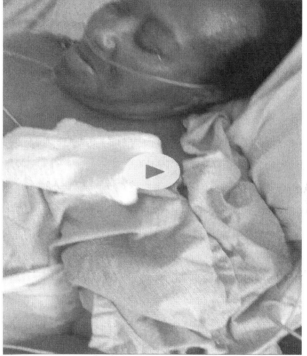

My first day waking up after being in a coma at Doctors Hospital in August, Georgia. My son, Otis, recorded the miraculous event.

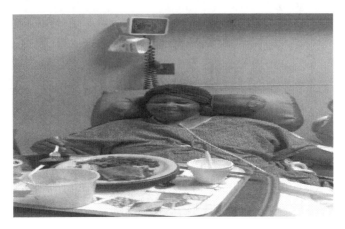

Two weeks after being Select Specialty Hospital

EMTs who picked me up on May 19, 2017—Lindsay Hughes, Rebekah Echols, and
Dennis Weaver

The Next Time I Go To Heaven I Will Not Be Back!

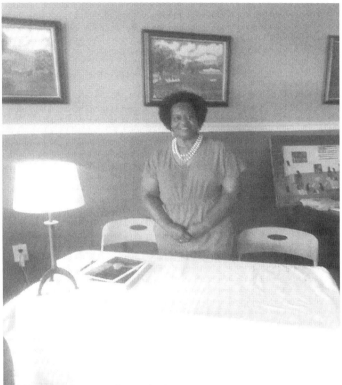

This is me today at my first author's event in Washington, Georgia 2019

ABOUT THE AUTHOR

Willie Agnes Chennault is a native of Washington, Georgia. She resides with her husband, Lazarus Chennault Sr. They have been married for 45 years. They have four children together—Lazarus Jr., Otis, Pastor Henra, and Dr. June. Willie and her husband have six grandchildren—Semira, Hannah, Callie Blue, Caia, Otis Jr., and Olivia. She enjoys gardening, fishing, reading her Bible daily and going to church.

Made in the USA
Columbia, SC
26 March 2022

58188060R00369